KU-507-889

THE GOLDEN AGE

BOOK II

EMPIRE

Conn Iggulden

PENGUIN BOOKS

PENGUIN BOOKS

UK | USA | Canada | Ireland | Australia
India | New Zealand | South Africa

Penguin Books is part of the Penguin Random House group of companies
whose addresses can be found at global.penguinrandomhouse.com

First published by Penguin Michael Joseph 2023
Published in Penguin Books 2024

001

Copyright © Conn Iggulden, 2023

The moral right of the author has been asserted

Typeset by Jouve (UK), Milton Keynes
Printed and bound in Great Britain by Clays Ltd, Elcograf S.p.A.

The authorized representative in the EEA is Penguin Random House Ireland,
Morrison Chambers, 32 Nassau Street, Dublin D02 YH68

A CIP catalogue record for this book is available from the British Library

ISBN: 978-1-405-94967-5

www.greenpenguin.co.uk

MIX
Paper | Supporting
responsible forestry
FSC® C018179

Penguin Random House is committed to a
sustainable future for our business, our readers
and our planet. This book is made from Forest
Stewardship Council® certified paper.

To John Souter and Michael Whitehead.

The Greeks saw lives as threads: washed, teased, spun, woven – and at the last, cut. Each one stands apart at first, but becomes whole cloth. I believe a love of stories is one of the great patterns. When we catch a glimpse of it, we know we are part of something vast and strange and complex – and greater than ourselves alone.

N

THRACE

MACEDON

*Thracian
Sea*

THASOS

Hellespont

▲ *Mt Olympus*

THESSALY

*Aegean
Sea*

LESBOS

• *Artemisium*

Thermopylae •

EUBOEA

SCYROS

IONIA

Delphi •

Gulf of Corinth

Thebes • *Tanagra*
Marathon •
Athens • ATTICA

PELOPONNESE

Corinth •

SALAMIS

Argos •

DELOS

PAROS

• *Sparta*

*Ionian
Sea*

CRETE

The Ancient World

Byzantium

PERSIAN EMPIRE

...lis

...ARA

Eurymedon
River

RHODES

CYPROS

0 20 40 60 80 100
miles

Pronunciation

Military terms

	Ancient Greek	Ancient Greek Pronunciation	English Pronunciation	Meaning
archon	ἄρχων	ark-own	ark-on	Ruler, leader.
epistates	ἐπιστάτης	ep-ist-at-airs	ep-ist-at-eez	Chairman in the Athenian Assembly.
lochagos	λοχαγός	lock-a-goss	lock-a-goss	Rank equivalent to captain.
phalanx	φάλαγξ	fal-anks	fal-anks	Body of heavily armed infantry.
strategos	στρατηγός	strat-air-goss	strat-egg-oss	General.
trierarch	τριήραρχος	tree-air-ark-oss	try-err-ark	Commander of a trireme.

Underlining indicates stressed syllables.

Locations

Agora	Ἀγορά	ag-or-a	ag-<u>or</u>-a	Open place, market.
Cypros	Κύπρος	cou-pros	<u>sigh</u>-prous	Island of Cyprus.
Delos	Δῆλος	dare-loss	<u>dee</u>-loss	Island birthplace of Apollo and Artemis.
Pnyx	Πνύξ	p-nooks	p-<u>niks</u>	'Packed in'. Hill. Meeting place of the Assembly in Athens.

Characters

Agariste	Ἀγαρίστη	ag-a-rist-air	ag-a-<u>rist</u>-ee	Mother of Pericles.
Anaxagoras	Ἀναξαγόρας	an-ax-ag-or-as	an-ax-<u>ag</u>-or-as	Friend of Pericles, natural philosopher.
Archidamus	Ἀρχίδαμος	ar-kee-dam-oss	ar-ki-<u>dame</u>-ous	King of Sparta.
Artaxerxes	Ἀρταξέρξης	art-ax-erks-airs	ar-ta-<u>zerk</u>-sees	King of Persia.
Aspasia	Ἀσπασία	asp-as-ee-a	asp-<u>ays</u>-ia	Hetaira, companion to Pericles.
Cimon	Κίμων	kim-own	<u>ky</u>-mon	Athenian general.
Ephialtes	Ἐφιάλτης	eff-ee-al-tairs	eff-ee-<u>al</u>-teez	Athenian politician.
Nicomedes	Νικομήδης	nik-om-air-dares	nik-a-<u>meed</u>-eez	Regent to Pleistonax.
Pericles	Περικλῆς	per-ik-lairs	<u>per</u>-ik-leez	Leader of Athens.
Pleistarchus	Πλείσταρχος	play-star-koss	play-<u>star</u>-kous	Spartan king, son of Leonidas.
Pleistonax (Pleistoanax)	Πλειστοάναξ	play-stow-an-ax	<u>play</u>-stow-nax	Spartan battle king who succeeded Pleistarchus.
Thetis	Θέτις	thett-iss	<u>thee</u>-tiss	Wife to Pericles.
Zeno	Ζήνων	zairn-own	<u>zee</u>-no	Friend of Pericles, natural philosopher.

Prologue

Arion waited on one knee, nervous in the presence of kings. After all, Pleistarchus was the son of Leonidas himself, a name all men knew. More, Pleistarchus looked like a warrior born, his limbs powerful, his every movement in balance. Yet the Spartan was one of two royal figures in that place, nor did their ephors kneel to either of them. It was a strange system to the watching eye of Arion. Though he had heard they were of common stock, the five ephors had real power, even in the royal palace.

From beneath his fringe, Arion watched them discuss the plea he had brought. There was clearly some difference of opinion and he wondered if he would be sent away again. He had been summoned and dismissed twice before, until he was repeating all his answers and his voice had grown hoarse.

He understood they wished to test his story, to judge from repeated details whether he had told the whole truth. He would not have wanted to lie to such men, he realised. Arion was no clever courtier, no bard or poet. He was just a young man, a runner, sent to ask for help from the greatest warriors in the world.

'Your king still lives? You say you saw him alive?' one of the ephors directed to him. It was the oldest one, scrawny-looking with deeply tanned skin and scars like stitched leather. Arion blinked as they all turned to hear his answer.

'As I said it, master. When I left, King Hesiodos was alive, though defeated. The League fleet had Thasos surrounded on all sides. They pulled down the walls of the royal palace . . .'

'Some goat pen, I would imagine,' one of the ephors muttered to another.

Arion flushed and stopped talking.

'An entire fleet at anchor around Thasos, yet you escaped,' the oldest one said.

Tendons stood out in his neck as he watched the young messenger for any sign of evasion. Instead, Arion answered with barely controlled exasperation. He had spoken the truth. Though he feared them still, he was weary of their suspicion.

'I took only a coracle, a fishing boat any man can carry on his back. I waited in the woods until dark and then slipped across. I have fished those waters and I know them well.'

The ephor shook his head, his eyes black.

'He lies. It is a trap, some game of the Athenians.'

Arion breathed out. He did not know what he would have done if he had actually been lying. The truth was his only shield and so he repeated words he had come to know as well as his own name.

'King Hesiodos sent me to ask for help. No one else has the strength or the will to throw a rein on the men of Athens. Persia is no threat to us now. Only the League demands silver or ships, with threats of violence if we refuse! Who then is the tyrant? I was told to say, "Sparta leads the Hellenes, those who know the gods and the words of men. We do not ask for aid; we ask for justice. Nothing more."'

He watched as they turned back to their discussion. Three of the ephors raised their hands, with two shaking their heads. A subtle tension left the group then. A decision had been made.

After a beat, it was King Pleistarchus who responded.

'We will take up your cause, Arion of Thasos. You have come to us in proper humility, as is right. We will restore the balance – and Athens will be made to answer for the crimes of her people.'

Arion felt a shiver go through him as he listened, awed at what he had brought into the world. Men would die because he had reached that place.

In the distance, a rumble began, a sound like distant thunder in the mountains that cupped the city of Sparta. Arion had taken ship for a good part of his journey but run the last days, coming through high passes where wild deer grazed. The floor trembled and he rested his palm on it. Such things were common enough in that land. He felt his stomach tighten even so. It was as if something approached, something huge that made him afraid.

'Master . . .' he began.

'The earth shakes,' the other king said as if to a child.

Archidamus was young to have such power in that group. Yet they were respectful, as far as Arion could see. He'd understood the man was somehow a king of Spartans outside the field of war, though he could still lead in battle. Pleistarchus was the battle king, though he could apparently rule on civil matters as well. It was more complicated than the island of Thasos, that was certain. Arion shook his head, waiting for the trembling to stop. He had known such things before, along with the sense of utter wrongness that went with them. It never lasted long.

'Master,' Arion said again. 'I think . . .'

They all turned as a great crack appeared in one of the

walls. Arion could see dust shimmering along the polished floor, invisible before, but suddenly there, rising and falling. Another crack appeared, spreading in veins. The two kings looked at one another.

'We should go outside . . .' Archidamus said.

The ephors were already moving when the true earthquake hit.

Arion found himself on his back and realised he had been thrown. The ground had risen under him, rippling like water. He gaped at sunlight as the roof tore apart. Walls were falling and he heard one of the ephors cry out, the sound cut off as he was crushed.

Kings and men alike ran into the evening air, the royal palace crashing down behind them. Even as they moved, the ground surged again, hurling them from their feet. The air smelled foul, of damp and sickness released, as if they breathed airs of the underworld. Dust covered them all, billowing from the palace. It coated their skin grey, with splashes of bright blood where they had been scraped or cut. Arion saw kings of Sparta standing with weapons drawn, as if they could fight an invisible enemy who flung them like children.

All the while, the rumbling increased. They stood on a hill, looking down a street as it collapsed onto those who lived there. As the sun set, the entire city of Sparta bucked and kicked. Arion saw temples and houses made rubble. Somewhere nearby, screaming sounded, the high voices of women and children, of pain and shock.

'Go to the barracks. Bring the army,' Archidamus ordered.

His battle king raced away, weaving between fallen blocks of marble as more walls fell and broke apart. Dust filled the street and there were already figures staggering, bloody and confused.

Arion looked for orders. He was a man of Thasos rather than Sparta, but there was something about the sheer scale of this that meant he did not hesitate.

'What can I do?' he asked the Spartan king.

'Help the trapped,' Archidamus said without hesitation.

A clatter of running men made them both turn. Twenty Spartan soldiers came through the dust with swords drawn and cloaks swirling. Archidamus snapped orders to them, sending them into fallen houses along the street. As Arion watched, they heaved masonry away with astonishing vigour, revealing flopping limbs that looked almost part of the dust. Some of the injured stirred as they felt a touch. Many more would clearly not move again, already stiff in death.

The rumbling died and crying and shouting grew to fill its absence. Arion was almost knocked from his feet by a stranger scrambling past, the man made blind by blood pouring from his scalp. Half his hair hung on a torn flap of skin, with a sheen beneath that might have been bone.

'Is it over?' the man called. 'Is it over?'

Arion did not know if he would even hear an answer. He turned to Archidamus with the same question. The young king shook his head.

'There will be another,' Archidamus said with dark certainty. 'They come like waves on the shore.'

The king's bleak expression eased as Pleistarchus returned from the barracks, leading hundreds of Spartiates. Some wore no sandals, Arion saw. Others bled from lost skin. They too had been caught by surprise.

Arion joined another group as they began to heave

rubble away, responding to the sobs of a trapped child. No one objected to him being there. The dust made them all one.

Arion choked on grief as the sound weakened. The little boy was limp by the time they reached him, his chest crushed. It was a wonder he had made any sound at all. Arion felt tears sting his eyes as he moved on to the next and the next. Sparta had fallen. Street upon street had been reduced to rubble. *Nothing* stood, for as far as he could see.

In the distance, in the twilight, a different roar sounded, more anger and fear than some spasm of the earth. Arion came out of the rubble to see what was going on. Sparti-ates near him had all put away their swords. Yet he could hear the clash of iron and bronze, the shouts and fury of the battlefield. It made no sense.

The royal palace had been built on the crest of a hill, with roads stretching down to the city proper. They were not far from the acropolis there, where people gathered to pray and hear kings or ephors in more normal times. Hun-dreds were streaming to it as he stared, but they looked back in fear then, as if something hunted them.

'By the gods, no . . . *no*,' Archidamus muttered.

King Pleistarchus was nearby and the two men ex-changed a look that had horror in it. Arion stared from one to the other, but he could read no answer in them. He was an outsider and they cared not for him.

'The helots,' Pleistarchus said. 'If they riot . . .'

'*You* command the army,' Archidamus snapped. 'So give the order. Kill them all – before this madness spreads.'

'If I give that command, they will overwhelm us.'

For an instant, Pleistarchus glanced at Arion, the for-eigner who watched with his mouth open. In that heartbeat of time, the ground began to shake again, building fast in intensity. Every fallen stone or tile jumped and bounced. It was as if the earth shook flies from its flank and they were powerless before it.

'Can't you hear the fighting?' Archidamus shouted over the rumbling. 'They are *already* killing our people! What do helots know of discipline, of obedience? Give the order, or I will.'

'We can contain it. They are not soldiers,' Pleistarchus said angrily.

'There are seven of them for every one of us – they do not need to be! Give the order, Pleistarchus!'

'No. The army is mine. Take the women and children to the acropolis. It is high ground there. You will be safe enough. I will set the army to containing the violence – I will be ruthless with any helot who takes up arms. But I will not slaughter them. We'll need them to rebuild.'

'Ephors! A decision!' Archidamus said.

There were only four on the street, with one still crushed in the palace. In normal times, no equal vote was possible, but those four could cancel one another out.

'Pleistarchus commands the army in time of crisis,' the oldest said.

One of the others looked angry, but nodded even so. The third and fourth bowed their heads. They were common men of Sparta, elected as a check on the power of kings. They did not look away from Archidamus as he glared at them.

'Very well,' he said. 'Though if it spreads, you will have the blood of Spartans on your hands. We are, what, a forty thousand? Five thousand Spartiates, as many perioikoi, the rest children and women? Yet more than a *hundred thousand*

7

helots live in Sparta as our slaves. If they revolt, even we will be swept away.'

'Still, it is my decision,' Pleistarchus said, his voice cold. 'Save who you can. Take them to the acropolis and tend the wounded. I will keep order.'

They all heard a great roar go up a few streets over. The sun had dipped below the western hills and the last light was fading. Archidamus shook his head.

'If you can,' he said grimly.

PART ONE

'Circumstances rule men;
men do not rule circumstances.'

– Herodotus

I

As Pericles rose to speak, he knew he held a man's life in his hands. Banishment, ruin or death. All three were there, in Cimon's steady gaze and the twitching muscle in his jaw.

With a jury of four hundred Athenians, they stood on the Pnyx hill, a breeze ruffling hair and robes. Cimon had endured three days of witnesses and accusations, organised by two prosecutors chosen by Ephialtes, strategos of the city – and enemy to Cimon. The man himself watched from the side of the hill, his back to the Agora of Athens below.

Cimon had defended himself well enough. He had explained every decision with calm expertise. He had sworn on the gods that he had taken no bribe to free the king of Macedon on Persian land, showing only the mercy that was a victor's right. Those who would not have done the same would doubt his word, of course. Some of those present knew only spite or greed as their masters. They would never believe there were higher standards than their own.

Pericles touched a fist to his lips. He had joined the accusers, then chosen not to speak until the end. He could feel all eyes on him – in suspicion or surmise. They knew Cimon had been his friend, some of them. Yet for the right offence, that would be no protection. Any Athenian would condemn a man for impiety or treason. In such a case, even his own family would consider it their duty to see him killed or banished. As a result, no one there truly knew what Pericles would do. He cleared his throat.

'I have listened to all that has been said,' he began. 'I have heard. Since the beginning of this trial, in the evenings, I have been approached by many who have known Cimon since his youth. Wherever I go in the city, I am stopped – by those who wish to remind me how Cimon commanded ships at Salamis, or how he took the war back to the Persians, breaking their great fleet and army at Eurymedon. How he brought the bones of Theseus home, the king of Athens who slew the Minotaur. All this is known.'

Over to one side, Strategos Ephialtes looked sour at such a recitation of honours. As well he might, Pericles thought, with so few of his own.

Pericles looked up as the breeze increased. The wind was turning, coming from the north. It carried an odd note of spices and dust he could taste on his tongue.

'Yet we hold our people to the highest standard. Any man may be a juror in Athens, to sit in judgement on any other – whether he be strategos or carpenter. That right to trial and judgement is the beating heart of our city, a living freedom. We are not tyrants, to condemn a man merely on some code of laws, or the word of his enemies. No. We gather, we listen, we decide.'

He looked around, at the implacable faces of his people. The men on that hill took their responsibility seriously. Cimon's fate hung on their judgement and he did not know yet if he could sway them.

'So I say to those who claim Cimon stands too high to be judged: all men can be judged. His father marched with mine from this very place, to fight and win the battle of

Marathon, but what of that? My father spoke against him at his trial, despite their friendship. Miltiades reached too far in the end. He was judged in this very place, here on the Pnyx – and he was found guilty. He died in prison.'

Cimon's stare was cold then. Pericles swallowed, his throat suddenly tight.

'You may say Miltiades deserved better.' He waved a hand as if searching for examples. 'You may say Archon Cimon fed the poor for years in Athens! That does not matter here. Perhaps he made his friends hand over their cloaks to those who shivered in the cold months. Put all that from your mind. The past does not matter. In this court, on this day, only these accusations stand.'

Pericles held up a single finger.

'Was Cimon within his rights as the victor of Eurymedon to free a king of Macedon, an ally of the Persians? Cimon did not have the time and peace we have today to decide the issue, not on that battlefield, with the smell of blood and smoke on the air. It was not his role to make new alliances, to turn enemies to friends with an act of mercy! That is for the council of Athens, for the people themselves.'

He paused, seeing them shift uncomfortably.

'The second accusation. Was Cimon correct not to continue the campaign deep into Persia, to pursue and destroy more of the king's fleeing army? I dare say his decision saved a few lives. There are some in Athens today who would surely have died in that pursuit into unknown lands. What of it? Men die in war! I have heard some say Cimon was in command, that the decision was his alone, but we sit in judgement of those decisions today. Far from that river plain, without the pain and exhaustion they knew

13

then. Perhaps he *should* have taken that risk. Well, you will decide, no other. Not Cimon, not Strategos Ephialtes, nor I will make that judgement. If you find Cimon guilty, it will be because his service to Athens displeases you. That is your right, as free men. To judge. As prosecutors, we will ask then for death or banishment for these errors – if errors they are judged to be.'

Every single eye was on him, he realised, as if he had lit himself on fire and they watched him burn. Pericles wanted to smile, but he had learned sternness from his father and he only nodded and held up a third finger, folding in his thumb and smallest.

'The last. The accusation that Cimon took a great share of Persian gold as his own, from Cypros, from the camp at Eurymedon. It does not matter how many of his men came home with pouches of coin or new coats! An archon is held to a higher standard. I have listened – to those who say Cimon wears no gold, that he lives like a Spartan. To others who say he broke a Persian threat that would have sacked and burned Athens for a third time. We know Cimon returned great sums to the city treasury, but who can say how much was kept back? His men brought earrings and gold to the city, spending like Persians themselves. Oh, Cimon may live simply, but he has his family land, his tenant farms still. His family paid the fine that helped build our fleet! They had wealth then. Gold may not grow corrupt, but men certainly can. I say wealth desires wealth and always has.'

He paused, worried he was making the point too well. He'd done all he could and deliberately chosen to speak in the last moments before the vote. A pot of water timed his speech, streaming into a second. It was already faltering.

14

Where had the time gone? Had he said all his lines? It was hard not to think of plays he had known. This too was a performance, though with considerably more at stake. He searched for a final word, something they might remember as they voted on his friend's life.

'This accusation rests on those three pillars. If even one is too weak, it all falls. You must not set Salamis and Eurymedon and Theseus against them, but decide on its own merit where guilt or innocence lies.'

The water died to a trickle and Pericles bowed his head. The magistrate directed the crowd of jurors to their deliberation. Elected for that day alone, the man was delighted to oversee such a serious trial. Pericles swallowed nervously as jurors walked away to discuss the judgement. It would not take very long. In just a few moments, they would raise their hands and decide whether Cimon walked free or not.

He did not look in Cimon's direction. From the instant he had put himself forward to prosecute, Pericles knew he'd walked a very dangerous path. If Cimon saw him as an enemy, their friendship was over. Yet he did not think Cimon would accept a subterfuge on his behalf either. The man was almost more Spartan than Athenian, with the same unbending sense of honour.

Pericles had understood from the first that Ephialtes wished to bring Cimon down – that his friend needed help. Whether it was simple dislike of his noble class or some stray word Cimon had said to sting Ephialtes' pride, he did not know. Nor did it really matter what drove the man. The strategos had thrown a knife by bringing that trial. Ephialtes would not, could not relent after that. So Pericles walked through thorns as he tried to bring Cimon out safe.

The great Themistocles had commanded at Salamis. He had saved the city while a Persian king watched from shore, and *still* been banished. Aristides had been a man of the highest honour. He too had been sent from his home, like a cur kicked from its bed.

Athenians were suspicious of all their leaders. They would not allow tyrants to rise again. That was Pericles' secret fear. He had sown doubt over the accusations. He had reminded them of Cimon's service and honour. Yet the truth was, they might bring him down as a reminder where power lay, or even for sport.

They had come to that place with clay dust or goat blood on their tunics. Many were working men, their hands rough with callus. Pericles thought he understood them. They loved the eminence of Athens, scorning lesser cities. Out of pride, they put themselves forward as council members and rowers, as jurors and magistrates. His people. Yet as much as he loved them, he feared what they might do.

Strategos Ephialtes did not trust him, of course. The man was not a fool. That was why he had set two others to make the case against Cimon. They had cast every doubt they could on the campaign in Persia, though it had made Pericles squirm to hear the way they twisted the truth. It had hurt to remain silent, but he had not said a word. His name was down as first prosecutor. In the end, he knew he had to be allowed to address the jury. He'd seen that awareness in the others, with every day and hour that passed. Time and again, they'd looked to see if he would rise, in support or rebuttal. He had only shaken his head. In that way, when they had run out of words and spite, his voice had been the climax, the last they heard before the vote.

Pericles stared at the ground, waiting. He hoped he knew his people. He had walked the running track in his local gymnasium over previous days, reciting aloud to prepare for this. Yet he could not tell if it had been enough. Some of the jurors looked over at him, but there was no way to know if enough had been swayed, not really. A few would have been in the fleet, even on the field at Eurymedon. For all he knew, they could revere Cimon, or despise him. Cimon's father had been found guilty by men just like these! Pericles could only whisper a prayer that history would not repeat itself. He found he was sweating, though the breeze had grown in strength. The day was hot, but it was more than that. Perhaps he was just afraid.

The jury returned to their places, facing Cimon. The breeze fluttered robes and cloaks, making a snapping sound in the silence.

'Jurors. Are you ready to pass judgement?' the magistrate said. His voice was strained. Dozens nodded in response and he darted his gaze to the sides. Scythian guards waited there, employed by the city to keep order.

The magistrate took up a tablet and read from it. As one elected to a position of power from sunset to sunset, he needed to know the correct form.

'The vote will be by show of hands,' he read aloud. 'I will call "Guilty" and "Innocent". Scribes of the city will make a tally. If there is a dispute, you will remain until a clear majority is declared.'

He paused, handing down the tablet.

'On the matter of Archon Cimon, of the deme Laciadae and family Philaidae, son to Miltiades, do you find him guilty?'

Hands rose. Pericles held his breath, beginning his own

count. It would clearly be close. Ephialtes was smiling to one of his group and slapping another on the back in congratulation. Pericles shook his head. He knew a little about theatre. It was just a show for the crowd, but sure enough, a few wavering men raised hands in response. Pericles saw others drop before they were counted. Condemning the greatest Athenian general to death or banishment was no small thing.

When the scribes had the first tally, the magistrate accepted their tablets. He took a breath and asked for 'Innocent'. Once more, a host of hands rose. Pericles heard murmurs as those who agreed or disagreed growled in reply. A few voices could sway those around them, he realised. Juries were just men. Pericles bit his lip as the scribes compared the totals. They gave nothing away in their expressions, treating the entire event as a sacred ritual. As it was, dedicated to Athena and watched by the goddess from her temple on the Acropolis. Pericles raised his eyes to the ruins there. The Persians had burned and broken all they could. They had begun to rebuild, but . . .

'The verdict is clear,' the magistrate said in obvious relief. He touched a sleeve to his forehead, mopping up sweat.

'Archon Cimon, by judgement of your peers, this jury finds you innocent of the accusations against you. Go in peace. You are free.'

The jury cheered and though some groaned or cursed, they were outnumbered and had no chance to start violence. Ephialtes was quick to leave the Pnyx hill, trailing disappointed supporters.

Pericles felt relief sweep through. It had been a dangerous course, for the highest stakes. He could not say aloud that he had hoped for Cimon's freedom. Not in that place. Such an act would be seen as dishonour and perhaps even bring about his own trial. His would remain a private victory.

He walked to the steps that led down to the Agora. Sensing something, Pericles glanced back, finding Cimon's cool gaze. There was no thanks there, no acknowledgement. Pericles dipped his head, understanding the cost had been the friendship he had known. He turned away. If that was the price of Cimon's freedom, he was content.

With his foot on the top step, Pericles felt the ground shake, a rumble that spread across the city. He stared in horrified fascination as something passed through streets and markets below, the ripple of a stone dropped into water. He saw dust rise and roofs collapse. Shouts sounded and jurors rushed to the edge, risking a tumble down the slope. Below, the streets filled with people coming out to see what was happening.

It passed. It had been stronger than any Pericles had known before, but it passed. Dust hung over the open Agora and he shook his head, wondering if it meant the gods were pleased or angry at Cimon being free. He vowed to make offerings at the temples that evening, just in case. Pericles walked slowly down and as he went, the ground shook twice more. It felt like an echo and he wondered where the upheaval had begun – and where it would end.

Aspasia looked onto the street through bars of painted iron, so close she could barely fit her hand between them. She could hear the mother's voice calling her name, but there was no harm in looking out, not really. At seventeen, the rules and strictures of the house seemed either point-less or designed to annoy her. The garden was beautiful enough, with trickling water and a fine growth of flowers that made the air rich with scent. Yet outside – outside! – the city was alive, with noise and dust and the strange shaking that had broken one of her pots. Black earth had spilled across the flagstones of the little garden. Her hands were dark from clearing it up, her fingertips like those who used henna to mark their skin or dye their hair. Aspasia snorted at that thought. Her own hair was thick and true black, a mane that hung in a single bond. The weight was something she could always feel, especially when the other mothers presented her in her red dress. The colour was meant to represent virgin's blood, so the other girls whis-pered. Men were said to value such things. Yet one of the mothers had given away her first quick pain to one of the servants – allowing Aspasia the choice of them. Aspasia was still not certain what all the fuss had been about. It had been enjoyable enough, though he'd seemed more excited and red-faced than she'd felt herself. There had been a distant tremor, she recalled, as she stared onto the street. Like the shaking of the ground that day, it had hinted at something greater, perhaps happening to some-one else . . .

'*There* you are, Aspasia! Oh, look at your *hands*! What have you been doing?'

They called them 'mothers', in the hetaira house, though none were related to the young women who resided there. Aspasia liked only the youngest of the three, the one she pretended was her true mother when she needed comfort. Unfortunately, the lady who had found her was one of the others, the pair she called 'the crones'. Aspasia knew her actual mother had sold her. She did not like to think of that.

'Did you feel the earth trembling?' Aspasia asked, trying to distract her. 'One of the pots broke!'

She looked out again through the bars, seeing a tall young man striding past. Her heart thumped in her chest then. She had seen that one before, always walking into the city from somewhere else. He looked so stern.

'Can't I go out?' Aspasia said without turning, saying anything that meant she could continue to stare, to drink in his movement. She knew some of the girls dreamed of favourites sometimes. She wanted to dream of him, no, to have him see her.

Her voice carried into the street. The mother who stood in her shadow reached out and pinched her arm. Aspasia ignored both the sudden pain and the hard words that followed. The man had heard! She saw his head turn. What would he see, she wondered. Her garden coat was clean but worn. Her eyes were dark, larger with the kohl she applied. The great tail of her hair was thick in its bind, swinging as she moved. She watched him become aware of her gaze.

In the moment before their eyes met, Aspasia was yanked back with a squawk from the little square of bars. She struggled, but the mothers were all extraordinarily strong. The women of that house seemed obsessed with her obedience, as if the world might end for a stolen hour in the garden.

Aspasia swore under her breath as she was tugged away from the light into cool shadows. The house was not large. In normal times, she shared her small room with another. That month though, she was alone. They said Marete had been accepted as an acolyte to Athena, though Aspasia had heard that a few times and was suspicious. The men who came to purchase hetairai did not seem like priests.

'*Really*, Aspasia!' the mother said. 'I know you heard me! I think you should go without dinner this evening. Discipline is the *first* requirement, not an afterthought! How can we ever find you a place in a good temple, or with a good Eupatridae family, if you are so wilful? I will be asked about your character and I *cannot* lie. Do you understand? If they say to me, "Is she meek and biddable, this one?" – all I can do is remain silent. And they know very well what that means.'

As she stepped inside her room, Aspasia spun to face her accuser. The mother looked her over.

'You *are* beautiful, dear. Your skin, your figure . . . your teeth are strong, your eyesight is clear. That hair! It has a life of its own, I sometimes think. We should have found you a place last year. You are the oldest in the house, now! There is a new one coming tomorrow to replace little Marete. Now there was a daughter! Marete was a year younger than you and she will represent us in one of the richest temples in Thessaly.'

'And what will she do there?' Aspasia said.

The woman blocked the door and she felt trapped in her own room, denied the warmth and shade of the garden. That little patch of green was the closest place to freedom in the hetaira house. She felt she could breathe there.

'She will pray, of course, and play the lyre. They have slaves to scrub and clean and cook, so I imagine they will train Marete in the secret rituals of the temple, that she may one day become a priestess.'

'Not just a whore then?' Aspasia demanded.

The mother's face hardened subtly, her eyes growing sharp.

'A hetaira is not a whore, Aspasia, no,' she said. Her voice was deceptively gentle, as if under great strain. 'We take girls whose parents could not feed them, who sold them to keep their brothers and husbands alive. Some fall away – the *very* stupid, or those who cannot learn obedience! The rest we train: in music, in posture, in dance and conversation. We raise clever girls to be wives – and companions of great men.'

'And those men pay you well enough. Do they buy the whole woman though, or just this?'

Aspasia grabbed at her crotch in the crudest gesture she knew. She hated to be trapped and the conversation was bringing on tears. She wanted the mother to leave. Instead, the woman folded her arms, pale with anger.

'They buy service, Aspasia. They buy your advice and your skill and attention. By the gods, how they crave attention! We taught you to read and to write. No mere whore needs such things! Indeed, if you knew just a little more about the world, you would know how rare it is. You honestly believe this is a whorehouse? I thought you were one of the brighter ones. It seems I was mistaken!'

She saw tears glistening in the girl's eyes and her expression softened.

'Aspasia, you have misunderstood. This house is paid, yes, money we use to feed and clothe those who live here. Unless you think those pots we sell are enough?' The woman sighed and shook her head under that accusing gaze. 'Our girls probably do go to the beds of the men we find for them. And yes, perhaps some of them sell that part you were grabbing, if all else fails. What if they do? The world is a hard place, Aspasia. There is no one to help us when we are hungry. We do what we have to, to live. In this house, we try to match intelligent girls with the lives they should have had. I have visited homes where the husband dotes on the one we found for him, where their children play and are loved.'

'*Everything* you say is a lie!' Aspasia shouted. 'You tell these stories to keep us all quiet – and when you sell us like slaves, we never come back. Why have I not seen any of the ones who left? They could tell us all about their wonderful lives, their warm and loving husbands, their fat little children!'

Tears were streaming then and her voice had grown harsh. The mother leaned against the doorway and crossed one foot over the other.

'Perhaps they feel ashamed, Aspasia, of the place that raised them. Or they don't want to be reminded who they used to be. They have new friends, most of them. Who knows? Every woman is different from the next. No answer will suit them all. Yet they – and you – are bound together, Aspasia, by one thing.'

Aspasia glared in silence, just wanting her to leave. The woman nodded.

'They want to do better than their own mothers. I remember that part, when my sons were born. I wanted to *show* her.' She smiled, but there was a world of grief in it. 'Well, I know a little more now. My eldest died in a fall, the other was killed in the war. My loving husband? He held his chest one day and was just . . . gone. Can you imagine? I sold his shop. He made shoes and I did not have the skill. Without that, the whole place was just tools and some

24

leather. So I came back to this house, Aspasia. And I was welcomed here. Even if you hate it, it's still your home.'

'I just want to get out,' Aspasia said miserably.

'Oh, we'll find you a husband, I don't doubt. Or you'll end up running this place and telling us all what to do. One or the other, before I kill you myself.'

She waited for Aspasia to smile, then stood away from the door.

'Come on. There is white fish and lemon for dinner.'

'I thought you said . . .'

'I say lots of things. Splash some water on your face before you come down. I don't want the others to see you've been crying. And clean your hands, Aspasia! I could grow vegetables under your nails.'

The older woman closed the door gently and went down the stairs. Another crisis smoothed over. She remembered the high dramas of her own years in the house, in that very room, though Aspasia did not know it. Life was hard. She had not lied about that. The hetaira girls were both freer and better educated than any women in the city. If the price of that was letting a few keen dogs get under the fence, it did not seem too high.

2

Sparta burned. As night came, a thousand different fires could be seen. They lent a red glow to the dark, with shadowy figures moving through it. Spartiates still worked in the centre of the city, by the cenotaph for Leonidas and the open forum. They searched through rubble with bloody hands, sending any wounded they found up the hill. Many of the women had gathered food and bandages on the acropolis there, as well as any children who wandered in alone. There was little enough to eat, even for the youngest. The rest endured with just cold water. There were worse things than hunger in the night, after all.

The aftershocks had died away, but no one dared seek shelter, not then. Too many had been injured by pillars and roofs suddenly dropping, betrayed by their own homes and temples. There were no walls left they could be sure would not fall. Instead, they huddled in the open, in groups of surviving family and clan. Army physicians tended wounds and splinted broken bones as best they could.

There was no silence on the acropolis. Children sniffed and murmured, shushed by their mothers. Others muttered prayers, fearing yet more anger from the gods. Lone men called aloud for their families, looking for those they had left to bring back a blanket or a jug of water. Or those who would never answer. It was chaos on the hill, but Spartiate warriors were there too, grim and watchful. No one would storm that place, and for that those who made it there were grateful. The people looked to King Archidamus and the ephors, taking comfort from their presence. Torches were lit, a symbol of life against the night. No Spartan king would cower in the dark. Where the ephors stood, where the civil king held court, Sparta still lived. Yet the helots were not there.

A few had run with the families who owned them, seeking out authority in the first wild rush. Some of those had heard a distant call then and simply vanished as darkness came, slipping away in shadows. Others remained, though they were treated roughly and searched for weapons as they protested their loyalty. Many had been killed, even over the protests of their Spartan families. The mood of that crowd was grim and outraged, without the luxury of mercy while helots still roared and hooted in the city night.

Little by little, Spartan women and children crept closer to Archidamus and the ephors, almost without thought, until the king's party was surrounded by his people. It would be a long night. They had known the earth to shake before, of course, a thousand times. The helots had not rioted then, not like this. That night though, they had become feral. Families whispered of betrayal, of horrors greater than pools draining into cracks or the rippling ground. It had never been as bad, not in all their memories and tales.

In the forum far below, King Pleistarchus reacted to the sound of struggle. He was stalking along the edge of the market square when he heard scuffling feet and hard voices. With just two of his personal guard, he raced towards the sound, leaping over the fallen statue of a king. The three of them skirted the corner of a burning building, crackling away above their heads. Too many temples and homes had kept charcoal braziers. Beams and roof slats had scattered coals as they dropped; the result was fire everywhere, with red embers drifting on the wind.

Pleistarchus had both his short kopis blade ready and a shield on his left arm. He had never dreamed he would go armed for war in the middle of Sparta, but he moved as if towards an enemy. As they had been trained, his companions joined him on both sides, swords drawn and shields raised. Only one had a helmet. The other was bareheaded and wore no sandals. His feet were already swollen and burned, but he did not complain.

Pleistarchus saw four men and two women struggling. He did not hesitate and roared a challenge, stunning the little group to stillness. The attackers tried to scatter and Pleistarchus cut them down in neat and savage blows, dropping them to the cobbled ground.

Two Spartans remained, a man and a woman. The woman sank suddenly to her knees, crumpling over a wound. The man dropped with her, crying out. His arms were running with blood and he had no weapon. Pleistarchus cast a glance at the helots he had killed. They had carried cleavers from some kitchen or shop. One of the things lay at his feet, old iron sharpened to a bowed edge.

As he watched, one of the helots moved. The man's wound was terrible, but he clung to life, trying to rise. They were not as powerful of frame as a Spartan. Lean and wiry, they wore dark and greasy cloth, stained by years of labour. No one would ever mistake a helot for a man of Sparta, Pleistarchus thought. Even in the firelight, he had known them.

One of his guards raised a knife to end the grunting struggle. Pleistarchus touched him on the shoulder. The helot had been cut deeply under his ribs. One of the man's thighs was gashed right through, a hobbling blow. He would not live. Nor could he escape, though he seemed not to know it. Pleistarchus watched him crawl, leaving a red trail. He shook his head, disgusted at the display. Helots were not warriors. They were barely men.

'What happened here?' Pleistarchus asked the pair.

The Spartan pressed his lips to the woman's hair, lost in her. He shook as if he had an ague, a chill. There was so much blood dripping from his arm, Pleistarchus thought he might pass out. Yet he held the woman tight while she too paled. Her hands were clasped over her stomach, dark and wet.

Pleistarchus looked around in frustration, for anyone else to come and take them to safety. Half his guard were escorting women and children to the acropolis, bringing them safe through streets of savagery. Pleistarchus had already witnessed a hundred scenes like this. He could feel drying blood on his face and he still could not understand it. There was a kind of madness in the air, borne out of fear or the depths of the earth. He remembered the strange damp smell that had rolled through the city in the first hour. Perhaps it had driven the helots insane, making them beasts.

He remembered the fears of Archidamus as he looked around at burning buildings, breathing air that stung his skin with its heat. The fires were growing taller, fiercer. The night concealed brutal acts and he could hear cries and thumps and screams all around.

Pleistarchus felt weariness sweep through him in a dark wave. He looked in frustration at the couple sitting on the stones of the street. If he left them, they would be helpless for the next loping group of helots. Oh, they scattered before shield and blade well enough, but he had seen them vanish down alleys and side roads, only to return, howling and peering at those actually trying to save the city.

'Give this man a sword,' he said to one of his companions.

It was an order and the guard did as he was told, the perfect example of *peitharchia* – the total obedience all Spartans learned. Only then did Pleistarchus realise he had no other weapon. In silence, he cursed his own inattention.

The man on the cobbles accepted the blade, understanding what it represented. He still held his woman in bloody arms, willing her to open her eyes. Pleistarchus could see she was dead. There was a stillness to her that he knew only too well. He dropped to one knee.

'She is gone,' he said. 'Come with us now. I will see you safe.'

'I can't . . . I can't leave her,' the Spartan whispered. His eyes were glassy, unfocused. He had no idea he talked to his king. Still, a man had the right to choose his own death.

Pleistarchus patted him on the shoulder and rose. Weariness tugged at his wits again, though he gave no sign. A king had to appear untouched by weakness. His men needed that, no matter what it cost. The truth was he needed to rest, to eat and sleep before he fell. Yet the night was full of screaming and he could not stop.

At his feet, the man holding the fallen woman suddenly slumped. There had been some other wound there, unseen, his tunic sodden with blood. He had showed no pain as death settled softly on him.

With a sigh, Pleistarchus took back the sword, returning

it to his guard. He looked up as more shrieks sounded, closer than before.

'Find whoever is making all that noise,' Pleistarchus said. 'We were too late here. Let's move a little faster this time.'

A hundred thousand helots, or even more. The slaves had lost thousands at Plataea, he recalled. The Athenians had somehow persuaded them to fight against Persian soldiers. They had been cut down then, butchered like goats. Pleistarchus took a grip on his hilt and settled his shield. It felt heavier than before, but he would not set it down. There was no flat edge below, where a man might rest for a time. No, Spartans stood and faced their enemies. He glanced at his father's massive tomb, a block of polished limestone and bronze. The cenotaph of Leonidas had neither ashes nor bones within its brooding mass. He felt his father's spirit even so.

Around a corner, a dozen helots came, laughing and howling like wolves. They halted when they saw his little group. For a moment, Pleistarchus thought they might scatter, but they saw just three battered Spartans and sprawling bodies on the ground. The numbers favoured them and Pleistarchus could see their smiles widen. They carried clubs and blades and they wore dogskin caps and dark cloth. They watched him as rats might watch a wounded animal, made bold by the smell of blood. They were not afraid. Perhaps for the first time in their lives. He clenched his jaw and readied his kopis blade.

'Stay close,' he murmured to the two others. They had sharpened up at the threat facing them, discipline stealing weariness. 'Watch for anyone coming up behind. Ready? With me when I move.'

The Spartans charged, surprising the helots. Pleistarchus smashed his shield into the face of one and cut another with his kopis before they could even react. When they struck back, they met shields and darting blades.

In moments, six of them were down. The helots may have been used to hard labour, but they faced soldiers who had trained in fitness and skill from the age of seven. Pleistarchus and the others went through them like a summer storm.

The survivors managed to run, vanishing into flame-coloured darkness. Pleistarchus turned to his companions as the one with sandals collapsed, the man's mouth opening in shock. He held a hand to his neck and Pleistarchus could see it was wet with blood. Even rats could bite, he realised. He stayed with his man as he died, giving him that honour, though cries sounded all around them. The helots were coming back, Pleistarchus thought, or calling more. He could hear tramping feet and voices giving orders.

For the first time, Pleistarchus faced the thought of his people being wiped out. For all their skill, their armour, their tactics, the Spartiates were few, had always been few. They could not face so many, not wounded and battered by the quake as they were. Without food, they would grow weak – and one by one, the helots would drag them down.

The king rubbed his chest, feeling pain throb there, a ragged beat. It was probably just some muscle aching, though he feared it. His father had died in glory at Thermopylae, standing for all Sparta, giving his life for enough time to bring the army out. Yet Pleistarchus had not been the one to secure the final victory at Plataea. That had fallen to the king's regent, Pausanias.

Pleistarchus would *not* be the last battle king of Sparta. He swore that on Apollo and Ares themselves. A man imposed his will on the world. As Pleistarchus took stock, the night burned.

His remaining guard had taken the sandals of their fallen companion, ever practical in the face of death. Oddly, it gave Pleistarchus hope for his people.

A woman's voice pleaded nearby. He could not ignore it, though he felt very alone in that place. He could hear the howling of slaves too, as savage and frightening as the flames. Pleistarchus clicked his tongue to his companion and the two men walked towards the sound of weeping.

The first light showed blackened ruins. For the final hours of darkness, King Archidamus had set his people to bringing water from the river. They had kept a few temples on the acropolis from being destroyed, but more importantly, it had given them something to do. By morning, some of them had even slept. The worst fires had burned out and only thin trails of smoke rose over most of the city.

Archidamus had not slept. He'd spent the night sending messengers out to their allies, to Corinth and Argos – to Athens. He'd organised patrols of Spartan warriors in full kit. They had orders to drag anyone back who might be called a leader of the helots. The rest were to be killed, on his orders. Pleistarchus had not returned the night before and for all anyone knew, he had not survived the fighting. Archidamus had made that point to the ephors who remained with him, as hungry and miserable as anyone else. The four of them had agreed at last, granting him responsibility. He smiled in memory of that. He was a king and a grandson of kings. Some men feared being tested in fire; Archidamus had always longed for it, to show what he could do.

It made him proud that his people exercised that morning. They made themselves alert with sprints and weapons drills. The women ran until they were flushed while their children cheered them on. Strong women raised strong boys, so it was said. The women of Sparta would never go meekly, Archidamus thought, not if every helot took up arms. If an enemy ever took a Spartan woman to his bed against her will, he would never sleep again, for fear of what she would do.

He tried not to lose heart at how few they were. Half the army was still out, restoring order in the city. Yet they had lost good men in a collapse at the barracks, while hundreds more had been murdered by their own slaves, their throats cut by men and women they had raised from children. It hurt to see his people so reduced.

They needed food, he knew. In normal times, his people ate in communal halls, taking in broths of grains and chicken or lamb, whatever they needed to keep them strong. The helots served in those places and, of course, they were all gone like morning mist. One or two remained with masters they revered, but the streets were empty and stomachs had begun to growl and complain. For all their discipline, they still had to eat that day or grow weak.

Archidamus looked for men to send out in search of food. His gaze fell on two of his personal guard, each one dragging a helot by the arm. The slaves had been battered almost senseless in their capture. They staggered rather than walked, and yet there was a glint in their eyes as they saw him.

Archidamus stood over them when they were thrown

down. One tried to rise and was pressed flat with a sandal on his back. The guard in question drew a sword and held it ready to strike. There was no pity in him. Slaves that rebelled were a threat to the order of gods and men. They had no value at all.

'Where are the rest of your people?' Archidamus asked.

One of the helots spat blood on the ground. The king shook his head. He needed to know and he had no time to waste on them.

'Put the sword in his back,' he ordered. He held up two fingers, outstretched. 'About so deep.'

His guard plunged the tip into the man's flesh, making him cry out.

'Where are your people? Where have they gone?' Archidamus said.

The king mimed twisting with one hand and the guard complied. The helot gasped as the blade turned in him.

'Hold your tongue,' the other muttered.

'If we find the leaders, we will kill only them, do you understand?' Archidamus said. 'If you care about your people, you should tell me who they are. Or I will have to go from village to village with sword and fire.'

He waved the soldier back. The sword tip came out red and Archidamus tutted, his voice becoming gentler.

'Come on, boys, it's over! There has been a lot of blood spilled, but I don't want to see any more. Understand? There are some who want to kill all the helots – to slaughter every last one. But who would make our bread then, or tend our fields? Who would rebuild our houses?'

That was how that fool Pleistarchus would have put it, Archidamus thought. The man traded too often on the glory of his father. Well, Archidamus knew what had to be done. The helots had earned a red-handed slaughter. He would leave only their youngest children, a meek new generation to serve.

'Lads,' he said kindly. 'All we want are the leaders! They'll have to die, you understand that much! But not the rest, not the wives and mothers. Come on, you can't be really thinking of living as free men! You'd starve without our fields and flocks, wouldn't you? Can you imagine all of you helots shivering in the winters without coats and blankets? Or do you think you could defend yourselves against those who would come?' He chuckled and it was a gentle sound, a father reproving his boys with humour and a little sadness. 'Come on. Where are they hiding?'

The one his man had wounded looked up, red-eyed.

'Mount Ithome,' he said.

His companion shook his head and sighed. 'You fool,' he murmured, resting his forehead on the dust.

'Mount Ithome is where your leaders are?' Archidamus asked.

The helot nodded, eager to please, desperate not to be hurt again.

'I know that place,' one of the ephors said. Archidamus turned his head as the man came closer. 'An hour's march west. Two peaks and a ridge between. Very steep. Can't be taken easily, not if they want to hold it.'

'How many helots have gone there, into the hills?' Archidamus said.

The man was *weeping*, he saw in astonishment. His helot companion glared, which Archidamus could understand, but tears? Helots were like children.

He looked up from his interrogation when a cry of joy

sounded. The name of Pleistarchus on the wind made him tense, but Archidamus felt no great pleasure when he saw the battered and blistered figure of the battle king approaching. A chill passed through him then, raising goosebumps on his arms. For just a moment in the dawn light, Pleistarchus looked very much like his father.

Pleistarchus walked through crowds of people all clustering close, trying to touch his tattered cloak. As he halted before Archidamus, the civil king had to summon his will not to take a step back. Pleistarchus had gone out the night before as an untested man. He smelled of smoke and blood then as he stood on the acropolis before his people, his eyes dark with sorrow or anger. Archidamus could not help feeling his own clean cloak and armour somehow rebuked him.

'Most of the helots have pulled back – heading west,' Pleistarchus said. 'The ones who are left have blocked off entire sections of the city. They are building new walls with rubble and mortar. They say they rule there now.' He was breathing hard and swaying, utterly exhausted.

'They'll starve then,' Archidamus said. 'Or we'll break in like foxes among chickens. We must make an example of them all, a lesson for the rest. When we have established order, we can take the army to Ithome. That's where the leaders are.'

'You haven't seen it, Archidamus,' Pleistarchus said. 'There are too many of them. They've gone mad.'

'Then we restore order, street by street! I have sent runners to our allies. When they come, we will take back the city.'

The dawn seemed to grow cold as Pleistarchus turned to face the civil king.

'You did not ask me first,' he said, his voice dangerously soft.

Archidamus shook his head.

'The ephors agreed, but it was my decision.' He pointed. 'You were down there, in the city. I spent the night tending the wounded and counting the dead. Have you any idea how many we've lost? More than Persia ever managed!'

His voice dropped as he gave voice to the most secret fear of Sparta.

'We have always been too few, Pleistarchus! Two thousand Spartiates are dead or missing – as many wounded. We *need* support. What good are allies otherwise?'

'All right,' Pleistarchus said. There was no point arguing about a decision already made. 'It will still be days before anyone comes to aid us. Perhaps I can restore order before then.'

He glanced at the two helots still lying on the ground. They had heard every word, of course. Pleistarchus gestured sharply and they were killed, their cries cut off. The bodies were dragged away by their heels.

'We need food most of all, then wood for warmth and shelter,' Archidamus said. He nodded to Pleistarchus, feeling an accord between them. 'More weapons, salvaged tools . . . everything.' He looked at the rising sun. 'We have light. Let us use the day.'

3

The Spartan runner halted at the walls of Athens, looking around in frustration. There was nothing like those huge constructions at home. There, men themselves were the walls. A line of carts and farmers waited to enter through a massive gate, guarded by soldiers and watched from wooden towers above. It was all vanity, as far as the Spartan could tell. He walked to the front of the line. One or two of the farmers looked up, but there was something about him that held their tongues.

The runner was utterly filthy, legs black to the knee, skin scratched and scraped. He wore only sandals and a red cloak twisted to rope around his waist. For a Spartan to have driven himself so hard could not be a good thing. The merchants watched him like thoughtful cattle, unblinking.

Still panting, he unrolled his cloak and secured it around his shoulders. The wall guards had already sent a runner to the city council. Its officers were chosen from whichever tribe held command that month, so they did not know yet who would answer the call.

The epistates who came to the gate was a stranger to the men there. Short and barrel-chested, Andreas of Antiochis stared at the silent Spartan. Despite the filth and sweat, the runner wore disdain like a second cloak. From ancient instinct, all those watching prickled with dislike.

'Who is in authority here?' the Spartan demanded of

the crowd. His voice was hoarse and one of the guards held out a skin of wine and water. He ignored it, his duty still unfulfilled.

'That would be me,' Andreas replied, stepping forward. 'Andreas of Antiochis tribe, epistates to the council, at least until sunset. If you bear a message, I can summon the council or the Assembly.'

The Spartan blinked. He had not been to Athens before. It seemed at least some of the wilder rumours were true.

'Take me to Aristides, or Xanthippus,' he said after a moment. Those were names he knew, from the conflicts of Salamis and Plataea. To his astonishment, the Athenian shook his head.

'Ah. I am sorry to say both men have gone on, to Elysium and sunlit fields I do not doubt. They have crossed the river. No one here can call them back.'

'Do all of you speak this way?' the Spartan demanded in frustration. 'I come from Sparta, from the side of King Archidamus! I left yesterday and I have run all night and morning, without food or rest. Would you delay me now, with the news I bring? Take me to your kings or great men!'

The epistates looked again at the dust and sweat that clung to the lean-limbed runner, his hollow eyes and obvious exhaustion. The Athenian made a decision and nodded to the guards. They stepped back, still magnificently ready to bear spear and sword against a single stranger. The Spartan seemed utterly oblivious to them as he came through.

'I will take responsibility for this man,' Andreas announced for the benefit of the crowd. 'Resume your vigil here. I will send a skin of wine and some olives and bread out to you.'

The guards smiled and thanked him as he guided the Spartan into the city. Andreas did not see the crude gestures that rose and fell once his back was turned. He was epistates for just a day, after all. They felt he took the role too seriously.

Another messenger was despatched to summon the council. On hearing that, the lone Spartan relaxed subtly, so that he staggered. His long trial was almost over, and he wondered if Sparta lay destroyed behind him.

'When did you say you set out?' the epistates said.

The swaying red cloak was drawing a crowd, stallholders and passers-by all staring at a Spartan warrior in their midst. The cities may have been allies, but they had been enemies too, in the past.

The Agora opened up before them, with the hills of the Pnyx and the great Acropolis looming over all. The Spartan looked in astonishment at signs of wealth on all sides, at gold jewellery and fine cloth. Even beggars seemed to have sandals as good as his own.

'Yesterday night . . .' he replied, drinking in the sights of a city he had known only in stories.

'Perhaps you exaggerate. It is four days' march to Sparta. Of course, our runner Pheidippides ran to Sparta and back in just three days, then marched to Marathon.'

'And died on his return, as I heard it,' the Spartan said. 'Athenians should never try to be Spartan.'

The epistates looked sour, saying nothing else as he reached the council building on the edge of the Agora. There, officers of the Boule council were gathering for an emergency meeting, with hundreds more coming in. Across the city, five hundred representatives had put down tools or walked out of shops, running to hear the news as

41

word spread. The seats of the great debate chamber were filling like water into a jug.

From the side facing the Agora, the Spartan looked in at them, past columns of polished stone.

'These men will hear me?' he asked.

'Well, to a point,' the epistates said with a shrug. 'The floor is yours, once we have given sacrifice. When you are called, you may speak. We will decide then whether to call the full Assembly of Athens – up to twenty thousand free citizens. You may then be granted a chance to address that greater body, if your cause is judged worthy.'

'How can men live like this?' the Spartan murmured.

Andreas of Antiochis decided he did not like the fellow's arrogance. He pretended not to have heard.

'What about emergencies? War or . . . destruction?' the Spartan said more clearly.

The epistates looked at him, sensing desperation as well as anger. He firmed his jaw.

'You have come for our help, have you not? Perhaps then, you should assume a humbler manner. Ask and we will answer. But you will not make stone less hard, or water less wet. We are Athenian – men of honour.'

Silence had come. The Spartan looked at Andreas of Antiochis in red-eyed exasperation, then walked to the centre of the hall to address these men of Athens. He held the rostrum tightly, as if it prevented his collapse.

Pleistarchus could hardly believe what he was seeing. The battle king ordered two officers and sixty warriors to split off and seek a way to flank new barricades. The helots had learned from the first bloody encounters. They refused battle now whenever it was offered, no longer daring to attack Spartiates in the open. Instead, they dragged rubble and beams across open roads and pelted his men with bricks, tiles and sling-stones.

Pleistarchus had seen more of his men injured – when he could not afford to lose a single one. While his Spartans trained for war, helots worked as carpenters, bakers, potters and farmers. They had both bladed tools and murderous intent. More than once, his men had overwhelmed a position where they were melting lead to form sling-shot, whipping finger-length pieces high into the air as fast as they could cool them. The helots struck in packs, then ran, without armour to slow them down.

Pleistarchus wiped what he thought was sweat from his forehead. His forearm came away red and he blinked at it. Someone else's, he realised numbly. The helots were still developing their tactics, but they were overmatched in every way. More than once, they had simply failed to understand how fast Spartans could sprint in chestplate, kilt and greaves. The helots had paid a savage price for that. The trouble was, there were just so many of them! He'd lost one of his best men that morning, with another three so badly wounded they had to be sent to the acropolis. Archidamus had extended safe territory there, taking back the city street by street around that hill. Yet the helots knew the roads as well as they did. They scrambled away when odds turned against them, then returned, whipping slings to a blur.

'Three unit – lock shields and advance.'

Six men moved immediately out of line. Pleistarchus held up a hand to halt the rest. He had two large groups out flanking, the rest in reserve. Helots were like children, or wild boar. They had no understanding of tactics . . .

43

One of his men cried a warning and the air filled with stones flung from behind. Another force of helots had come across them and attacked, or . . . He felt a chill at the thought of them evading his flanking groups, detouring around a huge part of the city to come up from the rear.

The king snapped an order to turn and attack. The result was rapid, without hesitation. The entire unit moved as one, trusting one another, racing to kill. They kept shields ready, with spears raised, driving all before them.

Pleistarchus showed his teeth, tasting metal on his lips. The helots wanted none of what they saw coming. Instead of standing like men, they ran, sprinting in all directions. He saw his warriors catch and spit a few, silencing their cries with hacking blows. They too could be butchers. Yet a Spartan fell senseless, struck by something. As he passed, Pleistarchus saw the man's nose had been broken, an eye crushed.

He swore to himself. He and his men had killed four at too great a cost. It could not go on. He wondered if he would be the first Spartan king to lose the entire city. To retreat on a battlefield was bad enough – even just to regroup. No Spartan threw down his shield to run! *E tan e epi tas*. Come back 'with it or on it', as their wives and mothers said.

To be forced to tuck tail and run by mere slaves would be the end, Pleistarchus was certain. Even if order was eventually restored, he would not survive the judgement of the ephors. It was better to die than bring shame on Sparta. That was a king's role too.

A horn sounded nearby, a battlefield blare that made his heart sink. Corinth had come, responding to Archidamus. They had to have marched without delay to be there so

44

soon. Pleistarchus saw hoplites in golden armour intercept one group of fleeing helots. They cut them down in dozens, suddenly just there, blocking the road. Pleistarchus smiled at that, though it turned sour as he considered how reduced Sparta must look to foreign eyes.

The earth was long still, like a dog that had bitten and retreated to its spot by the door in guilt and fear. Yet the damage was done – the city lay in ruins, a dusty maze where young helots and Spartan soldiers played cat and mouse. Bodies sprawled everywhere and the entire world was disrupted. In his despair, Pleistarchus wondered if he could even feed the men of Corinth.

He welcomed their officer, a tall man in his forties. The Corinthian was looking around in disbelief as he introduced himself, kneeling to the son of Leonidas.

'You are welcome, Nestos,' Pleistarchus replied. 'As you see, we are working to set the city to rights. How many have you brought?'

'Just the four hundred with me. I wish it were more, Majesty. Our king sent as many as he could at once, with others to follow. We were not sure then of the extent of the threat.' He looked around as he spoke and his expression was troubled. 'I did not expect such . . . destruction.'

'This is a hard land – it breeds hard men. We can rebuild easily enough,' Pleistarchus said with a forced smile. 'As soon as we have put down this rebellion. I'm afraid our dogs have gone wild.'

'I saw,' Nestos responded drily. He was still taking in the battered appearance of the Spartans. In normal times, each of them would have gone to war with helot slaves to tend his kit. Without that support, they seemed a rougher and less polished force. He could sense an outrage in their glares, a consuming anger. The Corinthian general looked away.

'I am at your command, Majesty, on behalf of my king. Corinth stands with Sparta.'

'Good. There is a stronghold of them in the western part of the city. They bring food to it each night from the mountains, where they have villages and towns of their own. Perhaps we let them grow too many, Nestos. Either way, I must cull them now. With fresh men, we can break their barricades and drive them beyond the city bounds. When we are secure here, my people can restore the city, while you and I take the fight into the hills.'

'Will you reach an agreement with them? Is there any bargain to be made?' Nestos asked. He waved a hand over streets of rubble and leaning walls.

Pleistarchus wondered how he could prevent the man finding out how terrible the losses had been. For the first time in his lifetime, in *centuries*, Sparta had been fatally weakened. His people had just lost too many in the quake and the uprising that followed. The power of Sparta lay in her army, but the earth and fire and wild children had stolen their strength.

He knew there would be enemies ready to take advantage. Even an ally like Corinth might wonder if their time had come. The god of war had no favourites, so it was said.

He kept his voice light, without weariness or despair.

'Don't hold back on these streets. My orders are to kill anyone who dares to face us. But when we have driven the helots into the hills? Spare only the children. A man doesn't kill all his mules, not while there is still a load to carry.'

*

46

The air was warm and still on the Pnyx, the torches kindled as the day's light began to fade. The Athenian Assembly took time to call. For their usual monthly meetings, a red rope was used, held between Scythian guards as they shepherded citizens to their duty. They had not had to dip it in dye that day. Word had spread and the entire city seemed to have turned out to hear what was happening.

Cimon made his voice carry. If he had submitted to their judgement just days before, perhaps he was stronger because of that. Certainly, they did not shuffle or mutter when he spoke, as they did with some. Cimon had broken fleets and armies before. Now that Aristides had crossed the river, he was the most experienced strategos and archon they had.

'I stood on Delos,' Cimon said, 'when the great oath was taken, when the League of Hellenes was created. I was there, with Xanthippus, with Aristides. They rest now, while we remain in the fight and the dust.'

He was a good speaker, Pericles thought, watching him. He and Cimon had shared a thousand discussions on board ship. It was something men did on the night watch, when the waters were calm and they rested safe in a great fleet. Some repaired and polished their kit. Others talked, telling stories or teasing out ideas. Pericles and Zeno had often found themselves arguing one side against Cimon and Anaxagoras. That training showed then, in the way Cimon ordered his thoughts.

'That Great League brought cities together in the face of a Persian threat, as men will always band against a common enemy. Yet it survives while Persia is quiet, licking the wounds we gave her.'

He was too modest to mention the part he had played,

Pericles thought. Yet words unspoken could still be heard.

'I saw something in that dream, that alliance of cities. I saw brotherhood – and it included Sparta, though they were not there. I accepted Spartan command of the navy, because I had come to realise they too are my brothers. We took Cypros with them, the jewel of the east. Those of you who remember Plataea will know what it means to stand alongside such men. They honour the gods and all our customs. They know the mysteries of Eleusis and the oracle of Apollo at Delphi. They run against us at the games! And they lose to Athenians, often as not!'

He chuckled and the crowd smiled with him, losing a little of their fierceness. Pericles knew that was something Zeno had taught, to let the crowd know it was time to smile. When Cimon frowned, the air felt colder and they leaned in to hear him.

'The Spartans are allies and brothers. We have fought beside them too many times – and yes, we have faced them down as well, more than once. I call myself first an *Athenian*. Not petty, not small. Not venal or full of spite. No Athenian is those things! So I call on the Assembly to respond to brothers, to allies, to friends. To brothers, to allies . . . to friends. Let me take the army to help them in their hour of need, to rebuild and restore order. Let us show Sparta what having Athens on your side actually means. Let us be friends, let us be allies, let us be brothers!'

It was a fair ending. Pericles saw his friend Zeno nodding at the use of three, and simple repetition. Many in the crowd cheered as Cimon walked down the few steps, passing Ephialtes. The strategos had been reappointed in his annual role, his support in the city growing every year.

He climbed to the speaker's stone with no more than a cool nod.

Ephialtes held up his hands to quiet the crowd as they shuffled and muttered to one another. Those who kept talking were elbowed sharply by his supporters.

'Gentlemen, Athenians, it falls to me to make the case we all know in our hearts. What happens in Sparta is not our concern.' Ephialtes shook his head as if disappointed. 'Oh, *Archon* Cimon speaks true when he talks of allies, but not for men like you or me. No. The nobles of Athens would have you give your lives to serve the nobles of Sparta, I do not doubt! He calls us small and petty? Oh, they know their own – and they answer the call of their own. They would happily spill the blood of common Athenian men in response to that call – and for what? The gratitude of Spartans?'

He chuckled and shook his head. The very idea was amusing and many in the crowd responded. Pericles glowered as the man waved a hand to indicate Cimon below.

'*Archon* Cimon has always favoured the Spartans, the Lacedaemons, over his own. What did you call your son? Lacedaemonius? And you carry a Spartan kopis blade on your belt . . . Of *course* you speak for them!' He shook his head, dismissing Cimon. 'Well, I speak for the people here. If there was an earthquake in Sparta, let them rebuild without us. If there is a slave rebellion, let their nobles put it down, without one drop of Athenian blood!'

Ephialtes stood down to some cheering, though there were arguments too in the crowd. The mood was darkening as different factions clashed. Before he had a clear plan, Pericles raised his hand. The epistates saw him and heard the cries of 'Speaker here' from Zeno and Anaxagoras as they pressed him to the front.

Neither Cimon nor Ephialtes was sure which side he would support, Pericles realised. He looked out on some twenty thousand of his people, all crammed into that place and down the gentle slopes. When they voted, the result would truly be the voice of the city. Right or wrong, it was the authority of men, under the gods. He swallowed and breathed.

'Brothers, allies, friends,' he began, deliberately echoing the words from Cimon.

Ephialtes scowled and looked away from him.

'What do Spartans see when they look to us? To Athens? They see our great port, our trade, our potteries and workshops, the wealth that flows in. They see our magnificent fleet, paid for by the League. They see power and influence that grows every single year. When men talk of Hellenes, they speak of Athens.'

He paused as the breeze lifted, smelling sweat and mint.

'Yet when the subject is war, they talk of Sparta. I saw Athens burned twice when we could not stop the armies of Persia. Do you remember? With many of you, I watched from the island of Salamis as King Xerxes stood on this very hill. We could not stop him, not then. The Spartan army took the field at Plataea – shamed into it, as I recall. Yet they smashed that host. No single day will ever mean as much again, not in my lifetime. Well, this is a chance to repay part of that debt, to show honour to the gods and to our allies. If you wish, to show all Hellenes what it means to have Athens on your side. Archon Cimon . . .' He said the title without the sneer Ephialtes brought to it. 'Archon Cimon has the right of it.'

He paused as if a thought had just occurred to him, though it was the reason he had risen to speak.

'For those of you who still scowl, I think you will enjoy reminding Sparta that they had to call for our help! That will be a gift for our old age, I think!'

There was some laughter at that. Pericles nodded to the epistates, and the man looked for more speakers. The day had fled, with a break only for lunch around noon. There had been dozens of speakers, with repeat performances and questions asked and answered. Yet it seemed to have come to a natural end. They were ready to vote and, once again, Pericles would be the last to address the Assembly.

When it came, the actual vote was quick. Officers of the council counted – and the result was close, but clear by seven hundred votes. Cimon would lead hoplites to Sparta. The exact number would be decided by the city, so that the walls were not stripped of all those who might stand in defence. Yet Cimon was pleased. He nodded to Pericles, and the younger man chose his moment to approach, though a crowd of well-wishers still clapped Cimon on the back.

'I would like to come with you, if you'll allow it,' Pericles said.

Cimon turned his head to stare and Pericles did not look away. They had fought side by side in Cypros. Each owed the other his life and that was a bond, perhaps one even a trial could not break.

'Your father was a man of honour,' Cimon said. 'In

his memory, I accept. Be here at dawn. I will not wait for you.'

It was a slight easing of the chill between them. Pericles felt relief as he nodded. The evening was already late and he would have to fetch his father's shield from the estate. He sighed at that. His wife was there. If Pericles thought he'd known cold before, her welcome was the very heart of winter.

4

The moon had risen by the time Pericles arrived at his home outside the city. He rapped his knuckles on the iron door and waited while someone shuffled up the inner steps. It took an age, though Pericles waited patiently. Manias was no longer the man Pericles had known in his youth. He had been a slave then, before his own labours freed him. The estate had paid him a wage since the war. As a result, Manias had taken a wife and rented a small house in the Ceramicus area of the city. His health had always been good, right up to the point of the spasm that had ruined him. These days, he rolled as he walked, half-dragging a leg, while he held his right hand curled into his chest like a claw.

Pericles looked up at one who would always smile to see him. Manias' face was all eyebrows and nose, his hair white and hard-cropped. Yet the old man beamed, revealing a few remaining teeth.

Pericles waited as Manias made his slow and careful way back down. When the door opened, he stepped into a courtyard of cut limestone, leading to a path and the main house beyond. He reached out and took Manias' good left hand in an awkward grip. The man's face drooped on one side and he had trouble speaking and eating. It was all a long way from the one who had carried Pericles and his brother around the paddock, snorting and pawing the ground like the Minotaur.

It was quiet in the darkness, with a warm breeze from the back field. Pericles breathed it in: his home, where his mother Agariste and his wife Thetis endured their own long war. He paused when he realised it had been at least a month since he'd seen either of them. He spent most days in the town-house in the city, his father's bolthole and refuge, rebuilt after the Persian invasion.

With a grunt, Manias shoved the bar back into place, patting it to be sure it was secure. Pericles noticed his left bicep was wrapped in a stained cloth, marked with a coin of blood.

'Are you hurt, Manias?' he asked.

'It's nothing. Just a fall.' The old man's voice was slurred and he looked embarrassed. He spread his arm wide, ushering Pericles further.

'A fall from where?' Pericles asked as they walked.

'Just a fall. I was cutting out some rotten wood. The ladder slipped.'

'I thought I'd made it clear you were not to work,' Pericles replied.

He frowned. Both slaves and free men grew old. Some families put them out at the end, to beg or starve. There were a few temples that provided a bowl of soup and a little bread, but the elderly rarely lasted longer than a single winter.

Pericles knew his mother would not have gainsaid his word. There was only one other who could have sent the old man up a ladder or onto the roof.

'You know,' Pericles said as they walked, 'I've seen you build walls and fences with the strength of men half your age. I've seen you take up arms to defend this place as well, to protect my family.' He stopped for a moment, halting Manias with a touch. 'There is no shame now in letting others take the weight. This time it's just a gashed arm. What's next, a broken neck? Was it my wife who sent you up?'

'A house always needs work, kurios,' Manias replied without looking at him. It was not an answer.

'Not from you, not any longer. You *will* rest, Manias.'

'All right, all right,' he said, grumpily.

There was still pride in him. That was part of the problem. Pericles followed him to the front porch. Voices could be heard calling inside, rousing the kitchens and the mistress. The master was home.

Pericles sighed. All he really wanted was to retrieve his father's shield and weapons. He knew Cimon was telling the truth about not waiting for him. When the sun rose again, the Athenians would march – with or without Pericles.

Voices called as he entered the house and he smiled for the first time. His sons arrived like a battle charge, and he bent to embrace them. Both of them had grown, he noted. They were as much young men as boys, though Paralus still rushed in with a cry of happiness, butting his father in the lip with his head, telling him a dozen things in a great torrent. Xanthippus stood back, frowning, though Pericles held out a hand to him. It had been too long, he realised. He held Paralus too tight, until the boy began to complain.

'You should both be asleep at this hour,' Pericles told them, laughing as he rose. He nodded to Xanthippus and his son returned the gesture. Not everyone could rush into the arms of another, Pericles thought a little sadly. He had been the same as a boy.

Xanthippus had been named for the father Pericles had adored; Paralus for a hero of Athenian history. As he looked them over, he felt pride in the men they were becoming. They were easily the best thing to have come from his marriage.

Pericles looked up as he sensed his wife's gaze. Thetis stood in a pale robe, leaning on a doorpost, almost like a ghost in the moonlight.

'Come on, lads,' Pericles said.

He was about to send them to bed when he realised he would not see them in the morning. Instead, he ignored the woman standing in disapproving judgement.

'Boys, I am going away for a time – not to war, but to help rebuild Sparta. They had a terrible earthquake and they need my help. I'm leaving at dawn.'

Both Xanthippus and Paralus were silent as he explained, then the youngest turned sharply away, knuckling tears from his eyes. Paralus did not want his father to see.

'I thought you were going to stay this time,' Xanthippus said. He didn't try to hide his resentment, from his tone or his expression.

'It won't be for more than a month,' Pericles said. 'I've been away too long recently, I see that. I'll make sure I spend more time with you.'

Paralus was looking nervously from one to the other, sensing a great tension between them. Xanthippus and his father spoke as if they were delivering battle reports. Yet neither would give way.

'I have taken up carving, Dad,' Paralus said loudly. 'Manias says a man should know how to use a chisel and a mallet.'

Pericles ruffled Paralus' hair.

'And Manias is right. Now then, boys. I need to sort out a few things. Go to bed now, please. I'll see you when I get back.'

Pericles watched as Xanthippus turned away without another word, taking his brother off into the dark of the house. There was anger there! Had he needed a father when he was the same age? Pericles wasn't sure. He promised himself a few days uninterrupted with his sons when he came back.

He turned then to where his wife had stood. Thetis had gone, vanished into the darkness of the sleeping house. Pericles clenched his jaw. In the council building, he knew exactly how and when to speak. It all just . . . worked. Yet in his own house, he was met with waves of scorn or dislike. All he wanted was to fetch his shield! For a moment, he was tempted to ignore the challenge, to just find his kit and head out to the rally point. Yet he could not. Manias still watched and Pericles shook his head as their eyes met.

'Bring me my shield and spear, would you, Manias?' he said softly. 'I must have words with my wife.'

Manias nodded in silence. Pericles took a deep breath. Perhaps it was the unreality of night, where nothing seemed as good or true as it did by day. Or simply that he was about to leave the city he knew. He found a certainty growing in him as he made his way through the house to his wife's rooms.

Thetis had been sure Pericles would come, always knowing him better than he did himself. She waited in bed, knees drawn up and some bolster wedged behind so she was almost armoured fore and back. A little lamp burned with a clear flame at her bedside, crackling only lightly. It was the good oil then, that cost twice as much as cheap tallow. She had grown used to such things, Pericles thought.

He sat uncomfortably on the edge of the bed. She did not look at him, but he sensed her anger in every line.

'Was that the truth?' she said at last. 'You're going to help the Spartans – or to fight?'

'I wouldn't lie to the boys, Thetis. They'd hear it from their friends if I did. Sparta is damaged – some great tremor of the earth. Their slaves are in revolt and we'll go armed for war, but I think it will be mostly to help rebuild. We'll take food and tools, some coin, as well as architects and carpenters. The Assembly has agreed to fund all of it.'

'You haven't been here for over a month and now you are going *away*?' she said. Her voice was like a lash and he recoiled. 'You leave me here like a prisoner, while you enjoy the plays and the drinking houses in the city – and the women, I don't doubt.'

'Well, there's cold welcome here!' he snapped. 'All I get are bitter looks or arguments. Or the details of some foolish dispute with my mother. Did you tell Manias to fix something on the roof? Was that how he hurt his arm?'

Her face twisted and he wondered how he had ever found her attractive.

'Oh, has he been carrying tales to his master? That crippled old dog should be put out of his misery. He forgets half the things he's told to do. Who knows how he hurt himself? I doubt even he can say for certain.'

'I told you, Thetis, he has earned a peaceful retirement. He has worked for us all my life and he deserves a few quiet years on the estate. You forget he is not a slave, not any longer.'

'Nor much of a servant either, if he won't work.'

'I remember when you had *no* slaves or servants!' he shouted at her. 'Have you forgotten how things were when I found you? You had *nothing*.'

'And you were just a foolish boy,' she retorted. 'Well, there are times I wish I had not come to Athens! I saw your father was dying and my heart went out to you. If I'd known this would be my life, that you would abandon me here, with just your mother and slaves as my companions . . .'

'I have not abandoned you,' he said. 'There are women in the city who would give everything they have for your life here.'

'And you know all of them, I suppose. Well, I married you, Pericles, in my pity. I was never your whore.'

'No, that was just for Cimon,' he said. He regretted it as her face pinched and her hands clasped the covers. She drew them up with her dignity.

'I am the mother to your sons,' she said.

'They are the only good to come from this marriage,' he replied. The words came too quickly. His anger had sprung from her saying she pitied him. He would have taken it back if he could, but it was too late.

'Oh, get out,' she said softly. 'Just get *out*! Why do you sit on this bed? You are the stranger here, not me! Xanthippus said so just the other day. The boys hardly know you.'

He stood slowly and felt a weight ease from him. He almost swayed as he stood there. Even in her fury, she saw the change in him. She frowned, suddenly afraid.

'Get out,' she said more softly, looking away from him.

He said nothing for a time, looking for doubts. No, it was right.

'If you had paid a dowry, I could return it to you,' he

said at last. 'Instead, I will settle funds and property on you, enough to be comfortable.'

'You . . . you are *divorcing* me?' she said.

He nodded. The words had to be spoken aloud.

'I am,' he said. 'I divorce you.'

Thetis shook her head in silence, then words came pouring out.

'You poor fool. I thought at least you had the character of your father, that you would see to the end whatever you began. But no, you can't even do that. I should have known, when you stopped coming to my bed. You *had* the sons you wanted! And all your clever friends, with their talk and laughter. Like geese, cackling away! What could you possibly need me for, that you could not find in your precious city?'

'You can have the town-house,' he said firmly. 'There is a small staff there, enough for you to live at ease. I'll find somewhere else.'

She was weeping, he saw. For a moment, his resolve softened. Yet saying the words had been right. He'd married her in a moment of madness, before heading out to fight Persians. He hadn't known then if he would return, or die as his brother had died, broken on a strange shore. The reality of marriage to Thetis was more than a grand gesture. It was years and years . . . of this.

'You deserve better . . .' he said. 'You aren't happy with me, Thetis. You never have been.'

There it was again, the barb that snagged in each other's skin when they talked. He could hardly remember looking on her without a sense of regret.

'So you will cast me off,' she said through tears.

She buried her face in the covers and sobbed. When she looked up, her eyes were red, her face swollen.

'Go on then!' she said. 'Go to your Spartans, your noble rescue. Leave me here, again, as you always do, with only slaves to talk to.'

'You'll have a month to move out,' he said, suddenly stern. He would not let her ignore what had been said. The words were out, but he knew she could turn the night into a dream, almost. Some women could remake reality, but he could not let her do it, not this time.

'Manias knows the town-house,' Pericles said. 'I'll leave word there to let you in. I'll leave the deed as well, with Xanthippus named on it. He will inherit, of course.'

'So I will have nothing,' she said.

'You have my word, Thetis. I'll come to see the boys when I return. They still need tutors and I'll pay for all of that. You'll get a small income from the estate, at least until you marry again.'

She spat curses at him then, a furious stream of sound that made him grit his jaw and leave her to her sobbing. He wondered how long that would last when he was not there to be affected by it.

As he drew the door gently shut, he saw his two sons were in the dark corridor. His mother too had come to see him. The three stood together, Paralus with his mother's arm around him. He had been crying, Pericles realised. In the silence of the night, no doubt they had heard everything.

'Ah. I'm sorry, lads,' he said. 'Your mother and I were arguing. I'll come to see you when I return.'

'You're throwing us *out*?' Xanthippus demanded.

Once again, Pericles heard the tone of the man he was

becoming, the seething anger. He was only defending his mother, he reminded himself.

Pericles shook his head, exchanging a glance with Agariste. His own mother was as white-haired as Manias, though age had touched her more lightly. Of all of them, she seemed least distressed by what she had heard.

With a sob, Paralus suddenly put out his arms. Pericles gathered him in. He could smell clean grass in the boy's hair.

'I am not throwing you out,' he said. 'This house is your *home*, and always will be.' He felt them trembling, caught up in waves of strong emotion. 'Do you understand? Your yaya would kill me if I tried to keep you out, don't you think? You are my blood, boys! That is unbreakable. You are my father's line – my sons.'

'My grandsons,' his mother added.

Pericles smiled and nodded.

'There is no place in the world where I will not welcome you at my side. I swear that on Athena herself – and she is a goddess of the hearth, the home. She would never forgive a broken oath from a father to his sons.'

'What about mum?' Xanthippus said. 'You are casting her off? How can you?'

He was unrelenting, his eyes bright with angry tears. Pericles could still remember how his father had seemed to him on the day he had gone out to fight at Marathon. The armour warm from the sun, the smell of oil and sweat.

'Your mother and I . . . have come to the end of our road. She will be fine, Xanthippus, I will make sure of it. She will live in the town-house in the city – and you will live with her. But your rooms will *always* be here if you want to come back . . . I wonder though, will you help her to settle in? She will need you to look after her, at least for a while. You'll make new friends and go to tutors in the city – friends of mine like Anaxagoras and Zeno, or the musician, Damon. Or the architect, Phidias. And of course, sword drills and fitness – the spear and the shield. I should have arranged it before now. My word, there is so much to learn! You'll be busy and your mother will need you. Can I depend on you to help her?'

Paralus nodded. Xanthippus pulled away and vanished into the dark. Pericles stared after him.

'He will understand in time, Paralus,' he said. 'I know you will not let me down. Go on, go back to your room now. There will be a lot to do in the morning.'

Paralus raced after his brother, not needing light in the place they called home. Pericles was left alone with his mother. He could no longer hear the sounds of sobbing from his wife's room, he noticed. Of course, she could still be listening.

'I can't stay longer,' he said. 'Will you speak to Xanthippus when I'm gone?'

'I'll put him straight. They'll get over it,' his mother said. 'Are you sure though?'

'Don't pretend you aren't delighted,' he said wryly.

'Oh, I am, but it's still an ending. There isn't a way back, Pericles, not from this.'

'I know,' he said. He took a moment, then shook his head. 'I feel lighter. It's right, I am certain. I cannot regret marrying her, not with the two boys. I would not have them if not for Thetis – nor would you.'

'That is true,' she said with a smile. 'Good crops can come from bad ground, it seems. Very well. I pray you'll find happiness apart – as you never could together.'

*

The sun rose on a host of spears. Bronze shields of gold and vividly painted colours were carried on their backs, slung on leather straps. Four thousand Athenian hoplites had been allowed to join Cimon on the mission to Sparta. With them went at least another thousand, those with skills a city might need to rebuild. Carpenters, lead workers and tilers stood and chatted with brickmakers and potters. Grain and salted meat or cheese lay stacked and wrapped on wooden cart-beds. There was even a portable forge, drawn by asses, tended by a master smith and his apprentices.

It had all been put together at astonishing speed. Just the food alone had been commandeered from ships unloading down at the docks, a flurry of forced purchases that would have to be redeemed when presented to the council. The men's wages too had been taken on by the Assembly. Every day away from the city meant a huge sum in silver that had to be set aside. They were not slaves, but free Athenians.

Pericles waited with them, his father's shield on his back, a spear in his right hand. The length of Macedonian ash felt good. His father had held that same grip at Marathon, after all. Every piece of his kit was inherited, polished, repaired and loved. It had saved his life more than once in the heat of battle, when he had last stood at Cimon's side.

The journey from Athens to Sparta took four days in normal times. Pericles had heard Cimon was determined to get there in three. The hoplites could do it, he thought. They ran every day, as fit and lean as hunting dogs. Only the carts and equipment would slow them down. There were few real roads between the two cities. In places, the ground was little more than broken stones. Yet, left too far behind, the carts would be vulnerable to bandits and thieves.

Pericles was staring at Cimon as he thought. It caught the man's attention and Cimon studied him in turn for a moment, then gestured. Pericles approached, unsure what to expect.

Cimon looked him over and, for once, all the certainty was missing in him. Pericles raised an eyebrow and Cimon shrugged.

'I don't have many friends,' he said.

'*Any* friends,' Pericles corrected immediately. They both grinned.

'Well, I am more careful than you in those I keep around me. I find I miss Anaxagoras and Zeno – and Aeschylus and all the conversations we used to have.'

'They are with me,' Pericles said. 'We . . . I miss all that too. I am sorry about the trial.'

'No, you had to do it,' Cimon said. 'I think I understand. Are we friends then?'

'Of course. I have every intention of spending my old age telling you how you should have done things differently. We'll be old men sitting together, with a jug of wine, a little cheese and some black olives.'

Nothing more needed to be said. Cimon clapped him on the back and all was well. Pericles wished things could be so easy with women. There were times when he enjoyed the sheer challenge of working out how they thought, of persuading them round to his point of view, or just as often accepting he was in the wrong. With his friends, it was as if he knew the shortcuts. It saved on time; it saved on words.

Horns blared and the hoplites moved off. Pericles left

the pieces of a marriage behind him and yet found himself walking with a light step. He realised he was not the only one. The mood was oddly cheerful in the ranks, perhaps because they did not march to war. They laughed and talked as they went, with the sun casting long shadows ahead.

5

The huge peninsula that contained Sparta, Corinth, Argos and a dozen other regions and cities was separated from the rest of Greece by an isthmus, a narrow tongue of land – and in past times, a wall, manned by Spartan soldiers. Cimon had been astonished to find that construction of the Persian war in ruins, reduced to rubble by the forces that had ripped through the earth. The outlines of the Spartan camp beyond were still easy to make out, with its toilet pits and training circles, but the isthmus was abandoned, with no sign of life. Every soldier and camp follower had been recalled.

Whatever light mood the Athenians had known drained away as they marched. Corinth was the closest city to the pinch point and they had no business there, so kept well clear of it, heading south to Sparta. Yet they saw individual homes in the hills, still broken, with men or women peering from crude shelters.

Hour by hour, signs of the quake grew worse. Temples that had stood by the road lay scattered, their sanctuaries broken open, their statues fallen. The men were silent as they passed those, for fear of offending furious gods with a careless word.

Crops too had been ravaged. Pericles saw hundreds of fruit trees lying flat in one valley, as if blown by a great wind. It was a vision of forces he could hardly imagine. Every fence and sign of man had been knocked down.

More than once, some farm animal ran past, bleating in panic, its owners nowhere in sight. A couple of chickens were snatched up by quick-handed soldiers, necks snapped and feathers plucked as they marched along, ready for the evening meal.

Cimon set a brutal pace, as if in response to the wrongness of the landscape. Pericles recalled he had been to Sparta before, in the wake of the Persian invasion. Those men of a far empire had come with fire and iron. Yet any Athenian could understand what drove them. There was something worse in having the earth itself turn against those who farmed and lived on it.

By the evening of the third day, Pericles was limping, sore-footed and weary. According to Cimon, Sparta was just a few miles further and Pericles was not surprised to see red-cloaked soldiers coming out to meet them. The worrying thing was how long it had taken, compared to normal times. For an army of Athens to reach so far into the region of Laconia without being challenged showed more than anything how the world had turned upside down.

It was hard not to feel a thrill of fear at the sight of Spartans coming up the road. Pericles could see it was a small force, no more than four or six hundred. Yet they brought their legend with them. These were the warriors who had conquered entire peoples of the peninsula, one by one. It was said their helots were descendants of some ancient tribe, broken to slavery when they had chosen to stand against Sparta. Not even Persia had been able to crush that army. The entire military forces of King Xerxes had been undone at Plataea. In that moment, Pericles was pleased Cimon was there. No one else in Athens could claim to have stopped Persia in the field, to have taken the war to them.

'Show no weakness,' Cimon muttered at his shoulder.

In that moment, Pericles wasn't sure if the words were meant for him or for Cimon himself.

The Spartans halted before the much larger force. Their men wore their helmets down, as if for war. Pericles found the image disquieting. He thought suddenly of the masks in the theatre and the sense of unease slipped away. Helmets were meant to be frightening, but they were still masks, designed to fool other men.

'Who commands here?' one of the Spartans said.

Pericles saw the speaker wore a scuffed chestplate and a kilt of leather straps that left his legs bare. His helmet had a plume of black horsehair, the bristles tight with wax. He did not seem intimidated. Pericles wondered if that might be another kind of mask, or whether the Spartan believed he and his companions were somehow the superior force. It was a chilling thought.

'I am Archon Cimon, son of Miltiades,' Cimon replied. 'By authority of the council of Athens and the Assembly of my city, I am in command.'

His voice carried well, as one who has known the battlefield. The Spartan turned sharply as he spoke.

'Well, Athenian, I have no orders . . .' he began.

His manner irritated Cimon enough to speak over him, for the others present as much as the man himself.

'Your king, Archidamus, called for our aid – and I have staked my reputation on bringing it to you.'

He glared at the Spartan, waiting for the man to continue. When the officer opened his mouth, Cimon went on over him again, his tone furious.

'You'd speak to me without giving your name? Are manners dead in Sparta? It was not so when I stood last on your acropolis, when Archon Xanthippus and I spoke to Regent Pausanias before Plataea. Well, the oldest son of Xanthippus stands with me today – and I have returned as an archon of Athens, in goodwill, to answer your call.'

Pericles blinked at being singled out in such a way. He wondered if there was truly a thaw between them, or if Cimon had wanted him along just for his name and line. He frowned as he considered it.

Facing them, the Spartan looked to one side, giving way. Cimon followed his gaze and noted another who stood a little way back. The second man was much older. He wore no armour or helmet, only a robe. There was certainly no plume to show his authority, yet it was there, in the calm way he met Cimon's outraged anger.

'My apologies, Archon Cimon. I remember you, though you were just a youth when you were here last. Like Regent Pausanias, gone to his reward. I am Axinos, senior ephor to the kings of Sparta. You are welcome to make your camp here this evening, but I cannot let you enter the city. I have King Pleistarchus' permission to express our gratitude that you have come. It speaks well for Athenian honour and it will be written in the record. But the crisis has passed. You may camp, as I have said, but if you remain here beyond tomorrow, we will consider it an act of war.'

The old man spoke as if he described the weather, without special emphasis. Yet the words rocked Cimon. He shook his head in amazement, a slow flush spreading along his face and neck.

'You asked for our help,' he said at last. 'At great cost, we came . . .'

'Athenians consider the cost of everything, yes,' the ephor replied. A sneer coloured his tone. 'The crisis is over, as I have said. No matter how many of your coins you have spent, there is no need for your presence here. Can you understand that, Cimon of Athens?'

'I was appointed by the Assembly . . .' Cimon began.

As he had done with the first Spartan, the ephor spoke deliberately over him.

'And I was elected by the people of Sparta, Athenian. What of it? I advise the kings of Sparta. In my city, we know an order when we hear it.'

'You do not give orders here, not to me,' Cimon said, his voice dropping. He held up a hand when the ephor looked as if he might argue the point. 'No. There was talk of an uprising among your helots, of blood in the streets. You came to us for aid. If that is now to be refused, I must hear it from a king of Sparta, or I will enter the city.'

Without any apparent order, the Spartan front ranks raised shields and dropped their spears down, points facing the Athenian lines. No one moved on the Athenian side, though a ripple of shock went through them. They had come to lend their strength, with carts of food and supplies. To be faced with a Spartan force apparently ready to attack brought a terrible tension to that place – and rising anger. They were heartbeats away from shedding blood on dusty ground.

Cimon turned his back on the Spartans.

'Make camp!' he ordered. 'Post guards and get something cooking. We'll stay here tonight.'

His face was pale, Pericles saw. There were different masks, beyond those of bronze. When Cimon turned back to the Spartans still standing there, he affected a look of surprise.

71

'Axinos, was it? I have told you what I will do. I suggest you go back to Sparta and tell your kings there is an Athenian relief force waiting to be admitted. Perhaps one of them will have the good manners to come out and speak to me, without sending his dog.'

Axinos said nothing, though Pericles saw him twitch to be described in such a way. The man had spent his forty years in the army and he would be no stranger to the calls and alarms of war. Yet he *had* given permission for the Athenians to camp. Pericles saw Axinos share a look with one of the others. They would expect ruses and cleverness from Athenians, of course.

The Spartans were left standing as the Athenians broke rank and strolled off. The moment seemed to last a long time before the ephor waved a hand in disgust, giving his men the signal to return to the city.

Pericles watched as the Spartans marched away. No one looked back, though they must have known all eyes were on them. He frowned as Cimon came to stand by him.

'They can be a difficult people,' Pericles said.

'Not if you know them,' Cimon said.

'You were so certain they wouldn't attack? You didn't feel your bladder getting tight at all?'

'My bladder was fine,' Cimon said. He saw Pericles still looking at him and sighed. 'Perhaps a little, I admit. I have never seen Spartans so . . . ragged? Unnerved? Their usual confidence has gone, hidden by brashness and threats. They have been shaken. I don't yet know what it means.'

Pericles snapped awake in darkness, looking up at stars glittering overhead. On all sides, men were running, shouting. He rubbed his eyes as he rose, reaching for the spear and shield that lay close to hand. He buckled on a sword belt and stepped into his sandals, fastening the straps without seeing them. It took just moments and his bladder ached. No, there was no time for that. Instead, he sought out Cimon. Whatever was happening, Cimon would be at the heart of it.

The Athenians had set guards the night before. Those men blew ram's horns to rouse the rest, giving the camp time to come alive. Lochagoi officers bellowed commands and their men formed around them. There was no complaining, not with talk of helots rampaging through the land, slaughtering women and children. The men gripped weapons with relish at the thought of taking those on.

Pericles looked over his shoulder, pleased to see the grey light of dawn revealing the mountains. It would be some time before the sun passed the peaks, but it meant he had slept for a good stretch. If he had to fight all day, he would not be falling down with exhaustion, easy prey to anyone fresh. His father had always insisted on fitness, sleep and good food for anyone in his command. Pericles swallowed. It was still strange to be in a world without his father and brother – and a man never felt more alone than when he faced a sudden alarm in the dark. It was why those around him called questions and shuffled close together, waiting to learn the nature of the threat.

The news of red-cloaks spread like a breeze through the Athenians. They whispered the name of Sparta with stomachs sinking. The growing light revealed more and more until they stood slack-jawed.

A huge force surrounded them, on all sides. Spartan warriors in armour faced their Athenian counterparts wherever anyone looked, at first as shadows in plumed helmets, then with colour bleeding into the scene as light grew. Pericles had taken his position on Cimon's right hand and he could only curse the fate that had brought him to that place in trust and innocence. The Spartans matched their number and there was no one in the force from Athens who believed they might win. It showed in the way they stood, in the slight dip of spearheads, or the wavering of shields. The Spartans carried their reputation before them – and of course they knew what effect their presence would have.

Dust swirled and Cimon turned his head to see two Spartans walk out of the massed ranks. He recognised them, Pericles could see that much. He felt his eyes widen as he realised he did too, at least for one: Tisamenus, one of the few Spartans he had encountered. No, Pericles recalled. Tisamenus was not a son of those mountains but some other place.

Cimon bowed deeply as the pair halted. Pericles stayed where he was, his father's memory making it impossible to bend.

'I present His Majesty King Pleistarchus,' Tisamenus said.

Cimon bowed again on hearing the name, though his expression remained dark.

'Your Majesty,' he said by way of greeting. He nodded to Tisamenus. 'Soothsayer.'

'That is an old title,' Tisamenus replied. 'There are some who say it was just while Pausanias lived.'

'We heard of his passing in Athens,' Cimon said softly. 'I was sorry to hear it – and the manner of it. He was a good man.'

'Yes, he was,' Tisamenus said. His tone was cold. If

there had ever been liking or affection for Athenians, it was absent then.

Cimon nodded, turning back to the battle king of Sparta and son of Leonidas himself.

'Majesty, I am honoured. Yet I must ask – are we still allies? I told your ephor that I wished to hear it from you, but I cannot understand this. Why do so many of your warriors face us in battle array?'

Their lives hung on the answer, Pericles realised, which Pleistarchus knew very well. It was to his credit that he did not wait too long.

'This? These men are but a small part of my forces, Archon Cimon. No, I heard you scorned my ephor and I was not far off. I came only out of courtesy – to echo his words, I'm afraid.'

Pericles watched the man's gaze take in the carts and supplies at the rear of their square. Was there regret there? It was hard to say.

'We have already begun to rebuild. Before the season turns, we will have repaired and remade our city, greater than before.'

'And your helots, Majesty? We heard they had rebelled and begun a great slaughter.'

The king chuckled.

'Stories grow in the telling. Our helots certainly needed to be culled this year, as a gardener must trim dead wood to encourage new growth. It is just the way of things. I cannot deny the labour has been hard, but the worst is past. You have honoured us with your response, but we have no need of you now.'

There was something in his tone that made Pericles bristle, unless it was just the presence of thousands of

Spartan warriors still facing them. They were perfectly still, as a cat will drop to its haunches while some hapless bird sings unaware. There was an air of menace to that place and Cimon was very aware of it.

'I will head home this morning, Majesty. If you are certain there is nothing we can do. I've brought smiths and builders with me, with food, salt, wine. We could leave those labourers to make their own way back, or even just the rations, to support your people.'

A muscle twitched in the king's neck, Pericles saw. Pleistarchus only smiled and shook his head.

'The kindness of Athenians is well known. Perhaps you'll leave us the bill as well, eh?' He chuckled, though there was bitterness in it.

'I assure you . . .'

'Go on your way, Cimon. There are some in my city who don't like an army of Athens this close, where one has never stood before. I have thanked you for coming so far and fast, but you should leave. Now.'

Cimon was stiff as he bowed once again. He had been dismissed and it showed in the furious glitter of his eyes.

'Very well, Majesty. I hope you never again need to call for our help.'

It was a reasonable enough thing to say in the circumstances, but also a threat, depending on how it was understood. Pericles hid his satisfaction as he nodded to Tisamenus. That man had an expression as hard as any winter gale. There was no friendship in that place, not for them. It was a mystery and he began to think it through as he had been taught. Anaxagoras and Zeno would not abandon a problem until they understood it. Nor had his father.

Faced with a clear command, Cimon had no choice but to withdraw. He bellowed orders to his people, and if anything showed in their faces, it was mostly honest relief they were not about to be slaughtered.

The camp followers and all their equipment were eased to one side and the first hoplite ranks went through, forming as a column with spears upright and shields swung to their backs. Cimon remained at what became the rear as his people moved away, still observing all he could. Pericles too looked into the distance, to where the city of Sparta lay. He wondered if he would ever stand in its central square, or whether this was the closest he would come.

When it was time, Cimon turned and marched with the rest, leaving the massive force of Spartans behind with their king. The Athenians showed their backs to them all and raised dust as they headed north.

Pleistarchus clenched his fists as the column dwindled in the distance. Tisamenus looked at him, having some sense of the strain the younger man was under. There was no sympathy in the soothsayer's gaze. Years before, Pleistarchus had been given a chance to save his own regent, when the man returned to Sparta under a cloud of accusations and rumour. If Pleistarchus had been half the man his father had been, Tisamenus thought he would have overridden the ephors and pardoned Pausanias, the victor of Plataea. Or perhaps let the poor, broken man go into exile. Instead, a spiteful boy had allowed his rival to be destroyed, walled up in a temple to die of thirst. Tisamenus had seen that place reduced to rubble with so many others. He had been pleased about that.

Pleistarchus was sweating, he saw. The king knew very

well what was happening in his city, every moment he remained there to block the road.

'Majesty, should we . . . ?' one of the officers ventured at last.

The Athenians were just a smear of dust by then, heading north with no sign of deviation. They had certainly been offended by their treatment, but Tisamenus thought they had been frightened too. That was what the king had wanted.

'Just wait . . .' Pleistarchus said. 'I want to be certain they can't return on some excuse, to undo all we've brought about.'

That was enough for both Spartiate and perioikoi warriors to remain in perfect silence, staring north until all sign of the Athenians had vanished. He had needed every one to assemble that force, stripping the city.

Tisamenus found he was sweating as well. The previous week had been brutal on all of them, especially when the dead began to bloat. The city buzzed with flies, rising in huge clouds. It was a place of murder and vengeance, where they hunted helots and were hunted themselves. Yet Pleistarchus had abandoned the fight for an entire day, just to make a show of force for the Athenians.

'They are gone,' Tisamenus said at last. Of all the men there, he knew he was most precious to the king. The gods had promised Tisamenus five victories – and he had still won only four. The soothsayer's voice seemed to start Pleistarchus from his reverie.

'Then we resume the fight,' he said. Weariness showed in him. He closed his eyes, one hand rubbing his chest, where ribs met. When he spoke again, his gaze was grim.

'Gentlemen, the helots will have advanced in our absence,

recapturing districts we left undefended. We will have to take them back, street by street. There can be no accommodation, no terms of surrender. We must annihilate them, or everything we love will fall. I ask for everything you have, for your last strength and final breath – for me, for my father . . . for our people.'

They raised a great hoarse roar in return, though they were as tired as he was. Tisamenus had seen them made ragged by exhaustion and lack of food, but they still stood. He only wished Pausanias could have been alive to see it.

'Was bringing them out here worth it?' Tisamenus asked.

Pleistarchus turned to him as they returned to the city.

'It was,' he said with certainty. 'If I had let the Athenians see . . . If they understood how reduced we are, we would have lost more than a few districts! The pride of my people is not so easily thrown away. Who knows what Athenians might dare to do? King Archidamus called for help when the city was burning and our helots were red-handed and running mad. I will not blame him, though some might say he shamed us all. If you had been born a Spartan, perhaps you would understand. Today, I showed the Athenians strength, because without *strength*, we have nothing.' He shrugged. 'I know who our allies are – and who they are not.' He rubbed his chest with his thumb, as if he scratched an itch, breathing slowly all the while. 'This year will pass. We will rebuild. That is what matters.'

6

The column that entered Athens had none of the laughter and light talk from when they had set out. Crossing the isthmus once again left the great peninsula behind, but there were many thoughtful faces in the ranks. None of them had faced armed Spartans before, certainly not been surrounded by them. They had gone out as allies, and the insult stung – to themselves and to their city.

Pericles walked with Cimon and his friends through the Dipylon gate, then on, to the open Agora and the council building along one edge. The seats there were already full, as news of the column winged ahead of its arrival. The elected representatives of Athens waited inside to learn why their hoplites had come home weeks early. No doubt a thousand rumours were being whispered in the markets and shops at that very moment.

Pericles shook his head at the change in Cimon. His friend had been humiliated, sent away like a whipped boy. The Spartans should have fallen on his neck with tears of gratitude, but of course they had not. They went their own way, no matter how perverse it seemed.

Pausing at the foot of the steps, Cimon looked up at the council hall. The Agora lay at his back and crowds were gathering, wanting to hear. From their raised position, Scythian guards glowered out, fingering sword hilts in nervous anticipation. They were not much loved. Any riot that broke out always involved them getting a beating.

'Just tell the truth – and if they dare to argue, ask what they would have done,' Pericles said.

His friend Zeno nodded.

'Or ask if they are willing to do Sparta's will,' he added.

The others turned to him in question and he shrugged. The little man had grown up in Greek colonies south of Rome. He had one of the most incisive minds Pericles had encountered – at least the equal of Anaxagoras, who was looming over him.

'Cimon has always supported Sparta,' Zeno explained. 'They appointed him their representative in Athens, which is why he wears that kopis blade. They would surely have known he would lead any aid column – and so lose the most status when it was sent home again.' He looked at Cimon. 'Is it not possible they want to bring you down – to damage the authority of an Athenian archon and strategos?'

'Why would . . .' Cimon began.

Anaxagoras spoke over him. When he and Zeno argued, their thoughts moved so fast it was sometimes hard for anyone else to get a word in.

'You think it's war?' Anaxagoras asked. 'Or vengeance for Pausanias?'

Anaxagoras had been born in Ionia, in the Greek shadow of imperial Persia. He had taken his restlessness to Athens to make a life for himself. For his trouble he had seen the city destroyed twice. Like Pericles, Anaxagoras had a young family. They all had. The mere possibility of conflict with Sparta was like a cold wind in that place.

One of the Scythian guards gestured impatiently for them to ascend. Another had his head turned inside, listening to some instruction from council officials.

'We destroyed Pausanias,' Zeno said thoughtfully. 'He raced home to Sparta to face accusations of corruption *we* brought about – and they walled him into a temple. We should not underestimate such men, either in their intelligence or the depth of their hatred.'

'I should go,' Cimon said, speaking quickly before a full-blown discussion could begin. 'I do not believe this is some great plan of theirs, nor that Sparta threatens us. There was something . . . ragged about the ones we saw. I suspect the earthquake was much worse than we were told. You saw the homes and temples on the road south. Imagine how it must be in the city.'

'Perhaps they didn't want us to see . . .' Zeno said.

'They have great pride,' Anaxagoras nodded. 'That might explain why they were willing to infuriate their strongest ally.'

Cimon looked from one to the other in exasperation, then to Pericles.

'So they could be weak . . . or strong! That's very helpful, lads. Any more advice? The council will want someone to blame for the waste of all their silver. I expect it will be me.'

He saw Zeno dip his head in simple agreement and sighed, striding up between the columns and into the chamber. The crowds were growing in the Agora and the three he left behind followed him quickly. There would be no seats, but the Scythian guards would allow them to stand for a coin or two.

Pericles let his feet drag as he walked out to the estate. He strode along with the spear held upright, using it like a shepherd's staff. His father's shield was on his back, without any new scratches to add to its history.

The sun was setting and the day had been long. Nor had it gone well. Pericles could hardly believe the way Ephialtes had savaged Cimon in the council chamber, pouring scorn on every decision he had made. Though it proved once and for all that there was some personal dislike between them, the burly strategos had clearly built a great deal of support. Ephialtes had called for a decision from the full Assembly and it seemed a majority in the council agreed with him.

Cimon had been ordered to appear on the Pnyx once again, his fate in their hands. Pericles swore under his breath as he walked. He passed a group of merchants and they seemed to know him, bowing their heads and then following him with their eyes. He smiled at them, for all the world a man at peace. Inside, he seethed. He'd saved Cimon once from the schemes of Ephialtes. There had been counter-arguments before, with a huge victory over Persian forces to set against it all.

Pericles reached the iron door in the outer wall of his estate and hammered on it, waiting for the shuffling steps of Manias. The expedition to Sparta was hard to justify, given how it had turned out. Ephialtes had read out a list of costs, staggering sums. Pay and food alone for five thousand men might have beggared the treasury of a lesser city.

Cimon had led the original debate to go to the aid of an ally, only to be humiliated. Whatever Sparta had intended, the council and Assembly were still lashing out, driven to anger by way of indignation. They could not rebuke the

Spartans, so it seemed their wrath would indeed fall on one of their own.

As he waited, Pericles chewed his lip. Cimon was a friend, but he was also the best war leader Athens had. If Zeno was right and war was coming . . .

He looked up. He had expected to see Manias by then. After a moment, he thumped the door again, making a ringing sound.

'Manias?' he called.

He heard steps at last, but they were quick and light. The head that appeared at the top of the wall was young and tousle-haired, one of the house slaves.

'Open up the gate,' the fellow called to someone inside.

Pericles frowned as the bar was drawn back.

'Where is Manias?' he asked.

He felt his heart sink as he guessed the answer. Suddenly wearier than before, Pericles lowered his spear and made his way to the house. He had told his wife she had a full month to leave. It had been barely ten days. He knew he was not expected and yet the place already seemed different without Manias on the gate.

'Pericles!' he heard. His mother's voice. It made him a child again, just for a moment, until he embraced her and was reminded how small she had become. Agariste had always been slender. She seemed as fragile as a bird as she rested her head on his shoulder.

'We didn't expect you back so soon. I'm afraid Thetis is still here.'

She seemed strained, he saw, with dark hollows around her eyes.

'What's wrong?' he asked, suddenly suspicious.

'It's not . . . it has not been easy,' she said. 'Your wife . . . she has been angry with all of us, all the household.'

Pericles felt coldness steal through him. He had been concerned with saving Cimon and the business of the Assembly. He had not thought to come home to something worse.

'Are the boys all right?'

Relief was cold in him as she nodded quickly.

'Of *course*. I would never let anything . . .'

'What happened to Manias?' he demanded.

Her face was tight and pale. He knew he had the heart of it.

'I . . . Thetis sent me into the city two evenings ago, to settle some account or bill she swore needed my presence. I didn't know anything about it. The moneylender had not been told to expect me, and by the time I returned . . .'

When his mother trailed off, he took her by the arms.

'What?' Pericles said. He held himself very still rather than shake her.

'She called an *anassa euthana* – a lady of the good death. Thetis paid for her to come out to the estate. They say it was quick, Pericles. The old ones don't suffer when she visits them.'

He let go of her arms, wincing slightly to see the pale marks he had left.

'What does she do, this lady?' He knew by then, but he still made her say it.

'They usher out the dying, when they are weak or in pain. A single hammer blow to the temple, or strangulation. Some consider it a mercy, a duty to the gods. I'm so sorry, Pericles. I would have stopped it if I had been here.'

'Had Manias grown worse then? He seemed happy enough when I was here last.'

'He was the same,' Agariste said.

He looked at her and said nothing more. They both understood. After a time, Pericles went into the house, to the central courtyard. Stairs led from there to the bedrooms above, but he halted at the sight of Thetis, waiting for him. She sat on a wooden bench by a pool, looking perfectly calm.

Pericles was no longer the young man she had known. Nor was she his wife. He breathed softly, gently, crossing the open space. He sat next to her.

'Where are the boys?' he asked.

Thetis crossed her legs, adjusting the cloth with quick twitches of her fingers before she replied. She was nervous, he realised. With good reason. He had not been expected home for weeks – and when he finally came, Manias would have been long in the ground, all her spite buried with him.

'They are out at the town-house, settling in. I was not told you would be coming home so soon, Pericles. I would have left with them if I'd known. You did say I had a month.'

'And is it right that you summoned this *anassa euthana*, this lady of the good death? Was it just to hurt me, Thetis?'

She turned a hot gaze on him, her eyes very dark in the gloom.

'You were not here. I called her out of mercy. Sometimes, it is the right thing to do when the old linger past their time. I think Manias understood at the end.'

She looked away and he had the sense she was remembering terrible events. Pericles swallowed uncomfortably.

He dared not ask for details. Hearing that Manias had fought or called his name would haunt him and still not bring the old man back.

If Thetis had wanted to cause pain, she had a perfect victory. Yet she was still mother to his sons. He rose, understanding there was only one path left to him. The quality of *praotes* was something he had learned from his father – and from Manias himself, who saw it as the highest virtue. It was strength through calm, the control of emotion under the worst pressures. It served him well then, when the only alternative was to draw a blade and kill her.

'As I have returned early, Thetis, I will have the rest of your things taken into the city tomorrow. The boys will stay with you. This will remain their home, however. I will arrange tutors for them both, during the days. Until you marry, I will meet the costs of your household.'

He smiled suddenly and her eyes narrowed in response. This was not the reaction she had wanted and that gave him the will to go on.

'I remember when this whole place was filled with lights and people, Thetis, all talking and laughing and drinking too much wine. I met Aeschylus here for the first time, long before we won the Dionysus festival with his plays, before the theatre burned! By the gods, we had some good times here! I will think of those when I think of you.'

She rose to her feet. He could see rage in the way she held her hands, but there was nothing more to be said. She shook her head in disgust and walked out, leaving him alone in the moonlight. After a while, he sat down once more and wept for the childhood friend he had lost.

*

Cimon stood on the Pnyx hill, listening to Strategos Ephialtes do his best to destroy him. The sun was warm and he felt sweat trickle down his ribs under his robe. Cimon had never liked the man. Whatever he felt was clearly returned tenfold. Ephialtes certainly made no secret of his beliefs. With a consuming passion, he detested the Eupatridae nobles of Athens – the landowners and old families. He hated archons most of all, though their council could only advise and no longer had any real power in law. The Assembly was the final arbiter and Cimon wondered if they would even remember the service of his family while Ephialtes harangued them.

Pericles claimed to understand the people – both in the Assembly and down in the city – but if the ungrateful bastards sent him into exile, Cimon would find it hard to look on them with anything but contempt ever again. He had a vision of Athens. It included the poor, the women and children, the working districts, even the urchins and thieves who stole from the docks. When he had led the fleet for the League, it had been as the representative of them all, not just Eupatridae families. Yet . . .

He sighed and shook his head. They infuriated him. Ephialtes talked of the common men as if they were a different sort of Athenian, one Cimon could never understand. The strategos brought up the wealth of Cimon's family over and over, while his service to the city went unmentioned. What did it *matter* if Cimon's ancestors had owned farms and horses and silver mines? No man chose his father! Cimon's family had staked all they had on creating a legacy – and Cimon had allowed the very poorest to be fed from his fields, his granaries. Ephialtes seemed to think they should resent the very hand that fed and clothed and protected them. Such a font of bitterness was forever a mystery to him.

Six of the officers from the expedition to Sparta had spoken for him. Pericles too had done his best under the cold scorn of Ephialtes and the anger from some parts of that crowd, whipped to indignation.

Yet there was a tide in the Assembly and it was turning against Cimon, he could feel it. They had banished Xanthippus and Aristides, men famous for their honour. What chance did he have? It was madness – and the only thing he could say in their defence was that they had no kings. If they lashed out, it was by their own order, not a royal bloodline. No, it was themselves: their votes and their appointments. After all, beyond violence and the gods, there was no other authority.

The latest speaker stepped down. The epistates called for others, but the crowd was restless and more than a few voices called 'Vote!' from the safety of the mass. Cimon hardly listened. He turned his face to the breeze and closed his eyes. Some twenty thousand stood on the Pnyx that day. Ephialtes needed only six thousand to see Cimon banished from the entire region of Attica for a decade. Men had survived such votes before, but there was no counter-vote in support, nor had Cimon been given the opportunity to speak in his own defence. If the total was reached, he would be out, with no chance to appeal.

He watched as lines formed. Many in the Assembly stood back ostentatiously, folding their arms and glaring at anyone waiting to drop a piece of tile into the voting pot that stood before them all, much repaired with strips of iron or bronze. It would hold every one of the ostraca of broken tile, enough to ruin him.

The day wore on, with the sun sliding onto the horizon. Cimon had not eaten since the morning. He was both hungry and thirsty, but he did not leave the hill. No matter the outcome, he told himself, he would watch every piece of tile dropped in, each with his name scratched on the surface. It was designed to give a voice even to the poorest, and Cimon could only wonder at it. There was nowhere else in the world where a royal court wouldn't have laughed to see such a thing. Yet there it was – and they voted on his life.

The count was kept and called aloud. When it reached five thousand, a new tension crept into the crowd. They watched each man step up then and open his hand, dropping in the broken piece of some old pot. Some of those with Ephialtes began to chant the numbers, laughing while Cimon could only watch. The lines were thinning and he did not know if they had enough. One single vote short and he would walk down a free man.

He watched the last dozen without blinking, so that his eyes stung. Or so he told himself. The officials of the council called 'Complete' and the vote was over. A few still waiting tried to toss their pieces into the pot, but they were sent away. The count was finished and Cimon lowered his head.

Pericles came to stand at his shoulder, looking grim. Zeno and Anaxagoras were there to glower at the crowd and those around Ephialtes. Some had got what they wanted, of course. Yet for every gleaming smile, there were two or three who stood stunned.

Gently, Pericles turned him around. Cimon was grateful he was there as he reached the steps heading down. He had until the following sunset to leave the city, forbidden to set foot there for ten long years. Cimon blinked sore eyes as he looked out on Athens, trying to keep the view in his mind. It would be a comfort to him in the time to come.

'I'm sorry,' Pericles said. 'Ephialtes seems to get his own way more and more. He makes alliances and deals all the time now.'

'Well, he wanted me gone – and he has that. Be careful of him. He talks too much of the people.'

Pericles nodded, though he was not sure Cimon was right. He knew his friend was only then understanding what had happened, the full import crashing down on him. Cimon had given his life for Athens, and the response seemed both cruel and petty. It was a huge blow to the plans Pericles had begun to make on his way back from Sparta. Cimon had been a vital part of his group, but all that had changed in an hour. Pericles looked back as he walked down, seeing Ephialtes there, smiling and laughing with his supporters. Pericles swallowed. A man made the friends around him. Enemies made themselves. Yet with Cimon gone, he would need Ephialtes.

7

The tavern where they met was near the Dipylon gate, to the north of the city. The owner had run a family fishing business before the war, owning every stage from boat to plate. Pericles suspected the wine was some way off the claimed strength, and if the fish was as fresh as the sign said, he was a dancer from Corinth. Yet the tavern did come with rooms above and a parlour at the back that could be hired for privacy. It was there Pericles waited for the others.

Anaxagoras and Zeno arrived first, already deep in discussion. Anaxagoras held a wooden skewer of meat to his lips, purchased from some street vendor. The tall man sniffed it in between bites, still unsure though it was already half gone. Pericles had ordered a jug of wine and cups for the table and he watched in amusement as Anaxagoras folded himself into a seat. Zeno had no such difficulty, of course. The little Roman-Greek kicked his heels and waited for about the space of a single breath before he spoke once more.

'Who else have you called here? This is a part of the city I usually walk through with a hand on a weapon.'

'Forget your weapon and have a drink,' Pericles replied.

The truth was, he did not know if all those he had invited would come. He was hopeful, however. Curiosity was a powerful force, for Greeks more than most. Half their favourite stories involved someone wanting to see what mysteries they might discover on a strange island.

Aeschylus entered next. They heard his voice addressing the tavern owner long before they saw him. The playwright had fought at Marathon and seen his brother killed there. He was still powerfully built and bearded, though it was for his insight Pericles had asked him. Aeschylus had won the great festival of Dionysus half a dozen times since their first meeting. In that moment, he was one of the most famous men in Athens. Of course, it meant the tavern crowd would be wondering what he was doing, but there it was. Pericles would have asked them to meet at his town-house if he hadn't passed it over to his wife . . . his ex-wife. He smiled at that, so that Aeschylus raised an eyebrow as he sat down.

'It's nothing. I was thinking of happier times,' Pericles said. 'Try the wine. It is a red Lemnos.'

'Truly?' Aeschylus said. He raised the jug to his nose and sniffed deeply. 'Ah, very good. The wine Odysseus used to subdue the Cyclops. I heard of a shipment coming in last month. Not cheap, Pericles, even in a place like this, even watered.'

Pericles found himself flushing. Aeschylus was abstemious in character – not normally the sort he would have asked to an evening of drink and song. Yet he respected the man's experience. More importantly, so would his other guests.

'I wouldn't give bad wine to good friends,' he replied.

Aeschylus seemed to accept the point. He gestured and a tavern servant poured him a cup that Pericles suspected would last longer than anyone else's.

The architect, Phidias, was one Aeschylus already knew. Phidias was in his late twenties, a long-fingered scribe of a man compared to Aeschylus. Yet he understood stone almost as a living thing. It was said he could pull a shape out of a block as if it had always been inside, just waiting to take his hand. Phidias looked around in confusion at his presence in that group, but Pericles introduced him and made him welcome.

'Are there others?' Aeschylus asked over the noise of talk and laughter. 'You said this would be a gathering of friends.'

Pericles put his head out into the main tavern. The light was deepening. The day was not yet at an end, but he felt a pang of disappointment. He shook his head as he came back.

'I had hoped . . . No, it does not matter.'

He caught the eye of the servants who stood against the wall and thanked them. The others watched them file out, exchanging glances as the room became theirs alone.

'My friends,' Pericles continued. 'For those not with us on the march to Sparta, I will describe what we saw. One or two things became clear . . .'

He paused as the noise in the outer tavern suddenly died away, so that he found himself speaking too loudly. Pericles glanced at the door and smiled as Cimon came in, closing it behind him. The archon looked around at their astonished faces and shrugged.

'I have until sunset – and fast horses waiting. Let them chase me if they want. Before the light goes, I will drink a last cup with you.'

They cheered him as they sat back down and even Aeschylus thumped him on the shoulder.

'Thank you,' Pericles said as they quieted again. 'I asked Cimon here because I know he saw the same things. We have lived too long in fear of Sparta, gentlemen. I witnessed an Athenian force surrounded, threatened by a Spartan king who had never set foot in Athens. I realised then they have no idea how powerful we have become – can still become – within the League. For this season, they are blind to us. Yet if they see us reach for *kleos*, for glory, they could still march. You know how they are – determined to preserve a world where nothing changes, year after year.'

He took a moment to drink, feeling the wine warm his stomach.

'I saw it, suddenly and clearly, as they showed us spear and shield. The threat of Sparta is always there, every spring, whether they actually march or not. Until we find a way to smother that threat, to counter it, Athens cannot become the city she was meant to be.'

A few of those present glanced at Cimon, to see how he was taking it. He nodded, giving his approval.

'I have been reluctant before,' Cimon said, 'to set Athenian against Spartan. I looked for better ways than a knife in the dark to handle their regent Pausanias, when he tried to take command of our fleet. Pericles has persuaded me, gentlemen. I came here to show I stand with him.'

'Despite your banishment?' Aeschylus asked.

Cimon turned to him.

'My wealth remains. What Pericles will suggest requires a huge sum in silver. We will certainly ask for costs from the council, but you know them better than most. Silver we own is spent quickly and well. Silver we are promised? That is a much slower beast, if it arrives at all.'

Aeschylus chuckled at that, as a man who liked a turn of phrase.

Zeno actually checked the room was truly empty of strangers before he spoke.

'You are not suggesting war with Sparta? I was there too, Pericles, in my cheap armour and the spear I bought in the Agora, held together with bronze wire. I knew real fear when the Spartans appeared in the dawn – more than I care to remember. If they come, how can we stand against such men?'

'I don't believe we can,' Pericles said. 'Though they are not gods, my friend! They do train every day – in a city that has honed the art of war for a thousand years. All their losses are in the past, as I understand it, before they created the forms and tactics that bring victory. No, if we face them in the field, we'll fail, just as the Persians did.'

'Then what?' Zeno said. 'They know better than to face the League at sea – and if they did, sooner or later we would have to land. Wars are not won on water. I don't understand. If they see Athens grow too strong and decide to march here, you say we *shouldn't* face them?'

'I am convinced of it,' Pericles said, his voice gentle. He had risen to speak to them and he rested his knuckles on the table. 'If we take the field against Sparta, it will be the end.'

'We have city walls,' Phidias said. The architect was pale at what he had heard, but he was interested too, in the problem Pericles was laying before them. 'I oversaw part of their construction, with Themistocles. I don't believe any force of men could break through, not with a defence of arrows and stones from above. The main gates are more vulnerable, but if they can be kept wet, there is no real danger of fire – and there are walkways and towers for archers over each one. I will not say it cannot be done, but they would lose many men in the attempt.'

'They don't *need* to break our walls,' Zeno said over the others. 'All they need to do is surround us, to cut us off from water and food. Within a month, we'd be eating the last dog and rat. You know by then some of the people would be clamouring to open the gates. That is how cities fall – even cities like Athens.'

Pericles used his father's memory to hide any sense of satisfaction, though he could have grinned to hear them follow his own path so closely. He had come to the same conclusion – and then gone one step further.

'That was my thought . . .' he began, glancing at Cimon. 'If we . . .'

'What about building walls *between* the city and the port?' Anaxagoras said.

Pericles stopped.

'That was my intention,' he replied in exasperation. They were like cats in a bag sometimes when wine and ideas flowed, all squirming, noisy life. Crammed into the small back room of a tavern, Pericles had to speak over Zeno when the man began to run with the idea.

'Yes . . . *yes*!' Pericles said loudly. 'Two walls, as high as those around the city, with towers, but no gates of any kind. All the way from Athens to the sea. We can enclose an area of open land between them.'

'I believe that is what I was saying . . .' Anaxagoras said.

'The *cost* though,' Aeschylus added, scratching his beard. He dipped his finger in his wine and began to sketch lines on the wooden table. 'If we put towers here and . . . here . . . with the range of a bow, it would cover an area to the left and right, do you see? We'd have to space them so there would not be any gap between where a man could stand . . .'

They all stood, crowding each other to look down on the lines Aeschylus drew. Phidias interrupted that when he pulled a slate tile from his bag and made neat strokes on it with a piece of chalk.

'It would be like this,' he said. 'We can work-out the overlapping arcs, then set the towers at the centre.'

Pericles said nothing for a time as they talked and laughed and drank. He had assembled an extraordinary little group that evening.

'The cost just for labour . . .' Phidias said, chewing the end of his stylus. 'For quarrying limestone, transporting the blocks . . . for mortar, the wooden towers, steps up to them – walls thick enough, *high* enough to resist an army? Each one could be compared to the wall we built around Athens! I think I remember the sums for that were huge. For two of them?'

'This is why I asked Cimon to be here,' Pericles said. 'He agrees, Phidias. You can build it, if we can find the silver. How much will it all be?'

'As a very rough estimate, we are looking at a talent of silver a day just for labour. If you want it done quickly . . .'

'There's no question about that,' Pericles said. 'Once Sparta hears, they will understand what those walls mean. They'd have to be blind not to. They will protest – and when we refuse to stop, they will either watch their authority dwindling by the day . . . or they will attack, before the walls are finished.'

There was silence in the little room then, already

uncomfortably warm. The stakes were as high as the survival of Athens.

Aeschylus drained his cup and let Zeno refill it.

'But if we *could* finish,' Aeschylus said, 'it would mean we are free, for the first time in history. We would have a fleet they cannot match – and a safe road to the port! There is no limit to what we might do after that! I vote to build the walls!'

Pericles nodded, smiling.

'It was my thought to put it to the Assembly tomorrow. Cimon will stand surety for the initial funds, but if we move, it will have to be fast. We'll need the Assembly to appoint new strategoi, as if we are heading to war. There is an opportunity here, if we can just seize it. Sparta is in disarray, rebuilding the damage of the earthquake. They will not be as willing as usual to cross the isthmus. We may have a year or so – and when have we needed more?'

'In all my life,' Aeschylus said, silencing the talk around him, 'I have never known the Spartans to leave home for more than thirty days. Not for Marathon, not Thermopylae, not even for Plataea, when they fielded their entire force, or so some of us believe.'

He leaned in and they copied the angle, so their heads were close.

'I heard once that they have so many helots, they live in constant fear of an uprising. It is why they almost never send the full army – and why when they do, they force-march, fight and return before a month has passed. It's worth knowing, is it not? If we build these walls . . . and if they march, we may not have to hold them off for a season or a year. Three or four days each way gives them two or three weeks at most to shout and raise shields before our walls. If we have to, we can hold them that long.'

'No one ever has,' Zeno muttered, making the others scowl. 'What? I want to see the walls as much as the rest of you, but I am not a child or a dreamer. If they come, it will be hard and bloody.'

'A Spartan king marched right into the Agora of Athens once,' Cimon said. 'He came at our request, but then he refused to leave. The people turned out against him, with blades or broken tiles, filling every street but one. The Spartans saw they could not win against so many and they went home. Well, we are more now – and we have more to protect. I vote for the walls. Let Pericles persuade the Assembly. This is a chance to make Athens free.'

Cimon had been watching the light as it came through a small window set high in one wall. It had taken on a darker gold and he clenched his jaw, his eyes shadowed. Pericles saw and understood immediately. The others gave up their conversations and stood to honour one of their number, forced to leave the city he loved and still tried to protect.

'My father was called back from exile,' Pericles said. 'As was Aristides. I will keep your name in their mouths, Cimon. Don't lose hope.'

They clasped hands and embraced.

'I have a place in Thessaly,' Cimon said, his voice suddenly hoarse. 'I will send word when I arrive, with orders for the funds you will need, at least to begin. A talent a day . . .' He shook his head. The sum was more than most men would see in a lifetime.

'We couldn't do it without you,' Zeno said.

Cimon nodded, suddenly brisk.

'Sunset calls me away. I hope this isn't the last I see of you all. My friends.'

He turned and was gone.

Pericles was thoughtful as he took his seat.

'A talent a day?' he said, hearing the sum aloud.

'For labour alone,' Phidias reminded them, adding numbers and rubbing them out with a chalky palm. 'Cutting that much stone would double or triple it. We'd be better off buying the quarries before the prices start to go up.'

'And how long would we have to bear that kind of cost?' Aeschylus said. 'It took two years to build the walls around the city. Even if we doubled the workforce and had them build without rest . . .'

'We could cut the blocks without raising suspicion,' Pericles broke in.

'Could we?' Aeschylus said. 'If you are right and Sparta is, for once, too wrapped up in their own affairs to see what we do here, there is no time for subterfuge or hidden stores of stone. If the Assembly agree, we'll need every able man in Athens on this job. We'll need thousands – every potter, mason, builder and carpenter in the city, all on this, without rest.'

'It's too much,' Pericles said. His eyes had taken on a faraway look as he considered. 'Cimon can give us a start, but if he can find forty talents, I'd be surprised.'

'We'll need at least three hundred more,' Phidias said, glancing up from his slate. He looked pale, even to say such a sum.

'That's it then. It's impossible,' Aeschylus replied. 'That is why only wealthy cities have walls and why it takes years to build them between the normal work of a city. Even Athens can't fund something like this.'

The light had darkened further in that little room, as if a candle guttered and had begun to fail. When Pericles heard voices raised in greeting in the main tavern, he became aware of it, so that he stood to call for lamps.

The man who opened the door and stared in made them all grow still.

Aeschylus was the first to rise, his mouth opening in anger.

'Peace, gentlemen,' Pericles said, though he had more cause than anyone to object. The man peering at them was Attikos, close servant to Strategos Ephialtes. Pericles and Attikos had almost been friends once, before the wiry little man attacked his wife. Though Pericles couldn't be sure, he thought Attikos had also left him for dead with a Persian charge thundering down on them.

Having looked around the room, Attikos ducked out of sight, reporting to his master. Ephialtes appeared immediately, nodding thanks to his man.

'I asked Strategos Ephialtes here,' Pericles said, still watching Attikos as he sidled around the outer wall. 'Or did you think we could win the favour of the Assembly without him?'

Ephialtes stopped just inside the room, looking over the group facing him with some interest. Cimon's chair was empty and Pericles indicated it.

'You are welcome, Strategos Ephialtes,' he said.

'Sunset has come,' Ephialtes said. 'Was that Archon Cimon I saw haring off down the road? My man Attikos was convinced it was. I'd say Cimon will be hard-pressed to reach the border of Attica before dark.'

Pericles breathed deeply, allowing his anger to show.

'Strategos, I must ask that your man remove himself from my company. I do not trust him.'

'Nor I,' Aeschylus added. 'You keep strange company. He's no friend to any of us.'

Ephialtes blinked as the others nodded. The strategos made a quick decision and hardly gestured before Attikos was heading out of the door, anger in every jerking movement.

'As proof of my trust and goodwill,' Ephialtes said.

He seated himself as the door closed, looking pointedly at the jug of wine. He was a large-limbed, florid man and Pericles thought he was also a hard one, who looked on the whole world for how it might profit him. Pericles summoned his *praotes*. The warrior's calm was not needed on a march, or in the company of friends. It was called on only in a crisis.

'Thank you for coming, strategos,' he said. 'Cimon has agreed to fund part of what we need, but without the approval of the Assembly, we cannot begin the work.'

'Which is why you need me . . .' Ephialtes said.

He leaned back in his chair and gestured to Cimon's cup. It was Aeschylus who filled it for him. As a playwright, he was more familiar than most with the need to please patrons.

'Exactly, kurios,' Pericles said, giving him the title.

The detail was not lost on Ephialtes and his smile widened as Pericles went on.

'We believe we have an opportunity – to build something new, a chance to change the balance of power.'

Ephialtes drank the wine poured for him and nodded, waving a hand for him to continue.

Pleistarchus looked in fury at dozens of kneeling men, lit by the camp burning behind them. This group had fought well enough at first, with the tools that served them as weapons. Yet when their barricade had fallen, they'd run away down the narrow pass – right into the arms of his reserve force. Hundreds had died, while others threw down their blades and surrendered. At their backs, his men kicked down the last of their crude stockade and stormed through.

He knew by then that he and the ephors had allowed the helots to thrive too long. Like coiling weeds, they strangled good crops – and no matter how many he killed, they cost him men he could not replace.

This band had been surrounded and rushed, panicked by an attack on two fronts. Pleistarchus was proud of that success, having sent Spartiates off in search of a goat path before the sun set. There were days when he could still remember the frustration he had once felt, watching the entire army march out to Plataea. He had remained behind that day, safe from death and glory both. That unscarred boy seemed far off in those mountains, as he wiped blood and soot from his hands.

Pleistarchus blinked eyes that stung, from dirt and smoke as well as a weariness that weighed on him as if he had been turned to stone. He had pursued helots through the mountain passes, risking ambush and rockfalls as they went. The slaves had driven him to a grudging respect for their endurance. Perhaps it was because he offered no mercy, he did not know. Most fought on when there was no hope, no rescue, no reinforcements, preferring a quick death to surrender. Not that it made any difference. Pleistarchus flexed stiff fingers, where the forearm muscles had grown tight from holding a sword. He was marked in filth. More, he was weary and half-starved. Yet he could hear scrambling feet somewhere nearby. The rats were coming back, looking to take a few more with them.

The barricades he had broken had been one part of the fortified hilltops around Mount Ithome. The helots had laboured like pack animals to bring rocks and baskets of earth to block his way, all while he hunted them. Pleistarchus had chosen the task for himself, while the ephors and Archidamus put the city into some sort of order. This was his role, after all. He still burned with indignation on behalf of his people. For helots to stand up like men, to refuse to obey, was like spitting in the face of gods. Pleistarchus was the agent of Apollo in that place, his right arm. He was justice, for broken oaths of fealty and obedience. That was why he endured.

One of his men struck a spark into tinder to light a torch, blowing on his cupped hand. Pleistarchus felt his eyes widen as he understood the sounds from above meant they were up there, watching.

'Put that out,' he snapped. He could already hear slings whirring and jammed his helmet down, one edge scraping his cheek raw. Pleistarchus raised his shield and heard the crack as a lead piece hit it. Of course they looked for him! The helots knew Spartan plumes and cloaks. They knew his customs as well as he did, or even better.

He glanced over to the shadowy figures of his prisoners, still kneeling on the rocky ground. Perhaps he had captured a few sons and daughters this time. He'd killed a large number of helots a week before as they tried to rescue a different group. He supposed even rats cared for their pups.

'Leave a clear path to the prisoners,' he murmured to one of his officers.

The man understood and grinned, though he had blood running down his neck where something sharp had caught him. In moments, the Spartans had secured three sides of the kneeling group and left the last completely open. It was a trap a child could have seen, but . . . there. He heard them coming, relying on the dark as they rushed in, hoping to free their own.

'On my word, stand ready . . .' Pleistarchus said softly, letting them commit. It was not a battle shout, to echo back from the hills around. He felt hemmed in and overlooked in that place. One of his men had been killed in a pass just like it, his skull broken to softness by a stone from above.

Pleistarchus clenched his fist on the sword hilt once more, listening to the scrabble and rush of helots creeping in. He smiled. Their children were herded down to the city whenever they were found. They would be the hands that rebuilt. The adults though, could not be allowed to live. That was his final word on the matter. They had killed Spartans and that could not be forgiven or allowed to spread.

Perhaps a tenth of the helots would survive the great cull, he thought, straining to hear in the dark. They were coming, without a doubt, approaching his prisoners and whispering to them. He could rebuild Sparta with that many. In just a dozen years, he would restore the city to everything it had been. He rubbed his chest as an ache grew there, making it hard to breathe. The world could never learn how weak his people had become, how close they had come to annihilation. That had to remain their most important secret, until they were strong again.

8

The air in the garden was heavy with moisture. It had rained the night before and the leaves still shone, the soil darker than usual. The sun was rising and Aspasia was there, ready to cut dead flowers and leaves away. Each one of the plants had been selected and grown by her hand. She had a touch for them that made that garden a place of peace and delicate scent all summer. She knew their stories too – of how Hyacinthus had been a Spartan prince, killed as he practised throwing his shield. Apollo had loved him enough to weep – and those tears had sprouted into flowers. Or the purple and pink anemones, born from droplets of blood as Adonis lay dying, cradled in turn by the goddess of love. Asters too came from tears . . . lilies from the breast milk of Hera . . . Aspasia loved all the stories. It meant she was surrounded by wonders.

She paused before a bush of dianthus by the outer wall, red and splendid in the morning. That was a darker tale, of tragedy and rage. The goddess Artemis had failed in a hunt and seen a mortal man daring to smile at her. In rage, she had torn out his eyes, tossing them away. Dianthus had grown from those, its flowers the colour of blood.

Aspasia had learned some of the tales from the woman who sold seeds and bulbs in the market. Others she had heard from boys who delivered food to the house. One of them had offered knowledge of the gods for kisses from

Marete. Aspasia had hidden close when he came, listening to the entire transaction.

A thought stopped her as she leaned over the dianthus. Marete had gone. Who would kiss the boy now, to hear a story? She felt herself flush at the obvious conclusion. She rose slowly to the level of the little barred window onto the street – and froze.

The man standing there was the one she had seen many times. In truth, the reason she came so early to the garden was the knowledge that he walked into the city shortly after dawn each morning. He seemed always in thought, with the weight of the world on his shoulders. To have him actually looking at her was as shocking as watching a statue get up and walk.

'I've seen you before,' he said. 'Your garden is very beautiful. Are you the one who tends it?'

Aspasia nodded silently. She felt her hair swishing back and forth and reached behind with one hand to keep it still.

'I always smell flowers when I reach this place in the road,' he said. 'I look forward to it.'

He was looking at her with a sort of intensity that made something tighten inside. His voice was just as she had imagined, deep and warm and strong. He was wide in the shoulder, like a soldier, she thought, yet slim at the waist. He had grown a beard since she'd first seen him. She liked it. His skin was unmarked and his eyes were the deepest brown, almost black, but with touches of gold at the heart . . .

'Do you speak?' he said suddenly.

'Yes,' Aspasia replied. 'I've seen you . . . walking.'

'Have you? And will you grant me your name? I can't keep calling you that girl in the garden.'

'Aspasia,' she said. Having spoken, the stiffness vanished. She smiled at him. 'And yours?'

'Pericles, of the Acamantis . . .' He had not yet been made an archon, nor a strategos for the Assembly, a fact which suddenly annoyed him. It was ridiculous to want to impress a stranger, but there it was. 'My, er, my father was Xanthippus. My mother is of the Alcmaeonid family.' He began to stammer under that unwavering gaze. 'Her, er . . . uncle . . . Look, I just wanted to say how much I liked the garden.'

'Thank you,' Aspasia said.

She turned away when one of the mothers swooped across the paths, ready to defend her from whichever rough man was at the lattice. Aspasia didn't see Pericles roll his eyes at his own tongue-tied embarrassment. His flush matched her own, just about. Yet when he looked back, it was to see a hawklike expression in a much older woman.

'And what do *you* want?' the woman demanded.

'I-I'm, nothing untoward! I was merely asking about the blooms.'

'Oh yes? And who are you to be talking to one?'

'What? No, the flowers! The g-garden. Kuria, I assure you. I am Pericles of the Alcmaeonid family. My mother is . . . Oh, by the gods. Look, my intentions are perfectly innocent, I assure you.'

The woman who had replaced the young vision from before slowly lost her narrow-eyed suspicion. Her eyebrows rose.

'The Pericles who was divorced not so long ago?'

Pericles was surprised at a stranger knowing such a thing, though he supposed it had been the gossip of the market for a time. He nodded and the woman smiled at him.

'Come to the front, kurios. Yes, yes – come.'

She vanished as he made his way around the house. The door was opened by unseen hands and the woman stepped out.

'There! I'm sorry I was curt before. You'll understand we do get mere boys looking in sometimes. All for nothing, of course, but it doesn't stop them.'

'What . . . is this place?' Pericles said, leaning back to look. He had only ever noticed the little barred window into the garden. The building seemed solid enough, on two floors. To his surprise, the woman took his arm in the most natural way, turning to look back with him.

She had been beautiful once, Pericles thought in confusion. The morning light was hard, but she had the posture of a dancer. When she spoke, she looked into his eyes as if there was no one else in that street and not half a city heading to work or opening stalls and shops all around them. Mornings were always busy in Athens, before the sun became too hot.

'We bring good men and women together,' she murmured, as if imparting a secret. Pericles had to bend his head to hear, so that he felt her breath on his ear. 'In fact, I have a symposium planned for tomorrow evening. Just a gathering, for music, talk and wine. No wives.'

She smiled and Pericles did the same, then frowned as he understood.

'Ah . . . I think. I didn't realise, er . . .'

He glanced back to the lattice in the wall, where he had seen the girl – Aspasia – so often, where he had walked slowly past and wanted to ask her name a dozen times.

He'd imagined many lives for her, but not this one. He knew his father had been to houses in the city where women could be bought for an evening. Pericles reminded himself guiltily of his own experience, when he had been blind drunk with Cimon once. That night had involved vomiting and lost sandals – flashes of grim pleasure and not much joy. He shook his head.

'I'm sorry, I have too much to do . . . Please pass on my thanks to Aspasia.' The words kept coming, though he could hardly believe it. 'How, er . . . how much would it be?'

'How much would what be?' the woman asked, stepping back.

He looked at her in confusion.

'To . . . I can't believe I am explaining this – to purchase her time for an evening!'

He said the last in a rush and stood in surprise as the woman laughed, actually leaning back from the waist and bending her knees.

'This is not a house for bought women, kurios, for *pornai*. We raise *hetairai* here. Companions. If Aspasia likes you, her time will cost nothing at all. If she does not, you could offer a talent of silver and still be sent home.'

'Truly?' Pericles said. His scepticism was written on his face and the woman's expression hardened.

'If I had a drachm for every man who thought all he had to do was offer a little more, I would have that talent of silver right now. We raise *wives* here, Pericles, not street girls. We find them, we train them – the most extraordinary women you will ever meet. If one of them likes you . . . well, you'll never want another. Hetairai are rare and valuable, kurios. They are not to be rented like a horse or the poor drabs down by the docks. Our girls are adored, as rubies and gold. They are a treasure of the city. Do you understand?'

'I don't think I do, no,' Pericles said bluntly.

His previous embarrassment had vanished in the face of the puzzle this woman presented. He narrowed his eyes, determined not to be made a fool. He had not forgotten the young beauty he'd glimpsed in her garden, the perfect setting for her with her hands dark and a smear of earth across her brow where she'd wiped away sweat. That had been real, he realised.

'Invite me then,' he said suddenly. 'And I have friends who will want to join me, if they will be welcome?'

'That depends. Wild young men? Those who will drink too much and paw at those who serve them? I will not tolerate bad manners, kurios. Tell them that. This is a *respectable* house. Is that understood? Good. Then I will leave your name at the door, with . . . two others? Be prepared for wonders. I will see you then.'

She watched him go, his gait clumsy while he sensed her eyes still on him. The road was growing busy and the mother nodded to herself. It seemed Aspasia's little garden had lured a bee, after all. As she went back inside, the mother sent a prayer to Athena, that the girl had the sense not to let him escape. She put the thought aside then. There was much to do if she was to put a symposium together by the following evening. Music, food, actors, all the right guests. There was little time and not enough money, but with good oil for the lamps, the best couches, wine borrowed from a local merchant with promises to repay . . . they could indeed make the house a place of wonders for a single night. For such a fine bee.

*

The boy sat up in the night. His dreams had been disturbed again. He hadn't slept for weeks without waking at least once with images of flames and blood. No matter how hard he pressed the heels of his hands into his eyes, they remained, gleaming green and gold.

He slept on his back, with a wooden block shaped to his skull to support him. He knew some of the older Spartans lay on cloaks or even blankets to ease their bones. Yet Pleistonax was small for his age, much lighter than grown men. He lay down like a cricket on the floor each night, trembling with cold until his spot warmed under him. The dreams did not disturb him, not really. Like the others, he slept lightly anyway, always ready for a sudden clash of sound. Spartans could not be surprised, so the trainers said. Two of those men had been killed when the barracks collapsed, crushed by falling blocks and a roof beam that had crashed right across one of their pallets. Some of the boys had laughed about that when they heard.

Pleistonax's group had been fairly lucky. A few had broken legs or arms, but only one had been killed. He sniffed and rubbed the back of his hand across his nose. That was one of the images that came to him as he slept, the way that little boy's head had ended under a column of stone, smashed to blood and hair and fragments. At times, it was hard to remember his face, at least without seeing the pieces and the way the dust darkened around him. There had been a lot of dust. The boys had been marched away from the city when the rioting started. They understood why without having to be told. They were the future of Sparta, the city's most valuable resource.

Four hundred boys had gone west from Sparta, heading to the training camp where they hunted and ran, where they endured thirst and physical extremes to collapse. It was not a happy place and their expressions had been grim.

Pleistonax rubbed his face hard. He was awake, though the moon was still high. One or two of the other boys sat up slowly in the darkness, then lay down. The night was warm and the tree crickets were singing. Even earthquakes and riots hadn't quietened those.

He knelt to put on his sandals and scratch his groin where sweat had stuck cloth to his skin. He needed to pee, though the trainers forbade anyone from doing it near camp. It meant heading out into the night, where lions or wolves might be waiting. He supposed that was the point. They lost one or two boys in the wilds each year, but the rest had tested their courage and survived. Or pissed in the dust near camp and given up their honour. If they were caught, they were sent home to become perioikoi – those who lived around Sparta but were not of the elite. To Pleistonax, that was a prospect worse than death.

Something moved nearby, a sound he recognised. Even in his half-sleeping state, he knew it was the noise that had woken him. No alarm had been raised, but these were not ordinary times. The trainers manned the perimeter of the camp as if they were in hostile territory and not on a training expedition.

Pleistonax picked up his knife belt and secured it in silence, his jaw set. If it was the helots, he would not run. They had killed good men and women and they would never see him coming in the dark. It was one way his small size had proved useful over nearly seven years in the agoge. He could not hit as hard as some, though he practised turning with his hip and shoulder until he could rock bigger boys back on their heels. But he was quick – and he could surprise a stranger with a sudden strike.

He heard steps coming closer and that was enough.

'Up, lads. Enemy, enemy!' Pleistonax shouted.

His voice was still high and if they'd known who made the call, they might have scorned him or thrown things. Given who his father had been, he was not popular in that place. Yet all they heard was the warning and they rolled out and up in instants. Almost before he had finished calling, the long room was filled with forty standing children.

The silence was unnerving. Any other group might have called out or asked sleepy questions. These ones waited for orders. Pleistonax wondered if this was how his father had felt at Plataea, when he led the army against a Persian host. It was a good feeling.

'Movement outside,' he said. 'No alarm given. Enemy or exercise, but there is someone there.'

'Who is that speaking?' came a gruff voice.

Pleistonax felt his heart sink. Dorion was older and the *eiren*, or herder, of their group. Pleistonax dreaded being singled out by him, but whatever happened later, there was no hiding in the darkness, not then.

'I did. Pleistonax,' he said. He could almost hear Dorion rolling his eyes.

'Bad dream, was it? Your mother forced to kneel again for all those nasty soldiers?'

Pleistonax said nothing as his face grew hot. Dorion delighted in the discomfort he could cause. There had been a few fights at first – not everyone liked the one chosen to lead them. Still, a few of Dorion's friends laughed, making the sound dutifully. Pleistonax hated those.

One of the boys near the door made a hissing sound

and all movement stopped. They heard low voices and stood to attention by their beds. Pleistonax had won them a little time and he was pleased about that. Being found asleep would earn a beating or a missed meal. The trainers were cunning sods as well, with all sorts of tricks to catch them unawares. This time, the boys had to struggle not to grin as the men came clattering in.

'Up, lads! Enemy, enemy!' a voice they all knew roared. On another night, it would have been followed by a mad scramble while he used his hand lamp to light a larger one. This time, the spreading gleam revealed row upon row of standing boys and young men in chiton tunics or loin-cloths, sandals already on.

The trainers had all been named for different animals. They delighted in the nicknames and at times, the reason for them was obvious. Tragos – the goat – was wiry and agile, with dark hair and wide-set eyes like his namesake. He walked into the room and Pleistonax wondered if he looked for signs of guilt. The trainers prided themselves on knowing every ruse, every trick the boys might come up with. The man was clearly wondering if the display of readiness was some sort of mockery.

Tragos halted before Pleistonax and the boy's heart sank. Dorion made a snickering sound a few rows over, his voice somehow unmistakable. How did the trainers always know? Yet the man who tormented them in daylight hours didn't show his usual dark delight. The face that bent to stare into his eyes was carefully blank.

'Come with me,' Tragos said, his voice a soft growl.

Pleistonax stepped out of line as he had been taught – a single pace, then turning on the spot to follow. Dorion muttered something else and Pleistonax saw the trainer's back stiffen. Tragos darted back suddenly and backhanded the older boy, knocking him into those around him so that three or four went sprawling.

Tragos flexed his hand, looking at a new cut on his knuckle where it had connected with teeth.

'Say what you have to say to a man's face. Never to his back. You'll get worse than that in the older group if you try that again, believe me. Or should I hold you back another year in this one?'

'No, kurios,' Dorion said. He had resumed his previous stance, though blood trickled from a broken lip.

The trainer nodded in grudging appreciation. He put a hand on Pleistonax's shoulder. At the door, he took up the hand lamp but left the other burning, though the sun was showing over the eastern hills. The trainers usually hated that sort of waste. It was a small thing, but it disturbed Pleistonax as much as anything else.

In the training yard, he saw a group of three men. He recognised Nicomedes immediately, a bearded block of a man. He thought too that he knew the one standing with him. The name came to Pleistonax and he whispered it – Tisamenus, whom men called the soothsayer. Pleistonax realised with a start that the third was one of the ephors, though the name would not come. That one seemed skin and bone compared to those with him, all his hard-won muscle sagged into pouches. Yet he stood straight and his stare was clear in the dawn.

'Pleistonax, son of Pausanias?' the ephor said.

Pleistonax nodded. He did not kneel as he stood there. Tisamenus had been a friend to his father, but the ephors had been part of the judgement against him. Pleistonax would not kneel to any of them, whatever it cost. He knew that with certainty as hard as the ground beneath his feet. Instead, he smiled at them, making the ephor frown.

'It's him,' Tisamenus said, drawing his eye.

Pleistonax looked over, but the soothsayer was staring into the distance.

'Your father Pausanias was the oldest son of Cleombrotus,' the ephor went on. 'He was nephew to King Leonidas, cousin to King Pleistarchus. You are his only heir.'

The ephor fell silent though his mouth moved, as if he could not bring himself to go on. It was Pleistonax's uncle Nicomedes who spoke, his voice gruff.

'The king is dead, boy. He drove himself too hard and his heart failed.'

Pleistonax blinked, the words a roar in his ears.

'I don't . . .' he began.

The ephor had recovered enough to finish.

'King Pleistarchus had no heirs. You are the inheritor of the line of kings, Your Majesty. It is decided. The ephors have voted, but it's not as if there was a second candidate.'

The man's mouth worked again, choosing to speak his mind rather than exercise caution.

'I would not have had the son of a condemned traitor and coward as my king, but there it is. There is no one else.'

Pleistonax could see the man's bitterness consuming him. He supposed it was the bravery of the very old. When death had closed its wings over your head, a man could say whatever he wanted.

'I am fourteen years old . . .' Pleistonax began.

The ephor waved a hand in the air, speaking over him.

'Your uncle Nicomedes will be regent until you complete your training in the agoge. When you are of age . . .'

'Am I king?' Pleistonax said, his voice hard.

The old man stared.

'Because if I am, you should keep your tongue still in your head. Unless you think to insult my father again? Do that, ephor, and my first order will be for my uncle Nicomedes to draw his sword and run you through with it.'

There was a long moment of utter silence, as if the hills around them held their breath. At last, the ephor nodded and bowed.

'Majesty, the gods have made you king. I spoke in grief, as I loved Pleistarchus like my own son. With your permission, I will withdraw. We are rebuilding the city. There is much to do.'

The boy nodded to him, gripping one hand in the other behind his back so they would not see how he had begun to shake. The ephor turned away first, heading to a group of horses that waited for them. Tisamenus and his uncle remained.

'It is a bad time to lose a king,' his uncle said. 'After the earthquake and the helot revolt. It feels as if we are cursed . . .'

He glanced at Tisamenus, as if he might have the answer. Yet the soothsayer watched the boy.

'Your father was a good man,' Tisamenus said, 'and no traitor. I swore an oath at the end, one I repeated to Pleistarchus and now to you. I was promised five victories by the oracle at Delphi. Pleistarchus used two, to secure his reign. With Plataea and Cypros, I have had four of them. The last I reserve, in your father's name. It was the Athenians who brought about his end. If Sparta ever takes the field against Athens, I must be there, in your father's name.'

'Uncle Nicomedes?' Pleistonax said, looking up. 'Do you hear?'

His uncle was a stranger to him, a Spartan warrior in his prime. Yet he accepted the order, bowing his head. The ephors and the gods themselves had chosen this boy. Spartan *peitharchia* – obedience – was the only response.

'As you wish, Majesty,' Nicomedes said.

Pleistonax waited until they too had mounted and ridden away. When he turned, he was startled to find the trainer still there with his lamp. Of course Tragos had listened to every word, unnoticed as a pillar. The man had been a bully and a tyrant for all the years Pleistonax had known him. Yet he too was a Spartan. Slowly, the one known as Goat dropped to one knee, his head dipping to his chest.

'Please get up,' Pleistonax said, suddenly embarrassed.

Tragos rose with a calculating look in his eye.

'If you are to be the battle king of Sparta, lad, I will have to train you harder than all the rest. It will be a challenge, but I will not have my class found wanting, not by anyone. We'll make you *iron*, son.'

For an instant, Pleistonax considered taking a high tone with him. The man had knelt, after all. Yet there was a glint in the old bastard's eye. Tragos was waiting for it, Pleistonax could see, just waiting for the opportunity to knock him down and call it his first lesson. After seven years, Pleistonax knew him too well.

'All right,' he said. 'Do whatever you have to. I am king by blood. Make me worthy of the name.'

The trainer lost his glint and swallowed back whatever he had been going to say.

'Well, the sun's up!' he bellowed, turning away. 'You'll

run the hard path before you eat! Get out here, all of you. I see you skulking in the shadows. It seems you'll run with a king today.'

Pleistonax groaned, though a part of him wondered. The so-called hard path was brutal, but it suited his small frame. He was usually in the final six or so, while those heavier with muscle faded in the heat. He suspected the trainer had decided to offer him a win, if he chose to reach for it. Well, he did. He felt the certainty in his bones. No matter what, he would leave them in his wake.

9

The Boule council was packed that morning. The ten tribes of Athens sat in their fifties, though there was barely enough room for them all. Some stood on steps or crammed themselves onto benches with no stone showing. The crush was said to be deliberate on the part of the designers. They could not sit apart as they made decisions. It created a sense of life in that building by the Agora, of massed voices rising and falling as each issue was brought to a vote or passed to the Assembly the following day.

Pericles loved it. He'd listened to his father speak there, as well as great names from the past. He was part of the new generation and he took his seat with those of the Acamantis tribe, nodding to those he knew and liked. He made a point of remembering the names of his colleagues in that place, as well as their interests and families. It was such a small thing, but he was surprised how few others seemed willing to make the effort. It meant he could always find a seat, as men he'd greeted a dozen times made a space for him.

Acamantis was not in rotation that month, unfortunately. The officers of the council all came from Leontis. They had reached their greatest influence when Themistocles had led them, and they were still a shadow of their previous eminence. The wheel turned.

Pericles nodded across the hall to Zeno and Anaxagoras. As citizens made and not born, it was typical of them to take such an interest in the council and the Assembly. There were many in Athens who regarded the work as a chore to be avoided, while his friends attended every meeting, to listen and occasionally to speak.

As he settled himself, the epistates called for a vote on the matter of Megara. Pericles cursed under his breath when he realised he had missed the debate. That was what he got for sighing at a hetaira! He felt his face growing red as the issue was settled then and there. Pericles matched Anaxagoras when the other held up his hand to vote. Athens would support Megara in some dispute with Corinth apparently, offering them protected status. That suited him well enough and he relaxed as the debate moved to another subject. It pleased Pericles to see such confidence in that building. The power of Athens was increasing – in ships, in trade, in the flood of wealth and new buildings, in the decisions they made. It showed in the faces of the young, in the laughter. This building, this five hundred, was the heart of the League. His father had called it a nation, but there were times when it seemed even more, its reach increasing with every year that passed.

The officers listened to half a dozen petitions for reduced League payments, one after the other. Those votes were quick enough, dismissing each one. The amounts had been set by the states themselves, after all. In ships or men or silver, they paid their tithe in exchange for fleet protection. The treasury on the island of Delos supported the ships – and, of course, Athens commanded them.

It had been years since Pericles had set foot on Delos, right at the beginning of the great enterprise, the joining of allied forces. Given its importance, he thought he should ask for ships from the council before the end of summer, to take a small group there to check on the arrangements.

His musings were interrupted as a rowdy debate on sending a military force to an island near Thrace came to a vote. They would see six ships within a month, bearing League banners. A strategos was appointed and left the room to collect his written authority from the clerks. The council broke for lunch then and it was some time into the afternoon when the debate finally turned to the reason Pericles was there. He and his friends had kept their preparations quiet, but they were ready.

The epistates announced the subject as 'new construction in the city', as unremarkable a description as Pericles had been able to think of. Yet it was Ephialtes himself who rose to speak – and his friends who called for the strategos to be heard. Others took up that call easily enough. Ephialtes was well known in that place. In the absence of Cimon, there was no one else with so many supporters in the Boule or the city beyond those walls. That was why Pericles needed him.

'Gentlemen, archons, strategoi,' Ephialtes began, 'I believe an opportunity lies before us, a task that could change the course of history – for this city and for all Hellenes.'

The epistates leaned over to whisper to his clerks, confusion clear on his face. He had not been told anything important was on the docket. Ephialtes glanced once to the water-keeper, waiting as the man pulled a clay stopper and water began to drum into the pan below. The tension of the moment brought silence to the hall, for the first time since Pericles had entered. They sensed something was up.

'Sparta has been weakened both by tremors of the earth

and a slave revolt. May the unseen one welcome those who have fallen into his domain. We sent men, silver, salt and food to our allies – and they were refused by too-proud Spartans. They scorned Cimon and he lost his place here as a result. A noble Athenian, stolen from us by their games of power.'

Pericles nodded. He had discussed the speech Ephialtes would make, making suggestions. The man may have been proud, but he knew a good phrase when he heard it. Pericles had thought Cimon would be the one to carry that particular crowd, but Ephialtes had his own following, in the markets and the potteries, in the poor streets. It did not show as strongly in the council building, where Eupatridae nobles still held a balance of power. No, his strength lay with the Assembly, when the common men of Athens lent their vote.

'Athens grows wealthy, gentlemen,' Ephialtes went on. 'Many of you here have seen silver flooding into your coffers since the League was formed and Persia denied our waters. For the first time in centuries, the seas are free both of pirates and the old enemy. Our potteries blaze day and night to meet demand! League ships roam the Aegean and as far west as the new colonies. All in our name, with our strength – and our silver.'

He waited for a beat and Pericles clenched a fist. The man was a better speaker than he had been before. It was actually uncomfortable to see his own techniques used by another. Pericles hoped he had not created a tyrant in his struggle to keep the city safe. The gods loved it when men brought about their own destruction.

Ephialtes spoke in a lower voice then, his tone a portent of dark years ahead.

'There is one ally who will not allow us to grow too rich, too powerful. You know their name and what they can do. I have come to accept we cannot face them in the field.'

He nodded in acknowledgement to Pericles then, singling him out in the crowd. Torches were being lit as twilight came, but there was no sense of weariness in that council, no shuffling.

'I have consulted with architects and builders,' Ephialtes went on. 'I have sought solutions to the problem. We are Athenian! The workshop of the world. Nothing is beyond our imagination, our strength. If it can be conceived, we can make it. And yet – how can we live and trade and bring goods into this city if Sparta marches against us?'

He took a deep breath, savouring the moment. Pericles found his hands were trembling.

'Come on,' he whispered.

'City walls can be surrounded,' Ephialtes said at last. 'But if we build *new* walls, from the city to the sea, no force of man – no, not even those of Sparta – will ever trouble us again.'

There was noise then, as hundreds bent their heads to explain or mutter in response. Pericles kept an eye on those closest to him. They were men who had volunteered for these meetings and discussions, giving a full month out of their year to the work. They tended to be from wealthier classes in the city and he could see them frown at the thought of the costs falling on their shoulders. Such a momentous decision would have to be sent to the Assembly, that had always been clear. Yet it had to get through the council first.

'How much?' someone shouted. A hundred voices roared some agreement with that. The idea of walls thirty stades long – two of them! – was almost frightening in its ambition.

Ephialtes patted the air and some of them did quieten, while others were so lost in their own debates that they went on, red-faced with fingers jabbing. Ephialtes had to shout to be heard, but the rostrum had its own sort of power and they gave way with bad grace.

'. . . archer towers will defend them, without gates. In that way, a ship will unload at the Piraeus onto carts, then travel an hour into the city, without ever being in the open. A Spartan army could stand and howl at those walls all day if they wanted! No, it is not a hostile act! We are a trading city. We want to live in peace, to grow and trade in peace. Is that too much to ask?'

He responded to another shout from the crowd, making Pericles wince. He'd counselled Ephialtes to ignore such things, rather than encourage more and more.

'Your fear of Sparta is *exactly* why we should build these walls!' Ephialtes said, jabbing the air with his own finger. 'There will never be another year like this, where they are distracted and weakened. If we do it – and we can, of course we can – Athens will know a golden age. We will be safe, without threat of war. No one can attack us at sea, not with the ships we command. Enemies *must* come by land – and these walls will stop them. I give my support to this.'

It was the signal for Pericles to rise. His name was called by Zeno and Anaxagoras as well as some of those around where Ephialtes sat. Ephialtes glanced over and half-bowed, as if he merely gave way. It was all a performance of a sort, but the epistates chose Pericles and he walked to the rostrum to face them.

'Gentlemen of the council. Athenians. I spent part of my youth watching Persians burn this city to the ground. Twice. This very building still smells of sap and oil because it is new. In our history, soldiers of Sparta have entered Athens and stood in the Agora just outside. Oh, we called them, yes, but once they were in, they did not leave easily! Aristides saw them fight at Plataea. He said the Persians could not hold them. And I saw them surrounding the force we sent in aid, with spears lowered. If they are allies, it is like having a lion in the house.'

He smiled and changed his tone, as if the idea had just occurred to him.

'That would be a glorious thing, would it not? No one would dare steal from you! Until you move a little too quickly, or drop a pot – and the beast springs upon your family and tears them to pieces. No, gentlemen, you have had your turn. Ephialtes has spoken – and I believe he is right. You know this cannot be decided here. Such an undertaking will have to go to the Assembly, before the people who will have to build it and pay for it.'

He nodded sharply.

'I can secure pledges for forty talents,' Pericles said.

The amount brought a hiss of shock from the assembled council.

'I welcome more, from Eupatridae families who wish to save the lives of their fellow men and be praised for generations. There will have to be new taxes, yes – for the duration of the build and not a day longer. From the ships that land cargoes, from the foreign metics who benefit from homes in our city – even a liturgy offering from every citizen, until it is done. We do not compel our people, gentlemen! They pay what they can and they are praised and loved for it. These great walls will belong to all of us, after all. Rich and poor alike will thrive once they are built. This can be our great work, gentlemen. Ephialtes has the right of it. Two walls from here to the coast will mean we are *safe*. Two walls will mean we are *free*. Imagine it for a moment! Imagine being able to work and trade and talk and live, without fear of a Spartan column coming to impose its will on us! I say we can do this – in a year or less. If the Assembly passes this motion, we can build these walls. We can be free.'

He shook his head, in silent awe at the word. There were other voices calling to speak and he bowed and left that spot. They would debate it, but he saw a great part of the crowd had listened. Ephialtes had carried some of them; Pericles had brought more. The promise of forty talents had smothered the first demands to know who would pay for such a thing. Of course, when the true costs became evident, they would complain, but the walls would be rising by then.

Pericles knew Ephialtes was watching as he walked back to his seat. When he looked up, it was to see the man studying him. They smiled, but it was like two fighting cockerels, each weighing the strengths of the other, neither completely liking what he found. Pericles settled back to hear the speeches. If he had to intervene again, he would, with arguments he had kept back. All that mattered was that the council would kick it up to the Assembly. As night follows day, only one objection really mattered: when Sparta heard what they were doing, they could march. The threat of that could be howled down for a while, with talk of Athenian pride and strength of arms. Yet it remained.

He frowned to himself. Sparta could not stay in the field

for longer than thirty days, if Aeschylus was right. There had to be a solution, a way to deal with them. He just didn't know what it was.

Pericles plucked at his clothing as he stood in the street. He felt unusually, almost painfully clean. He had mentioned attending a symposium to the staff at his gymnasium and it had opened doors he had never seen before. In moments, the entire staff had appeared, taking an interest and discussing his needs. He had been bathed, oiled, scraped and bathed again. His nails and hair had been clipped, shaved and oiled in turn. One of the staff had lit a taper and run it over his ears, to the pungent smell of burned hair.

Zeno and Anaxagoras stood in the street with him, about as scrubbed and awkward as he was. As neither was native to Athens, they had expressed a desire to see a hetaira house and all the mysteries within. Zeno reached out and patted a statue of Hermes set by the door. Overhead, two bronze lion heads gaped at the street, their open mouths ready to direct rainwater away from walls and gutters. Pericles was still not sure his friends were the right companions for such an evening. Cimon would have been a better choice. He knew this world. Pericles swallowed and walked up two steps.

The door was opened by a serving man, broad-shouldered and very powerful of frame. Pericles announced himself and the fellow gestured silently for them to enter. Pericles assumed it suited a house of women to let guests know they had at least one hulking brute on the premises.

He and his companions swept inside to the sound of music. The lighting was very low, lamps casting a dim glow in the corridor. A woman of great beauty gestured for them to come further in. Zeno gaped at her, but she was not Aspasia and Pericles passed by, going on to the centre of the house.

The roof was open above, with a small pool below. It was not on the scale of his home outside the city and he might have been disappointed if not for the lights that glittered everywhere. A hundred tiny lamps warmed the air. One wall had been built with protruding stands no larger than a coin from floor to ceiling, spaced apart so that flames flickered like constellations of stars. Some sat behind glass of different colours so that they gleamed red or blue without any clear pattern. The air too was strange, thick with a perfume that pleased his senses. Pericles had to breathe slowly as a wave of dizziness washed through him.

He saw only three women in that shadowed room, lounging like cats on the couches. He had the impression of long bare legs and draped cloth of gold, of eyes large with kohl in the Egyptian style. Of gold bangles on wrists and ankles. Of jewels and the scent that filled him with every breath. The flowers of the garden were part of it, he was certain, though the combination was somehow stronger, darker.

Aspasia was not there, he realised with a pang of disappointment. If they thought to hide her, he would not stay long, he was almost certain. He accepted an invitation to sit and a goblet of wine was placed in his hand. It was stronger than he was used to, he knew that from the first taste. The entire experience was. Yet the day had gone well and the Assembly would not meet until the following evening. He drank deeply and saw Zeno doing the same. Only Anaxagoras waved his cup away. He was looking around him in fascination, but then Anaxagoras had known a few such places in Ionia, or so he said. He had offered to keep a clear head, for which Pericles was grateful. There were always thefts and murders on dark streets and he did not want to fall into some trap, his senses all befuddled. With Anaxagoras sober, he could relax for the first time in months.

One of the women lifted a languid hand and a servant drifted over and put a lyre into it. She brushed the strings with her fingertips and Pericles felt himself shiver at the sight. He noticed his wine had been refilled, though he had not seen it done. They were good, the servers! He wondered if they could be hired if he ever had another party at his estate.

The music was lulling at first, so that he sank back into pillows and bolsters, relaxing and drinking. Another of the women put a double pipe to her lips and accompanied the lyre player. Little by little, the music grew faster, so that Pericles felt his pulses tugged along. He knew the extraordinary power of that from the theatre, where a whole crowd could be lured into sorrow or surprised to raucous laughter with just a few chords. Yet it worked. It did not hurt that the women were both beautiful and lithe. Having them play gave him the excuse to stare. If these were hetairai, Pericles decided he approved.

The third woman produced a tiny pair of metal discs that she clashed in time with the music. Pericles felt his gaze drawn from the lyre player to the pipes to the last in a sort of daze. Someone had refilled his cup again. The air had thickened with warmth and scent and his limbs were deliciously heavy, almost without sensation. Yet the music grew faster still, building to something as the women in the room all looked to a doorway, in shadows he had barely noticed. Silk sheets swayed there, touched by currents of air. Pericles glanced with them and then froze, breath catching in his throat.

Aspasia spun as she entered the room, so that her hair moved and twisted around her. It had been bound in gold thread and shimmered. Her arms were bare and her skin had been dusted with something that caught the light. She *gleamed* as her robe flared up around her. It was long, the sort of dress an Athenian noblewoman might wear. Her leg appeared through it, drawing his eye. Pericles found he was holding his breath.

As she reached the centre of the room, the lamplight made her gold. She moved in patterns of steps Pericles could not predict, while the music swelled and built, faster and faster. Her eyes were huge. He sat at the heart of it, utterly entranced as her foot caught the edge of the gown and tore right through. For a moment, Aspasia hung in the air, still splendid, her expression turning to shock.

'Horse*shit*!' she shouted as she collapsed in a tangle of cloth and kicking legs. The music died with a screech as she knocked into the pipe-player, causing the young woman to swallow the first part of her instrument.

Pericles was already laughing as he turned to Zeno, finding his friend wide-eyed, with a cushion pressed against his mouth. He rose then to help Aspasia free herself from the tangle of dress and some length of drapery ripped from the edge of a couch. The lyre player was still strumming along, but idly, the tune forgotten as she looked for someone to tell her what to do.

'Are you all right?' Pericles asked.

Aspasia was flushed, visibly mortified. She let him take her hand as she stood up and he saw her skin had indeed been dusted with some shining powder. He rather liked the effect, even as he struggled to keep his composure.

'I'm *fine*, thank you,' she said.

She was distracted by the effort of freeing her foot from the robe. He saw her glance down to where he still held her hand. She left it there for a beat, then withdrew.

'Will you dance again?' he asked. 'I thought it was going very well . . . at first . . .'

Despite his efforts, he knew he was grinning. The expression seemed to pull at her, widening her own smile even as she tried to be serious.

'Yes, well . . . as with falling from a great height, the first part isn't really the important bit.'

He blinked, entranced by her.

The crash had summoned the three mothers. They poured into that room, taking in the chaos of the scene with a single frozen glare. In moments, one of them was directing servants to straighten up and another was tending the girl who had hurt her mouth on the pipes. Pericles was ushered out with Zeno and Anaxagoras by a thin-lipped woman he didn't know. He looked over her head to where Aspasia still stood, burning in embarrassment.

Before he could truly marshal his thoughts, he was on the street with his two friends. Zeno had somehow managed to hold onto his cushion. The woman snatched it from his grasp, retreating inside.

'When can I come back?' Pericles called as the door closed. It did not open again.

10

The Assembly was a more raucous beast, with hard currents of anger or mockery. Pericles and Ephialtes took the lead in the debates, one answering the other so that their arguments built like a wave, crashing over objections. Despite himself, Pericles was impressed by the strategos. Ephialtes had risen in opposition to noble families like Cimon's or Pericles' own. In the process, he had grown in stature and ability, learning from the Assembly and the council how best to sway them. He had become a formidable speaker and Pericles had to be at his best to match him. Together, they brought a new excitement to the Pnyx hill. Each meeting was packed and those who wanted to speak in support or to object were all heard, though time trickled away like water.

On the second night after the symposium, Pericles let his thoughts drift while Ephialtes spoke, answering half a dozen points raised that afternoon. The crowd murmured as he dismissed each one, in acceptance or denial. Yet he carried them, or as many as mattered. The vote was coming closer and instead of focusing on the debate, Pericles wondered what Aspasia was doing at that moment. Why did the door of the hetaira house remain closed? Were they punishing Aspasia? Perhaps he should gather a few lads and kick that door in! He imagined her face when she realised he had come to rescue her. Delighted, obviously, draping her arms around his neck. He could smell the rich scent again as he stood there on the Pnyx, so that he actually turned to be sure she wasn't standing behind him. A burly oarsman looked back, tilting his head in question. Pericles sighed. Imagination could be powerful, but it was no substitute for the real thing.

Ephialtes took a question and Pericles felt his thoughts sharpen.

'What will the Spartans do when they hear? What if they march before we are finished?'

Ephialtes glanced across the crowd to Pericles, giving him the chance to answer. Pericles nodded and Ephialtes gestured for him to step forward.

'I will defer to my colleague in this, if you will allow it.'

Hundreds in the crowd murmured assent as Pericles took his place at the rostrum. Built from the wood of a Persian warship, it was the very symbol of war – and the destruction that came in its wake. That was not something he had to explain to the Assembly of Athens.

'Thank you,' he said to Ephialtes. 'The proposal before us – the Long Walls – will change the balance of power between Athens and Sparta. That is clear to us all; it will become clear to Sparta when they see them go up. I do not believe we can hide the purpose and intent of such a great enterprise. We are free men – and we choose strength, so we can live without fear of attack. Only the strong can make that choice – the weak have their fates decided for them. That is why we are gathered here, why the entire city is poised to begin. Every man in Athens must be part of this effort. Every foreign metic within our walls will put aside their usual work for this. Every ship will bend oars to feed and clothe us, every woman will organise food and tools, every slave will carry blocks and saw or dig. Every child will carry errands and news! We are as one on this, until it is done – if the Assembly votes to begin.'

He bowed his head for a moment, showing humility before them.

'If we vote to take that leap, beginning as soon as dawn tomorrow, I believe those walls will rise faster and stronger than any others ever built. In a few months, there will be an unbroken barrier from here to the sea – and another, enclosing land that will *always* be free. You ask what if Sparta comes? What if they march here?' He shook his head in disgust. 'Is that not the exact reason we stand on the Pnyx tonight? Why should Athenians live and breathe only at the whim of Sparta? Did we not fight Persia to remain free? I know I did!'

He hunched forward over the rostrum, leaning on his elbows. It made no difference at all to their ability to hear him, but it lent his words a subtle power, as if he shared secrets.

'Our advantage is fleeting and soon gone – as you have heard from Strategos Ephialtes. For this year alone, Sparta's soldiers are fighting their own and rebuilding shattered temples and homes. For just a season or two, we have a chance to change all the years ahead. If we take it. To answer you, I do not believe they will come. Some of you know how reluctant the Spartans are to leave their home region. They fear their helots will rise, with good reason. They live on a knife-edge of uncertainty every time they march! So *if* they come, it will be for just a brief season.' He let his voice fall deeper. 'And if we have to, I will lead the hoplites of Athens out to that new wall, to protect it.'

He paused, letting his promise soak in.

'I do not believe it will come to that, however. Not if we move with all the energy and talent of our race. The gods have given us much, gentlemen, but we must still struggle. Look around you! Look what you have already achieved. Now imagine what it could be for your children, without a Spartan knife at their throats!'

They cheered that, so that he faced thousands of glittering eyes. It was a heady feeling, as if he was back in the symposium that remained so close to every waking thought. Why hadn't the hetaira house asked him back? Had he ruined his one chance with his laughter? It had not been . . . He pulled his thoughts back to the subject, realising weariness had fogged his mind.

'If they come . . . we will find a way. I cannot share all our plans tonight, not with ears twitching that might end up on a road to Sparta. Yet I stake my honour on this. I am the son of Xanthippus and I will see it through.'

He glanced at Ephialtes and saw him dip his head. They were ready.

'I call for a vote,' Pericles said to them.

The epistates rose to judge the mood of the crowd. It took just a moment for him to nod and summon the clerks. Pericles felt his heart beating. If they agreed, he would leave a mark on the world that would secure Athens for generations. Even if they said no, they were stretching out, feeling new strength. That could not be undone. He made himself breathe slowly, imagining Aspasia looking on him with awe. The clerks announced the vote and around him hands were raised in a great host. The result was clear in the first instants. Pericles bowed his head to the will of the people. They would build.

*

The six ships that approached the island of Delos were intercepted before they were in range of the dock. The League kept a wall of oak and oars around the sacred island. Pericles gave the order and his small fleet dropped anchor with the shore still just a pale blur. Three days out from Athens, his crews were fresh, though they had rowed most of the previous day when breezes fell to nothing and the sails flapped. They'd made good time, only to sit and wait for the port officers to come out. Twelve warships of the League had taken a bearing to block their path, ready to ram and sink anyone trying to break through their constant patrol. The rest of the fleet spent winters in safe docks rather than risk being sunk by tempests and sudden squalls. Yet the ships around Delos remained on station. If they ever were driven in to port, it would only be in a storm so bad no one else could survive.

Pericles exchanged a glance with Zeno as small boats approached. One by one, three senior captains came on board, climbing with the sort of easy agility he always envied. There were no greetings or introductions. They looked furious.

'We've had no word of League ships coming,' one of them said.

The man was ready to defend himself, Pericles realised, with a hand on his sword.

'Plans change,' Pericles said. 'I was appointed by the Assembly of Athens four days ago.'

He held out a thick medal of bronze and the man's eyes widened. It symbolised the authority of the citizens of Athens and was given to all strategoi.

The trierarch captain examined it, then passed it to his second in command before handing it back to Pericles. He looked as if he might have spoken again if another boat hadn't bumped against the side. Pericles was pleased when Ephialtes appeared. He had been outnumbered on his own flagship. Regardless of bronze tokens and the six ships he had brought, Pericles knew he would need Ephialtes to do what they had come to do.

The three League trierarchs clearly felt ambushed. They turned in suspicion at the second strategos arriving on that deck. For his part, Ephialtes strode towards them, holding out his own bronze piece as proof of his authority.

'I am Strategos Ephialtes of Athens, gentlemen. We come with new orders from the Assembly.'

'I have not been told of this,' the first replied.

Ephialtes halted and raised an eyebrow.

'That is the nature of new orders. Consider what you have seen this morning. Strategos Pericles and I have brought six ships here, crewed and commanded by men of Athens. You have seen the twin proof of our authority, have you not? The correct response is to say, "What *are* the new orders, strategos?" Then I will explain them to you.'

The man exchanged a glance with those he commanded. Pericles wondered how many months they had been there, circling the island of Delos, watching for anyone foolish enough to come close. It was both brave and vital work, if undemanding.

The trierarch stood clenching and unclenching his fists. At last, he bowed his head.

'Very well, though I cannot say if I will accept them, strategos. Tell me what new orders there are, that bring a fleet of warships to the sacred island.'

'I was here when the vow was made,' Pericles said before Ephialtes could reply. 'With my father, Xanthippus, with

Archon Aristides, with Cimon. I watched as the first tithes were brought and silver poured into the store.'

The trierarch glanced at him, unsure where he was going.

'I was there. I sailed with your father,' he admitted grudgingly. 'Xanthippus was a man of honour.'

'Then you will know that that silver is to maintain the fleet. The treasury of Delos is for the alliance we formed that day, the Great League. Our members supply ships or men – or silver – as their part in the enterprise.'

'I know this,' the man said, frowning.

'Then you will know the treasury is not bound to Delos. The oath was taken here, but the sums have grown too vast. The order of the Assembly is to remove the treasury and store it in Athens, safe from pirates or foreign states.'

The man gaped, but he saw Ephialtes nodding, confirming.

'Where will they go then, members of the League, when it is time to bring their tithes? Will they come to Athens?'

'Why not?' Pericles said with a smile. 'We are the centre of the world. Not Delos. This place has been quiet since Apollo and his sister were born. It will be quiet again once we have gone.'

The man still looked stunned, but he made no more arguments. If anything, it was as if a weight had been lifted.

'Shall I . . . are we to return to Athens then? To leave Delos?'

It was Ephialtes who rested a hand on his shoulder and looked into his eyes.

'You have done your duty, kurios. It is at an end.'

To his surprise, Pericles saw tears appear in the captain's eyes, wiped roughly away.

'Then . . . you have permission to land, gentlemen. I will give orders for my men to help move the treasury.'

'I have oarsmen of six ships,' Ephialtes said in surprise. 'I hardly think I need more.'

The trierarch of Delos looked at them.

'Come and see, before you decide,' he said.

Boats returned like bees to take their captains away. Pericles joined Zeno in the bows of one and was rowed to shore, with Ephialtes in a second. Anaxagoras was back in Athens, setting up a school. Pericles only wished Cimon could have been there, as one who had witnessed the original League oath. Yet Cimon had settled into his new home outside the border of Attica. He would wait out his banishment for ten years, unless Pericles found a way to get him home. Such things had happened before, though it had taken a war with Persia.

As the boats were tied up on the island quays, Pericles was confronted once more by hoplites, ready to defend the island with spear and shield. He had gone slightly ahead of the news and had to wait for officers of the Delos squadron to land and order them to stand down. Pericles and Ephialtes were made to show the bronze tokens once more, with Ephialtes raising his eyes. Yet Pericles understood very well why they were so cautious. If they lost the treasury to thieves, it would certainly mean all their lives.

The island looked better kept than when his father had first chosen it – the very centre of the Aegean Sea, within range of Athens. Only priests had lived there then. Now, the garrison of hoplites was as permanent as the ships around the island, a constant presence to protect the League treasury.

As Pericles walked with Zeno and Ephialtes up the path

towards the temple precinct, he wondered again if this was the right choice, or simply the only one. He'd argued in the Assembly that the fleet guaranteed the safety of League states – and Athens paid the bulk of those costs. As long as they continued to do so, what did it matter if they moved the treasury to Athens, or even spent it on the Long Walls? He winced as he rehearsed old arguments. There would be trouble when the news spread, he was certain. There were already some who said Athens acted like a tyrant over smaller members. Yet to build those walls in such a short time, they had to fund the entire city, to pay every worker who might otherwise have given his days to earn a wage. It would be for just a short time, but the sums involved beggared the imagination. There was no choice, he reminded himself – and for all he knew, Athens becoming the centre of the League might be a very good thing.

'How many members are there, in the League?' Zeno asked.

Pericles listed them in his thoughts, counting aloud.

'Around a hundred and eighty,' he said.

Zeno looked shocked and Pericles shrugged.

'Peace leads to trade. Trade leads to wealth . . . wealth leads to strength. The numbers have grown, the fleet with it.'

'And they have all been sending a tribute in silver to Delos, year after year?'

'Or ships, if they have them. A few sent their young men in the beginning, but we had to train them. It was easier to let Athens build and crew the ships . . . Silver is the most common tithe.'

The League trierarchs halted just ahead, exchanging passwords with another group of hoplites in armour, weapons bristling. Pericles had begun to realise the level of fortification in Delos since he'd last stood there. An entire new wing had been added to the temple of Apollo – and if it looked more like a fortress, that was because it clearly was one. He whistled as a gate as thick and tall as anything in Athens swung open before him. With an awed glance at his companions, they went through into a sunlit courtyard. The gate was closed and barred behind them and Pericles felt a prickle at the back of his neck. He knew there were archers on the walls before he turned to see them. It was what he would have done.

'What is this?' he said.

The senior trierarch looked back and his frown cleared as he understood.

'Merely caution, kurios. You will see. Come.'

He led them out of the sun and down new steps cut in stone. The air was cooler below ground and Pericles could only wonder at such a place chipped from the rock, deep as a mine.

His legs were aching by the time he reached a paved floor once again. The trierarch and his companions indicated a row of storerooms, each one barred and locked. They were all filled with chests, of wood and iron. As the two Athenian strategoi stood and watched, the men opened the bars of the closest and threw back the lids of a dozen chests.

They were all full, of silver or gold. Each one would hold four or five talents, Pericles estimated, his mouth suddenly dry. He could see . . . thirty chests to a room and . . . He swallowed. There were at least a dozen rooms.

Ephialtes was as round-eyed as a child in the gloom.

'I had no idea the amounts were as great as this!' he said.

'No wonder you look so strained, trierarch! I don't think I would sleep if I had all this in my care.'

'It has been a weight of responsibility, strategos,' the man agreed. 'It has also been my honour, but I would not mind laying it down.'

'Is there any way out, except for that winding stair?'

'No, strategos. The designer thought it would be a good idea to make it difficult.'

'He was right,' Pericles said softly. 'But it will take for ever to get all this to the ships. We'll need your men, carts, mules, bags, anything you have.'

'Very well, strategos,' the trierarch said.

He actually smiled as he spoke and he looked younger. Pericles could see a bounce in his step that had not been there when he'd come on board. He could understand the change. The responsibility for so much wealth was like a weight settling around his neck. It was true the fleet cost fortunes in pay and supplies, but there was clearly a massive surplus to have built up so much over the years. The silver of Delos meant safety, freedom. It meant they could build the walls.

He blinked as a thought struck him. If the members of the League ever saw the amount gathered in their name, they would want to be released from their annual tithe – with good reason. He would have to be discreet, as if moving so much silver and gold could ever be done quietly!

'We'll have to search the men at the end of every shift,' he said, his mind racing. 'They'll have their hands filled before they've gone a dozen paces.'

'Or we could melt lead for new seals,' Zeno replied, 'and bind the chests closed before we move them.'

Ephialtes nodded at that, though it was with a sort of vagueness. He looked at least as shocked as Pericles, his eyes gleaming with possibilities.

'Come on,' Ephialtes said. 'We'll work it out on the way back to the docks. There is a week's work here or more, gentlemen. The sooner we begin, the sooner we can sail home.'

11

The weather turned cold, but the walls still rose, higher every day. They built in a sort of frenzy that was hard on both men and tools. The injuries were terrible, from arms crushed under a block to splinters of stone lodged in skin. There were few days where someone wasn't killed or so badly hurt they could not work again. The council paid compensation to the families of those who did not survive, but it was not enough to keep them from poverty.

Though Pericles knew the costs in blood and silver, the sheer wonder of the progress never failed to steal his breath. Each morning, he walked into the Agora through the cemetery that lay just beyond the city walls, passing the tombs of his father and brother and paying his respects to them both. When he climbed the Acropolis and looked to the south, he could see the foundations dug and blocks assembled to be laid down, all the way from the city to the sea. The work had already begun in earnest and every day brought a dozen new problems.

Tens of thousands of labourers rose at dawn and dug or lifted until they were exhausted, stopping only for food and darkness, coming faster each day as the winter wore on. They knew Sparta would have heard by then. The only response was to raise the walls before red-cloaked soldiers marched into view. Yet they ran out of sand or mortar or wood or stone, or loads were delivered to the wrong place, so that one part of the walls had a surplus while a dozen others had to stop work. It was all maddening and Pericles had Anaxagoras and Zeno working day and night to keep the supplies flowing. He paid them for their labour and they relished it. There was still a shadow over every day and every stone laid.

With the vast sums from the Delos treasury, Pericles had expanded the port section of the great build, creating new warehouses and dock buildings there. They would fall under the protection of the western wall when it was complete. The second great wall was to the east of the port, coming in from the sea to join the city walls at an angle. Pericles was not too happy with its location, but there was no time to revise the plans, not then.

Rain turned good earth to slop and interfered with lime mortar, but they worked on under makeshift shelters, shivering and counting every day as a win against an unseen enemy. Not since the city had been evacuated to Salamis had all Athens united in a single aim. The red-cloaks were the threat that sent children to bed, that had men staring into the distance, wondering if they would see another year. There were no cheering crowds in the Agora in those months. The council organised the work alongside the trials and laws of the people. The entire city waited – and built, as fast and as well as they could.

Pericles felt a little guilty at how happy he was. The mood in the city was one of dark expectation, fearing the worst, while he walked with light steps, at least when he could visit Aspasia at the hetaira house. He had never known a woman like her and he was still not quite sure how much of her was real and how much artifice.

He stood before the open door, with one of the 'mothers'

watching him through narrowed eyes. Aspasia had agreed to walk with him into the city, where they would find a place to eat. He had met her only half a dozen times since the first symposium disaster. She seemed to have grown in confidence since then, as if her association with him gave her status in the house. With more than a little smugness, he supposed it did. He had been made strategos that year, after all.

When she came out, his breath stopped. She wore a simple dress, tied at the waist. Her arms were bare, but with the chill in the air that month, she had put on a cloak, wearing it around her shoulders. It was a dark red and suited her, he thought. He was not aware of how his smile had spread, though the mother in the doorway rolled her eyes as she turned away.

Pericles reached out to offer his arm, then hesitated as he saw the burly figure of the house guard coming out after the young woman.

'The lady does not need a companion,' Pericles said. 'Go inside.'

The man returned his gaze. Aspasia shook her head.

'Orcas is deaf, Pericles. It's considered a great thing to have a deaf slave in a hetaira house. He cannot repeat secrets.'

She gestured to the man, her hands moving. Orcas shook his head firmly and Pericles frowned at him. He had worked for a month to get permission to take Aspasia out. The idea of being followed around by some muscular clod was not at all what he'd had in mind.

'You can speak to him?' Pericles said.

Aspasia shrugged.

'When he chooses to understand. He knows a few

gestures, but he is loyal to the mothers. I think we are stuck with him.'

Pericles dropped his hand to the sword he wore on his hip. In a normal year, it would have been a surprising choice for a city street in daylight, but with the constant threat of Spartan retaliation on the horizon, half the people in Athens wore blades.

The hetaira guard looked at him in amusement. Orcas moved one leg slightly back and rested his own right hand on a sword hilt. The man's intent was clear and Pericles felt blood rushing in the presence of a threat.

'Please don't hurt him, Pericles,' Aspasia said. She laid a hand on his bare arm, warmer than his flesh. 'Orcas is a simple man and he has his orders.'

Pericles nodded, delighted at her assumption. He hadn't liked the look of the guard, nor his confidence at the prospect of swordplay. Still, he scowled at Orcas as he led Aspasia out to the street.

'At least he won't spoil the day with talking,' he said. 'Come on, I want to show you the Acropolis – and the theatre. You've truly never been?'

'I . . .' She hesitated and he slowed down, confused.

'What?'

When she didn't respond, he reached out and took her by the arm, feeling the shape through the draped cloth. He was aware of Orcas stepping closer in response, but made a point of ignoring him.

'Please, Aspasia,' he said. 'If you don't tell me, I can't pluck it from the air.'

'Very well!' she said. 'The mothers told me I should let you show me the city, as if I had never left the house. They said men like to share what they know with women, that it makes them happy to do so. But I don't want to lie to you. So, yes, I have been to the theatre! I saw all the festival plays last year. There, I have said it! I love all the stories, the masks, the music, everything. So if you bring me to meet Aeschylus today, I do not want to lie and say I have never seen his work. Do you see? It was impossible. Why are you smiling? What? Do you not want to tell me about the city, to show me wondrous things as if I spent my entire life in the garden?'

'I want to know you,' he said. 'Not some idea of you. I'm still learning about hetairai, Aspasia, but I don't want to be fooled.' He became serious for a moment as he considered his own words. 'That is true. I cannot fall in love with a picture someone else has painted. You are either completely real, or of no interest to me. Do you understand?'

She smiled – and it was a grin as wide as his own, rather than the delicate smirk of an Athenian lady. It turned into delighted laughter and she clenched her fists with the pleasure of it.

'I am Aspasia, Pericles. I will be eighteen in a few days and I would love to meet your friend Aeschylus.'

She put out her hand and in the madness of the moment, Pericles drew her in for a kiss. Callused fingers wedged between them as Orcas stretched out his arm. Pericles stood back, flushing deeply.

'This one though . . .' Pericles said, 'he has to go.'

Aspasia nodded, widening her eyes at him.

The theatre of Dionysus lay alongside the Acropolis, at the heart of the city. As a sponsor of past festivals, Pericles was greeted with pleasure wherever he went, leading

Aspasia and her silent companion into areas the crowd never saw.

He found Aeschylus discussing lines with half a dozen young actors. The playwright broke off the rehearsal the moment he spotted Pericles looking in. He crossed the room like a warship, bowing deeply to Aspasia and taking her hand. When the bodyguard grunted, Aeschylus turned and crowded him.

'Why do you frown at me?' he demanded. The playwright was as quick to temper as ever and Pericles had to intervene.

'Orcas is a guard for Aspasia, my friend,' he said. 'He is deaf as well, so ask him no questions.'

'I see. Well, he should not come into my theatre and stare like some angry boy,' Aeschylus said. He had been a soldier before he'd become the first playwright in Athens. He carried violence with him, Pericles thought, always close to the surface.

Aeschylus stood back and really looked at Aspasia. She coloured slightly under the scrutiny.

'You don't need guards, my dear. Not with Pericles giving you those big cow eyes. The way he talks, I think he'd fight half the city for you.'

'Aeschylus, please!' Pericles said. 'I'm sure anything I said was in confidence.'

'Really? You were not very clear, with all that mooning around and asking me for lines of verse. I put a lovesick youth in a scene afterwards, so I owe you thanks for that.'

Pericles said nothing, though his mouth hung slightly open. Aspasia looked at his expression and laughed.

'He is delighted, kurios, I can tell. I hope to see it in the spring.'

Aeschylus focused on her, his brows drawing together. 'Truly?'

'I love it all, kurios. I was telling Pericles before. I saw your *Seven Against Thebes*.' She sighed in happy memory. 'It was wonderful. I wept when the sons killed each other at the end. When I think of it . . . !'

Tears came to her eyes and Aeschylus lost all his gruffness and bull-like manner in the presence of one who loved his work. He beamed at her.

'You must call me Aeschylus, dear girl, no more of this formal "kurios". I see both beauty and wit in you. Why on earth are you wasting your time with Pericles?'

Aspasia laughed, but she took a moment to answer.

'He asked me to be honest with him,' she said, seeing how Pericles stared.

Aeschylus nodded as if it was all perfectly clear.

'That was just an hour ago,' Pericles said.

'Well, that was when I knew,' she replied.

Aeschylus watched how they gazed at one another and he did not look away, because he used almost everything he saw or heard. He smiled though, at what he witnessed growing between them.

'Come,' Aeschylus said, suddenly back to his booming normal. 'Have lunch with the company. I'll have them speak the new lines for you.'

'Can you find someone to distract our companion?' Pericles murmured.

Aeschylus looked up as a couple of brawny young lads went past.

'Gentlemen! Would you gather a few mates and escort our friend here onto the street?'

He indicated Orcas. The hetaira guard had no idea

what was happening until four of them took him by the arms.

'Be gentle with him, please,' Aspasia said. 'He is a good man.'

Aeschylus passed on the order with a nod and they moved Orcas away. He opened his mouth to protest, but only a strange yowl came out, dwindling as they walked him off.

Pericles turned to Aspasia as Aeschylus stomped towards the smells of broth and bread. They were alone for a moment, and before he could speak, she stepped in close and kissed him. It seemed to take a long time and she was slightly breathless as she stood apart. His hand reached for her, clutching air. She took hold of his inner forearm awkwardly, almost like two soldiers.

'I . . . er, I thought we should get that out of the way, now Orcas has gone. But . . .'

'Yes,' he said. They kissed again and it went on and on, his hand drawing her in by the waist.

As the sun rose, two messengers ran towards the city. On damp ground, the men made no dust trail, but they were sighted far from the walls. Coming from the north was news in itself, so that all Athens woke to shouts in the street. Tens of thousands of workers gulped down a little milk and a few sweet figs, or a barley cake with honey and cheese. They asked what was happening as they reached their spots on the building sites, laying out the tools they took home with them each evening. There had been thefts in the beginning, with a whole new industry based on reselling them. Ephialtes had forced that part of the market to close with threats and a judicious application of violence.

With the sun still a wire of red gold, gossip spread like fire in dry leaves. Pericles came awake when a house slave knocked on his bedroom door. He opened his eyes and turned to the one who lay next to him. Aspasia had unbound her hair at some point in the night. It seemed to have grown in the process, dark and unbelievably wild. His gaze drank in the slight curve of her breast as she lay on her stomach, snoring lightly. It took a moment for him to realise the sounds of the city were wrong. His senses sharpened from a lover's drowse. He had not been too long in that part of Athens, a smaller place than his father's town-house, where his first wife now lived. Yet he could hear shouts interrupting an odd silence.

Aspasia woke as he leaped up, heading for the door.

'What is it?' she called after him. 'Is something wrong?'

Pericles had similar questions for the house slave.

'It's the Spartans, master. They have been sighted.'

Pericles swore under his breath. He looked back at Aspasia and part of him yearned to return to the warmth and welcome there.

'I have to go,' he said.

The slave handed him a fresh chiton tunic, with another bringing sandals and armour. The last was clattering up the stairs under the weight of his shield and sword belt. The spear would remain by the front door, too awkward to use indoors.

Pericles held up his arms as they buckled him for war.

'The Assembly made me strategos, Aspasia. I must go out to them.'

She had not seen him in his hoplite gear before. She watched the transformation with wide eyes.

'Will there be fighting?' she said, sitting up.

He could not help but stare. The slaves kept themselves very busy for a time, brushing and securing every tie.

'Perhaps,' he replied. He felt rather fine in chestplate, kilt and greaves. After all he'd said the day before, he actually did want her to be impressed. He knew by then that she would roll her eyes at any boasting, so he took a more modest path.

'I'm sure there is no danger. I'll come back and join you here for lunch.'

Aspasia began to reach around for clothes she had discarded.

'No, I'll go back to the house. The mothers will want to know.'

Pericles stopped, suddenly unsure of himself.

'You won't . . . stay?' he said.

Aspasia pulled on her dress and stood to tie the belt. Her feet were bare, he noticed. She came around the bed and touched him on his arm, looking into his face.

'The mothers will already be furious with me, for escaping Orcas, for spending the night with you. I owe them an explanation. But . . . what do you want? From this? Do you know?'

The thought of her not being there was strong in him as he replied.

'I want you with me,' he said, his voice little more than a breath. 'I've made mistakes in my life. Too many of them. I want to have a second chance – and I don't want you to leave.'

Aspasia leaned in and kissed him on the crook of his neck.

'Well, that works,' she said. 'Though I will have to return to the house at some point. I have clothes there and

156

scents – and a few friends. I owe them, Pericles. They are my family.'

Pericles left the house with the perfume Aspasia wore still on his skin. He could smell it as he hurried through the streets to the north gate. There was a drift in the crowd that seemed to be heading in that direction, but it was still with relief that he saw men he knew in hoplite armour, trotting along in files. One or two nodded to him and he fell in with those, matching their pace. The faces on the street were all serious and he wondered what he would find at the city wall.

At the Dipylon gate, the crowd was being ordered back by red-faced officers, forced to leave a clear space. Pericles was recognised and let through to an open space where Ephialtes stood with the epistates of the day and most of the other strategoi present in the city. Pericles looked for the man's servant, Attikos, but there was no sign. That was unnerving for one who knew him. Attikos usually clung to his mentor like a limpet.

Two archons from the noble council had made it through the shield line to join that group. Even at first glance, it was clear to Pericles that Ephialtes excluded them subtly, his back half-turned so that they stood outside his circle.

'There you are!' Ephialtes said when he approached.

Pericles saw the big man was sweating as he nodded to one of the senior hoplites present.

'Tell it again, for the latecomers,' Ephialtes ordered, clearly in command.

'We have six hundred Spartans standing outside the city wall,' the man said. 'There's no sign of any greater force, though I've scouts out looking. They've made no approach and no attempt to enter the city, not yet.'

A little of the tension seeped out of the group. An approach by the entire Spartan army would have meant a call to arms and immediate action. A smaller group suggested they had come to talk or negotiate. Either way, the sense of imminent violence faded.

'I'll go out and see what they want,' Ephialtes said. 'I think we all know what it will be.'

'How many men do you need, strategos?' the officer asked.

Ephialtes glanced at Pericles, inviting his opinion. They had learned to trust one another.

'All of them?' Ephialtes said. 'We could send them a message – and a reminder of our strength.'

'I think that might be a mistake,' Pericles murmured. 'Our aim is to win time, remember? Once the new walls are finished, they will have lost this power over us. So we should keep that in mind. Send just a few, half a dozen, as if we aren't aware they could be a threat. They're meant to be allies still, I think. Offer to show them the walls and explain their purpose. Waste days on a tour of the work! After that, agree to anything they ask so they go home – while we complete the walls.'

'Very well. Will you stand with me?' Ephialtes said. He seemed pleased at the thought of having Pericles alongside. 'Mind you, if they decide to make an example and kill us, who will keep Athens safe then?'

'I imagine the council will invite Cimon back,' Pericles said.

The idea did not seem to please Ephialtes particularly, though he nodded. Pericles did not seem worried at the thought of walking out to face a Spartan force, so Ephialtes would not either. His sweat continued to shine, however.

Ephialtes explained the situation to the others around them and secured offers from two of the strategoi and two more of the archon council. Six of them would go out.

Pericles swallowed his nerves as orders were roared and the gate opened, a crack of light that became a bar. He heard Ephialtes sniffing.

'Are you wearing *scent*?' he asked.

Pericles smiled ruefully and rubbed his neck.

'She was,' he said.

Ephialtes chuckled.

'Where's your man Attikos this morning?' Pericles said.

'Ah. I let him go,' Ephialtes said. 'I asked him some questions about his previous association with you – and Archon Cimon.' For once, there was no sneering tone in that title. 'I didn't like some of his answers.'

Pericles nodded.

'I think that was wise,' he muttered. It had been neither an apology nor an admission, but he was still pleased. It was certainly one more sign that Ephialtes had become closer. Whether it was the great walls, the absence of Cimon, or simply that the strategos had grown into his role and his authority, Pericles did not know. He was glad of it though. Without allies, he could do nothing.

The gate opened wide enough for them to walk out. In the distance, they could all see a line of red-cloaks standing, waiting for them. There was a breeze that morning and they seemed to ripple.

'I hope this is not our last foolish act,' Ephialtes said. '*Praotes*, gentlemen. No matter the provocation. Calm.'

They went out, to face whatever Fate and the Spartans had in store for them.

12

'There is no going back from this,' Regent Nicomedes said. He watched as a dozen Athenian ships burned in the port of Argos. The flames reflected gold in the hills around the docks, reaching into the city. Six warships and as many heavy merchantmen – together, they were a new sun, lighting the night around them, even up to the hill crest where he stood. He saw it in the faces of the men standing with him, all gold and shadow where darkness had hidden them before.

Those on board had not expected an attack, believing themselves too strong. Their arrogance grew with their walls, perhaps. Certainly, neither warships nor merchants had been properly guarded. If the crews had been Spartan, Nicomedes knew he would have had the officers killed for that lapse, with the men whipped and sent home. He could hear shouts of alarm by then, with bucket chains forming along the docks. It was too late, he thought. He felt a twinge at the damage to the docks themselves, but there was nothing he could do about that. His biggest regret was that half the Athenian crews were still in the city, whoring and drinking while their ships were destroyed.

On the hill bluff over that part of the Peloponnese, the regent stood with just a few senior men, enjoying the satisfaction of hard work well done. The soothsayer was absent for once, which was a mercy. Nicomedes did not like the man, nor his certainties. Tisamenus had said he wanted nothing to do with any small action, in case his precious fifth victory was taken from him.

Nicomedes winced at the thought. The man may have been called a Spartan, but he was not one. Tisamenus still believed he could somehow use the prophecy he had been given at Delphi. It had defined his entire adult life, after all. Nicomedes wondered if he should send the poor fool away before he did any more harm. The gods were not there to be used, not by men. No, they were capricious and frightening. Apollo was as cunning and dangerous as any of them, with his oracle, his priestesses and all his veiled promises. Nicomedes knew Apollo punished arrogance of the sort he saw in Tisamenus. Indeed, the god seemed to exult in it. Until the prophecy was resolved one way or another, he thought he would be wise to keep the fool at arm's length.

The light of burning ships along the shore was glorious, but it was not a battle victory, not yet. Nicomedes had brought only sixty men to that place, covering a vast distance in a single run. In the darkness, they'd gone through the docks like shadows, killing anyone who saw them. That too was a regret. Some of the guards and sailors had been men of Argos, without a doubt. Nor was it how he preferred to fight. With the advantages of night and surprise, it had been like setting leopards amongst boys.

Skins of oil and shuttered lamps had been all it took to start each blaze. Sailors feared fire with reason, above even storms and Persians. The sun made timbers dry enough to split and crack, sucking away oil into its depths. When they were set aflame, they burned like a torch, unstoppable in moments.

Nicomedes smiled as he saw figures leaping into the sea

to save themselves. Some would make it to shore. Many more would drown or burn. More importantly, the Athenians had lost valuable warships and some part of their crews. They'd feel the sting of that – and they would know they had brought it on their own heads with their damned walls. He narrowed his eyes against the glare as it built even higher, painfully bright in the darkness. The arrogance of Athenians! To raise walls like that was an insult to the natural order, an abomination in the eyes of gods and men. First, they had surrounded their precious city with them, higher than before. Sparta had objected, but of course, the leaders of the day had pressed ahead. That had been bad enough, the action of a future enemy rather than a true ally. The walls down to the sea were a different degree again. Every stone of those was rebellion, was scorn.

Nicomedes thought he could hear screaming below, echoing from the cliffs he stood on. He nodded sharply, satisfied. There was a cost to every decision – there had to be. They had refused to take down their walls. This was the war drum sounding in response. The Athenians would have to guard every ship on every shore after this. In a hundred ports, they would fear the same. That would cost them silver, as well as pride. It would cost them in reputation.

It was much more than just a dozen ships and a few dock bays. It was a weakening blow to their League, he thought. He shook his head. They should have taken down their walls.

'They do burn well,' his second in command said.

Nicomedes was still unused to the authority of being king's regent and he smiled, understanding the man wished to please him.

162

'They do,' he said. 'I tell you, wherever Athenians dare to dock, they will know fear from now on. Their allies, their merchants, their hoplites, their ships. And we'll hit them all anyway. We may not have the men to bring them to battle this year, but we can disrupt their trade, burn their farms, sink their ships, kill their men. They have welcomed in the whole world, so our people will riot in their streets and rob their strength. We'll make all Attica a field of destruction, until they pull down those cursed walls and beg our forgiveness.'

PART TWO

'The spring has been taken from Athens' year.'

– Pericles

13

The sun was weak, the day cold, with a breeze blowing. Nicomedes walked with his nephew through the great square in Sparta. The buildings around it were still being rebuilt, but the worst of the rubble and ash had been cleared away. When Nicomedes looked for signs of conflict, he saw marks remained, scorched into stone.

It had been at the funeral of the battle king when Nicomedes had first been sure his people would survive. In dignity and honour, the body of Pleistarchus had been consumed in fire while all Sparta mourned. Pleistarchus had pushed himself without sleep or rest to put the helot rebellion down. That labour had cost him his life, his people their king. Yet they honoured him, in prayer and ritual. Despite the losses they had endured, they were still Spartans.

Nicomedes stopped at the cenotaph for Leonidas, resting his hand on a bronze frieze that had survived all the fire and destruction intact. The likeness of the battle king had been cast there, his right hand on a sword. Those who passed often reached out and touched that spot, so that it had been polished gold.

'For luck,' Nicomedes said.

Pleistonax looked up in silent scrutiny. The boy weighed everything with the same expression. Nicomedes found it infuriating, as if his authority had always to be examined for cracks. At times, he wished Pleistonax would just do as he was told, but he was not certain of his own judgement. Perhaps Pleistonax was right to judge his uncle's words. The world was upside down after all. All that had seemed so solid had been made blood and ash.

He watched as Pleistonax moved on. The grave of King Pleistarchus was just a name carved into the stone of the forum, his ashes in the earth beneath. It was a simple thing compared to the cenotaph, but Nicomedes felt his throat choke as the boy knelt and traced the letters.

'He was a good king,' Nicomedes said, 'though the gods gave him little. Too young to lead at Plataea, he had to watch your father Pausanias win glory. I suspect King Pleistarchus will be remembered more for the earthquake and a helot rebellion, but I knew him. He was a brave man. Sparta was better for his service.'

The boy nodded. Pleistonax had grown since the king's death had been announced. Not just in height, but in toughness. Nicomedes knew the boy had endured everything the agoge trainers had put him through without complaint. Yet his eyes showed a new wariness.

As Pleistonax stood, Nicomedes wondered if he should pat him on the shoulder or ruffle his hair. The regent was not a demonstrative man, but he could sense the lad's pain. He almost reached out and then stopped himself. No. Pleistonax would be the battle king of Sparta in a few years. If they allowed kindness, or softness, they might make a man who would break. True kindness lay in forge work – in the creation of iron.

'Why am I here?' Pleistonax said suddenly. To Nicomedes' surprise, he seemed angry. 'The others are gathering. They'll think I am being given special treatment.'

'You are graduating from the boys' agoge today, Pleis-tonax. You'll join the older section now, until you are eighteen. I might not see you for months and I . . . told your mother I would speak to you.'

The boy looked at him.

'Well, you've done that,' he said.

Pleistonax clearly wanted to turn away, to go back to the group of agoge boys milling by the western entrance to the square. Yet he hesitated. Pleistonax was fifteen years old. He could not just turn his back on his uncle.

'Is my mother well?'

Nicomedes nodded.

'She is proud of you. As am I.'

'You?' Pleistonax said. 'I don't know you. You're only regent until I am of age.'

'That is my honour,' Nicomedes said, stung by the boy's tone. Would it be so terrible to cuff the ear of a future battle king?

'Yes, it must be. I will be watching, uncle. You are regent for me. I expect to be kept informed of every decision.'

'That is not . . . no . . .' Nicomedes said, hesitating. The conversation was not going the way he had expected.

Pleistonax shrugged.

'It's your choice, uncle. But if you keep me out, you'd better kill me. Or when I am king, I will come to you and make you regret it. Do you understand? Who are you?'

'I-I am the regent . . .'

'And who am I?'

Nicomedes considered and rejected a number of angry responses. The truth was, the boy would be king, perhaps for many years. It made no sense for Nicomedes to set himself against his nephew. All that mattered was whether the boy was good for Sparta! It seemed the gods and ephors had chosen wisely. Pleistonax had a strength of will that made his uncle wilt like wax in the sun.

'You will be king, Pleistonax. Very well.'

The boy regarded him for a moment longer, making sure the message was understood.

'Good. Now, what are you doing about the Athenians?'

Nicomedes blinked, but the decision was made.

'We ordered them to take down their walls. They didn't do it.'

'And then, uncle?' Pleistonax said.

The contempt was there again, in the curl of his lip. Nicomedes repressed a sigh.

'We don't have the numbers to take the field against Athens, Pleistonax. Not this year, nor the next! The older class of the agoge is not a tenth of what we need to get the army back to strength! So I have set men to destruction – in dozens, in thirties, in sixties, burning and breaking. It's what they care most about, the Athenians. I have hit them in their profits, assaulted their allies and supported their enemies. I have made our own allies affirm their loyalty – and I send ships where I can. Though the Athenians patrol in numbers now, looking for our sails. They still control the seas. Yet wherever men say they wish to resist Athenian tyranny, there are Spartans to advise and train them. It is a dirty war, Pleistonax, but do not think I have been idle. I'd give my right arm for the army your father had at Plataea. If I had numbers like that, I would stand in the Agora of Athens today.'

To his utter surprise, Nicomedes felt relief. He had not been able to speak to anyone in such a way. His nephew may have been a boy, but he would be king. It was like removing a burden he had hardly known was there.

'The other cities should fear what we will do,' Pleistonax muttered. 'It is the heart of respect and strength.'

'They should! But they see the walls going up, from Athens to the sea. We've disrupted the work where we could. I've had those loyal to us rioting in their streets, murdering their master masons, whatever they could do. Yet they continue. Word of those walls is in every market, from here to Thrace. And there is some new rebellion against our Dorian people in the north. They sent word for our aid, but we need every man here. If I march three or four thousand out of the Peloponnese, Sparta will be defenceless, never mind attacking Athens.'

To his surprise, the boy put out a hand to rest on his arm. The act was so ludicrous, it succeeded in startling Nicomedes back to steadiness.

'Sparta rules the Hellenes,' Pleistonax said. 'If they cannot call on us, we have no authority. That was your priority, uncle. Not Athens! If you cannot send three or four thousand, send one – with a call for allies. The Dorians are the ancestors of our race. They have the right to call on us. Let other cities see Sparta at war once again. Perhaps it will stiffen their backs.'

Nicomedes breathed slowly, in relief. He nodded and, on an impulse, went down on one knee. When he raised his head, Pleistonax had turned and walked back to his age group, all graduating from the agoge that day. Nicomedes watched as the trainers lined up, joined by their fathers and brothers, as well as women and strangers who cared about raising the new generation. Nicomedes too would take a place. He untied a stick from his belt, swishing the air with it.

The final trial had actually begun that morning, with a punishing run through the hills, whipped on by the trainers as they went. The last part wound through the city streets and out to the temple of youth, rebuilt from rubble. Every step then would be marked by a stripe from some cane or river reed. Yet the running boys would remain silent, offering no defence. By the time they reached the temple to Artemis Orthia, they would be running with blood and stumbling in exhaustion. Perhaps a few would even cry out. That would be the end. Those who did were sent away on the instant, never to live as a Spartiate. The standard was brutally high, Nicomedes thought. It meant they were always small in number, but a breed apart. He suspected his brother's son would survive the trial.

The regent walked over to a place in the lines, seeing them form as a great snake across the square. The ordeal would show the boys who they truly were. It would renew them in blood and pain and brotherhood. Nicomedes remembered his own triumph with enormous fondness. Unconsciously, his hands traced thin scars on his arms and chest, faded like memory. He smiled then. Youth was a wonderful thing.

Pericles could not understand why Sparta hadn't marched. It was the thing they understood most – the threat of force to achieve what they wanted. All their allies and enemies understood that. Yet they had not come.

After the first angry meeting before the walls of Athens, they had sent a second delegation a few months later, to demand to know why promises had not been kept and why the work appeared to have continued without break or pause. The arrogance of it! The Spartans honestly expected them to tear down the walls on their command. When they had refused, a campaign had begun against their allies and their holdings, wherever they claimed land and influence. It was driven by spite and rage – and it had hurt them.

Spring was the season for war. All winter, Pericles had known the Spartans could appear as soon as the weather turned. They were not fools! They clearly understood what the walls meant – freedom from their control, their tyranny.

The air was warm outside. By all the gods, they should have launched an attack by then! It made no sense. Spartan authority slipped away with every stone that went up, with every archer tower finished. There was a point in the construction where a single man would have had trouble getting over. In places now, the walls were twice that height. Pericles thought in a month or two they would have every last weak place shored up and the Long Walls would be complete. He could feel it all coming to the boil – in the riots and attacks on their workers, in the growing sense of violence in the air. Their enemies were desperate, but the walls still rose. By the end of summer at the latest, it would be done and Sparta could complain then and demand all they wanted.

'It doesn't make any sense,' he said to Aspasia.

She had brought plants to their little house and she was watering them, filling the room with the smell of blossom. He saw her fingers were stained gold with pollen, so fine it remained like a tattoo on her skin. The colour suited her, he thought.

'Zeno says they must be weaker than we know,' she replied idly. The little philosopher was clearly infatuated with her, to the roughly equal embarrassment of Zeno's wife and Aspasia herself.

'Perhaps,' Pericles said. 'Though underestimating the Spartan battle king comes with a cost. We've angered them, Aspasia, insulted them even. There were terrible riots last week in the Agora here – and the call was to pull down the walls. They have supporters in the city. I don't know how many will rise up when they come against us. Too many.'

She turned to him, listening. She knew he liked talking things out with her – and that he listened when she gave some insight into his friends or the matters that concerned them. She had been right too many times for him not to, though it still seemed as if he had to be guided rather than told. He closed down when she let her voice rise. Honestly, it was very annoying.

'How long before the walls are finished?' she asked.

He grimaced as he considered the problem for the thousandth time.

'It has taken longer than I thought it would. Two months – three if the last quarry fails and we have to open the new site. And the costs! If we'd built them like city walls over years it would have been hard, but this? All Athens busy here instead of their normal work? They say you can't get cloth now, or leather for shoes. I see wealthy men with holes in their cloaks, for want of anyone to spin and weave. We can't endure this madness much longer.'

'You'll get it done,' she said, with such simple confidence in him, he had to grin. He put his worries aside and looked again at her.

'Are you over at the house this evening?' he said.

She nodded prettily, making her hair shake. He had

bought out the hetaira mothers and let Aspasia run the establishment the way she wanted. Young women were still trained and educated as she had been, taught music and dance, but it was now her decision alone when it came to finding husbands for them – or anything else that went on. She chose only the best girls to train and her symposia had become fashionable in the circles of Athens, with invitations as valued as a good seat at the theatre. Pericles felt sometimes as if he'd managed to tame a beautifully coloured bird. He suspected he did not deserve her, or the benefits of some parts of her training, which she would undertake with agreeable goodwill. She liked to please him and to refer to him as 'her man'. It suited him well and he was so indecently happy, it worried him.

He stepped out into a street of workers all heading out to their section of the wall. It was true the city was suffering. If it wasn't for the fleet, they'd have run out of food, though farmers were exempt from the work. All the shops he passed were closed, without even street vendors to hawk fried meat. He joined a crowd going in the right direction and walked with them for a time, feeling how weary they were. Some of them talked to their mates, but the rest were silent and grim with worry. He understood that well enough.

He heard his name murmured by those who recognised him. When he looked up it was to see smiles in his direction. They didn't blame him yet for the great task he'd begun. He nodded to them and, to his surprise, one reached out and patted him on the shoulder.

'It will be all right, kurios,' the stranger said.

Pericles felt tears prickle without warning. He nodded in thanks. It was a moment of kindness from an anonymous older man, responding to worries he'd worn more openly than he had known. His people. His city.

Most of the crowd filed away as they reached their sections of the wall, heading off along side streets to begin the day's labour. He was proud of them, of all they had done, though the sense of a storm coming was not something he could shake. There was no greater military force in the world than Sparta – and Athens was attempting to tear herself free. It was as if a wolf had them in its jaws. If they managed it, they would have won a great victory, but the cost could still be terrible.

Pericles reached the Agora and loped up the steps to enter council rooms within. The sun was up and he saw Ephialtes was there, waiting for him. Pericles made himself smile and saw it reflected. It was hard to forgive his hatred of Cimon, but no man scorns an ally when the storm comes. Pericles clapped his fellow strategos on the shoulder, unconsciously copying the touch of the stranger in the crowd.

'It will be all right,' he said.

Ephialtes stood very still and then nodded. The words seemed to have an effect on other men, Pericles realised. Perhaps they all needed to be reassured.

'You heard then?' Ephialtes said as they went in.

Pericles saw the assembled strategoi of Athens were in the room, along the side of the main chamber. He frowned as he saw Aeschylus, Zeno, Anaxagoras and all eight of the council of archons present with them. Together, they were his faction in the council. He swallowed a lump in his throat.

'Heard what?' he said, though he guessed.

'The Spartans,' Ephialtes said. 'They've been sighted. They're out.'

Pericles held up his hand to quiet the rest. They had spent part of the morning discussing what to do, but it was all wind and bluster, as far as he could tell. There was only one choice – as clear as mountain waters to him. He merely had to persuade them.

'We've had Spartan soldiers attacking our allies, firing ships, killing and disrupting – anything but face us in the open. Their actions reek of weakness, though they do not seem to see it. Burning ships alone was an act of war, but we agreed in this room to endure – while the walls rose. This council and the great Assembly voted to hold on, not to rise to their provocation. That was right, I'm certain. It won us vital time.'

He looked around the room at men he had grown to trust. Only Cimon was missing and he felt that loss like a broken tooth. With war coming, Pericles needed him as strategos. He glanced at Ephialtes, seeing how the man met his gaze. Perhaps enemies did make themselves, but no man was a block, unchanging. Pericles had learned that much. Reality and truth were found with the gods and in a woman's arms. The rest could be changed – for better or worse.

'Gentlemen, we are already at war,' Pericles said. 'Sparta has made that clear. I cannot say why they have not attacked in strength, but this could be a chance to weaken them. I've counselled caution before, but we're so close now. It could win us the last months we need to finish. It could set them back for a generation, while our League only grows stronger. That is the dream we all feel – Athens as the heart of a nation. Or an empire of Hellenes and all the peoples of the Aegean. Why not?'

'You want to bring Sparta to battle?' one of the other strategoi said.

The man looked ill at the prospect. For some, there would never be a right time to go out, Pericles realised. They had vowed to endure attacks on their possessions and allies while the walls were built, but in part it was because they *never* wanted to face a Spartan line in the field. Pericles lowered his tone, choosing his words carefully.

'Our scouts say there are no more than a thousand of them, fifteen hundred at most.'

'They'll pick up more from allies,' Aeschylus muttered.

Pericles inclined his head.

'As will we. If they were strong, they'd be coming here, not heading north. No, this could be a chance to tear the heart out of Sparta, once and for all. If the council appoint a polemarch and strategoi, I will ask for every man with spear and shield to assemble. We can put, what, ten thousand in the field?'

'With Megara, more like twelve,' another of the strategoi replied.

Pericles nodded. He could feel a cold hand clutch in his gut at the words he was about to say.

'Then with that twelve thousand, we should move to destroy the Spartan force. If they have marched in support of allies, we will reveal their weakness to every wolf of the Peloponnese. We'll have kicked their nest, but by the time they move against us, our walls will be finished. From that day, Athens will rise and rise.'

'Unless it is a trap,' Aeschylus said. He shrugged when

all eyes turned to him in irritation, the spell broken. 'Well? They know us. If they are not as weak as we believe, this could be a feint to draw us north – while the rest of their army attacks Athens and destroys our precious walls. You know we can't do it again. The silver and labour cost has brought us to the point of disaster as it is. There are riots every day as families go hungry or women cry out for their men, killed in the work. And the chant is always to "pull down the walls!"'

'There are Spartan sympathisers in the city,' Ephialtes added. 'I have a dozen men in cells, waiting to be brought to trial. They were all caught trying to set wood stores on fire or breaking scaffolds. They'll be executed, of course, but more escaped. I agree with Pericles. We won't have another chance.'

'We'll keep a few of our people on the Peloponnese and watching the isthmus,' Pericles said. 'If it's a feint or a trap, we can turn back. With fast horses, we can get a warning back in time. But can we miss a chance to weaken Sparta? To show their allies they are no longer the beating heart of Greece? It's worth the risk.'

Pericles looked around. There were no more objections. He dipped his head. The council were still gathering in the main chamber. They expected news, and instead he would bring them a call to war. He rose to his feet and Ephialtes spoke suddenly, as if the words had been crammed in and released all at once.

'I would like to lead the army out, as polemarch . . .' he said.

Pericles froze. Though he had come to a truce with the strategos, he had not forgotten how inept Ephialtes was when it came to leading men in war.

Ephialtes sensed the hesitation and coloured.

'I *am* a strategos of Athens, gentlemen. Without direct responsibility for the walls, as Pericles has. Who else would you make polemarch for this force against Sparta?'

The answer was Cimon – and Pericles almost snapped the name in his irritation. Yet he had to persuade the other man without hurting his pride. He smiled.

'Strategos Ephialtes, you are first among us – especially when it comes to the Assembly and the crowds of Athens. They trust you. *I* trust you to command calm and order in the streets. Believe me, that will be a most dangerous time with the army away in the field. Those factions you describe will see it as a perfect opportunity. You have ears in this city, for all the whispers and secrets, so you can block their schemes better than anyone else. I don't want to come back to a city on fire, not again. Please, strategos. Keep the city safe while the walls are completed.'

Ephialtes was flattered. Yet he was not a fool and he had not missed the implication of Pericles' words.

'You are not thinking of leading them yourself though, Pericles? It should be someone senior.'

At least he was no longer putting himself forward, Pericles realised. Disappointment surged in him. He *had* hoped to lead Athenians against Spartans. His father certainly would have done. Yet Xanthippus had been part of a generation that seemed born to authority. For those who came after, it was harder.

Pericles looked around the room. His gaze settled on a senior strategos, Myronides. The man had led a dozen small actions over the previous ten or twenty years. He had also been a strategos at Plataea under Aristides, which counted well for him. Myronides had a reputation for competence, though in every other way, he was utterly unremarkable. Pericles could not bring himself to say the man's name and quash his own chance to lead.

Ephialtes saw his gaze and spoke the words anyway.

'What about Myronides? Would you be willing?'

The older man nodded, considering.

'It would be my honour,' he said. In that, Myronides was the model of a modest man. The honour had come to him without having campaigned for it. Pericles could have strangled him.

Outside, the council was getting noisy as they filled the benches. Words would not come, so Pericles bowed his head to Myronides and went out to them.

Tisamenus was not a great rider, though he could sit on a saddle well enough – better than most Spartans, in fact. He went slowly, however, rather than risk his neck or bruise himself too badly. Nicomedes had left him behind at his own request. The regent seemed oddly relieved when Tisamenus reminded him of the prophecy. He simply dared not risk his last victory on some minor dispute.

The words of the oracle had given Tisamenus value in Sparta, at least when Pausanias had been regent. It had won him his citizenship, unique in that entire region. He'd thought his value was clear to all. Yet the oldest ephor always scowled when he saw Tisamenus, as if he was some eavesdropper or a stranger there.

Perhaps it was that Pausanias had fallen from grace. When the wheel of Fate made his only son king, Tisamenus had thought he would rise again with Pleistonax, to sit at the boy's right hand. Yet his presence seemed to irritate the young king as much as the ephors. They would not cast him out, not until they had used him up. For Plataea alone, they should have given him women and wine! Instead, they made no secret of their dislike.

Tisamenus shook his head as he rode, mumbling curses no one could hear. He knew he would never understand the Spartans, not when it mattered. They had used his prophecy well enough, hadn't they? The victories he'd been promised? Where would they even be without him? They hadn't scorned his help at Plataea or Cypros! Of course, that had been with Pausanias. The bastard ephors had walled him up on nothing more than accusations.

Tisamenus squinted into the distance. The land was very dry there, but it had rained the night before. He had refilled his waterskin from a little stream dribbling over green moss, clean and cold. As he came through the pass, a plain expanded before him, huge and open, with air so clear he felt he could reach out and touch the distant mountains.

He saw a smudge of red cloaks – the column with Nicomedes. Even they were made small by the land, he realised. The ephors thought sending Tisamenus out to take a report was some fool's errand. He had no doubt about that. Yet he was happier having ridden for days alone. Their frowns and insults had worn at his spirit and he felt refreshed away from them. They had not intended that, he was sure!

The soothsayer rode on for another hour, digging in his heels and kicking the horse when it stumbled. Little by little, he gained on them. It looked like chaos ahead, but of course the Spartans were only one part of that force. They had marched to relieve some attack on the Dorian people, honouring ancient oaths and the call of blood. Those who wished to be called allies had come out of their towns to join them. Tisamenus shook his head in grudging appreciation at the thought. The red cloaks still commanded respect.

He narrowed his eyes as something changed ahead. The rear of the column was spreading apart, coming closer? Were they . . . ? For a time, he watched in confusion, his horse trotting along. The ephors had told him Regent Nicomedes would be marching east and north. Yet the scene before him did not look like a peaceful march, even with . . .

Tisamenus reined in hard, turning the horse's head with main strength so that the animal reared and almost fell. He spun the animal in place, turning right and left to stare. There was a battle going on, at that moment! Whether Nicomedes had closed with the enemy at a furious pace or simply met them earlier than anyone had planned, the result was still being fought. Even as Tisamenus stared, he realised the figures coming closer were running. Most of them had cast down spears and shields and were just haring across the grassland, anything to get away from the red-cloaked maniacs slaughtering them.

For an instant, Tisamenus felt only interest, then a cold horror stole across him. He had hoarded his fifth victory for years, waiting for war with Athens. They were the ones who had brought down his friend, no matter how Pausanias met his fate. If the gods played fair, they would have let him save his final victory for them!

Of course, the gods did not play fair. As he closed with them, Tisamenus watched Spartans destroy the last of a personal guard. Those men were cut to pieces trying to protect their master – some doomed king who had thought it was the season to steal Dorian land and cattle. Perhaps he had believed the Spartans were too weak to come out. Tisamenus winced as the king's head was hacked off and jammed onto a spear.

The Dorians were already cheering and raising their hands, wiry little men with shields and bloodstained smocks. Had his presence delivered their victory? Or had it been secure before he arrived? Tisamenus rode slowly through them all, sick with private uncertainty. This was how the gods punished pride, he thought.

14

Gathering an army was no small undertaking. Pericles sent word to Megara, then had to wait. He had to give an ally time, though he bit his nails to the quick. Every day he remained in Attica was one in which forces of Sparta roamed free, unchallenged. Unbroken.

The men of Megara arrived a few days later, dusty from their march. The greater surprise was the two thousand hoplites of Argos anchoring at the Piraeus port the next morning. They had travelled further, but with sails and rowers doing the work.

Pericles and Ephialtes went down to the docks to greet them – and assess their loyalty. Argos was an ancient city, older than either Sparta or Athens. Perhaps because of that, they had remained neutral more often than not.

Ephialtes wore the robe of an Athenian strategos rather than hoplite armour and helmet. The senior officer who stepped down the dock bowed deeply to him.

'I am Danaos, leader of Argos,' he said. 'I had word from League captains that you were taking the field against Sparta. I pledge two thousand to your command.'

Ephialtes stared, at both the man's title and his bluntness. He had dealt with Spartans and Corinthians before, but not men of Argos. Perhaps the way of speaking was something all the peoples of the Peloponnese adopted.

'Ephialtes, Strategos of Athens,' he said faintly. 'If you

will take a binding oath of loyalty . . . you will be made welcome.'

'Done,' the man replied. 'Show me your most sacred temple and I will swear.'

Pericles cleared his throat, wanting to slow the man down. The fellow's brusque manner seemed to be rushing them all to war.

'I am Pericles, son to Xanthippus. You are very welcome. However . . .' He chose his words carefully, not wanting to give offence. 'Argos has been neutral in the past, many times,' Pericles said. 'You did not take the field against the Persians. Nor did you join the League of Delos. It falls to me then to ask why you have decided to join us against Sparta – your neighbour and ancient ally.'

There was a glint in the eyes of the newcomer as he looked past them, examining the huge wall that led from that port right into the city. His gaze followed the line of it, right to the Acropolis looming over Athens.

'Sparta defeated us in battle over thirty years ago. It was a period of shame for my city, when we felt helpless. Yet we have not forgotten. Since that day, we have taken up no cause and answered no calls to arms.' His mouth twisted as if he'd bitten something sour. 'It might have continued, but then men of Sparta burned ships in our port. That was an insult too far. This is my response.'

'Then disembark your men, Danaos of Argos,' Ephialtes said expansively. 'We are leaving tomorrow morning.'

The man turned on his heel and went back to the ships docked along the quays. Ephialtes and Pericles watched as boards clattered down and two thousand hoplites came out, forming on the new cobbles.

'Argos,' Ephialtes murmured in thought. 'There was

the ship, of course, with the Argonauts – our own King Theseus among them. Wasn't it . . . also the name of Odysseus' dog?'

Pericles chuckled.

'Yes. The one that waited for him and died as he came home. Argos was loyal.'

They shared a glance at that.

The following morning, fourteen thousand men marched out of Athens with spears and shields. The air was warm and the fields showed green, with crops growing busily in the sun.

Pericles felt a little guilty for the way he had manipulated Ephialtes into staying behind. The man was so delighted at the city being left in his sole care that he didn't count the loss. In the end, it had been a simple request, quickly granted. Ephialtes was first a politician, it seemed, a dealmaker.

As he marched away from Athens, Pericles knew it was also possible he was storing up trouble for the future. Power was a pleasure to wield, it always had been. Like enemies, tyrants were made, not born. It had not escaped his notice that Ephialtes had been left behind without any real opposition. Having all the Athenian strategoi away at war would not prevent new laws being passed. It was a risk, but so was racing north to ambush a Spartan army.

There was no sign of any enemy as the Athenians reached the foothills of a mountain range. Beyond a few huts owned by madmen or outcasts, they were alone. The slopes were thick with laurel, oaks and wild olives, as well as banks of thorns to snag their skin.

Pericles watched scouts vanishing into green shade. He had not yet reached the higher slopes and they loped ahead with horns around their necks, while Myronides and the strategoi trudged after them. At the same time, they left riders stationed behind, watching the west and the isthmus that led to Sparta.

No one trusted the Spartans. It had become rare for a week to pass without news of some disaster: of warehouses burned or innocent merchants slaughtered. The Spartans usually disdained cunning, but Pericles could no longer trust that part of their character. If this chase was some ruse, he and the others were ready to race home to defend Athens.

When he looked right and left, the army seemed more like thousands of golden beetles clambering up the hills. It was rough terrain and he felt vulnerable there, too dependent on the scouts. At least the council had opened the city store of kit and equipment. Zeno and Anaxagoras wore better armour than either had known before. As well as bronze helmets and chestplates over strip-leather kilts, Anaxagoras even had a set of greaves that fitted him. His friends looked like hoplites, but more importantly, they had trained, in fitness and sword drills. They would never be as natural as men like Pericles, but neither would they embarrass themselves. Pericles had tried to persuade them to remain in the city, not least because he needed to have eyes on Ephialtes. They had insisted.

Wild animals crashed away ahead of the lines, as deer or boar or bounding hares became aware of the presence of men. Birds too erupted overhead, calling in alarm. Pericles winced at the thought of a Spartan force being alerted before they were in view. None of the scouts had come back, he reminded himself.

He looked across at Myronides, the one appointed as

polemarch. The man used his spear to steady himself as he climbed. In fact, Myronides seemed utterly relaxed, as if on a hike through the mountains. Pericles was still not sure if it was merely a lack of imagination, but Myronides actually was a calm presence, a valuable quality in a leader heading to war with Sparta.

The camp that night was cold, with dried meat and water to restore their strength. Pericles slept better than usual, with the comfort of guards and scouts around him. He woke to rain on his face and sat up, coughing into one hand and feeling stiff. Clouds had thickened in the night and he heard thunder rumble in the distance, with light flashing. After each burst of light, men muttered in fear. He sighed, rising to walk among them. Pericles was a strategos, and though he felt as if he played the role, part of it was to be seen, to reassure. He strolled through his thousand as if he hadn't a care, careful not to flinch when the lightning lit the sky. He greeted many of the men by name, all while the storm grew in power and volume, stealing away the dawn.

The rain died after a time, but the clouds kept roiling and pouring, driven by heavy winds. Pericles could see the men were growing more afraid. Many of them prayed aloud. The night before, they had been impressive in their skill and endurance. With a few flickers of lightning, they were made as children before the gods.

'On your feet,' he shouted. There was comfort in routine and gruff officers, he recalled. 'Up! There's light enough now. Check the ground for kit and coin. We'll leave no sign we were here.'

It was make-work, to keep them distracted from the storm. Yet as they began to do as he'd ordered, the sky went white, bright as noon, followed by a crack of sound. The storm was above them and a gale whistled through the trees. Pericles smiled. The air smelled different, almost sour. He felt alive in it.

'What does it mean?' Myronides shouted over the sound of thunder. 'Is it a good omen? You don't seem afraid.'

Pericles almost made a light reply, but caught himself when he realised how many of the men had turned to hear his answer. All they knew was violent sound and light. It frightened them. He glanced at Anaxagoras and saw the man make an exasperated motion, as if he struck an invisible flint. Pericles nodded.

'We are heading to battle, Polemarch Myronides. It may be that Apollo beats a drum for us, to fire the blood. Can you smell the air? It is . . . alive.'

He saw that the man Athens had appointed to lead them looked absolutely terrified. Pericles lost patience and drew a flint from his boot, striking it against his sword. The blade was dry and the sparks lit up that part of the camp well enough.

'Or it could be sparks like those, kurios. Whatever it is, we should be moving on. Until we know where the Spartan forces rest their heads.'

Myronides lost some of his visible distress. The scorn of a younger man seemed to have reached through to him and he was gruff as he bellowed orders to break camp and move on. Pericles saw some of the men miming the flint strike to those who had not heard. It brought smiles forth and as the storm passed, it took their gloom with it.

The morning was spent in forests so deep and thick that Pericles wondered if they would ever see an end to them. Only the position of the sun told them they were still heading in the right direction. They crested hills and descended fields of broken scree in blinding sun, skidding down as if they rode waves of dust and stones. Myronides kept them together and the going was not too hard as they came down a gentler slope, sighting a low pass that led out to a plain beyond. Pericles looked up and froze at the sight of a runner coming in.

The man raised a plume of dust and in response Pericles' throat felt suddenly dry. Myronides called the halt moments later and the army settled down to tend kit, taking the time to rest and prepare. Their mood was calm enough. They had come to that place to hunt down a small Spartan force. Perhaps a few had hoped they would search without end. Others like the men of Argos were determined to pay the red-cloaks back for old dishonours. They were fourteen thousand strong – and they trusted their shield and spear lines. The Spartans were hated in that place, so there was a certain amount of anticipation and good humour.

Pericles made sure he was standing by Myronides when the scout reported. The other strategoi came in to hear, while their men waited.

'A camp lies ahead, kurios,' the messenger said, gasping. 'There are signs a battle has been fought – I could see bodies, with birds still feasting on them. No more than a day or so back, if I'm any judge.'

'What of the Spartans?' Myronides said.

'I saw red cloaks – perhaps a thousand, it was hard to be sure. They have others with them. Many more. I would say another six or eight thousand.'

The young man had been trained to gauge numbers at a distance, but it would still be a guess. Pericles felt his heart sink. He'd expected to ambush a much smaller force. Instead, they faced an army – one with Spartans at its heart.

To his surprise, Myronides grinned and clapped his hands together.

'Then we have them,' he said. 'They are a week's march out of Sparta, while we can set supply lines right back to our walls. We are barely a day from Athens! This is our land, gentlemen, not theirs. We can cut them off from home and they will have to engage us to break out. We're too far from the sea for them to summon ships. No, they *have* to get past us, without any reserves of food and water. Excellent.'

Pericles blinked, understanding for the first time that this was no ordinary venture for Myronides. The man had been part of many small actions over the years, but never against Sparta. He seemed excited at the prospect, more vital than Pericles had seen in him before. Pericles nodded, giving him visible support. In response, Myronides clapped him on the shoulder.

'Well, shall we go out to them?' Myronides said. 'I'd like the Spartans to see hoplites in this place – in our Attica – where they thought they could march and work unseen. Let us face the boar, gentlemen. Show him the spear we will use.'

If the mood amongst the men had been strained before, it eased at his words. Pericles was pleased to see teeth flash as they gathered their kit and formed into ranks to march through the final pass. He stood with his Athenians and felt pride surge. He carried his father's shield and spear. Many of them did.

They tramped through the gap onto a green plain,

where fruit trees drooped with new growth and an army of their enemy was preparing to head home – an army that had dared to come into their territory. Pericles felt his heart beat faster and he too showed his teeth. He was with his people; they were with him.

Nicomedes was tired of dealing with foreigners. It was bad enough having to appease the allies he had gathered, though it felt at times like conversing with women. It was worse that he had to endure the indignation of one who was not Spartan born yet had the temerity to raise his voice in the presence of his betters.

'I was *promised* there would be no battle,' Tisamenus was saying. 'Your ephors sent me to report on your victory, but they swore it would be over. Instead, I find your people pursuing these attackers. Some of them ran past me.'

'You were in no danger, I'm sure,' Nicomedes snapped. Did the man think he had nothing better to do than listen to him complaining? There were times when he wished Spartan discipline could apply to the whole world. Perhaps if he sent Tisamenus to be whipped. That would surely temper his anger, like hot iron in a quenching trough.

'It is not the danger, Regent Nicomedes! The oracle promised me five victories. My fear is that the last was this petty dispute. Your king gave me his word I would not be called to war until it was against the Athenians. Until that day . . .'

He paused as a runner came through the ranks. The man leaned in close to murmur and a change came over Nicomedes immediately.

'Where?' he said.

The Spartan regent raised one flat hand to shade his

eyes and peer into the distance. In confusion, Tisamenus turned with him.

A golden line was spilling out of the hills to the south. Nicomedes bit his lip as he regarded them, the soothsayer's petty concerns forgotten on the instant. He and his allies had repulsed the attack on the Dorian people, slaughtering their enemies – and proving once again the value of having Sparta on your side.

Now, warning horns were sounding across the ranks, each a different faction, with his fifteen hundred Spartiates at the heart. Commanders who had looked to him in awe just hours before were coming in, needing to be reassured.

Nicomedes could only watch as lines of hoplites formed up in the distance. It had to be the Athenians, he realised, the damned League. No one else had an army of that size.

'It seems Athens has come to try us,' he said. 'This may be your chance, soothsayer,' he said.

Tisamenus looked ill as he understood.

'Unless it has already gone,' he said softly.

Nicomedes muttered a curse. He knew it had been a risk coming so close to their region. Attica had been quiet for a long time and the Athenians had seemed determined to stay behind their walls, hiding from war like rabbits in a burrow.

He clenched his jaw. That misjudgement was the sort that could kill a king's regent, never mind some foreign soothsayer yammering on about promises and oracles. The plain of Tanagra was surrounded by peaks and high passes. It was a perfect field of war and Nicomedes had delayed there, accepting the plaudits and thanks of lesser men.

He thought of his allies. They would not have been his

first choice, most of them. Nicomedes had picked them up in the northern Peloponnese as he passed by. It was the oldest part of their relationship, that they sent men to war when Sparta called. They were not the elite, however. They never were.

Nicomedes felt fresh sweat trickling down his neck. Fifteen hundred Spartiates could not be thrown away, nor could they retreat before a force from Athens. If he refused to engage, all the good work he had done putting down the attack on the Dorian people would be lost. No, it would be worse than that. Every city-state and region would hear the Spartans had run from battle. It would be a blow at the foundations. On top of the quake and the helot revolt, it might bring everything crashing down, just as they had begun to recover.

He looked round sharply, realising one of his allies had asked him something. A Spartan commander was expected to be fearless. Nicomedes had to act in a very particular way, even if it cost him every man he had brought to that place.

'Send scouts close to their lines – do not engage,' he ordered. 'Bring me numbers, factions, whatever they can discern.'

Good. That was all in keeping, of course. He swallowed again. How had his throat become so dry?

'Regent Nicomedes,' one of the others said.

The man knelt when Nicomedes looked at him. Arcadians, he recalled. They had sent four hundred to march with him.

'Kurios,' the commander said, 'my lads are not ready for war with Athens. Can we not withdraw? You have only a small force of your people with you. Mine are farmers and potters for most of the year. They carry shield and spear for a season, when I ask it of them. They are not hoplites like your men or those of Athens.'

Nicomedes narrowed his eyes. The fool would have been better saying nothing. Now he had to respond, forced into his role whether he wanted it or not. He commended his soul to Apollo, god of the sun.

'I would wager my Spartans against ten times that number,' he said.

Sweat stung as it reached his eyes. Was the day warm enough to excuse it? Nicomedes wiped it away with a thumb. By the gods, was this what Pleistarchus and Leonidas had known, the awful loneliness of command? There was no one else to agree or argue with him. They all looked to him, but *he* couldn't be sure! It was an agony and Nicomedes hesitated for too long, sensing their confidence draining. It was the damned soothsayer, he thought. Everything had been going well until he had arrived. Nicomedes scowled at the man, standing there like a stunned calf. From the joy of an easy victory to despair! The Spartan wanted nothing more than to go back a day, rather than to meet the fear in the gaze of those around him. He could not. The responsibility was his.

'They stand in our path,' Nicomedes said. The truth of it was clear as he spoke the words. 'That is what matters. They have come to attack, believing they can win. We cannot reach one of the passes back to the Peloponnese without crossing their force, gentlemen, so put aside any thought of marching clear. We must fight, or leave our honour on the earth behind us. Do you understand?'

One by one, they nodded. They too had been congratulating themselves on the goodwill they had won. They had supported Sparta in a minor action and earned the respect of a king's regent. It had been a fine battle from their point of view, with allies relieved and an enemy broken. The blood of executed prisoners was still wet on the ground. Yet in an hour, all that was ashes. With no warning, they faced war again, this time against a powerful enemy. They looked to Nicomedes for leadership.

'Give the order to form up,' he said. 'In column.'

His gaze passed over the carts they had filled with looted kit. He shook his head.

'Leave everything – except weapons and armour.'

He took a deep breath, forcing himself to go on. The words sounded like his own death on the breeze.

'We will march to the south, towards the isthmus and the Peloponnese. If the Athenian force seeks to block our passage, we will engage and force a path through. Those are my orders. Move out now, gentlemen. I will lead you – and we will prevail.'

They scattered, the orders spreading with them so a new sense of urgency crossed the camp. Nicomedes wiped sweat once more as he noticed the soothsayer still there, shifting uneasily from leg to leg.

'Well?' Nicomedes demanded. 'You wanted your battle with the Athenians, didn't you? Take up a spear, lad. Find a shield and join the rest of the lesser ranks.'

A stunned Tisamenus went away and Nicomedes summoned his senior officers. At least the Spartans were implacable, showing only blank expressions. They would march and die at his order. That was not in doubt. He tried to swallow again and called for water. By the gods, his throat was dry.

*

Pericles stood in a silent rank, his helmet high on his head. Some of the others had pulled theirs down, but he preferred to let the breeze cool him. In the distance, he watched the forces of Sparta and its allies form into a column and march. Myronides was at the heart of the golden formation that faced them. He sent runners up and down the lines in all directions, passing on his order to shadow the enemy. Pericles gripped his spear, exchanging a glance with Anaxagoras and Zeno. The men of Athens had come to fight. They would not let the Spartans march clear without blood.

Pericles took a deep breath, forcing himself to calm. His soldiers were looking to him, expecting him to speak. He was nervous, but he had trained for this – with his father, with Cimon, even with Ephialtes in the Assembly.

'Act today as you will say you did,' Pericles called to those around him, 'when you raise a cup to this battle. That is for tomorrow. All I ask is that you do this first, and well.'

Some of the men were frowning in confusion. He could almost hear his father's voice. *Keep it simple, you fool!* His heart was hammering. Very well.

'Today, Sparta is our enemy – and we can bloody them. We are the League! Who are we?'

'*Symmachia!*' they roared back. League. Alliance.

That was better. He had found the words. He still thought of them as Athenian, but the men of Argos and Megara were something else, something that was still growing.

There were scouts on horseback on that field, on both sides of the plain. Pericles did not think much of just one more, even as the distant figure took a great loop around the enemy forces, avoiding two scouts who raised hands and tried to stop him. He could ride, Pericles thought. At full gallop, whoever it was risked his neck. A single rabbit hole could bring both man and beast down, hard enough to kill them.

There was something about the figure ... Pericles shaded his eyes as he watched him approach. A messenger from the north made little sense. Stranger still, the rider wore a shield on his back. It was almost as if ... He froze in disbelief.

Cimon swung his leg over and dismounted. The Athenian had no spear, but he was kitted out for war and wore his shield on his back. As he collected himself in front of an astonished Myronides, Cimon jerked it round to his left arm.

Pericles jogged across the ranks to greet his friend, though he was filled with foreboding. Cimon glanced at him and seemed pleased enough, though his expression was tense.

'Polemarch Myronides, this is ...' Pericles said as he closed on them.

'I know very well who this is,' Myronides snapped.

He glanced back at the lines of men watching. They had not been given an order to halt and so the three of them had to move or be lost in the formation as it went through. To his visible irritation, Myronides was forced to wave Cimon alongside.

'I put myself under your authority, polemarch,' Cimon said. 'On my honour, I swear to follow your orders.'

'You cannot!' Myronides replied.

Pericles realised he was furious. Myronides gestured towards the enemy that still slid west across the plain ahead of them. Cimon was busy keeping his horse from cropping at the grass underfoot as Myronides took him by the arm.

'Archon Cimon, you have been banished by the Assembly. I cannot allow you to remain here! It would mean my life, my honour. Have you no respect for the law?'

Cimon flushed a deep red and Pericles could not find words to help him.

'I am an experienced man, Myronides.' Cimon clenched his jaw. 'If I cannot lead, surely I can stand in line and fight as a hoplite? I know I can't simply stand aside while Athenians go to war!'

Pericles saw stubbornness in Myronides then.

'You must,' Myronides said. 'I wish it were not so, Archon Cimon. Yet the law is the law. I understand why you want to fight, but you were banished for ten years. I cannot allow you to join my forces. You flout honour just by standing on this land! This is Attica. I could have you taken up and executed and I would be within the law. I'm sorry, but that is my final word. Mount up and leave.'

Pericles saw his friend's distress, but Cimon only glanced at him, his eyes red. He nodded.

'I will watch, kurios. I know you will be victorious.'

It was a gracious comment and Myronides nodded to him as Cimon turned away and mounted.

'I will speak to the council when we return home,' Myronides said. 'I will tell them of your offer, Archon Cimon. It speaks well for you. I will do that much.'

From the vantage point of his saddle height, Cimon glanced over at the forces Sparta had brought to that place. He bit his lip in sheer frustration, but there was no choice. He had gambled on war loosening the laws of men. Myronides saw things differently.

Pericles watched his friend leave the field, cantering clear. If he had been polemarch, he would have allowed it, he realised. Those who made the laws could always see how fragile they were, as flawed as they knew themselves to be. It did not seem Myronides shared that perspective.

With a hard shove, Pericles lowered his helmet, so he looked out on the plain and the enemy through a narrow slit.

'For the League!' he shouted across the lines. They roared in appreciation. 'For Athens!' he shouted to his men. They raised spears and howled. 'For Cimon!' he added. They bellowed the name. He saw Myronides twitch at that, but Cimon didn't turn as he rode clear.

15

Though it was late in the day, both armies moved, easing across the plain. Pericles could see the red-cloaks march through their own people to his left – forming the right wing of their force. It was a battle formation, but they were not coming straight on. Instead, they seemed intent on a line west. He frowned, squinting into the distance. A pass rose into the hills there. It looked as if they were still considering leaving the plain of Tanagra, heading back to the isthmus and the Peloponnese without a battle.

Pericles nodded as Myronides adjusted their own path, cutting them off. There would be no chase through mountain passes. The Athenians had come for war and would not be denied. The plain was dry and firm, a true dance floor of Ares as they crossed it, pace by pace.

As the Athenian force marched, Myronides passed orders to strategoi and lochagoi, as well as the factions from Megara and Argos. The formations shifted to eight ranks deep across the line – and the drums began to beat. That was the true sound of war, the tugging pulse that made Pericles breathe faster. It had seemed a dream before, a vision. The drums made it real. They would beat every step to the enemy, until the sound was drowned in cries of rage and pain. He heard pipes shrieking from the Argos contingent, a harsh and discordant sound that set his teeth on edge.

Fourteen strategoi oversaw the change in formation,

with hundreds of lochagoi to shout in the ear of hoplites. In polished bronze, the forces they had brought looked like a snake or a glittering brooch. Pericles was close enough to hear Polemarch Myronides refuse Argos the left wing. They burned with a desire for vengeance, but that honour was not to be theirs.

At the outset, Pericles had been sent to the left. Planned or not, it had become a pivot point, he realised. Unless Myronides changed his mind, his Athenians would face the Spartan edge. He felt his heart beating harder, so that dizziness washed over him. For his whole life, he'd heard stories of those red-cloaked men. Some like Pausanias had impressed his younger self. Now he would bloody them, with spear and shield line, and all the ranks pushing behind. The pressure the phalanx created was immense, unstoppable. Men at the front either killed and went through, or died and were trampled.

Pericles whistled for water and a boy reached him with a skin. He merely wet his lips and then passed it on, while the boy tried to leap and get it back. The sun was warm and they were closing on an army. The world had become small.

'It falls to us,' Pericles called across the ranks, 'to face the old enemy. The ones who would tear down our walls and make us slaves. This is why you trained, why you worked so hard with spear and sword. We are *symmachia*. I would wager on us against these men.'

Those who heard growled assent, all while his words were repeated further down the lines. He nodded to two Athenian strategoi and the leader of Argos over on his right. For an instant, Pericles could not remember the man's name. It suddenly became very important that he did and he struggled with it as they closed to two hundred paces like the edges of an arrowhead coming together. Danos, he recalled. No, Danaos.

There were no archers on either side, Pericles saw. Nor were there cavalry to support the wings, not beyond a few scouts. No one would throw their spears, not when they were so useful in the charge. Yet the lines were growing ragged as men trembled, wanting the fighting to begin. In that moment, there was no thought of pain or injury, only the first massive blow, the strength they felt in their arms. They were fit and rested. They were young.

'Steady! Maintain your lines!' Pericles roared at his best volume. The drums were beating in time, measuring the last moments of their lives, sounding louder and louder. Every officer was bellowing the same, keeping men steady and firing the blood. 'Ready spears! Ready shields ... steady ... *shields*!'

Those who had not already done so loosened straps and brought them forward, taking the shields on their left arms. Pericles saw a few experienced men dip, rubbing dust on spear shafts where they would hold and thrust, anything to prevent wood slipping through their fingers. They wore swords, but the spears were the true killing weapons.

At forty paces, the drums were rattling hard and the pipes sounded like screeching birds. Pericles looked past the front rank to where Spartans had been forced to turn and face them. Had they hoped to march clear? He heard no orders on their side, as if they cared nothing for those they led. He hoped that was true. The red-cloaks were at least a thousand, perhaps half as many again. He watched as they overlapped their shields perfectly, each spear at the same angle. The Persians had known that sight, he thought, wishing he hadn't.

'Keep those shields up! Phalanx *ready*!' he roared.

Pericles had a glimpse of Zeno and Anaxagoras further along the line, marching together, grim-faced and pale. He sent a whisper of prayer they would survive and raised his own shield, touching it to his shoulder and left thigh as he marched on. His spear had been pointing at the sky the whole way across the field, but it was time. Across the front, the first two ranks lowered leaf-iron points towards the enemy.

The drumbeat blurred into one. Myronides was calling for them to charge and Pericles echoed it, his lone voice lost amongst thousands, bellowing rage and hate and cursing those ahead.

Front ranks crashed together with shields overlapped. Spears punched through with all their weight behind the points. They licked out like snakeheads, coming back red.

Pericles leaned into the bowl of his shield, pressing his bare thigh against the lower rim and bracing his feet on the ground. His helmet saved him from a glancing blow, a Spartan spear that reached out and scraped along his horsehair crest. When it snagged on a join, his head rocked back. Pericles wrenched away to one side, panting with strain. He doubted the one wielding it had even seen him. The phalanx began to heave against his back and the damned drums were still there, racing like his heart.

They had survived, he realised. He and his men thrust spears at red-cloaked warriors, but they had not been torn apart in moments. Some part of him had feared exactly that – had expected exactly that! As men compressed the ranks behind him, he felt relief wash through. These were not gods. The Spartans growled and swore and dripped blood, just as the men of Athens did.

'Who are we?' Pericles roared suddenly.

Enough of his men heard to answer him. '*Symmachia!*'

He grinned and went again.

'Who are we?'

The second reply was louder and they heaved forward at the same time, understanding what he wanted. Pericles swallowed, feeling a sense of awe. He hated the crush, but the phalanx could not be stopped. The eight ranks leaning all their weight and strength pressed forward blindly, knowing they had to go on. Those at the front could hardly move, even as many of them gasped and died. They jerked spears back and forth where they could, but the shields were a wall. A great groan went up, of men, of metal, of breath forced out in the press.

Pericles had to lean away when the unseen spear-wielder lashed out again. He would have given a fortune for a free hand to grab at it, but he could not. His left arm was buried in the shield bowl, his right held his own spear and heaved on it, forwards and back, seeking flesh. The scrape of iron tips set his teeth on edge, but there was no more movement, not against a Spartan line. All the time, the pressure at his back increased. He began to think he could not breathe. Panic eased in like a worm.

It came down to will, but even will can be crushed. Men were dying, one by one, all along the bloody gash where they met. When enough of them fell in one place, the ranks behind pressed blindly forward and the lines bowed.

Pericles had lost sight of the other strategoi, along with much sense of the battle. His world had become the men who faced him. He caught glimpses of them within the bronze helmets. They spoke words he knew, in anger. They caught his eye even as they tried to kill one another. The Spartans were matched by the hoplites of Athens and he could see that understanding grow in them. Dozens had lost their spears. The crush tore them from grips, for all they roared and strained. They drew swords then, or the shorter kopis blades.

Pericles ducked away from a Spartan with a bloody mouth who hacked overhand at him. The man wore the red cloak and seemed utterly calm as he sought out weaknesses. Pericles took a blow on his helmet crest, then barely avoided a blade aimed right for his eyes. He raised his shield a hand's breadth and the Spartan switched grip to hack across his greaves. It was hard not to flinch or give way. Pericles felt the man step on his foot and grind down. Two of his toes snapped dully and Pericles gasped.

His second rank were not idle. They could see the struggle and one of them waited, choosing the moment. His spear-thrust took the Spartan up under his ribs, cutting through leather as he turned to strike Pericles. Half the spearhead vanished and blood poured. With a strangled sound, the soldier let his shield fall and pressed his left hand to the wound. His fingers were red and slippery, but he still struck at Pericles with the kopis. One blow knocked his head to the side, dazing him. The second rose to cut into his neck. The spear-wielder lunged again, desperately, knocking the Spartan down. The man died at the feet of his battle line, his body kicked and rolled while his fellows filled the gap with one from further back.

Pericles could not turn to thank the one who had saved him. There was so little room, he could barely breathe at all. His spear had gone, he realised in dismay. As a Spartan sword cut a notch from his shield, he drew his own blade, lowering it across the upper edge. He glowered then at the red-cloaks pressing in to kill him. Slowly, he drew in a huge breath.

'Who are we?' he roared, shoving forward. His arms and legs were growing heavy, but he was as fit as anyone there. He told himself he was. His will was as strong as theirs. He told himself that too.

'*Symmachia*! League!' those around him shouted back. It was a crash of sound and they shoved at the same time.

The Spartan line wavered. It was not that they grew weary, but because of the sheer weight of men leaning on them. Eight ranks of Athenians faced only four on their side. They were being pushed back and Pericles stepped forward, a full pace. He grinned at the Spartans even as they went berserk.

His shield was smashed into his mouth so that he tasted blood and saw a bright flash. Pericles ducked into the hoplite crouch on instinct, so all they could see was helmet, shield and greaves. He bore a storm of blows and yet lived. When he rose again, it was to see them fall back another pace, bloody with wounds. Spears struck at the Spartans and too many of their own had fallen. Pericles took a third step without any choice in the matter. The mass of men leaning on his back forced him on. He felt his broken toes twist as they sank into mud. He dipped his head to glance down and found the ground sodden and red, soft underfoot where it had been dry before. He saw fallen men in the host of straining feet and legs, some with red cloaks. He swallowed and almost lost his father's shield as someone tried to pull it from his grip.

Pericles growled at that, jerking his sword around the rim so that fingers were cut free and a Spartan stood looking in shock at the wound. As Pericles watched, the man pulled a rag from his belt to bind it, but Pericles stepped forward, hacking him down in a flurry of blows that made his arms leaden and left him gasping.

The Spartans fell back. They guided their wounded to the rear and allowed the Athenians to advance step by step. Pericles had the sudden fear it was some sort of manoeuvre, some trick of the field. He let another hoplite step in front of him and used the respite to peer along the lines, to restore some sense of the whole battlefield rather than his own small part of it. His men were all looking to him. They needed to be led.

'Hold the line steady!' he bellowed. 'In good order now. Remember your training. If you are tired, ask yourself – did you train hard enough? Did you attend every fitness run around the city?'

It was ludicrous, as if he were speaking to them in the Assembly. Yet he saw a few shrug and blow air, admitting their own lapses. There were lulls in battle. Men could not maintain a white-hot rage for long. If they tried, they became exhausted and were slaughtered like hogs.

'If you see a spear, pass it to me,' Pericles went on. 'Or pick up any one of the fallen ones. They have no owners, or if they have, the dead won't mind. Check yourself for wounds when you get a chance.'

He paused, making his voice harder. They were breathing better, without the wild look of before. They were still facing Spartans.

'Now. We have pushed back a Spartan force, *symmachia*! League! Athens! Now make them run!'

The light was fading, he noticed in surprise. He had been hours in the press, with every breath a forge-heat and life beating out in moments. Across the field, the force that had marched from Athens was slaughtering the enemy. Only his wing had been held, but then no one else had faced that quality of men.

The Spartans had not broken, but they had lost hundreds. No one had ever seen so many of their dead on the battlefield, not even Persia. Turned and buffeted in their red cloaks, they lay like broken birds. Pericles saw the sun had dipped down to the hills. In the last light, he tried to press forward with the rest. The Spartans slipped away like shadows and ghosts, leaving their dead.

In darkness, Myronides rounded up prisoners. Torches were lit and dried food brought from the city behind them. Athens was close enough that hundreds of its people had come to see. Though the danger was not past, they walked the battlefield, mothers showing children the bodies of the dead. The ones in red cloaks were the most popular. Myronides set guards on them so they could not be stripped or hacked apart for souvenirs. The older man's experience showed then. It was not something Pericles would have thought to do.

There was no great sense of triumph in that place, even with the people of the city bringing food and wine. It wasn't possible to know the extent of the losses until the sun rose, but the battle had been hard, harder even than Pericles had known. His own world had been smaller, but both sides had fought with dark energy and no respite. The result was the spongy ground underfoot, that squelched and reddened the feet of those crossing it. Thousands had bled that day. It was hard not to think of their souls, still close, like bees in the air.

Anaxagoras and Zeno found Pericles with the thousand he had commanded. His section had lost over four hundred, their bodies laid out in dignity alongside whatever parts could be found. When a group of boys from the city came over to see, they were sent on their way with blows and curses. One of them tried to grab a finger on the ground and received a mighty kick that almost lifted him into the air before he ran off howling.

At first, the work was a way to sort out the experiences of the battle and simply breathe, growing slowly calm. Pericles knew Greeks liked to sing and drink wine after a fight, so he was pleased to hear 'Athena' rising under the stars as thousands of voices took up the words.

He wondered if the men of Megara and Argos would sing with them. Anaxagoras and Zeno did, though they had both been born far away. They had offered their lives for Athens, he thought. Out of love and sacrifice, they had become one of his people.

There was no possibility of sleep as the moon rose, not with an enemy force still roaming the hills. Myronides visited each spot on the field and seemed pleased to find the forces with Pericles in good order. The polemarch said very little, but gripped Pericles' hand and nodded in pride before moving on to the next. Pericles watched him, learning what it meant to lead in war.

When the first light showed, it revealed a plain scored and torn. More bodies than they had known lay sprawled. They too were collected and laid to be counted, a mounting tally that pleased no one. There would be thousands of shields returned to families in Athens that day, Pericles realised. They had come to that place to wound Sparta, to weaken them. The cost had been high.

In the end, just over four thousand would not return with Myronides. The forces of Argos and Megara had lost a good part of their men, but Athenian hoplites had paid the highest price. The light of day came without drums and pipes. Pericles felt as if he had sand under his eyelids. He had even dozed for a while, leaning on a spear. His foot had swollen and every step made him wince. All he wanted to do was get drunk and sleep. Yet he could not.

As the light grew, the scouts returned to say the remaining Spartans had withdrawn to the isthmus and their allies had scattered. They would not be resuming the fight. Not when they had lost at least half of those they'd brought to that place. The enemy dead were laid out in dignity, but the Athenians would not take them, nor spend time or oil building a pyre. Only the red cloaks and fallen shields were collected as trophies, rarer than hope in that place. Pericles had walked the line of Spartan dead with Myronides, seeing men drawn white and wounds to turn the stomach. The smell of opened bowels was strong there.

Pericles thought he knew one of the dead men. He had stopped, looking down at him, trying to bring the name to mind. The fellow wore no cloak, though he had been tall and strong . . . Tisamenus, he recalled. Some sort of soothsayer. Whatever he had been, Pericles thought, the end looked much the same.

Though he still felt both battered and exhausted, Pericles set his lochagoi officers to forming a column to march back to the city. The Spartans had been taken on and knocked back. In normal times, he would have feared their response, but by the time they came out again, the walls would be finished. That was the victory he and Myronides had won.

Even Persia had not done so well against the Spartans, he thought. He told that to the men around him and watched the words spread, spirits lifting like the morning breeze. It made it easier to take so many home to be buried.

16

The procession wound its way through Athens, with huge crowds following or shadowing its progress. No one worked in the city that day. The Long Walls lay abandoned, the workshops and potteries all still.

Each bier was drawn by horses or mules, the wheels turning slowly. Coffins or wrapped bodies were laid out: the sons of women. The ten tribes had decorated the cart beds with green branches, preparing dead men for the earth. The council had allocated a field by the main cemetery.

Pericles took each slow pace in thought, hardly aware of the city around him. Ephialtes was at his shoulder and together they led the rest towards the Dipylon gate and the northern wall of Athens. It was traditional each year to have a strategos deliver a speech for those Athens lost in her service, honouring their sacrifice. Pericles had expected Ephialtes to be given the honour, but he had not been there on the field of Tanagra. Perhaps, too, the scale of the losses had shocked the other man. Over two thousand would be buried that day. The bodies had been collected and brought back, each one laid out for identification by a weeping family.

Some of the wounds made that simple task impossible. As Pericles walked, the cart at his back was empty – deliberately so, for those they could not name, the unknown. It too was decorated and he could smell amaranth flowers on the air.

Beyond the city gate, the carts rumbled down the road, then onto the field in rows. Family members hefted the weight of fathers or brothers onto their shoulders and placed them gently in the ground. Priests of Athena walked among them, holding green boughs that whispered of hope – in Elysium, in what came after. Hours passed until all the carts had withdrawn but the one that had always been empty. Pericles had seen women and children draw close to it, reaching out to touch the wood in their grief. It was a symbol of the lost and it meant something to them.

By the time the last prayers had been said, the sun was setting and torches were lit across the field. Pericles looked up at a structure of wood, at steps he had to climb. His poor bound toes ached at the prospect. To his surprise, he felt Ephialtes grip his shoulder. The man leaned close and Pericles swallowed his nerves. A ball of iron had lodged in his gut. He could taste it.

'You'll find the words,' Ephialtes said. 'It is your gift, after all.'

'What?'

Ephialtes smiled.

'You must know! You always find the words that need to be said – whatever it takes to bring the rest of us together.' He saw Pericles lift a hand, starting to wave the idea away. Ephialtes shook his head, speaking again.

'No, it's important. Half of Athens would be at each other's throats if it wasn't for you. Or did you think men like Aeschylus would sit at table with me without you present? That Cimon would give his entire family wealth to your Long Walls if *you* hadn't asked him to? That I would support you in the council and the Assembly? It is your talent, Pericles. You bring men together, somehow. I don't really know how. The result lies before us – Athens, the League. What did you call it – a nation, even an empire? If I can give myself a little credit, it will be that I saw it in you.' The strategos chuckled. 'When we first met, I was determined to show the noble Athenians that I was worth as much as anyone. I thought you were just another gilded fool, but . . . when I met the men you gathered in your name, when I heard Zeno and Anaxagoras speak and saw how you welcomed them in the same room as Cimon!'

It was the big man's turn to look embarrassed and wave a hand at his own rising emotion.

'I might have been your enemy, Pericles. Perhaps I even was for a while, when I didn't know you. But I have listened. I have heard. What joins us is the same dream. We *are* Athens, you and I. The people, the fleet, the islands – the League. That is something new in the world, and I don't know where it will end . . . but I know you'll find the words today, because that is what you do.'

Pericles felt discomfort flow away. As Ephialtes had spoken, he'd decided to accept it. He'd seen men pledge loyalty to his father many times, offering their lives in service. Ephialtes hadn't used those words, but the sense was there. Pericles put aside a desire to say something quick or amusing. The other man had laid open his heart and Pericles knew he could hurt or heal with a word.

'I count you as a friend, Ephialtes. Yes, we are Athenian. Whatever that means, wherever we will go. That remains true. Hold to that.'

'You *see*?' To Pericles' surprise, tears glittered in the other man's eyes. '*Go* – go on, they are waiting for you.'

Ephialtes pushed him on, up the steps.

The wooden tower was small at the top. The rostrum nailed to one edge was as much to stop him falling off in the twilight as it was to rest upon. Pericles looked out on a crowd that stretched right across the field of graves. Torches fluttered and spat all the way to the city walls. Thousands sat or stood, just waiting. They were the grieving widows and sisters and children of the dead. He could feel their need in the warm air. What he said mattered that night. Perhaps more than it ever had.

The coffins had been replaced by heaped earth that would settle back in the months to come. Tombs and markers would rise there and grass would grow. Yet they would not be forgotten.

'In the past,' Pericles began, making his voice ring out, 'many have praised the tradition of this speech each year, given at close of day, to honour those who have fallen on the field of war.' He paused, listening to the flutter of torches. 'I do not agree. No words of mine can gild their service. These men have made themselves noble – and what they have given up does not rest on the words of one, delivered well or badly.'

He glanced down to where Ephialtes stood in the torch-light. Pericles saw Aspasia had come to stand by him. She had been joined by Anaxagoras and Zeno, as well as Phidias the architect. Aeschylus too was there, as well as a dozen others he knew and loved. Pericles nodded to them, his throat suddenly tight.

'It has been our custom to thank the ancestors who gave us this great democracy – true power in the hands of the people. In this place, with the sacrifice of brothers and sons and husbands, it has to be worth a life. I believe it is.'

He saw heads dipping in the crowd and emotion swelled in him, the words coming more easily.

'*This is who we are,*' he said, louder. 'Every one of us is equal before the law. When we raise a man, it is for his quality, not his class or his family. Those with talent can rise in Athens. We obey those in authority. We keep to the law, written and unwritten. When we rest from our labours, we strive in competitions, in sport, in recreation – in great plays and in love. We are different from our enemies! We don't rely on spies and threats and secrets to run our state, but the love of men and women for it – for her. We love beauty and the works of the mind, but it does not make us soft. No, it gives us purpose. The Spartans must break their children to make them warriors, but we are as brave, as willing to die, because it is for something much greater than ourselves. In Athens, wealth is to be used, not boasted about. Poverty is no shame, unless a man will not work to escape it!'

That brought a growl of approval and he smiled, carrying the crowd with him.

'We are concerned with politics. If a man takes no part in our debates, we do not say "He minds his own business", we say "He has no business here!" That is the city for which these men fought and died. I say to you all, remember their sacrifice every day. Make it noble in your own lives, in your work, in how you raise your families. These men were worthy of her, that is beyond dispute. I tell you, fall in love with Athens once again with their example. Fix your eyes upon her, for there is nothing like her in the world.'

He bowed his head for a moment, letting the crowd settle. He had not planned to rouse them up, but the truth of it lay in the mounds of earth stretching into the gloom. Men did not give their lives for worthless things.

'For those left behind,' he said more softly, 'for the widows and children, you should know that your husbands and fathers and brothers and sons were brave to the last. They had honour – and because they believed in our city, they made her great by their sacrifice. If Athena has blessed you with sons and daughters, raise them with those words and that example. The city will support each one to their majority. Not out of charity. No, it has been earned, by those who lie in the earth. If you have youth and strength, bring forth more children into the world. They can never replace the ones who went before, but they can honour them – and they can inherit the world they made.'

He smiled, feeling calm.

'There is no more noble act, no better men than these. Our city is an example. In the future, they will wonder at us, as men wonder now. Our spirit, our courage, has forced an entry in every sea, in every land. We go out – and some of us return to the earth too soon. Perhaps they had faults, these men, but if they had, they are wiped away like tears tonight. Let your hearts lift at the fame of the dead. They died for us. Their honour will not grow old. That is the crown and reward of our city. Where valour is given in love, that is where you will find our people.'

He stopped, but no one moved. In the torchlight, he could see faces turned to him and he was unsure, suddenly, how to end.

'This is your land, your field. When you are ready, come back to our city. Live the lives they earned for you – and for us all.'

It was enough. He went back down the steps and

staggered as Aspasia embraced him with great force. He could hardly remember some of the words he had spoken, and yet they pounded him on the back and crushed his hand. Ephialtes looked stunned. Aeschylus took Pericles by the head in both his big hands, shaking him, his eyes full.

'Come on,' Aspasia said. She took him by the arm, but looked back at Ephialtes, Zeno and the rest of the group. 'I have wine at home, enough for all of you.' They bowed to that.

She was beautiful, Pericles thought, her skin almost luminous in the dark, her hair a great serpent coil of gold wire. His second chance, whether he deserved it or not.

Aspasia noticed his gaze. He looked like that sometimes when he was drunk, as if he could hardly believe the wonder of her. Yet she frowned for a moment, her thoughts visible. Before he could ask what was wrong, Aspasia reached up, her hand very cool on his bare neck. Without conscious thought, Pericles bent to be kissed. Instead, she whispered into his ear.

'You did say to bring new children into the world, Pericles. Perhaps ours will be among the first.'

He blinked as understanding dawned. Aspasia nodded, pleased to see him smile.

'Yes,' she said. 'I am.'

She was young enough to be a little afraid, but he swept her up and spun her even so. His friends surrounded them in an instant. Zeno and Anaxagoras pounded Pericles on the back anew when he told them. He would have bruises later, he was certain.

As the group left the shadow of the steps, the crowd caught sight of him. In moments, they too were pressing close, clustering. Both Ephialtes and Aeschylus called for them to make way, but instead, more and more came. Those who grieved, who had lost, rushed across the field by the thousand to speak to him, to thank him. They called out in a clamour that only grew.

Pericles stared as unknown hands touched his arm or his robe. He had to draw Aspasia back, he realised, away from the weight of the press. It reminded him of the phalanx and he felt sweat break out. From the warm darkness, voices called to him, answering his speech, adding to it. He had one hand around Aspasia's waist. He raised the other to acknowledge them and found it grabbed and shaken, over and over.

Aeschylus was a veteran of Marathon. When the burly playwright voiced a command at battle volume, it was a blast from another time. Those who pressed too close all froze and fell back, shaken. Pericles felt his friends slip in to surround him with Aspasia, moving him through the mass of the people.

17

Pericles watched Ephialtes call for the vote. The evening session was running late, but he thought they had gathered enough support. There would only be one opportunity. His political tribe of Acamantis was back on rotation. If he tried and missed with his own people on point, that would be remembered. A second attempt would have less chance of success – and the Assembly would never allow a third. It was one reason he and Ephialtes had not brought matters to a head before.

The great vessel used for ostracon pieces was nowhere in evidence that night. It had no place in a vote to overturn a banishment. Under the flickering of the lamps, the will of the Assembly was all that mattered – the decision of the entire people of Athens, as expressed by those present. They were the ones who rowed triremes, or took up spear and shield in a hundred disputes. The war with the Spartan alliance dragged on at just less than boiling each month, never quite spilling into open battle, but always there. Wherever Athens sent her people to rule on a dispute or to enforce League authority, they knew there was a chance enemies would appear on the horizon. Every month, fresh graves were dug in the cemetery outside the walls. War could be an inferno. It could also be a slow bleed.

Pericles nodded grimly. He and Ephialtes had kept a tally of all those they could trust to speak for Cimon – until they were sure they had enough to sway the vote. Yet the possibility of his return rested on two pillars, rather than anything they could do. Every man in the Assembly knew Cimon had gone to Tanagra to offer his service, his life. It was a simple act, but it spoke well for him. The second was simply that they were afraid. The losses at Tanagra had been a reminder of how dangerous Sparta could be – and still was. Pericles doubted the Spartans called it a victory. Over seven hundred red cloaks had been collected from that battle. They had been cleaned and pressed and rolled in chests up on the Acropolis, in the huge temple to Athena that Phidias was building. No other city could claim such a token of victory, not even the empire of Persia. Yet the war went on – and Cimon was proven in battle. His banishment had been an act of peacetime, a luxury. They could not afford such things any longer.

Pericles watched as the epistates called the vote and the clerks readied themselves to mark tallies on their slates. He had spoken and the crowd had listened, though his mind had been half on Aspasia. She had grown large in the months since telling him. He smiled as he thought of that. She had worn pale yellow at their wedding, one of the first to be held in the unfinished temple of Athena Parthenos – the maiden. He did not think the pregnancy had shown, though his mother had maintained a rather arch expression throughout. Still . . .

'The votes have been agreed,' the epistates called in a clear voice.

Pericles looked up, colouring at the thought of being distracted at such a moment. Ephialtes nodded to him and Pericles relaxed, turning back. The epistates was not one of those who could read and he had to repeat the lines as a clerk whispered into his ear.

'Cimon, son of Miltiades . . . is granted leave to return, by the will of the Assembly of Athens . . . in recognition of his long service. His ostracism is at an end, from this moment. We welcome home a son of Athens . . . and restore all his honours.'

The crowd cheered, a deep wall of sound that showed little dissent. It had been a long day and they would return to their homes in weary satisfaction. Pericles found himself grinning and he crossed to Ephialtes, leaning in to make himself heard.

'Thank you,' Pericles said. 'I could not have brought him back without you.'

Ephialtes shrugged.

'He paid to start the great walls, Pericles. We all owe him for that. Though I wonder . . . no, it isn't important.'

'What? Are we not friends? Ask me.'

For a moment, he recalled the man Ephialtes had been when they'd first met, so consumed with desire to reset the scales that he could see no value in Cimon or Pericles or any other Eupatridae family. Yet Pericles had spoken the truth at the funeral oration. In Athens, men were judged by deeds before their name. His words had been copied down by another and then distributed so he had the chance to read his own thoughts. He'd been relieved to find he agreed with that version, or at least that it wasn't too humiliating.

Ephialtes looked him in the eye.

'I think Cimon had the security of the city in mind when he gave his wealth to the walls. He served at Salamis, after all. He watched Athens burn and perhaps that was reason enough to go along with it. But he is an archon and Eupatridae – the noble class.' He saw Pericles was about to

224

interrupt and raised his hands. 'I know, I know! Cimon is an able man. You said it at the funeral. We raise men for talent over class. It was a great thing to hear, Pericles, and I want it to be true. Yet the group who complain most bitterly about your walls are those same noble families.'

'They have borne the lion's share of the cost, of course . . .' Pericles began.

'It's more than that. They have land – farms and woods . . . estate houses that lie outside the walls.' Ephialtes knew very well that Pericles had such a home. The man's already florid cheeks darkened as he went on. 'If war does come, all that could be lost. They know it. The council of archons votes down the wall maintenance bill whenever it reaches them.'

'An advisory vote, ignored by the Assembly,' Pericles recited with a wry expression.

'Even so. I wonder if Cimon will see things differently when he returns. He is not like you and me, Pericles. He has no great love for the people, except perhaps as rowers and servants. His class believe themselves above the fray, above us all. In a way, I can bear the arrogance from the ones without wit or talent. They are too stupid to know what fools they are. Yet with one like Cimon, who broke the Persians at Eurymedon, who commanded a third of the fleet at Salamis! Who understood what you needed to begin the walls. Who risked his life and honour when he offered to stand in line at Tanagra? Cimon actually *is* a great Athenian – and his certainty of that rubs me the wrong way and always will.'

Ephialtes sighed and shook his head.

'I need you to be the bridge between us, Pericles. I think you and I have reached an understanding, but the last

Cimon saw of me was when I argued in favour of his banishment. If he comes back as my enemy . . . well, I can see things souring between us. That is what keeps me awake at night.'

The man's honesty was painful to see. Pericles had listened to Ephialtes arguing well for Cimon to be brought home – all while he worried what the man might do.

'I promise you, I'll find the right words. Cimon can be stiff as a board. I know that as well as anyone. I can reach him, however. I'll make sure I can.'

Ephialtes nodded. He had come to accept Pericles as an ally in the city – a connection to a class he knew looked down on common men like himself. He knew too that one day he would abolish the council of archons and its title. He would bring all their wealth back into the treasury of the city. If their sons could rise then without land or personal fortunes, that would be their right. Pericles had spoken the truth at the funeral oration, there was no doubt. Athens would be built on trade and love of the gods, with no noble class to drink the sweat of working men – to turn it into silver coin and unimaginable luxuries. Ephialtes did not think Pericles was ready to hear all of that, however.

'You could use your seal as strategos on the order to bring Cimon back,' Pericles said. 'If you are quick. The clerks are preparing it now, but if it has your seal in the wax, that will count for something.'

Ephialtes' eyes widened. He scrabbled in the pouch he kept under his robe, nodding.

'That will do, as a start!' he said.

Pericles grinned, clapping him on the back as he went over to join the group working on the order. It would fly from the city that very night, carried by a runner who would not stop until he placed it in Cimon's own hands.

By the time Ephialtes stepped out onto the Agora, night had fallen. He remained on the steps of the council building for a moment, just taking in the sights and sounds of the great open marketplace. The Long Walls were finished and the protection they gave seemed to have brought more trade, more work than before. All the jobs that had been left undone were now desperately urgent – it was impossible to hire a carpenter for any amount. Yet there was silver flowing into the city from all directions. The stoneworkers on the Acropolis spent wages like there was no tomorrow, while merchant crews came into the city each evening looking to exchange their pay for memories and a sore head. Ephialtes watched one such group pass by, a dozen young men with rolling gait. They were so certain of their own strength! He wondered if they would be so loud and cheerful in the morning. Athens had a way of punishing the careless. The Scythian guards employed on city funds rarely ventured out after sunset. On dark streets, it was wise to keep a hand on a hilt or be ready to run. He smiled at the thought, recalling a few adventures of his youth. That boy could not have dreamed he would ever stand there as a strategos of Athens. For a month or two, Ephialtes had privately considered himself the first man in the city. Yet his head had not been turned by it. He'd admired men like Aristides when he had been much younger. Ephialtes could still recall the man's ragged old robe and the way he disdained wealth. He patted his own stomach ruefully, feeling the extra flesh there. Ephialtes could never be as thin and wiry as Aristides had been, but he could try to be as humble.

Across the Agora, a cheer went up, smothering the squawks and indignation of a cockfight. Ephialtes strolled in that direction, deciding to see what was in the ring. Each cockerel had little bronze spurs attached, the better to gash and rake the other bird. They didn't often last longer than a few bouts, but it was great sport. Watching was free, though of course the owners tried to collect bets from everyone. Ephialtes kept his money in his mouth, as the saying went.

He passed some jugglers and balancers, including one who simply stood on his head and held an amphora upright on his bare foot, as still as a statue. Ephialtes nodded to him and the man smiled, upside down. Nearby was a seller of ferrets, with a collection of carrying cages and a man swearing they would clear any house of mice in a single night. He said he might as well rent them, as no one needed one for longer. Ephialtes chuckled at the line and moved on.

There were a few more hawkers and food-sellers around the Agora. Once the main stallholders had closed for the night, those who could not afford a pitch came in, hoping for coins thrown or earned. Many were newcomers to the city, making their living in a place where wealth flowed in a torrent. Ephialtes stopped by one old man who made little round toys for children that went up and down on a string. The fellow offered a pair of the things for two obols, but he waved them away, giving back the one pressed into his hand.

The strategos was pushed and buffeted by strangers as he passed, the crowds thickening. The Agora only really grew still in the small hours, or when the drunkest ones finally stopped singing. It was actually a relief to reach the edge of the cockfight and remain there, out of the currents and pressures.

Ephialtes craned to watch the birds leap and hack at one another, their wings outstretched for balance. They were brave little things, he thought, or perhaps foolish. One of them caught the other across its neck, the bronze needle snagging in the wattle so the other bird's head was forced down. The dominant cockerel pinned his opponent to the ground and raked at its face, wings shrouding them both and blood spattering.

A great groan went up, alongside a cheer from victorious gamblers. The dead bird was lifted to show them all, limp and dark with blood. The owners tossed it into a basket then, stripping off the metal thorns. The bird would still grace someone's dinner table, useful even in death. Ephialtes found himself smiling as one of the owners promised the crowd an even greater spectacle, a bird known as 'Achilles'. He decided to stay long enough to watch the spurs tied on and the birds readied for battle, their owners blowing into their beaks and ruffling their feathers. Just the proximity of another cockerel was enough for them to become enraged, Ephialtes knew. They were like dogs in that. Or men.

On his right, a darker street led away from the heart of the city. The note of the crowd changed there and Ephialtes turned his head, listening. He was not sure what had caught his attention, but in the midst of the noise of the crowd there were . . . cries of outrage, or anger. He had known battle and it was that memory that flared in him, ripping away his mood of contentment in a single breath.

He saw a great heave starting in the crowd and swore. For a moment, he felt his responsibility to those around him.

'Look there!' Ephialtes shouted, pointing. 'Watch out.'

It wasn't much, but many in the crowd turned and more than a few began to move away.

The rush of men sweeping through the Agora had begun in that side road. Ephialtes had heard it described before, but not seen it. Now he felt panic in the crowd around him and almost went over as someone bumped hard into his back. He struggled to keep his feet as memories of Persian soldiers swam before his eyes. His hand clapped to his waist but there was no sword there, not on a summer's night.

The attack was swift and brutal, like a sea wave crashing over the revellers. Ephialtes could see a front of no more than thirty or so, but they worked together and carried cudgels before them. When they met some burly group of merchant sailors, too drunk or slow to get out of the way, they went through them, cracking heads and snatching pendants and purses. They didn't stop to wrestle at rings; speed and shock were too important. At the slightest sign of resistance, they moved on.

Ephialtes could not keep his place as the crowd drew back, taking him with it. He saw young men tumbling as the line swung at them. Women yelled obscenities in fear, or clutched at blood on their arms where something had been ripped away. Ephialtes felt anger grow. He found himself waiting like a fisherman, one arm poised.

He lunged at a man who never saw him. The fellow was waving his cudgel and yelling at the top of his voice, adding to the tumult and chaos. Ephialtes grabbed him and hammered a huge blow against the side of his head. The man collapsed like a wineskin and a few of the cockfight crowd roared in support. They liked a bit of sport and Ephialtes found himself at the centre of half a dozen brawny men, up on the balls of their feet and ready to grab another one. A few more took the time to kick the one on the ground.

The line had gone on, but another man remained, watching him. Ephialtes felt the gaze and looked up, recognising the one he had called his manservant. Attikos still looked like sinew and muscle, and of course the moment he stopped running with the others, who could say he had been part of it at all? It was typical of the man, Ephialtes thought.

'Spare a coin, strategos?' Attikos said.

He was walking closer and one of the cockfighters was either too drunk or too excited to note the threat in him. The man swung wildly at Attikos and received a brutal punch into his short ribs in reply. The fellow made a horrible sound and fell, curling into his pain. Attikos looked up at Ephialtes once again.

'Coin for a veteran, kurios?' he called. 'To buy a little bread and wine?'

Ephialtes sensed the crowd turning to see him. They had come to watch birds tear into one another. This had something of the same taste to it.

'You were with them,' someone called in the crowd.

Attikos gave a terrible grin that quietened the rest down.

'Me? No, mate. I tried to stop those nasty men, didn't I?' he said. 'If you've charity in your hearts, you might find a coin for a veteran. I stood against the Persians, more than once. Come on, show a little kindness.'

His gaze never wavered from Ephialtes and the strategos felt his hand tapping away on his waist where a sword hilt might have been. He resolved then to carry one, or at least a knife.

On the other side of the Agora, a new roar sounded. The commander of the Scythian guards had decided enough was enough. Perhaps he'd finally been roused from his bed or heard a strategos was in the eye of the storm. Ephialtes swallowed, while Attikos stared at him.

'Nothing for an old friend, Ephialtes? I saved your life more than once. What did you do? What did you give me in return? Turned me out like a dog, to starve. All just a joke to your new friends, I suppose.'

The Scythian guards had come down to the Agora and were forming their own line, pushing the thief rush back on itself. The forerunners were already streaming away, deciding they'd had enough for the night. Ephialtes blinked as they passed by, some of them laden with armfuls. Not all would make it and those who were caught would be whipped the following morning, or taken as slaves to the mines. Yet Attikos had seen through to the reality beneath. If they ran, they were criminals. If they stood still, they were just Athenians once more. Attikos had always looked for an edge, Ephialtes remembered. The man had been a good soldier. Yet he didn't trust him, not even a little.

Attikos was very aware of the turning tide in that crowd. Ephialtes could see him deciding whether to remain and be one of the cockfighters, or vanish into the side streets with the rest. For all he knew, there would be pointing fingers and accusations coming closer with the Scythians, or perhaps a beating. Ephialtes saw his stubbornness surface, the sort of grim refusal to move that he remembered very well.

The strategos reached into his cheek and fished out a drachm in silver, half a day's pay for a skilled man, enough for both bread and wine. He tossed it through the air and Attikos caught it from instinct. His face changed then, suffused by rage. He threw the coin back with huge force. It struck Ephialtes under one eye, stinging him as it fell to the ground. When he looked back, Attikos was gone and the Scythian guards were passing through with swords drawn, growling and watching for the first sign of any resistance. If they had to leave a few bodies on the ground for the sake of public order, they did not seem worried by the prospect.

Ephialtes rubbed the spot on his face where the coin had struck. It had rolled away somewhere and he didn't look. Someone else would find it and be delighted, he thought. It was not a wound, not really, though it had hurt even so.

18

The estate was at a sort of exhausted peace, like the lull in the morning after a great storm. Pericles' sons Xanthippus and Paralus had been sent away to ride round the back field when Aspasia started to make sounds no young man should hear. Peace reigned once again and the new baby was quiet as it was rocked by a wet nurse, sitting in the corner. As Pericles entered the room, Aspasia was watching them both with a keen and proprietorial interest. The kohl around her eyes had been reapplied, he noticed. Her hair too had been brushed and retied. Whether it was her training as a hetaira or some quirk of her own, she was determined never to be dishevelled or unkempt, even after a long labour. On the whole, she looked as if she had run a long race, her skin faintly flushed. Pericles had expected complete exhaustion and physical wreck, but then his first wife had been considerably older. He could not help a slight feeling of smugness at that thought as he bent down and kissed Aspasia.

'I'd like to call him after his father,' Aspasia said, reaching up to rest her hand against his cheek.

It was a favourite gesture of hers and as always, Pericles nodded. Never a tactile man, a touch could pass through the private walls around him as if they had never been raised.

'Ephialtes is a lovely name, after all,' she went on.

Pericles froze and she gave a peal of delighted laughter.

'Very funny,' he said, still recovering. 'Very good.'

She beamed at him and he kissed her again, with more force.

'Is it all right to bring the boys in?' he said. 'They've been making a nuisance of themselves and they keep asking.'

Aspasia's gaze flickered around the room, but the midwife had cleared everything away and there was no sign of the battle. The day was warm and though she ached in every joint, it was, she decided, a fairly pleasant exhaustion. She nodded and Pericles put his head outside and whistled.

His two older sons brought the smell of fresh grass and earth into that place. They were turning into men and so they both stopped by Aspasia first to show respect, letting her take their hands.

Xanthippus looked sulky as he said, yes thank you, he had put the horse back in the stable and yes, he was looking forward to joining the Assembly. When Aspasia asked if they wanted to see their little brother, he looked uncertain.

'Half-brother,' Xanthippus corrected.

Pericles frowned.

'He is my father's grandson, Xan, just as you are,' he said.

His sons stood awkwardly as the wet nurse brought the baby close for them to see. The creature was tight-wrapped and fussing, wanting to be fed.

'We'll name him Pericles,' Aspasia said from where she lay.

Xanthippus winced and tilted his head.

'That is a great honour. Mother says . . .' he began. His father interrupted before the boy said something to ruin the moment.

235

'Whatever your mother says, the truth is that you are all my sons. Understand? I just hope you'll teach little Pericles here how to ride and fight – and debate! You can help with the things his tutors will overlook, I'm sure.'

It was an offer of peace between them. Xanthippus gave up some of his thunderous expression. Yet the oldest boy still wore unease on his face. Pericles could only guess at the things Xanthippus had heard at home. First wives could be scathing, especially when a second wife was making a new family. Xanthippus had grown further apart from his father with every passing season. There were times when Pericles saw a flash of the son he had been – when Paralus made him laugh, for example. Yet Xanthippus too had lost something in the divorce – innocence or certainty, Pericles didn't know. Perhaps it was just the knowledge that life did go on, beyond the end of the world. He reached out to pat Xanthippus on the shoulder and the boy swayed away from him. Pericles didn't try again. Paralus had discovered the baby would grip one of his fingers and wanted his brother and father to see.

Pericles felt sorry for his older sons. They would have to go home to a thousand questions and barbed comments. Thetis hadn't remarried, he'd heard. She seemed content with her new life, but he kept the boys as busy as he could, in part to keep them away from her.

His own home life was . . . a joy, to the point where it embarrassed him. Pericles couldn't honestly say he had wanted more children, but it was a public duty and Aspasia had been determined. Having a young woman bent on bringing him round to her way of thinking had been a most interesting experience. He looked forward to resuming the struggle the moment she was able. He had no daughters yet, after all. He recalled his father saying a man was not a man until he had a daughter. There was still time to make that right.

The slave who came to the door of the birthing room was new to the household, bought at auction and still being trained in the routines and labours of the estate. He was accompanied by Pericles' mother, the old woman watching every move and ready to pull him up at the slightest error. Very aware of her scrutiny, the man bowed deeply as he appeared in the doorway.

'Archon Cimon begs entrance,' he said.

'Kurios,' a voice hissed behind him, accompanied by the tap of a stick on the stone floor. He repeated it.

Pericles looked up in pleasure. His friend had been back for just a few months, but the results could already be seen wherever Athens raised a banner.

'Thank you,' Pericles replied.

His sons were fidgeting and ready to leave. Only courtesy and discipline kept them there. In fairness, the wonder of new life was probably wasted on them, he thought.

'Xanthippus? Paralus? I think it's time to give . . .' He caught himself, having almost said 'your mother'. That awkwardness would fade in time, he hoped. 'To give Aspasia a rest, I think.'

Xanthippus stared as if he might say something, then turned away. The two boys went out together, clattering down the corridor outside. Pericles hoped they would spend the rest of the day fishing rather than going straight home to report to their mother. He smiled at his wife and kissed her. He had not done so while Xanthippus was there to watch him, he realised.

When Pericles came out to Cimon, it was to find the

older man leaning on a fence bar, watching two colts frolic and mock-bite one another.

'I hear congratulations are due,' Cimon said, embracing him. 'A third son! The gods bless your line. Though of course, they say a man is not a man . . .'

'Yes, I know it. I will hope for a daughter as well, in time. Aspasia has plans.'

Cimon chuckled.

'I don't know what you did to deserve such luck, my friend. Perhaps it was your father at Marathon, or what we brought about at Eurymedon. If it was bringing home the bones of Theseus, some of that luck should rub off on me, surely? Either way, I am pleased for you.'

Pericles could see a tension in his friend, despite the light words. Cimon looked older, worn down by work and responsibility. It was dispiriting. More worrying was the knowledge Cimon would not have come out to see him for anything trivial. Pericles took a slow breath, putting aside his happiness. Cimon glanced up and nodded at what he saw.

'Persia has retaken Cypros. The news came in this morning, which means it is weeks old. That island! It has always been too close to their shores.'

'How did they even do it? I thought we had warships in dock there.'

'We did, but they have a new king, a son of Xerxes. They call him Longhand, for some reason. I don't know if it is a physical thing or some pun in their tongue. Either way, he has managed to kill all his brothers and take the throne. My fleet captains have all been saying the same thing – the Persians have been testing us again, even before this. For a few months now, they've been sending out fine new warships of their own. They won't face our triremes if we go hard at them, but they escort and defend merchants, patrol their own coasts. Around Cypros, they were more aggressive, probing our responses as it seems now. They rowed close enough to bring our crews out half a dozen times. Before the attack, it just looked like games and threats – nothing like an invitation to war. Then they staged a night landing on the island. I have only the one report so far and no numbers, but we had a garrison of a thousand good men there.'

Both of them recalled grim memories of landing on Cypros.

'You think they might still hold out?' Pericles asked softly.

Cimon shook his head. He had never been one to entertain false hope.

'No. If this new Persian king was bold enough to do this, I imagine he landed in force. If any of our people survive, they'll be prisoners.'

He cleared his throat, uncomfortable with the change in their relative authority. In theory, Cimon had returned to all his old honours and responsibilities, but the balance of power had changed in his absence and there was no taking it back. Pericles and Ephialtes controlled the largest factions in the council and the Assembly – with Ephialtes the more senior of the two. Cimon may have held the title of navarch of the League fleet, but he could not take the ships out without his old friend giving him the nod. Pericles could sense his frustration, but there was discipline there too. Cimon had always been as much Spartan as Athenian. If he needed to go on bended knee to take the fleet to Cypros, he would do so without a qualm. It helped that Pericles had never known a more loyal and ruthlessly determined man. When it came to Athens, to the League, Cimon was iron.

'What of Sparta?' Pericles asked. He hated to do it, but that was his role. If the navarch wanted to take the fleet east, it was Pericles' responsibility not to leave the seas around Athens undefended.

'That is ... why I came to see you,' Cimon said. He seemed to hunt for the words, speaking reluctantly. 'You know I've spent the months since my return looking over the walls and the fleet, our forces here and in every League city. We are overstretched, Pericles. I can't say why Sparta hasn't really tested us, not yet. But when they do, we will struggle to meet them.'

'You were away for a while,' Pericles began to argue. 'I don't think . . .'

'Please, Pericles. You know my judgement is sound. You know me. We are the Scythian guards for hundreds of small cities and League members. As things stand, it works, but the whole world is waiting for Sparta to decide they've had enough. You know how they are, better than most. They delay. They wait and wait, until the moment is perfect. Then they come out, destroy all their enemies at once and go home. It is how they marched against Persia, and does anyone remember how long they stayed behind their walls now? No. For Sparta, war begins with the food they serve their soldiers, then the training, the production of equipment, the landscape, the weather . . . all of it. By the time they actually take the field, they are *certain* of what they have to do and how to do it.'

'I know all that,' Pericles said.

Cimon surprised him by interrupting again, rather than

waiting patiently for him to make his point. More than anything, it showed how seriously his friend took the need to persuade him.

'They are not yet ready to move,' Cimon said. 'But when they come, it will take everything we have to survive it. Your walls will keep us safe, I believe it, but how long can we hide in their shadow?'

'A month may be all we need,' Pericles replied a little sharply. The walls were still his greatest project. To have Cimon dismiss them stung his pride.

'I hope so, but even in a month, our allies in the League will see we cannot protect them. That's what your father began, Pericles – what you continued. The League shadow protects and defends all its members. The fleet will come and answer a threat to any one of us. That is what our people on Cypros expect, what every member of the League demands in return for its oath and silver. In return for fealty to something greater than themselves. A nation of cities. An empire of the Aegean.'

He paused and gentled his tone.

'If we are forced to run for our walls every few months, to abandon the League . . . if I were a king in Sparta, I could ruin the authority of Athens in a single year. Do you understand? When they come – and they must come – it will hurt us more than anyone can imagine. It might even undo the League.'

'Well what then? What do you suggest? Ignoring the Persian attack on Cypros? That would wound and weaken our alliance just as deeply, wouldn't it?'

Cimon nodded.

'It would. I must relieve Cypros – and for that, I must be certain Sparta will not attack while our strength is elsewhere. They fear our fleet, Pericles. I can land men on the Peloponnese the moment they threaten our walls. They know that. Perhaps it is all that keeps them on their side of the isthmus. For me to leave for Cypros, I need a break in this cold war of ours. I need a truce with Sparta.'

Pericles blinked at the man he admired above all others, testing the idea in his mind. Had Cimon lost his wits?

'I know you saw the attack at Tanagra, Cimon. Ephialtes and I tried to weaken Sparta then. We brought what we hoped would be an overwhelming force – and though we bloodied them, they killed so many . . . You didn't see the funerals. The graves . . . I think it worked to weaken them, but since that day, they are the ones who burn our ships and confiscate merchant cargo, who join our enemies to advise and train. Do you understand? I would accept a truce with Sparta *tomorrow*! We'd still have our walls and our trade – the League is quiet except where Sparta preys on our people! By the gods, what I wouldn't give for peace! It is Sparta who prowls around the stockade, looking for ways to get the lambs. They are the ones who seethe and disrupt. *They* are the ones you have to persuade, not us.'

Cimon only nodded, widening his eyes and pursing his lips as the younger man caught up. Pericles was reminded of Cimon's experience in command, much greater than his own. No doubt this had all occurred to him already. Ah. He was being led. He felt himself flush, deciding to remain silent.

'I have friends in Corinth,' Cimon said. 'Men who have dealt with my family for generations, whom I trust to tell me the truth. They say the new king is rebuilding – forcing classes through their agoge schools, bringing on Spartiates before they are fully trained, anything he can do to bring his people back to strength. In a generation, it will be as if the earthquake and helot revolt never happened. Yet that is a problem for our sons, Pericles, not for us. I'm tempted to make him an offer in silver, for ten or twenty years of truce.'

'They don't use money . . . you know that, of course,' Pericles said, clearing his throat. 'Why do you think they would accept?'

'It's true they don't use coins in their normal lives. They do everything in common, from eating and sleeping in barracks to training. The state, though, has to have coin. They know the value of silver, when it comes to dealing with other cities. Sparta has a treasury like ours, though I imagine there's not much in it except for spiders and mice these days. Nor do they have the helots of old, to repair shields or build their walls. Yet if they want to employ master architects or blacksmiths from Argos, they need good silver to pay them. We have the mines at Laurium – and we want a truce. They need time and they need silver. For the right amount, I think I can bring both sides together.'

Cimon scraped the toe of one boot on the ground, looking embarrassed.

'In the old days, I would have gathered what I need from my own family coffers. I don't like asking the council for anything, Pericles, never mind a fortune large enough to tempt a Spartan king. Yet they trust me more than most Athenians. If I go, it must be with our best offer. One chance, and who knows, I could be back in a week with a truce sworn on the gods.'

'How much will you need?' Pericles asked. He dreaded the answer.

'Ten talents. I can carry that much on a cart.' He saw

Pericles hesitate. 'I don't need to remind you of the forty I put towards the great walls.'

'We spent nine hundred more,' Pericles murmured.

It was Cimon's turn to blink. The sum was more than he could comfortably imagine.

'The treasury at Delos?' Cimon said.

Pericles nodded. To his surprise, he saw Cimon's expression darken.

'That was pledged for the fleet.'

'And we *maintain* the fleet,' Pericles replied quickly. 'We have kept our oath. It does not matter if we spent the money on keeping Athens safe as well. We'll rebuild the League treasury – if we get peace. Very well. Ten talents. I'll put my name to it.'

'Good,' Cimon said. His sudden darkness cleared like the sun coming out from behind clouds. He held out his hand and Pericles took it in a powerful grip.

'You really think Sparta will agree?' Pericles asked before letting go.

'I will be staking my life on it,' Cimon said. He smiled, his worries vanishing. 'May I come in and see your son?'

'Of course,' Pericles replied. They left the sour air of deals and politics behind as they went inside.

19

Pleistonax rode with his uncle Nicomedes towards the isthmus. Though the horses were strong and fast, on the whole he would have preferred to run. There were times when he was only happy with a road under him in summer, barefoot and up on his toes, winding in the landscape like a spool of thread. He had won a dozen long races since he'd first learned of the king's death at the agoge camp. Perhaps that news had unlocked something within him, he didn't know. From that moment, he had not come close to losing. Fate and the gods may have made him king, but he was still determined to be worthy. A man willing to die in a race was hard to beat. Pleistonax had discovered that within himself. He thought sometimes it burned so bright it might destroy him.

He smiled in memory as the horse trotted along. On the first race around the hills after the news, he'd run without effort or strain for an age, hearing only his steps and slow breathing. He'd run like his feet had wings and felt only a sort of joy. Little by little, he'd left all but one boy far behind.

He hadn't been surprised somehow to see Dorion matching him, though the bigger boy had been labouring, arms pumping, head loose. The style seemed weak, though Dorion too was determined. Pleistonax had been intent on his own race, and so together they had drawn apart from the rest, step by step, until all the other boys were just a group running the last hill. He and Dorion ran alone.

He still recalled the silence of it, the sudden awareness of two sets of steps, two panting breaths that merged in pattern or eased apart. Both he and Dorion tried to break the spirit of the other with sudden lunges, pulling ahead in turn. They were both just flesh and bone. Each one had to endure worsening pain in his legs and lungs – then the slow humiliation of being caught. Each attempt cost more, hurt more.

They'd settled, Pleistonax recalled, into a sort of seething truce. A glance back had shown no one else closing. Almost in lock-step, he and Dorion had reached the bottom of the worst hill of them all, the last on the great track around the agoge camp. From its peak, a wide and gentle slope led down to the camp gate, but reaching that point was brutal, endless – just when the legs had gone and white spit gathered in the corners of the mouth.

On previous days, the trainers had come out to that hill to growl and threaten, to urge the boys on. They had not been there that time, Pleistonax recalled. He remembered wondering about that as he ran. These days, he knew the trainers were just men, with flaws and bad habits and even the tendency to gossip like old women, some of them. No doubt they had stayed in camp to discuss the news of a king's death while the boys ran themselves ragged. Yet at the time, that final empty slope had seemed part of the test, a challenge that needed no witnesses.

He put such memories aside as he reached the isthmus. The young king of Sparta reined in there, patting his horse on the neck and looking around. No sign of the Athenians, which was somehow typical. Pleistonax dismounted easily, looping the reins over the animal's head. He still remembered that damned hill! He had never pushed himself as hard before, until there was nothing in him but spit and will. He had begun to stagger and weave towards the end. Dorion had been just ahead and Pleistonax had felt his legs weaken. It would have been the easiest thing in the world to come to a stop, to let his tormentor have his petty victory. What did it matter who won a stupid race or came second? Perhaps *that* was the perspective of a king, to know what was important and what truly wasn't.

There had been voices in his ears, he recalled: whispers and promises, saying it was all right, he would still be king, that he could just stop. He knew them. They were his weakness, his fear. Under the sun, on a hill that went on for ever, he had burned them all out.

Pleistonax remembered the sound of despair Dorion had made as he passed him for the last time over the crest of the hill. The way he'd lengthened his stride then had been a sort of ecstasy. He'd felt a breeze drying his sweat as his speed picked up and no one – no one – could have caught him then.

When Pleistonax had passed through the gate, he'd come to a halt in the yard of the agoge camp. The trainers had been there, watching. In a strange way, they knew they were not part of it. They turned boys into Spartans – but some things could not be taught. They had to be learned.

Dorion had skidded to a halt, limbs flailing, dropping to one knee in the dust. A few of the other boys came in while he stayed like that, eyes closed and stinging, breath like a kiln. They too had run harder than ever before, trying to close the gap Dorion and Pleistonax had opened. For pride and the warrior's spirit, the entire group had driven themselves to complete exhaustion. It showed then. One or two were sick on the dusty ground. Others leaned over, hands on their knees, spattering huge drops of sweat.

At the isthmus, his uncle dismounted and took the reins. As he nodded thanks, Pleistonax found the memory was still strong, still clear, tugging at him. He knew what it had cost, in agony, to control his breathing, to stand as he imagined a king would stand. By the gods, it had hurt! Yet having won, having *beaten* them, he had found he could endure. His father Pausanias was long dead, condemned as a traitor. Pleistonax had no one to teach him the way of kings. Instead, from first principles, he had taught himself.

The trainers were busy with the new generation these days, putting them through the same drills and runs, forcing them to spar when they could hardly stand. Pleistonax grinned in memory. He wondered if there would be another who kept saying '*Autis*' – 'Again' – to them, when everyone else had given way to exhaustion. They had beaten his arms black with bruises and scrapes, his legs swollen. His ribs had cracked and his nose had been broken a dozen times. Yet he had picked himself up and spat blood, saying '*Au-tis*', gesturing for them to begin again until they could only stare.

Pleistonax looked back then, to the man who carried water and shield for him, who had ridden out from Sparta beside his uncle. Dorion had not yet dismounted. He was watching instead for enemies or threats. He noticed his king's glance and raised his chin in silent question. Pleistonax only nodded. They had been boys then. Training, sparring, lifting stones and iron had added ridges of muscle to their shoulders and legs. Dorion had become his most loyal companion, a trusted man. Pleistonax could only wonder at it, though he thought he understood. The boy who had been made *eiren* of their camp group had wanted someone to follow, needed it even. Dorion had found it in Pleistonax, but only when the boy proved himself. It had meant Dorion could give up his pride. Pleistonax smiled in memory. He had put out his hand to the kneeling boy, standing over him. Dorion had taken that hand and stood. He had been the first. Kings found their guards in the agoge, when they had tested them.

The isthmus between the Peloponnese and the mainland was a bare place, with a few gnarled olive trees that looked as if they might have stood when Homer was a boy. The sea glittered in the distance, Pleistonax saw, like grey beaten metal. The strip of land was not so very wide. Narrow enough to have had a wall across it once, though those blocks were almost gone. He wondered how many houses had new walls built after the quake, the stone taken from this place. It didn't matter, he thought. The wall had been built while an army of Persia roamed unchallenged, setting cities on fire. Sparta had broken that host – and they didn't need a wall after that. Once again, they were the walls.

Seeing the small group of Athenians approaching, he could not help thinking of the walls those people had built, all the way from their city to the sea. It was bad enough that they had ringed Athens in stone. That was an insult of a sort. The walls that stretched down to the port of Piraeus were worse. They were a challenge.

Dorion held the horses and Pleistonax walked alone with his uncle to meet the group. Three of them had come, with a small cart drawn by ponies at their backs. They had clearly walked from Athens and Pleistonax felt a moment's irritation at that. Was it significant that they had chosen to meet on the isthmus? They were said to be a subtle people. Pleistonax felt his youth and lack of experience like a weight. The Athenians were playwrights, debaters ... makers and traders. They were certainly cunning bastards, every last one of them.

Compared to him, they were also soft, he thought. He did not have to touch the hilt to know his kopis blade hung from his waist. It had been his father's once; it was a part of him. Pleistonax realised he did not fear their anger, only that they would somehow outwit him and make him their fool. He clenched his jaw. He had reached his majority and he was the battle king of Sparta. The ephors too had wanted to ride out with him. He smiled when he recalled their expressions as he gave his answer.

There were no chairs in that spot. Three Athenians faced two Spartans. The ones on either side of their leader were oddly mismatched, Pleistonax noted: one tall, one short. Neither stood like a soldier. The one in the centre had the look of eagles about him, however. He too wore a Spartan kopis. That certainly suggested a name, though Pleistonax had never met Cimon.

Pleistonax waited patiently. He would not speak first. The Athenians had asked for the meeting, even while war continued between their peoples. In silent interest, Pleistonax looked from one to the other of the group, taking in their tunics and robes, their sandals and rings. They were not armed for war, he noted. Perhaps that too was a message.

'I am Cimon, son of Miltiades,' the Athenian said at last. 'My companions are Anaxagoras and Zeno, both free citizens of Athens. Do I have the honour of addressing His Majesty King Pleistonax?'

Nicomedes opened his mouth to reply on his nephew's behalf. As he had with the ephors, the younger man held up an imperious hand. A Spartan king needed no one else to speak. Pleistonax carried anger in him, but also youth, in wide shoulders and powerful legs. He was faster and more dangerous than anyone else there. He knew it. It showed in the way he stood and smiled at lesser men.

'I am Pleistonax. You asked for this, Archon Cimon, under truce. I have come. What do you want?'

Cimon swallowed. The Spartan habit of speaking few words was something he usually appreciated. It seemed the young man who somehow loomed while standing still was of the breed. Despite his youth, Pleistonax bore white scars on his arms and legs, pale lines against his tan. His nose had clearly been broken many times. Cimon made himself breathe. He had discussed possible outcomes while he and his companions rode to the isthmus. Pericles had suggested the pair for their insights, but the reality of speaking to a Spartan king was like being plunged into a freezing river. All thought froze. If the Spartan saw weakness, he would surely refuse. Cimon spoke slowly, giving himself time to think.

'Majesty . . . I carry with me the authority of the Assembly in Athens. It is our . . . wish for there to be a truce between us. We have been allies before. War destroys what is good.'

Uncle Nicomedes cleared his throat, bowing his head over a fist. Pleistonax didn't look at him.

'Is that how you see it? I disagree,' Pleistonax said. 'War sharpens. I have a new generation now. They must be blooded, as their fathers and brothers were – at Plataea, at Tanagra.'

It was no accident that he mentioned the scene of an Athenian-led assault on Spartan forces. Cimon nodded as if considering the point.

'As with our ships burned at Argos, or our people killed . . .' he began.

'Yes. That is the nature of war,' Pleistonax interrupted.

He caught the edge of a warning glance from his uncle and took a grip on his emotions. The enjoyment he felt from needling Athenians was a luxury he could not afford. He pursed his lips. The truth was that Sparta was struggling. With a tiny number of helots, rebuilding was going incredibly slowly. Soldiers could carry bricks well enough, but mixing mortar, laying a roof, even shoeing a horse was work they did not know. The agoge was producing crops of young men to rebuild the army, but those numbers were still small. It would be years before all the squalling babies filled the ranks. Pleistonax had come to that place out of weakness, not strength, for all he might wish for something different. Yet the Athenians too were hurting, or they would not have asked.

'You came to me, Archon Cimon,' Pleistonax prompted. 'If a truce is what you want, offer your terms. I will decide then whether to accept them or not. If not, I will ride home.'

He waited, still playing the part of the dominant party. He only hoped the Athenians had no idea how desperate he was. The offer of a truce was like an answer to prayers.

'I am sure Sparta will find other wars,' Cimon said, smiling tightly. 'Yet for us, it is a waste, of both blood and silver. We would like twenty years of peace, Majesty – an agreement between Sparta and Athens not to take the field of war against one another or any of our allies for that time. We stood against Persia as brothers in arms. We should be able to find peace between ourselves.'

Once again, Nicomedes cleared his throat into his fist. Pleistonax refused to look to him. The man had been regent for just a few years, but he had ideas above his authority.

Pleistonax considered. Twenty years of peace would mean Sparta had all the time they needed to rebuild. Yet he could hardly imagine so far into the future. He would be an old man, just about. Nor could he shake the sense that he was missing something. The Athenians had come to him, he reminded himself, not the other way around. They needed a truce at least as much as he did.

'We are at war, you and I,' Pleistonax said. 'I can ride from here and gather my army – the thousands who broke Persia at Plataea, not some small column like the one you encountered on the plain of Tanagra. I could march them to Athens and bring those walls of yours down.'

'No, Majesty,' Cimon said. He shook his head. 'I think if that were true, you would be there now.'

As he spoke, he tried to make his tone a little less harsh. Calling a Spartan king a liar to his face was not how he had intended the conversation to go. Yet he could not let the boy have it all his own way either.

'We'll see, won't we?' Pleistonax said, apparently unperturbed. The young man shrugged. 'Words mean little, Athenian. When I stand before your walls, you'll know.'

Cimon gathered his thoughts. He had not wanted to lay his entire offer on the table, but the young battle king was just about arrogant enough to call off the truce meeting then and there. In the last moment, he remembered not to begin with a low offer. The Spartans hated bargaining.

'I have been given authority to offer ten talents of silver as a show of goodwill,' Cimon said. He gestured to the cart behind him. 'For twenty years of peace that will benefit us both.'

The amount was huge, but Pleistonax only shrugged.

'Twenty years is too long. I won't pledge my entire reign – not for a hundred talents. No, this is my offer, Cimon. Take it or walk away, I care not. Five years of truce for ten talents. That is two talents a year in tribute to Sparta. Well?'

Cimon held still, thinking. It was much less than he had hoped, but he knew he would not get a better offer.

'Very well, Majesty. Five years. The silver is there, in the cart.' He smiled, relief bubbling up in him. 'I am pleased. It is the right decision.'

He put out his hand and Pleistonax took it in a crushing grip. Cimon saw his own satisfaction brought no corresponding joy to the two Spartans. Uncle and nephew glowered at the sight of Athenians pleased with themselves. For all he admired them, Cimon thought, they could be a bloody-minded race.

When the Athenians had bid them an awkward farewell, Pleistonax was left with his uncle and Dorion. It would be Dorion who rode the cart, with his friend's horse on a long rein. He had checked the contents in awe.

'It's all there,' Dorion said.

'Athenians think everything has a price,' Nicomedes said. It was an old saying, but in this case, it was true.

'You were clearing your throat, uncle,' Pleistonax said. 'Was five years correct?'

'I . . . think so, Majesty. It was your decision.'

'Good,' Pleistonax said. 'Because I will not wait that long. The moment we are ready, I will attack. They took my father from me, uncle. There is still a debt to repay.'

Ephialtes walked through the Agora, on his way home after a long day in council. The open market was even more crowded than usual and he had to pause a number of times to let someone past or prevent some group of gawkers knocking into him. It was impossible to think in such a place, especially when he heard his name whispered or saw fingers pointing. He was well known in the city. Some said he was first amongst them, though it depended whom you asked. The noble Eupatridae called him an upstart and a rabble-rouser, one more at home in the Assembly than in debates of the council. He smiled at the thought. That had the benefit of being true. He was a common man! He loved the people of Athens in a way those like Cimon or Myronides would never understand. How wonderful it was to live in the heart, where mere common men could banish archons and strategoi, the moment they became arrogant! There was nowhere like Athens in the world and he . . .

He paused as a group of metic merchants pushed through, forcing Ephialtes to stand back. They were all armed, he saw with irritation. They seemed to sleep six to a room in the centre of the city, transforming the peaceful heart he had known. Silver drew them, of course. The opportunity to earn more in a month than they could in a year at home. Perhaps, too, they came for the rule of law that protected them. Ephialtes had an idea how rare that was. If a Eupatridae son took another's wife, say, he would not be able to scorn the judgement of the Assembly. No, he would be taken up and fined, even banished or killed. No king's court, no Greek city, no Persian satrapy could say the same, not in all the world!

Lost in thought, Ephialtes did not see the man who moved to slip in behind him, appearing out of the crowd. The strategos felt a sudden pain under his arm and he gasped and pulled back. He'd cut himself on something or snagged a piece of skin on a passer-by. The pain was sharp but already fading as he turned to see what had caused it.

Attikos stood there, a red-bladed knife in his hand. The man grinned as if he was pleased to see him. He reeked of sour wine, Ephialtes thought, wrinkling his nose. For a moment, he didn't understand what had happened. Then his eyes widened.

'You're for the workers, are you?' Attikos said.

His voice was blurred and growling, drunk on something. Ephialtes pressed a hand to where he had felt the pain and looked at wet red fingers in astonishment. He still wore no knife of his own. Attikos began to laugh, but it was a cruel thing.

'What do you know of men like me?' Attikos growled at him.

He darted in again, jabbing the blade into Ephialtes' side. Someone shouted nearby and Ephialtes tried to fight. Attikos was wiry and impossibly strong. He had a hold of the strategos and he would not let go. Ephialtes rocked his head back with a huge blow, so that blood spattered. The knife slit air again, gashing the hand the strategos held up in defence. Ephialtes found his breathing was choking off and he began to panic, lashing out, desperate to kick away the one who clung to him. He felt the knife go in again and he fell.

Attikos was panting madly as he stood over the fallen strategos. He could hear people yelling for the damned guards. They would be coming quick for one who paid their wages, of course. Attikos sneered at the man on the ground. Champion of the people? Men like him didn't need champions. They needed bread and wine and a roof and a woman. They needed work and not to freeze in winter. They needed pride – and that was not the gift of another.

To Attikos' astonishment, a stranger grabbed his wrist, the one that still held the knife. Attikos punched him, cursing. Another stepped in, looking for all the world as if he thought he would restrain one who had been a hoplite and a rower. Attikos striped his face for him, a deep gash to remember the moment.

'Out of my way, lads,' he snarled at them. 'You don't want any part of me.'

He'd stayed too long, he realised, his thoughts fogged. Too much wine, too much satisfaction. They'd formed a ring around him and he could hear shouts and a clash of armour coming closer. He swore, lunging at some weak sod with eyes wide. The man went over with a shriek and Attikos stepped past him. He didn't feel the grip on his neck until he was yanked backwards. Attikos landed badly, scrambling to rise.

They came in then, kicking and stamping like he was a mad dog. The knife was knocked out of his hand, and though he tried to get to his feet, they were merciless, red-faced and roaring. He couldn't hear them after a time. He caught one glimpse of Scythian guards shouting and pushing men back. When they saw Ephialtes lay killed, when they understood Attikos had done it, they turned a cold gaze on him. The light blotted out as the crowd surged in again.

By the time it was over, there was blood across half the Agora, taken away in a thousand footprints – and at the centre, two bodies. Ephialtes lay sprawled, the big man looking as if he had chosen to lie down. The other was more meat and bone than man, trampled to glistening rags.

Those who had done it walked away rather than explain themselves, some fearing retribution. Yet Ephialtes had been loved in that place. No one chased them or called out. Justice had been done and the Scythian guards too had been part of it. For the first time in their careers, men patted them on the back as they passed by.

20

Cimon stood on the docks of the Piraeus, looking out over the sea, judging the movement of the triremes waiting for him. In that thoughtful gaze, Pericles knew he would be assessing the way each ship balanced the iron ingots along her inner keel, how well the oarsmen beat to hold them against the wind.

There had always been salt in Cimon's veins, Pericles thought. His family money had created the first Athenian fleet. Perhaps that was the reason. He had certainly never been as happy as when he was in formation with triremes, beating the sea white. Just standing in that place brought back memories of the tomb of Theseus and the bones of a king they had both brought home.

'There's a sight to lift the spirits,' Pericles said.

Cimon nodded, his attention drawn back from vast distances.

'They'll do. The Argos ships are well run. Winning a dozen of those for the fleet is more than I'd hoped. I'll run that Danaos ragged, of course, while his captains learn the signals. We are only as strong as our slowest ship. I learned that with Ephialtes.'

That name cast a gloomy shadow over them both. Cimon rubbed his jaw. It was bad luck even to mention the dead, never mind to speak badly of them. He was clearly searching for something good to say about a man he had detested all his life. Pericles broke in first.

'He is greatly missed in the Assembly, I can tell you that. His faction still see me as one of the noble class. Oh, they treat me with respect for now, but there are new young men, all jostling to lead them, to replace him.'

Cimon raised his eyes at the words.

'I know they loved him,' he said carefully. 'And I know he was a loss to you. I was sorry to hear.'

'Honestly, he was a good man, once he let you see past all the anger. More importantly, he could get things done. I wish I had him now, with all I need to do! I have the annual accounts to defend – Phidias needs funds for a statue of Athena in the Parthenon temple, which is costing more than I can possibly believe, by the way. I tell you, Cimon, take no risks on Cypros. Without you, I am alone.'

Cimon snorted.

'I've never known a man less alone! You have Anaxagoras and Zeno, Aeschylus, Phidias – that musician Damon, who follows you like a lost dog. Then there are the ones who come to Aspasia's gatherings. Like that lad who wouldn't leave my side until I had told him everything I remembered of Salamis! What was his name? Socrates. Talked as fast as Zeno, just about. You gather them, Pericles. Or they find you, perhaps. Still, I wouldn't change places. I have the League fleet – and I am content. It is enough for any man.'

Pericles grinned at his cheerful honesty.

'Don't lose any ships then, my friend. We need them – and you.'

Cimon frowned and Pericles realised he'd come close to making his friend promise something that was not in his power.

'There is always risk,' Cimon said softly. 'Especially at sea – especially at war.'

260

Once again, he glanced over the waves, judging the wind and the waiting ships. There was a boat coming, Pericles saw, with two oarsmen sweeping the waters. Cimon smiled, though it was with a touch of sadness.

'I've learned that much – and so have you. Just when you think we have found peace, the . . . Persians invade, or a good man is murdered on a dark street. Or one of the League of Delos decides they don't need our help, that we are tyrants! Peace is just an illusion, Pericles. Never forget that. Our fathers, you and I, we built Athens on struggle – and the struggle goes on. There will never be a time when we can sit and eat olives and say, "Thank the gods we came through." What would our sons do then?' He chuckled. 'It doesn't end, not when you have something to defend, something worth defending. You know what matters? Not safety, or peace. All that can vanish in an instant. Courage matters – that's what I tell my men. The ability to stand up when the storm comes howling in. That is in our gift, Pericles. We can control courage, after all. I cannot stop my enemies rising up, or illness, or the great gale that tears the roof from my home. I *can* choose how I respond. Bravery matters more than peace, every time.'

His boat bumped against the quayside and Cimon clapped his friend on the shoulder.

'Look after yourself, Pericles. I mean that. There are too many angry men in Athens at the moment. And without you, who would I come to when I need new ships and crews?'

'You'd petition the Assembly,' Pericles said.

He saw a quick flash of irritation cross Cimon's face. The act of being banished rankled with him still. He saw it as a betrayal or an ingratitude. It didn't sit well with him that he could devote his life to Athens, that they could use all he had to offer and then just throw him away. As a single drop of vinegar could spoil a cup of wine, being ostracised had stolen something good.

Cimon took Pericles' hand in a brief, dry grip and then began to climb down to his boat. Pericles could almost see the weight lifting from him as he took his seat and one of his men pushed the hull away from the stone dock.

When the boat reached the League flagship, his friend leaned on the upright prow. Oars were taken in as the breeze freshened. Orders were roared and sails rose on the mast. The ship lunged into motion as they snapped taut, going from a wallowing thing to a bird or a dolphin, cutting through. Pericles smiled at how Cimon's heart must have lifted in that moment. He hated to be still. Pericles sent a prayer to Poseidon and Athena to protect his friend while he moved over the deep waters – and that the Persians would not see him coming.

Xanthippus smiled at the moneylender. A talent of silver was a huge sum, as much as a strong man could carry. It was certainly not the kind of thing he wanted to stagger with through the streets. He was just pleased his new friends had agreed to help, especially Tolmides. He had been the one who said gaining his majority needed to be celebrated. That it was only right.

The moneylender was a small and careful man, nervous around the group, though Xanthippus had seen the pair of armed guards lurking in his shop. The silver had all been counted out, sitting in fat pouches on the desk. Tolmides had made a show of biting a few coins, making them all laugh. Xanthippus had laughed, anyway. Tolmides knew about things like that. It had been his idea to go to the moneylender in the first place.

Xanthippus looked blearily at the pouches. There had been at least thirty of them. He had passed some back to the others and now there were just six. Was that right? The moneylender seemed to think so. He was handing over his book, with the name of Pericles of Acamantis written on it. Xanthippus felt a moment of fear then, seeing his father's name written on parchment. He realised the man expected nothing more than a cross and a ring's seal by the name.

Xanthippus glanced back at the guards. He found they were watching, both of them. The idea of rushing out without putting his name may have occurred to other customers. He could see something like suspicion in the moneylender's face.

Xanthippus dipped the pen and scrawled his own name, taking the time to form each letter. There. He was no ill-educated man! He held up his father's ring. Xanthippus had found it in a drawer at the estate and pocketed it. Once more, he felt the pang of guilt and shook his head to clear it. Just wine fumes. He was eighteen years old! His father was away on some business of the Assembly, of course. Xanthippus suspected Pericles didn't even know it was his manhood day. The first his father learned of it would be when he saw his son in the Assembly.

The moneylender cleared his throat and Xanthippus blinked at him. What was . . . ? Ah. He took a stick of wax and held it in the flame of an oil lamp. It blackened and spat as he kept it there for too long, so that the moneylender began to reach for it.

'It's fine,' Xanthippus told him, his voice thick. A few

drops fell on the page before he reached the spot by his name, but it didn't matter. He pressed his ring into it, and if the image was a little blurred, it would do. His father owed him more than a single talent, after all. His mother had said so many times. Pericles kept them all on barely enough to live, while he lavished luxury on his fine new wife and son.

The moneylender looked sour as he examined the parchment.

'The interest is due on the quarter day, kurios.'

'You'll get it,' Xanthippus said with a wave of his hand. He had a memory of some plan to pay the first part from the talent he'd borrowed, but the man could howl for the money, as far as he was concerned. It didn't matter. What mattered was his friends and celebrating his majority.

When he turned back to them, it was Tolmides who raised a pouch of silver as if making a toast.

'To tonight, Xanthippus. To joining the Assembly – and our own group.'

Tolmides too had been drinking all evening and had vomited once already. He was glassy-eyed as he glared around at the little shop.

'We need a name, lads. What about "The Fine and the Good" – the youth of the Assembly?'

They liked that well enough. The sound they made had the moneylender ushering them all out of his shop and onto the street.

'Please, gentlemen, it is late. I have neighbours,' the man said. His guards allowed no discussion and moved them out.

Xanthippus grinned with his new friends as they staggered onto the cobbles. Tolmides swore and kicked at the closing door. He faced the group of young Athenians.

'That was well done, Xan. We have funds now. The Fine and the Good. Why not? We'll show them all, lads. We'll be the gale that blows those dusty old men away.'

The Assembly meeting had thinned as the day came to an end. Most of the votes had been for minor aspects of city business – trials for corruption, new licences granted, a corps of archers Pericles wanted funded from the treasury. None of those fired the blood, Xanthippus thought. His father looked rather weary as he rose to answer objections or to give an opinion at the request of the epistates. Yet he was the power there, without a doubt. With Ephialtes in a tomb and Cimon away on campaign, Pericles was first speaker in Athens, no matter who had been elected that day. It could be seen in the way most of the Assembly fell silent for him.

Not Tolmides though, Xanthippus noted. His friend was not cowed or intimidated. Instead, Tolmides spoke with gentle scorn and humour. Xanthippus watched his father forced to respond to Tolmides, enjoying seeing the two of them spar. He imagined they fought over him, and that gave him a sense of pride even though it was not true. Not that Tolmides didn't value him! He *listened*, whereas Pericles hardly seemed to know he existed. When Xanthippus had spoken for the first time to the Assembly, Pericles hadn't even looked up. His head had been down to peer at sheaves of parchment. He'd actually jumped slightly when the faction cheered, Xanthippus remembered. His father had looked confused for a moment, as if he had no idea why they might make such a raucous sound.

Tolmides sat down and the epistates inclined his head, giving Pericles another chance to answer if he chose to.

Xanthippus watched his father rise with an unblinking expression.

'Epistates, members of the Assembly, I must advise against responding to every call for help – especially from the Boeotian states to the north. With just a little more experience, I believe my new-fledged colleague Tolmides will learn how often we hear of skirmishes there. One year half a dozen small states are at war with one another, the next, an entirely different group. Those who were allies are suddenly at one another's throats, while bitter enemies have become friends. Not for nothing do we call those lands the dance floor of Ares! No, I have learned to be patient when they ask us to intervene. I advise the Assembly to let the dust settle, at least until Archon Cimon has returned with the main fleet.'

Pericles sat and Tolmides jumped up on the instant. Those who called themselves 'The Fine and the Good' raised his name and the epistates gave way with barely concealed irritation.

'Athens leads the League,' Tolmides said quickly. 'The treasury is here, but also the responsibility. My colleague speaks of states calling us, as if they are wayward children, doing neither them nor himself a service in that description.'

Xanthippus smiled as his father looked up, stung by the words. Tolmides was thirty years old and in his youthful prime. He did not look away, not even from the first man of Athens.

'If I cannot prevail on this Assembly to send a proper show of strength, I will ask for volunteers. Perhaps the young of Athens will answer a call to arms. Perhaps they can even lead, where old men cannot.'

His faction shouted approval and laughter as he sat down, Xanthippus among them. His father looked flushed as he stood once more.

'I have known strategoi like Aristides, Themistocles, my own father.' For an instant, Pericles glanced at his son. Xanthippus felt skewered by his disappointment. 'Not one of them ever wished to rush into battle. If it was forced upon them, they planned and learned all they could. Time solved some of the problems then, before they moved at all. I advise you to rely on that ancient teacher, Tolmides. The Boeotians will still be fighting one another in a year or two, if it remains your desire then to go out to them.'

Tolmides rose, yet he did not speak. Instead he looked around at the thousands who still sat or stood on the Pnyx hill, waiting to finish and go home, their duty done.

'I call for volunteers,' Tolmides said. 'For good men with spear and shield. Let them see Athens will respond, will lend her strength when they call.'

The cheer was louder than Xanthippus had expected. He looked over at his father and saw the man shake his head and mutter something to one of his friends, Zeno or ancient Aeschylus. They were an older generation, all of them. Tolmides was right. They had forgotten what it was to be young.

PART THREE

'While you remain at home, they are abroad. They think the further they go, the more they will win – while you think any movement will endanger what you already have.'

– Corinthian delegates addressing Spartans, attempting to explain the Athenians (Thucydides)

21

Cimon smiled. There were times in a man's life when he had to surrender to chaos, when he knew suddenly and with fear that he could not control his fate. This was not one of those times ... He realised he was in danger of arrogance and reached down to touch the wooden prow, muttering quick words of apology. The gods punished pride. It had always been a fine line to walk for a strategos of Athens. He had to plan and organise and train, of course, but he could never be too confident. If the stories of the gods taught men anything, it was not to predict the future.

Three hundred ships could surround the island of Cypros. Around half of them would never stop patrolling the coast, watching for an ambush or counter-strike. No sane man trusted Persia in those waters. The walls of cypress, oak and iron would be his shield, while Cimon landed a vast force. The League was many things – a trading alliance, even a nation, as some told it. First and foremost, it was a hammer. As the sun rose in the sky, Cimon brought it down.

Twenty-two Persian warships burned at anchor on the docks of Cypros. The oily black plumes were proof of League training and discipline. Eight of them had managed to cut ropes and get away from his boarding crews. One by one, they had been rammed by League ships waiting for them, lit by the dying flames of others.

There was always a cost to any action, Cimon reminded himself. To that point, his losses had been light. He squinted, his eyes infuriatingly weak over distance. He could make out the main shapes, but not the details of the assault. For those, he had a young hoplite murmur a description for him. As Cimon listened, he prayed for the souls of the boat crews caught and killed on the enemy decks, cut down in the act of setting fires.

All along that bay on the coast of Cypros, League crews had beached their ships. As Cimon watched, hoplites poured out to stand in ranks, gleaming in the morning sun. His heart swelled at the sight. They had no way of knowing how many Persians lay waiting for them. The Persian fleet may have been small in comparison, but who could say how many they had ferried out in the months since first landing? Cimon found he was rubbing thumb and forefinger together, the skin damp. Persia could never be discounted in war. The Great King's resources were just too vast. Compared to that empire, Cimon had to account for every oar and coin spent, all while patrolling an entire sea. This new king, Artaxerxes, the one they called 'Longhand', he could be the spear if he chose. A man might sport a good shield and chestplate, but a single spear could still punch through, with enough force behind it.

A throat was cleared and he looked round.

'It is time, navarch,' the trierarch of his flagship said.

Cimon turned from his vigil at the prow and the man dropped to one knee, head bowed for the solemnity of the moment. That simple action restored Cimon's calm as he climbed down wooden rungs and stepped into his boat. The League trained and sailed and rowed together. Six thousand of his best men were forming on the shore ahead, phalanx upon phalanx. He told himself his nagging doubts were just the caution of any senior officer sending men to fight. A good commander accepted that weight on his shoulders. He appointed men of skill and experience, of course – six strategoi and hundreds of lochagoi to keep discipline. Yet it didn't change the burden he had to carry. Cimon was responsible. He was certainly the one the Assembly would crush if he failed.

As he wrapped his cloak against the sea spray, Cimon shook his head, casting off worry. It even worked, for a few moments. The sky was clear and the morning was warm. The hills of the island were in full bloom, with patches of red and gold.

His men rowed him in, finding a clear spot on the beach where two of his strategoi waited. They had watched for him to leave his flagship, of course. Cimon jumped over the side as soon as the keel rasped on sand. The waters were already cloudy from so many others doing the same, with brown fronds curling. Cimon staggered for a step and one of the strategoi took his arm. It would not be a good omen for the League navarch to fall, not then.

'Thank you. I have it,' Cimon said.

The man removed his hand and once again Cimon was ashore, standing on Cypros. Around him, lines of hoplites were ready to march, eight deep, facing forward. Voices still called somewhere close, dozens of them. It was not silent, but rather a living scene with ordinary men and kit and weapons of iron.

A horse had been brought up for him, held by a young groom. He stood ready, but Cimon felt the land under him and waved him back. Perhaps the spirit of Ephialtes spoke to him then. He made the decision to walk with the men for a time, seeing the world as they did.

Cimon glanced out to his ships. Some had anchored in that shallow sea, while others rowed or sailed beyond, blurred by distance. The island of Cypros was locked down. He murmured an order to the closest strategos. In turn, the man signalled a dozen horn-bearers.

Long notes sounded. Like a sword slowly drawn, six thousand armoured hoplites began to move. They had stood with stern expressions on the shore, knowing why they were there. Just taking a step forward eased some of the tension. They knew what they had to do. Some glowered as they marched. Others chatted to their mates in line, easing nerves or just ignoring whatever Fate had in store.

Cimon accepted his shield from another officer, adjusting it on his arm. From old instinct, he drew his kopis, the blade as long as his forearm. Not that a navarch would be expected to fight, he reminded himself. He knew he would be better off putting it away. Someone had to keep a clear head when all the rest was lost in sound and blood. The days of racing along corridors with Pericles at his side had surely passed. He grimaced at the thought. His knees ached, his right one in particular. He'd broken a bone in his heel years before, and though it had healed well enough at the time, the thing had recently begun to hurt again, with every step. Still, he was there to command strategoi and men in battle. He was there because he knew Persian tactics and how to counter them – and because Cypros was huge and valuable, as a base, as land for his people.

The scouts had gone ahead on foot, without armour. They were Cimon's eyes, more valuable in that moment than any other part of his forces. They had loped off even while the troop ships were landing, seeking out anything like high ground to let them see what lay before them. Cimon caught his breath as he noticed three of them returning. They had gone to seek the enemy. If they were coming back, it could only mean they had found him.

As he shaded his eyes, he saw the one in the lead was being chased by the other two. The Greek was scrambling down a low hill and those behind . . . Cimon blinked. The Persians had their own scouts out. Those two were intent on catching his man.

Even as he understood what he was seeing, one of the Persians drew a short bow from a case across his shoulders. All three kept running as he strung the thing and drew an arrow from the same slim shape. Cimon could only watch as the Persian scouts suddenly halted. His scout was waving his arms madly as he ran, pointing back. To the ones following him? In warning? Cimon could not tell. The young Greek was too far off to hear what he was shouting. All Cimon could do was watch as the Persians sent an arrow after him.

His man had opened a decent gap as they halted. For a moment, Cimon thought he would make it out of range. Some of the ranks at the front were yelling encouragement or warning, but the young man thought he was safe. As he reached their lines, an arrow took him between the shoulder blades. He skidded onto his knees, his face astonished. In response, the first ranks roared challenge as they passed by, swallowing him up.

Cimon felt sweat sting his eyes. He turned to the closest strategos.

'How many scouts did we send out?'

'Twelve, kurios,' the man replied.

Cimon swore under his breath. The two Persians decided not to face the hoplites raising spears at them. They turned and jogged back over the hill, but they had accomplished their intention. Whatever the scout had learned was lost.

Cimon suddenly felt afraid, blind as his men moved inland. For all the size and strength he had brought to Cypros, the island dwarfed them all.

He had landed close to where the Persians had built a fortress decades before. He'd thought that place might be the heart of a Persian position. Instead, he and his men had marched past broken walls and abandoned yards, leaving it all behind. He'd given orders for them to be ready, but there was no one hiding in those ruins. Beyond that place, the blue sea became glittering grey behind. The ground had sloped up for another hour and he'd begun to wonder if he would cross the entire island without seeing the enemy.

Ahead, he saw a commotion in the ranks. Cimon hadn't seen a second scout arrive, but the man was passed back, two hoplites taking his arms on their shoulders and bearing him to the navarch at such speed his feet barely touched the ground.

Cimon saw this man too had been injured. Blood stained the scout's tunic and he was gasping. Cimon raised his hand and the order to halt rang out. The League force crashed to a stop in three paces. Hundreds took the moment to adjust some part of their kit that had been chafing. Others stole a quick drink from leather flasks or put a piece of dried meat into a cheek to soften and give them strength.

'Report,' the closest strategos growled to the scout. There was no time for concern for his wound.

'Their camp is barely an hour ahead, kurios,' the scout said. 'They have archers, cavalry, spears and armour.'

Cimon could see the scout was drifting in and out. He wanted to grab him and shake the words free, like dried peas from a pot.

'How many?' Cimon asked. Everyone in range craned to hear the reply, the words that would mean whether they lived or died – or fought at all.

'Kurios . . . as many as us, with a thousand archers and around a thousand horse.'

Cimon swallowed. The scouts were trained to judge such things. Yet if he was right, perhaps the best thing to do was return to the fleet and turn out the rowers and the remaining hoplites. Unless this was a diversion, of course. As the others waited, he made himself think it through. If he stripped the fleet and left it vulnerable, a dozen Persian warships launching from the coast could tear the heart out of the League.

Cimon felt the others looking to him and kept his expression stern while he considered. They needed him to have the answers at his fingertips, to know instantly what to do. That was the burden his father had known – a life that ended in destruction and disgrace.

Go forward or go back. It was the simplest decision in the world, and yet he felt his heart pounding and his breath fast and shallow. Cimon nodded to the nearest man. Danaos of Argos, he recalled. Uncomplaining. Good fellow.

'Navarch?' the strategos said.

'Onward,' Cimon replied. It was right. He felt relief wash

across him. 'We came here to engage a Persian force – and we have found one. Send out more scouts.'

'Have you *any idea what your son has done*?' Pericles shouted. 'To my *name* in this city?' His ex-wife looked pale and worried, as well she might. It didn't help that he stood in his father's old town-house in the centre of the city. Pericles had called it home for a time, before the divorce. Everywhere he looked, memories tugged at him, sending his thoughts skittering back to happier times.

He'd come into that house like an invasion, pushing back the servant who opened the door and calling for Thetis or Xanthippus to come out and face him. Neither of his sons was home, which might have been a blessing as he could just about have strangled the older one.

'He is your son as well, Pericles,' Thetis said, coldly. 'And no, I don't know what you mean or why you have come barging in here. This is my home, not yours! You have no right to push your way in. Should I call for help? How would it suit your precious family name if I did that? Or will you sit down and stop baring your teeth like some castrated hound?'

The threat of Thetis wailing for help in the street was enough to bring him back to his senses. He ignored her description of him. She had always been good at seeding little phrases here and there as they argued, like wasp stings. They were never mortal wounds, but she knew how to hurt. He took a seat in the hall by the door, suddenly unwilling to come any further into a house he had loved.

'Xanthippus put my name to a talent of silver,' he said. 'A full talent! I don't suppose I would know even now if he hadn't gone off on that ridiculous expedition with his friends. The quarter day was three days ago, and of course he is not here, so the moneylender came to me.'

Thetis shrugged, though her colour deepened. He was not certain she had known, but she raised her chin, ready to defend her son even so.

'Was it so wrong?' she said. 'You've given us barely enough to live, Pericles. Perhaps Xan wanted to take some part of his inheritance early.'

Pericles blinked, appalled.

'He *stole* a talent of silver, using my name, Thetis! I could have him taken up by the guards and put to trial on his return. In fact, I will! That is exactly what I will do. If it was anyone else, if he were not my son, that's what would happen. Why should I hold Xanthippus to a lesser stand-ard? He'll be given a chance to pay it back and if he can't, he will sit in council cells until it is repaid. Or perhaps he will be banished, as my father was.'

'Xanthippus is eighteen, Pericles – and your first-born. You wouldn't dare.'

'Wouldn't I? He needs to be taught a lesson before he ruins my name in this city. No, I think that is the right thing to do. If I bring the charges myself, they'll see I had no part in it. He'll be wrenched away from his friends as well. You should see them in the Assembly! Preening cock-erels, all of them, with that damned fool Tolmides at the heart . . .'

'Enough! Stop talking!' Thetis snapped. 'You know very well you will not be bringing charges against your own son.'

'It is my duty,' Pericles said.

Thetis paled at his tone, understanding he was serious.

'Then you know what will happen. Not only will you

destroy what little respect Xanthippus has for you, but this house is his only possession. Or have you forgotten the terms of the divorce? He will have to sell it to clear the debt, and he and I will be on the street with Paralus – all because you can't forgive! It's not like you have been a father to him, Pericles! Why should Xanthippus or Paralus be filled with love and respect for you? All your attention has been on your *new* wife, your *new* son. That little boy knows you as his father. Xanthippus does not. Look to your own failings if you want to know how this happened!'

She was facing him as he sat there, both of them red-faced and breathing hard. It reminded him of the worst days of their marriage. With an effort, Pericles made himself calm. Thetis was a mother, trying to protect her son from his father's wrath. There was courage in that.

'He stole a fortune, Thetis,' he said more softly. 'And used my name to do it. How did he think it could possibly work? Can he not see ahead to the consequences of his actions? Is the boy so stupid?'

'He *doesn't* think!' Thetis almost growled. 'Perhaps if you had taken the time to teach him, as your father taught you, he might have learned to. He might be more of a leader than he is, less of a follower. There, that's the truth. He's not you, Pericles, though he wants to be, more desperately than you know. He's not your father either. He's angry and loud, and if you'd heard the things he has said to me, well . . . I'm glad you haven't. He follows that Tolmides around, hanging on his words . . .'

To Pericles' confusion, Thetis began to weep, pressing one hand over her eyes so he would not see. He frowned in response. He didn't trust her displays. She wanted to keep her house and her son out of the courts. He bit his lower lip as he decided.

'Perhaps he can work it off,' he said at last. 'The fences of the estate need to be replaced. That will keep him out of mischief for a month or so when he returns. I need someone to oversee the potteries after that. Yes, that will be good for him. He'll see how men have to work for the silver they earn. I'll pay him something, but the rest will go to repay his debt.'

'Thank you, Pericles,' she said, dabbing red and swollen features. 'I only wanted you to see sense. He's still your son.'

Pericles sat back in relief. His anger had gone, he realised. Perhaps it was because he could go from there and walk back to Aspasia and a little boy who beamed when his father entered the room, toddling over to him on unsteady legs. Life was simpler at that age, he thought.

'Do you know when he is coming back?' Thetis asked.

She still dabbed at her eyes, though they were dry. He wondered if she thought it was attractive.

'Those fools? In a month or so, I would imagine. Do you know what they call themselves, that faction? "The Good and the True", or something. Even before this business with the moneylender, I was going to say something to you about them. They dress alike, Thetis. Xan has taken to wearing a white robe trimmed in red along the edges. Honestly, I am embarrassed for him. It's time someone told him about influence and how it looks to have a son of mine . . .'

'It's not all about you,' Thetis said, her voice hardening again. She put down the cloth and glared at him. 'I don't much like the hold Tolmides has over him, but what can I do? What young man of that age listens to his mother?

And his father is nowhere to be found. What is it, a year since you spoke to him? If Xan hadn't taken that silver, would you be here now? I don't think you would. He admires you, you know. Above all other men, but you won't even look at him. Did you congratulate him on speaking in the Assembly?'

Pericles chewed his lip once more in thought. He remembered how annoyed he'd been to have Xanthippus clapped on the back by Tolmides and his faction, as if he'd scored a rare victory instead of making some minor speech on the election of magistrates. It hadn't even come to a vote. Pericles shook his head and Thetis sighed, shaking her head.

'He was delighted when he heard you would be there, did you know? He could hardly sit down as he practised the speech he would give. I must have heard it a dozen times.'

'I see,' Pericles said. Guilt was unpleasant, a sense of sickness deep in his gut. He could not put right what he had done wrong, he reminded himself. He *could* put Xanthippus to work. Perhaps he would even fix the fences with him, teaching him how to bind and nail and shape the wood. Or perhaps . . . The city needed a commander of archers on the Long Walls. That would be a position with some authority. He felt his mood lighten.

'When he comes home, I'll do something about it,' Pericles said.

Thetis nodded and in that moment there was something like peace between them.

'Where is Paralus?' he said.

Thetis pursed her mouth.

'I am not a jailer, Pericles. I imagine he is with his friends.'

He rose to his feet. There had been something evasive about her expression and he hesitated. Pericles wasn't sure if he wanted to push for an answer, but he hated it when she looked shifty and uncomfortable.

'Tell me!' he ordered, all his anger coming back in a rush. She winced at his tone, but her shoulders dropped. She could not look at him as she answered.

'He is with Xanthippus. They went out together.'

'He's not ready.'

'He's seventeen,' she replied, her face crumpling. 'Xan will keep him safe.'

'I pray you are right,' Pericles said coldly.

He left that house and stood in the street for a moment, clenching and unclenching his hands. Both his sons had gone to prove their courage. He understood that completely, but he could not escape the coldness in his gut, the sense of fear for them. They were not his father. They were not him. They were just boys.

22

Tolmides marched with his Athenian volunteers along a road in Boeotia – he wasn't sure exactly where he was, though the city of Thebes was said to be somewhere close. Of course, they would close their gates at sunset. No one would be allowed to enter after that, no matter how noble the cause. He scowled at the thought. His water was all gone and the Volunteers were dry-mouthed and gasping after a long day in the sun. At least that heat was fading as evening came.

He frowned at the horizon, realising it was later than he thought. Even if Thebes had been visible, they'd never reach it before dark. He was looking at another uncomfortable night outside, denied food and shelter. Denied the welcome he deserved.

Six hundred boys and men had come with him to settle the Boeotian dispute. A week's march north out of Athens, it felt almost as if they were following a storm, seeing only the destruction it left in its wake. The fighting had been savage, that was clear. Day after day, the young Athenians found burned villages, even a town where the gates hung open and bodies still lay in the streets. The flies and the smell seemed to follow them.

Tolmides and the others had surprised a young female lioness as she crouched over a dead child in the sacked town – and lost three companions to her claws and teeth before they drove her away. He had ordered graves dug for the ones they had lost, though the ground was dry and it was much harder work than anyone had expected. After that, when they saw crows circling, he ordered them to take a wide berth.

Tolmides was the most experienced. He at least had fought at Eurymedon, under Cimon. In the first evenings, Tolmides told the others stories of Persians, painting scenes of horror and outrage. Even those who had no direct experience of war knew the tales of Theseus or the other Argonauts. Like those, his Volunteers were strong and fit and bright with youth, ready to carve their own tales into the land. More importantly, they were Athenian, with all the authority that granted them. The League stood for something, but as Tolmides said, it had to be defended, by sweat and sacrifice.

Tolmides had allowed only those with shields and armour to come. They were the sons of Eupatridae families for the most part, young men reaching their majority like Xanthippus, or a few dozen who had lied about their age. Those fresh-faced boys strolled with them – heroes like Paralus, who walked with his brother. Tolmides had complimented the younger son of Pericles on his courage until he was blushing and overcome.

The road they followed was a track that led between rising cliffs of purple stone on either side, bare enough with just a few bushes on the flanks. Perhaps it was the path of some ancient river, or some mark of the gods, Tolmides didn't know. He didn't much like the look of the stone flanks, but the path led through. He was aware too of flasks tipped up around him, dry tongues hoping for some last drop.

He pretended not to hear when Xanthippus murmured

they really should find water. As if he didn't know! Tolmides had praised both sons of Pericles to the others. That was what a leader did, he thought. More importantly, it gave him something like status over them. As the one who clapped them on the shoulder and said how proud he was, Tolmides raised himself up.

Of course, he also needed them. Xanthippus had funded the new faction in the Assembly, buying their robes, parchment, anything they wanted. His name too was valuable when it came to impressing the younger ones. Yet he and Paralus were like puppies, so full of enthusiasm and bubbling ideas that it was all Tolmides could do not to punch one of them in the face. He didn't, of course. A Eupatridae family like that had power and authority. The name alone could persuade men to follow who would have scorned silver. It could . . .

Tolmides looked ahead. Something had moved, he was certain. Beyond the cleft in the hills, a copse of trees prevented him seeing further, even as the light failed and grew shadows. It was still some way off, but he had caught a flicker where there should have been only stillness. Dark-winged birds circled above those trees and he tried to remember if that was a good sign or not. Did such creatures seek out safe harbour in the evening gloom? Or were they drawn to carrion? He'd heard birds could learn to follow armies. Men marched with crows, in those lands.

Tolmides held up a fist and his little column halted. The light was dying and it seemed colder already. He cursed under his breath. A hundred voices started to ask why they had stopped and he could not roar at them to be quiet, not when he thought an enemy might be close by.

He needed scouts, he thought, someone to spring the trap, if it was a trap. No, it was better not to think of such things. Whoever he sent would find just an empty ridge and city walls in the distance, perhaps even kept open so they could eat and rest in safety. His stomach creaked at the thought. Thirst was a greater torment, but they had also eaten the last of the dried meat. Tolmides had no supply carts trundling along behind their little force. He'd thought it wouldn't matter in that region of Greece. In Athens, men called it the breadbasket! Yet the Volunteers had been on short rations and were growing thinner every day. Tolmides hadn't thought hunger would be such a part of the war experience. When he'd marched with Cimon, there had always been a stew of beans, cheese, wine and oats, every morning and evening. It had seemed the natural order almost, reliable as the rising sun. His stomach groaned again at the memory.

He saw Xanthippus bend to speak to his younger brother. It was Paralus who approached Tolmides then, head slightly tilted as he prepared to ask why they had stopped. Paralus was nervous in his presence, Tolmides realised. He found himself annoyed with both of them. It should have been Xanthippus who came over. Paralus didn't even bow as Tolmides ignored him. The young man stood awkwardly, unsure how to interrupt the strategos while he stared into the distance.

Tolmides kept him waiting, then spoke as Paralus scraped his boot on the ground, readying himself to break the silence.

'I thought I saw something over there,' Tolmides said. 'The light is going now, but I saw ... I don't know. In those trees. I need someone to scout. I was going to send one of the young ones, but with darkness coming, I need someone sensible, who won't go imagining things.'

'I'll do it,' Paralus said.

Tolmides nodded grudgingly, as if it had just occurred to him.

'Then pass your shield to Aeneas here.' He saw Paralus begin to object and spoke over him. 'Just while you are gone. You'll get it back.'

Paralus did as he was told, reluctance in every movement. He glared at the lad who followed Tolmides, his current favourite.

'I want that back,' Paralus murmured to him.

Aeneas was barely fifteen and he shrugged in reply. His worship was all for Tolmides, no one else.

'Helmet too,' Tolmides said.

'It wouldn't fit him,' Paralus replied, edging away.

Tolmides was on the point of enforcing the order when Xanthippus appeared at his brother's shoulder.

'What's going on?' Xanthippus said.

Though he was a dozen years younger than Tolmides, there was still something of his father in that tone, a hint of the authority that would surely grow in him. Tolmides half-turned to reply, though he had wanted to ignore Xanthippus and so punish him for sending his brother in his place.

'I have ordered your brother to scout ahead,' he said stiffly.

'Tolmides saw something on the hill,' Paralus added eagerly. 'I'm going up there to see if there's anyone on the ridge.'

Of *course* he would answer his brother, Tolmides thought in irritation. More annoying was that Paralus had failed to use his proper title. The Assembly hadn't actually appointed him formally as one of the strategoi, but as leader of the Volunteers, Tolmides had claimed it for himself – and they had all agreed. It was an insult now not to use it. He needed to remind Paralus who it was that actually led their force.

Xanthippus was squinting at the ridge, shading his eyes with one hand. He spoke before Tolmides could find the right words to put the brothers in their place.

'If there's someone waiting, they'll be watching right now, wondering why we're just standing here,' he said. He bit one lip, thinking. Tolmides didn't want to interrupt. 'The trees *are* thick enough. They could hide an army in there if they were serious about it. What is the plan, Tolmides?'

'What do you mean? Speak clearly,' Tolmides snapped. He saw Xanthippus frown as if the answer had somehow been surprising. When the young man spoke again, it was slow and measured.

'You said my brother should go forward and scout the position, but what then? What if he brings a host of raiders out after him? I don't like the idea of Paralus just wandering up and trying to count them! We need to decide now whether we'll attack or retreat. It's not far from being too dark to see, never mind fight.'

'There may be nobody there at all,' Tolmides said coldly. 'But if there is, we'll engage them – and defeat them.'

In the distance, they all heard a horse whinnying, unmistakably. The sound would have been lost in the noise of a marching column. Yet because they all stood still, they heard it. Xanthippus and Paralus turned to the ridge, listening intently. After a long breath of silence, it came again.

'Horsemen,' Xanthippus said. 'Pray it's just a few herders and not . . .'

He broke off. The trees on the ridge erupted, leaves flung into the air as a stream of armoured soldiers galloped into the open.

'Orders, strategos?' Xanthippus said.

Tolmides gaped at him. He had no idea how to fight men on horseback. They were the bane of foot soldiers everywhere. Tolmides shook his head, wordlessly.

'They are engaging, strategos,' Xanthippus said. The whites of his eyes were showing and his voice was tight. 'May I suggest a shield line in their path?'

'Yes! Shield line. Spears ready!'

Tolmides looked to see Paralus wrenching his shield back from Aeneas. The enemy riders were still pouring out as he stared, his heart thudding and his bladder squeezing tight. His own eyes had saved them from the trap, he reminded himself.

'They'll circle us,' Xanthippus said suddenly. He had to be just as nervous, though he seemed to have taken a grip on his emotion. 'We could back up against the rock face. That would give us a flank they can't get round, unless they drop stones from above.'

'Unless they *what*?' Tolmides asked in confusion.

His thoughts seemed to be moving slowly. The riders were thundering towards them and Xanthippus was calmly discussing their choices! Tolmides could see dust shimmering on the ground like an earthquake. He watched as the Volunteers tried to lock shields, but they had no experienced officers and they were afraid, fumbling spears so that they clacked together. Half of them wanted to run, edging back in terror. The rest were roaring at those, telling them they had to stand, had to raise their shields and spears and *stand still*, or they were all dead.

Tolmides pushed his helmet down, feeling the bristles of the crest crush under his fingers.

'We'll hold here,' he replied. Xanthippus glanced at his brother and Tolmides made it an order. 'Hold! Spears and shields ready!'

'We can't hold a position in the open, not against horsemen,' Xanthippus said quietly. He raised his voice then to growl at his brother.

'Paralus! Don't gape. Shield up. Stand by me.'

The riders were almost on them and Tolmides could not tear his gaze away. The enemy had bows, he realised in horror. They were bending arms back and aiming as they rode, sending arrows whirring through the air at his people. Others raised their arms overhead, using the terrifying speed of the gallop to launch spears. He'd always hated horses, Tolmides thought. They had seen his crest, of course, understood what it meant. Half a dozen shadows sliced the air towards him. He caught a glimpse of Xanthippus and Paralus, crouched behind their overlapping shields. Tolmides could only stand there.

Three of the spears struck him in the same moment. Tolmides was knocked backwards, sending his own men tumbling and crying out in shock. He could not speak; there was blood in his mouth. He died as he struggled to get back up, rolling onto one side while the veterans of Boeotia began to slaughter his brave lads.

Xanthippus grabbed his brother by the neck, dragging him to his right.

'Keep your shield up,' he grunted.

His brother cast one appalled look back to the figure of Tolmides, broken and half-rolled onto his side. There was one spear through his chest and another through his right arm. Blood was still spilling onto the dusty road, but Xanthippus was dragging Paralus away. More spears and arrows flew, cracking against the shields and helmets of those who clustered in panic.

There was no proper shield line, not after the first moments of chaos. Xanthippus barked a stream of orders in the voice he could make carry. The Volunteers heard and formed around that voice – a moving, straining clot of men with shields raised on the outside. The horsemen were hampered only by the lack of light as they rode around the group, sending arrows and spears darting in. Nor were they silent. Enemy riders roared and screeched even over the noise of hooves, making themselves a storm.

The Athenian Volunteers were desperate. They were jammed together, but they were inexperienced and afraid, beset on all sides. Each passing moment whittled a few away, so that the night was filled with terror.

Xanthippus held his shield over his brother. He and Paralus were in the centre of the moving formation. It meant Paralus had to hold his spear upright as the pair were shoved and battered in the gloom. Xanthippus took another deep breath, summoning the voice his father used when he was enraged.

'Phalanx!' he roared over their heads. The word was too generous, but it was the one he knew. 'Phalanx! Ease . . . right! Forty paces to the cliff. *Right*, I said! Stop panicking and open your ears! Ease right – until you feel the rock face on your shoulder. Sing out then and let the rest of us know.'

He almost sobbed when the entire force stepped in the same direction. Night had stolen upon them and he felt blind and afraid until his eyes began to adjust. He felt rather than saw the flank of Volunteers reach the cliff. They had listened – and the result was that the horsemen could no longer circle them and keep them pinned.

Xanthippus could hear cries of pain and shock on all sides. Some of the wounded had been carried along, though they were bleeding or dying as they stood there. He had the sudden thought that there was no way out from that place, no safe haven. They would all be cut down without even knowing the identity of their attacker. Just one more small, forgotten column, torn to pieces in a border war.

'What now?' Paralus shouted.

Pale faces turned to hear the answer. Xanthippus swallowed.

'Keep the shields locked! Hoplite crouch – nice and low. We can defend three sides till morning. Spears ready. If anyone comes in range, they get one in the guts.'

He saw spears jabbing out between the shields as panic eased in them. They made a crude formation with shields in a ring and the cliff at their back. Yet they were reduced. A trail of dark bodies marked the path they had crossed, hundreds of them. Xanthippus had not understood how efficient the slaughter had been until that moment, in the stillness and the dark. Over half their number had been cut down.

The horsemen understood the change. The Volunteers watched them dismount and form their own lines. They outnumbered the battered force of young men and Xanthippus could only watch in sick dismay as veteran hoplites put on helmets and drew swords, clashing them against shields to terrify.

'Spears ready!' Xanthippus roared across his people.

The enemy were so many! He would die in that place and all he could think was that Paralus would die as well. He had brought his younger brother with him and got him killed. His father would be furious, he thought.

'I'm sorry,' he said to Paralus.

His brother didn't reply. At least he looked like a hoplite, perhaps a little smaller than the rest. Paralus lowered his head so that the rim of his shield hid his mouth and chin. Xanthippus clapped him on the shoulder.

The Boeotians were experienced. They did not throw away a single life, but came in with measured tread and shields raised high. The difference in experience showed from the first moments. They cut through the Volunteers, hacking spears aside. Someone on the far side staged a sudden charge, as if wild courage would make a difference. Perhaps a hundred of them left the cliff wall. They were surrounded and cut to pieces.

Xanthippus had been trained by his father, and yet the darkness almost did for him. He could hardly see the enemy crowding him, barely avoided losing his arm. His counterstrike surprised the Boeotian in turn, catching the edge of a throat and ripping life away. Xanthippus squinted, hating to die in the dark, wishing Tolmides could have lived a little longer to see what he had brought about.

A dark shape loomed, snorting and knocking Xanthippus back. One of the horses had lost its rider and was panicking in the crush. Xanthippus drew in a sharp breath. He had ridden from his youngest years and he felt for reins in the dark, his touch soothing the animal. He knew these beasts. Just that great presence brought forth words he had known as a child, soothing its fear. Someone came at him in the dark and Xanthippus kicked out, hearing a stifled cry of pain. Bronze greaves could be weapons, for those who didn't mind denting them.

He moved, almost without thought. In the space of a heartbeat, he gripped the horse's mane and leaped onto its back. In that moment, he went from lost and alone in the dark to above it all, surrounded by a dying sea. He looked to where his brother had stood and saw someone fall there, smashed from his feet by a Boeotian shield.

Xanthippus dug in his heels, sending the startled animal forward against its will. The man who had knocked his brother down was raising a sword to plunge it into his chest when Xanthippus drew level and kicked him in the head. He'd broken toes, he was sure of it. Xanthippus looked down at Paralus under starlight, putting out his hand.

His younger brother reached up, his expression one of awe. He had looked death in the face and, in that moment of clarity, Xanthippus was suddenly there instead, on a horse the colour of night.

Xanthippus heaved his brother up behind him and wrenched the animal around. The column of Volunteers they had brought to that place had been reduced to just a few. Xanthippus realised the only reason he was free was because the enemy assumed he was one of their own. Slowly, he turned the horse's head from the fighting.

'Nice and quiet now, Paralus,' he murmured.

His brother was panting or sobbing, he didn't know which it was.

'They'll kill us . . .' Paralus whispered.

'Perhaps they will. They'll have to catch us first,' his brother replied.

He walked the horse south for a hundred paces, then another hundred. The enemy were looting by then, stripping bodies, despatching the wounded. Those boys had all been the sons of wealthy families, Xanthippus recalled. Their kit alone would be worth a fortune. More importantly, the Boeotians weren't looking for a single pair on horseback, riding slowly away. Most men couldn't ride, after all.

Xanthippus looked back when he heard a voice call a question after him.

'That's it. Hold on now,' he said.

He kicked in his heels and the wind built to a howl in their ears as the horse galloped away, allowed to run at last.

23

The Persian king was on the field. Cimon knew enough of their ways to understand no mere general would be seated in a pavilion like that one, high on a ridge, guarded by a thousand Immortals in white panelled coats. Artaxerxes had made himself comfortable, as was his right. He had chosen the field of battle, after all.

Years before, Cimon had faced huge numbers of ordinary Persian soldiers dressed as that elite regiment. His hoplites had been impressed, right up to the moment they'd started to batter them. The qualities of an elite force did not lie in a coat or a banner, or even a name. Cimon smiled, but it was a cold expression, born of too many years of war. It lay in the training they endured and the weapons they learned to use, for so many hours they could change formation or strike positions in their sleep. If those things were in place, they *might* then be sharpened and forged into something great – as the Spartans had done. Cimon shook his head. He was navarch of the League, with Athenians at the heart of his army. All his men needed was around four hundred years of never losing a battle.

The Persian position was not an ambush, not in the sense that it depended on surprise. Cimon suspected this king, Artaxerxes, son of Xerxes, the one they called Longhand, had known the Greeks would respond and simply prepared for their attack. How long had he had? Cimon had moved quickly enough to answer the reports from

Cypros. Perhaps he had interrupted the ferrying of Persian soldiers from the mainland to the island. He hoped so. The alternative was that the king had exactly as many men as he needed and had simply been waiting for Cimon to land.

Cimon felt his right knee begin to ache and muttered a curse. He had brought horses on board the flagship, walking them down long gangplanks to the shore. That had been good sense for a navarch whose knee might give out. It was harder to explain why he still walked alongside his men.

Cimon reached down to rub the sore joint. It felt as if a small stone had lodged within, fine for just long enough to forget it, then catching him by surprise with a sudden jab of pain. He glanced back to the horse his groom walked for him. There would be a moment to mount once again. He merely had to endure, until all the men knew he stood with them. They appreciated such things, he thought. Not all of them, but enough.

Of course, his own honour guard of thirty men surrounded him, marking him out in the hoplite lines. Beyond those, a dozen runners waited to pelt away with new orders, whatever they would be. Such things were necessities of command. The Persian king was literally above the fray, removed from the dirt and blood and stench. Cimon felt a touch of pride then. He was down in the fight, with strategoi and lochagoi, with all the men who looked to him. He wondered if the new Great King of Persia had any battle honours to his name. He hoped not. Men carried such things to battle like an incantation. They found endurance in . . . He grimaced as his knee jolted, catching his breath. At least the heel bone had gone quiet. Cimon had felt that happen before, when aches from old wounds just drifted away in the moments before a fight. It was a gift of Ares, so it was said. The god of war loved his servants well. Of course, all the old pains came back threefold in the evening, when a man could hardly bend a swollen joint or move his sword arm. There was always a cost in battle, even for those who survived. Cimon glanced back at his horse once more.

Ahead, the lines clashed in a blur of metal. The forces of Persia and the League began shedding one another's blood. Cimon might even have complimented Artaxerxes on his choice of ground. It was flat and firm underfoot, on a dry day, with a broad blue sky overhead. Something touched his skin and he smeared it with a thumb. A drop of red life, flung from a few paces ahead. He could see them all, heaving, savage and relentless. This was the good time, the best time – before they felt tiredness creeping in to make them afraid.

Cimon had chosen a depth of six ranks, with a thousand kept back as a moving support, ready to fill any breach. With horns blaring, the individual phalanxes plunged in together, strategos by strategos. Cimon was pleased with them, but the ones they faced were no false-coat warriors. These truly were the Immortals of Artaxerxes. He thought they would not run. Instead of a rout, the lines met like knife and stone, slick with blood, wearing one another down.

Overhead, all movement seemed to cease. The sun drained their strength, while men stabbed and died alongside their friends. Cimon had fought Persians for more years than he cared to remember. He still recalled the sea battle of Salamis, when men like Pericles' father had trusted him more out of desperation than anything else. Yet they had discovered how to fight fleets that day. His people loved intelligence and so it had not been so strange to have a man like Cimon wish to learn all he could of the enemy and their tactics. He knew the Immortals were ten thousand men, given the name because if they fell, they were always replaced. The number never fell below that total.

With those who stood with their king out of the fight, he faced around nine thousand of them that day. Cimon reminded himself that Leonidas had destroyed the very best Immortals at Thermopylae. These were just the sons of better men and they would not hold his hoplites. Cimon felt certainty grow in him, like ice. There it was, he thought suddenly, the last part of an elite fighting force – the absolute belief that they could carry the day. No matter how they were turned back or what disasters befell them, they would still come through. He swallowed, trying to keep that sense alive. It was a slippery, wriggling thing.

'Beware archers!' one of his lochagoi warned, pointing.

Cimon winced as he saw a few hundred lope up and bend bows. The sound reached him a beat after he saw the movement, a clatter like crow wings. A patch of sky had already darkened ahead and he looked up, hating this part.

The Persians loved their bowmen. By the gods, it was hard to face that whistling death, from far off, from above. His hoplites were forced to raise shields and of course that made them vulnerable to being stabbed by those below. The answer lay in perfect discipline. As Cimon looked through shields held overhead, he watched it happen.

The Persian archers shot six arrows at speed, so that they came like waves against the shore. That was well done, Cimon thought grudgingly. They would surely catch a few of his men in the lulls, too slow to raise a shield once again. For the rest, it distracted, unnerved them in their concentration. Front ranks fought on with shields overlapping, trusting that the Persians would not risk killing their own. Those just a rank or two behind watched the waves coming and raised the circles of bronze and wood in reply. The sun flashed off metal, rippling like beetle wings.

Arrows clattered and snapped across the Greek forces – and a few dozen vanished into gaps. Men choked or swore then, loud and long when they found an arrow had gashed their forearms or punched through a bare thigh or a foot. They endured the beats of arrows falling and a few always dropped. Those who did were left behind as the phalanx moved on, birthed like broken children from the rear. Wounded men snapped off shafts in their flesh or let friends bind the cuts with cloth. They muttered prayers for their deliverance, then leaned into the phalanx once more, eyes full of pain.

Cimon tried not to flinch as black shafts cracked against the shields overhead. He had dropped into the hoplite crouch from instinct, but he wore a helmet with a high red crest in dyed horsehair. The shafts were falling thick around him and he assumed the Persians were trying to hit the senior Greek commander. That was the chief danger of being present on the battlefield, of course. He knew the men took heart from having him stand with them. The other side of the coin was how many would panic if he fell. They believed in the gods' favour – and that could be withdrawn. Cimon clenched his jaw as Persian archers hammered his position, trying to change that balance in their favour.

In a lull, Cimon looked over to the hill where the king sat.

The man was leaning forward on his chair, apparently fascinated. Cimon would have given anything to send an arrow of his own up to that flapping pavilion, right through the man's seat. It would have been an impossible shot, especially with the breeze blowing. Still, the image was pleasant.

His hoplites were outnumbered, but his wide line matched the clustering Immortals. Enough of them had fallen already to give the lie to their name. Cimon felt every step forward as a victory, every step back as a surge of fear. Had he brought his people to their destruction? He had Strategos Myronides waiting back on the flagship, with a sealed packet of orders. If the League was routed, the Persian king would not get their fleet. Myronides would take every ship back to home waters and report to the Assembly of Athens.

Cimon had forbidden any attempt at rescue – and that gave him comfort as part of the centre failed and he had to send in his reserve, replacing exhausted and dying men. He hoped the presence of a thousand fresh hoplites dismayed the enemy. He showed his teeth as the phalanxes pressed forward once more. They were bronze and iron and no Persian king had ever seen them run.

Those had been the words Cimon had roared over their heads, as they'd sighted the enemy.

'Advance the League! We have made them run before! They have never seen our backs. Not once!'

The men had cheered him and, in that moment, he'd realised Pericles was right, that his father Xanthippus had been right. They were more than just Athenian as they cheered the navarch of the League and advanced against Persians. They were one people, a nation across the sea and land, an empire. He did not think that could be undone.

His heart sank as he saw Persian cavalry appear on both wings. They had been waiting for him to commit his reserves. Every man he had brought to that place would be risking a glance at those horsemen, wondering what they were up to, fearing encirclement. Cimon needed his damned reserve and he could not call those men out again. He wiped sweat from his face and began to snap fresh orders.

'Take this command to the sixth-rank lochagoi: "Detach and hold on my authority. Be ready to form on the senior lochagos and raise spears if the cavalry come. Shields and spear, defensive formation. Secure the rear. Courage."'

Four of the runners repeated his words and then went haring off. Cimon grimaced. He tried to turn the expression into a smile, but he hated dealing with horsemen. They were too fast to counter easily – and they could throw spears and bend a bow at speed. By the gods, they had little accuracy when they did, but they would cost him men.

Either way, he could not let his rear ranks feel panic when the Persians attacked. They had to know there were orders and plans. The alternative was chaos – and chaos destroyed an army.

He saw another drift of black specks lift into the air. Cimon glanced at the officer who had called warning before, but he had fallen. By the time others shouted warning, the arrows were coming down on men still craning to watch the cavalry. They were thickest around Cimon and he swore as an arrow struck his shield and snapped past him, slicing open his cheek. It was a perfect line, as if he'd been striped by a dagger. Blood spilled over the cut and he raised a hand to it, annoyed. He staggered a pace.

Danaos of Argos was suddenly at his side, pressing a

hand to the underside of his elbow. The strategos was serious and ashen-faced. Cimon tried to shake him off.

'Navarch, you have been wounded,' Danaos said.

He was looking back beyond the marching hoplites. As Cimon blinked at him in confusion, the man whistled, gesturing to the groom with his horse. Cimon showed him a red palm.

'It's nothing. I'll have it stitched when we get back.'

He could not understand the man's stricken expression until Danaos reached out to tap his collarbone. Cimon twisted, trying to see what caused the horror in his strategos. He felt feathers scrape his throat and understood at last, his hand rising to feel the thing in him.

An arrow had found the gap between his helmet and chestplate. It had to have come almost straight down to have struck at that angle. Could it be drawn? Cimon had known men die very quickly when arrows were yanked out.

His thoughts were in fragments, spinning around him. Cimon nodded to his second in command. He cleared his throat, suppressing panic. Was it harder to breathe? He had an arrow in his chest, vanished right to the feathers! With a twitch, Cimon tugged his cloak over it. Better not let the men see. He could feel it though, like a thorn right through him, sending shivers of pain and worry all over his body. He had not even felt it at first, in the thumping chaos. Yet something was wrong, he knew it then. Would he be able to sit down? The thought was suddenly funny and he began to laugh before pain seared him back to silence. He coughed once, wincing.

'Navarch,' Danaos said, 'I believe you should have that wound stitched on the flagship. You are too valuable, kurios. Please, your horse is here. May I help you mount?'

Cimon saw the man's eyes were desperate. He felt another cough building and he worried he would spray blood when it came. The Persian cavalry were still parading at the edges of the field. He could get clear if he went right then.

Bright lights flashed as he took the reins and bent his faithless knee to be helped into the saddle. Danaos lifted him up and Cimon flung his other leg over and sat straight. It was the effort of his life not to cry out as the arrow shifted. He felt bitterness gathering in his mouth and knew what it had to be.

'I take command, at your order,' Danaos said when the navarch did not speak.

Cimon nodded and turned the horse away. Ahead, the sea was glittering like snake scales in the sun. His fleet, his beloved fleet was there. It was not so far. He dug in his heels and felt something tear as the horse changed its gait.

Those who kept guard on shore ran to meet him, seeing the lone horseman from some way off. Cimon forced himself to speak then, though he felt a trickle make its way down from his mouth. One of the crewmen passed him a strip of cloth and he was dabbing at blood when he slid from the saddle. They caught him, holding him up.

Cimon was aware of voices calling in alarm. He felt himself carried to the water, the light suddenly blinding. More hands took hold of him there, lifting him into a boat. For a moment, he felt himself held aloft, while men murmured in shocked voices. As they lowered him down, the glitter of the sea overwhelmed him.

Cimon woke on board ship, knowing on the instant that he was in his own cabin. He was bare-chested, his tunic cut away. His cheek felt hot and swollen and he could smell sour wine. He blinked slowly at the surgeon wiping blood from his hands and forearms. Cimon felt fear uncoil, though he gave no sign. Strategos Myronides was there too in the gloom. His lips were forming words, over and over, some form of prayer.

Cimon cleared his throat, trying to see whether he would be able to speak. When it came, his voice was halfway between a growl and a whisper.

'How is the battle going?'

'Navarch, you should rest . . .' the surgeon began.

Myronides held up a hand.

'He needs to know.'

Cimon nodded, grateful to have him there. The older man had commanded at Tanagra, after all, against the Spartans. It was Myronides who had turned Cimon away when he had come to offer his help. That awareness was between them as Myronides sat on the edge of the cot and dabbed sweat from the navarch's forehead.

'The battle is going well, kurios. The men know you are wounded, of course. They fought like lions when the news spread.'

Myronides smiled, though it looked like cloth drawn tight.

'They are determined not to let you down.'

Cimon waved a hand and the strategos stopped mopping at his sweat. The cabin was uncomfortably hot, deep in the bowels of the flagship. Wherever he looked, there were things he knew: his maps, the sword he never wore, even his collection of stones and coins, taken from battlefields he had known. It was not much, but he was pleased to be there.

Cimon tried to speak again, but he felt something shift, as if he was about to vomit. He tried to turn his head, but pain swelled and he was helpless. Blood spattered from his lips as he choked and Myronides wiped it away as fast as it appeared, his eyes bleak. The surgeon handed over clean rags and, after an age, Cimon was able to draw another breath. He sipped air like wine, as afraid as he had ever been. This was death, and he could not turn from it.

'Don't tell the men,' he said, each word forced out. His gaze was terrible and the surgeon looked away from that awful intimacy. 'Not until . . . victory.'

As he spoke, the cabin seemed to grow lighter. His shaking fingers plucked and worried the feathers of the arrow still in him. Myronides saw his distress and turned to the surgeon in desperation.

'Are you sure we can't draw it out?' Myronides demanded.

The surgeon shook his head, his gaze firmly on the wooden floor.

'He'd die.'

'He's dying *now*!' Myronides hissed.

'I thought . . . he should go easy,' the man said. 'He is a great man, kurios. A man like this shouldn't have to die hard.'

'It's always hard,' Myronides snapped. 'So get your damned pincers and pull that foul thing out.'

Cimon felt his senses swim as the surgeon nodded and turned to a little table, laid out with the saws and tools of his grisly trade. The pincers he picked up were huge-looking and Cimon almost waved him off. Yet the arrow was a wrongness. He wanted it out of him.

Without warning, Cimon coughed and Myronides cried out as he tried to catch blood in cupped hands. More cloths were pressed in and Cimon felt blackness swelling like a great tide, rolling him under. He was gone for a while, tumbling beneath the surface. When he pulled in a little air and opened his eyes, the surgeon had the feathers gripped and was saying something. Cimon shook his head, but the man was tensing himself to wrench the foulness from his flesh.

'It has been an honour, adonai,' the surgeon said. A Jew then, granting him the term they used instead of 'kurios'.

'Don't tell the men,' Cimon rasped. 'Not . . . till they have won.'

Myronides nodded and the surgeon ripped the arrow out in one vast heave. Cimon saw the bloody length rise and rise until the light was blinding and he could see no more.

Myronides reached down to the navarch's throat then, searching for any beat or sign of life. There was none. His legs buckled and he sat on the edge of the bed, cleaning away blood and sweat.

'He's gone,' Myronides confirmed in grief. 'May the gods welcome his soul . . .'

He spoke without much awareness of the surgeon standing by, as if the words just slipped from him.

'You should have *seen* him at Tanagra, coming back from banishment, offering his life, though it was forfeit just being there! I sent him away. Can you believe that? I wish I hadn't.'

The surgeon nodded, patting him on the shoulder. There was silence then. The pain and struggle and fear had ended. There was a kind of peace in that small room with its low ceiling and the creaking sway of a ship at anchor.

After a long time, Myronides stood up and went out. On deck, he opened the package of order papers, sealed by the ring Cimon still wore. The strategos read those and passed on commands of his own. He climbed into a boat and was rowed ashore by grim-faced crewmen. He was as pale as milk, so they said nothing to him.

On the shore, Myronides mounted Cimon's own horse, though its neck and shoulder were spattered with coins of blood, still wet. He rode inland, making the animal canter though. The wind stung his chafed hands, cold on his skin as he reached the first bodies, cloak-wrapped and still. Some of the boys from the fleet had come up to walk amongst them, drawn by death or the prospect of a few coins. Myronides slowed to a trot and passed through a field of young men, torn and opened.

He found his people had pushed much further on, driving the enemy before them. The bodies came in patches then, ridges and sprawling heaps that marked each stand and reverse. Ahead, the Immortals still withdrew, in good order for the most part, accompanying their young king. He too had been forced to leave that place, Myronides noted with satisfaction. Yet the cost lay back in that sweltering cabin on the flagship. When he closed his eyes, Myronides could see Cimon's younger face as he stood on the plain at Tanagra, just asking to stand in line with shield and spear. Some men knew true *kleos* or glory before the end. Cimon was one of them, he thought.

The strategos of Argos saw him coming. Danaos guessed the news from his dark expression, from the flecked face and hands. Myronides dismounted and they embraced briefly as the older man confirmed it.

'We won for him, you know,' Danaos said, his voice choking.

'He knew. He didn't want the men to hear he had gone, in case they lost heart.'

They walked together in the wake of a routed force. It might have had the sense of a summer stroll if not for Immortal soldiers succumbing to wounds as they fled. Those men collapsed when they could no longer keep up with their fellows. Many were still alive as the battered phalanxes reached them. That was a grim business, with no mercy shown. The League rolled over men who had been roaring and chanting for their destruction just hours before.

'The battle is won,' Myronides said at last. 'Why are we still hunting Persians?'

Danaos glanced at him, seeing a decent and sensible man. Myronides was perhaps a little limited in his thinking. He was Athenian, though not as they liked to think of themselves, as other cities thought of them. Instead, Myronides was solid, somehow. A house built on one like Myronides would not fall.

'We have this island surrounded,' Danaos reminded him. 'With the Persian king present on the field. You tell me, Myronides. Even if he has ships hidden . . . How will he get home?'

Myronides paled as the man of Argos looked at him. He could not remain silent under that close scrutiny, though it looked as if he wanted to.

'I didn't . . . At the news of Cimon's death, I had orders to preserve the fleet. I'm sorry.'

'You sent them away?' Danaos asked. He closed his eyes for a moment.

'The orders were from Cimon, in the event of losing the battle. I am sorry, strategos. I sent them home. Only the flagship squadron remains, to take the hoplites back to Athens.'

Ahead, they could see the royal guard racing east, heading towards the shore at nervous speed. They had not fought for hours, of course. Like the king in their midst, they were fresh and young.

'There – do you see it?' Danaos asked.

He watched Myronides squint beneath a shading hand, then shake his head. The man of Argos sighed.

'Look along the shore . . . the ships in that little bay. Three? No, four. I doubt they can be seen from the sea. Those will be his. By the gods, we could have . . .'

He broke off, aware of the suffering in the man who walked beside him.

'I gave orders for the crews to rub soot into their sails,' Myronides said at last.

'We'll do the same,' Danaos said after a time. 'Perhaps it is for the best. The fate of kings is not for us to decide. You and I have done enough today. Today, we will mourn Cimon – and turn our sails black.'

Far ahead, the Persian king reached his flagship. Myronides could only imagine the bustle on those decks as they sighted the remaining Immortals loping along towards them. Perhaps a thousand turned to face their pursuers then, to give the king time. That too would be grim work.

Oars were already in the water as the young king boarded, casting off ropes, pushing them away from land. Their progress seemed slow at first, but they were free. As Myronides and Danaos watched, those four ships made their way out of the shelter of the hills and onto the open sea.

24

Dawn was close as Pericles stirred, rising from sleep. He had made it to bed in the small hours and felt as if he had grit in his thoughts. He sat up, groggily. Aspasia had gone to her own room, with his youngest son sleeping beside her. The little boy had been having nightmares.

Pericles rose to open a shutter onto the street below, letting cooler air in. He loved that time of day in Athens, before the sun's heat grew and the light was still more grey than gold. He yawned into a fist. The little town-house he had bought after his divorce was not really large enough for his new family and a staff. It was one advantage of the estate outside the city that guests could be stopped at the gate. He had time to wake up then, to bathe and dress . . .

He paused as a knock sounded again, at the street door. His thoughts sharpened. That was the sound that had dragged him up from troubled dreams. Yet it was very quiet. The house staff hadn't roused.

Moving with sudden urgency, Pericles splashed water on his face from the bowl left ready for him, running a bone comb through his hair to smooth it down. Whoever it was, they didn't want to wake the household. He hoped it wasn't some new crisis of the council that needed his attention. Ever since the murder of Ephialtes, he'd been forced to work every hour of the day and into the night, with little rest. It would be easier when Cimon returned, but until then, he had to endure a workload that appalled him. It was the hidden flaw in electing so many city officials, perhaps. There were times when he really needed continuity, not some new epistates or group of magistrates, blinking like newborns in the light. He felt sometimes that he was the only one in the city who knew how it all worked.

There was no time to shave. Pericles peed in a pot kept under the bed, pulled on boots and wrapped himself in linen with quick, neat motions, jamming a loose end into a belt fold and leaving his left shoulder and arm bare. He tried not to make too much noise as he came downstairs, but of course the steps creaked. From the kitchen, his cook called out in question. He at least was up early to bake bread and prepare breakfast for Aspasia and the boy. Pericles saw the man's head appear around a doorway and raised a hand in awkward greeting.

Pericles found himself standing alone before the closed door as the knock sounded again. He felt dread steal through him, like morning chill. Both his sons were out of the city. News of them, news of the entire world lay outside that door – separated from him by a single instant. He could hardly bear to open it.

His hands moved almost from habit while he watched. The door opened onto a cold dawn and Xanthippus and Paralus were standing there, battered and bruised but alive. Pericles made a strangled sound, without words. He reached out and grabbed both of them, drawing them in. He heard Paralus groan but didn't let go for an age.

They came with him into the house and Pericles put his head into the little kitchen where things were clattering on the stove and the air was thick with steam.

'Two more for breakfast,' Pericles said, smiling.

The cook echoed the expression, responding to the visible joy in the kurios.

'Come boys, sit,' Pericles said. 'Rest. There's food coming.'

He watched as Xanthippus and Paralus took their places at the only table. He could hear Aspasia stirring overhead, but Pericles was alone with his sons for a beat of time. He relished it before remembering he was furious with Xanthippus. Pericles lost his smile then. Both the young men noticed the change in him and exchanged wary glances.

'Have you seen your mother?' Pericles asked.

They shook their heads and he nodded, obscurely pleased.

'Never mind, I'll send a runner to her.'

He fixed Xanthippus with a hard gaze.

'I know about the moneylender, Xan. That . . .'

'I'm sorry. I know. It was unforgivable . . . my mistake. I'll pay it back, all of it.'

Pericles hesitated. The quick apology had stolen the wind from his sails, before he could build to a gale.

'Yes. Right. You will. You'll work on the estate with me all this summer, until the debt is paid.'

He waited for Xanthippus to nod. Perhaps it was because they'd been gone for so long, or that he had been so afraid for them, but in that moment Pericles was just grateful they were safe.

'And you should never have taken Paralus with you! Have you any idea how your mother and I worried? No, of course you haven't. It's this sort of selfishness I can't stand, Xan!'

'They're all dead,' Xanthippus said. His face crumpled and Pericles could only stare.

'What? Who is dead? The Volunteers?'

'I'm so sorry,' Xanthippus said. 'We were ambushed – horsemen. Cut to pieces.'

'All of them? Tolmides is dead?' Pericles said, still trying to take it in.

His sons nodded miserably.

'How did you get out?' his father asked. He felt cold suddenly, his stomach clenching for fear of what they might say.

'I ran,' Xanthippus said bitterly. 'There was a loose horse and it was dark and everyone was dying, so I just got up on it.'

'He saved me,' Paralus said, trying to head off anything Pericles might say in rebuke. 'I was done. Xan drove the horse back to me and pulled me up.'

Pericles looked again at his sons, seeing the differences in them. They had faced death and survived. Now that he thought to look, he could see it in them. It was a serious-ness, a lack of boyish laughter.

'It doesn't sound like you ran, Xanthippus,' he said after a moment of thought. 'It sounds like the battle was already lost and the gods saw fit to give you a horse. Is that how it went?'

He breathed out when they nodded. They had survived with something like honour. There would be no public disgrace, no tale of cowardice to follow them around the rest of their lives.

'You both fought?' Pericles asked in a lower voice. 'You killed men?'

It was a strange and bitter sweetness when they dipped their heads again, in thrall to his questions. He thought they would tell him the details in time, but on that morning they were trying to be men with their father – stern and disciplined.

'Well done. I may not have agreed with Tolmides, but I'd rather you came home than some other fellow. I still remember my first taste of battle, the exhaustion – the *joy* at winning, at just being alive after! The water I drank then was so sweet and clear I thought it was wine. And I would have got up on that horse as well, Xan! When a battle is lost, there's no honour in waiting to be killed, like some sacrificial bull. No, you did right. That's what matters – and the fact that you came back for Paralus. That was well done. You saved your brother. *That's* what matters! You saved my son.'

His approval was desperately important to both the young men at his table. It was as if a weight lifted from their shoulders, letting them sit taller as he spoke.

The cook brought out a platter of cut figs and goat cheese and the boys fell to like wolves. Paralus had half his face coloured in purple bruising and was clearly favouring one hand, fumbling his eating knife with the other. Yet Pericles could only breathe and stare, rubbing the knuckle of one finger over the bristles of his chin. They had survived. He had never worried as much for his own life as he had for theirs.

Steps coming down the stairs had both Xanthippus and Paralus scrambling to their feet. Pericles too rose to see Aspasia there, his third son on her hip. She looked radiant in comparison to the men of the household, hair brushed and singed and held with golden pins. Pericles caught his breath, giving private thanks once again to have been blessed in such a way. Every man deserved a second chance, he reminded himself. That applied to Xanthippus as well.

'The boys are safe,' Pericles said.

Aspasia smiled and nodded. She came down the stairs and handed the sleepy child to the maid drifting in her wake.

'And eating our figs, apparently,' she said, though it was a gentle thing.

Aspasia smiled and for the first time Pericles saw Xanthippus reply in kind. It was an odd sort of morning, Pericles thought, with all the normal rules undone.

'They'll have to see their mother. Gods, I haven't sent a runner yet! I'll do it now. She'll want to see both of you – and I imagine you'll want a chance to bathe and change. There is a decent bathhouse in the next street, lads. I go there sometimes, on my way to the Agora. Say I sent you.' He frowned suddenly in thought. 'This afternoon, Xan, you'll have to make a report to the Assembly. I can help you prepare for that.' He saw his son's sudden nervousness and went on. 'Don't worry. Your Volunteers had no official status. The Assembly can't punish you for being ambushed, not when they weren't paying the wage.'

'You warned us not to go,' Xanthippus said.

He was looking back into memory, his eyes glassy. Whatever he saw wasn't pleasant, judging by his expression. Pericles shrugged.

'That whole region is a hard place. A thousand feuds and alliances, and who can keep track of them all? In another year, Tolmides would have triumphed, I'm sure. What matters is that you made it back.'

He and his sons were standing by the front door, ready to go out into the street. Pericles kept a knife hanging from a leather loop there. He took it down to belt it onto his waist. Since the murder of Ephialtes, he had promised

Aspasia he would not go out without a weapon. The thought made him turn to Xanthippus.

'What happened to my father's shield?'

His heart sank as Xanthippus shook his head, embarrassed. The young man wore a torn cloak over a breastplate, but there was no sign of helmet or greaves, nor the spear and sword he had taken with him. All those had been left on a distant field. It was not so much the cost as the memories each piece evoked that made Pericles close his eyes in grief. His father had carried that shield at Marathon, painted with a roaring lion at his mother's request.

Pericles felt Aspasia touch him on the arm as anger rose in him. He had no love for things, he reminded himself, only the man who had carried them. The two youths looking at him so nervously were what mattered. He knew his father would have said the same if he had stood there.

Pericles blinked when a knock sounded, almost under his hand. He lifted the latch and flung the door back.

A young man stood there in a robe much like his own, held fast by an iron clasp on the shoulder.

'Kurios, the fleet has been sighted. They are coming home.'

Pericles looked at him in confusion. He had seen that particular youth before, in council meetings. He heard Xanthippus murmur a greeting to him. Yet the news did not explain why the lad panted like a woman in labour. The road from the port was barely an hour's run for a fit man, after all.

'Why come to me so early?' Pericles asked.

'I was sent by the council, kurios. They told me to say all the sails are black.'

Pericles felt blood drain from his face. He might have

staggered if not for the hand braced against the door frame.

'The sails are black? What does that mean?' his wife said at his shoulder.

'It means my friend is dead,' he said, his voice breaking. 'It means Cimon is dead.'

25

Pericles saw dark blues, browns and blacks when he strode through the streets of his city. A year after the funeral of Cimon, many Athenians still wore funeral colours, mourning the loss of a great man, as well as their own sons lost in battle. Pericles had given the funeral oration for them all, while flames roared to the night sky.

In private, he had spoken to Myronides and all the other strategoi as they'd come in, learning every detail of the Cypros victory. He'd been helped in that by an Athenian devoted to recording the events of each year. Thucydides was convinced stories needed to be written down, that if lads merely memorised works like the *Iliad*, they would eventually be lost. The young man had fallen out with another member of the Assembly over the best way to do it, almost coming to blows. Pericles shook his head at the thought of their earnestness. Men such as Thucydides were a new generation, filled with life and light. Yet scribes always thought stories were important. Architects thought truth lay in carved stone, artists in the scenes they painted. They were all wrong. Men remembered what mattered. When it ceased to matter, they would no longer remember.

By the following spring, Cypros had been rebuilt as a fortress of the League, manned by hoplites, guarded by ships and crews. Pericles had made sure of that, to honour Cimon's sacrifice. Many League soldiers had brought their families out with them and begun to clear land. Pericles hoped to develop a proper colony there, to live and grow green things without the shadow of war across their faces. Perhaps one day there would be markets and theatres as well as soldiers.

It was a dream, but he thought it was better to build and imagine what might be, rather than destroy. He knew some men saw their own ageing reflected in the world, as if all things faded, as if innocence and honour had died with the heroes of their youth. It was important to have children on such days, so a man could see the world through their eyes. Pericles had been present to hear Paralus speak for the first time in the Assembly. It had been a moment of pride and optimism for him.

The previous summer had brought an explosion of trade, so that Athens had hummed like a hive for all the hours of the day and half the night. Pericles smiled wryly as he passed the hetaira house. The garden still filled the street with scent there, though Aspasia no longer tended those particular blooms. She had bought two more properties and a public bath that winter. Those things were her own investment in the future – in the tiles and mortar and people of the city. The sea was safe for trade and the new walls from the coast meant the heart of the League was a fortress.

As Pericles walked, a group of scribes had to scramble through the bustling crowds to keep up. He had been made strategos again, year after year, more times than any other. Yet he still refused the title of archon. His father had held it, along with Aristides and Themistocles, men he considered giants of an age. Perhaps that was it. Or perhaps it was the abiding memory of Ephialtes, Pericles was not sure. The power of the city lay in its Assembly first and then its council, not the oldest families. Regardless of his title, Pericles knew he was first in Athens, as his father had been.

He walked briskly through the Ceramicus district, acknowledging the pot-sellers and craftsmen who greeted him. In those quick grins and gestures, Pericles thought he saw the reality – as real as any battlefield or trial on the Pnyx hill. Athens was *busy* – noisy and brash, with a hundred things sizzling on charcoal braziers and a thousand voices raised, wherever he looked. He passed women and men arguing furiously over prices and costs, gesturing sharply and claiming the deal would ruin them and beggar their children. There was nowhere else like it.

The light was somehow brighter as he reached the open Agora, with the great cliff of the Acropolis looming over all. Pericles knew every part and coin spent on the new gatehouse and steps up there, the extraordinary temple Phidias had finished at last, all to honour the city's patron goddess. Athena Parthenos rose from the natural rock in all her glory, looking over the city she had founded with her own hand.

Pericles had peered down curving lines where the stones had been cut to fool the eye, so they somehow appeared straight. It was a wonder of the mind and the heart – and Phidias taught other masters. There was a wild new energy in the city and Pericles did not know if it had been fed by the blood of the fallen, or some fortunate combination of great men and their ideals. Pericles had attended one speech on the steps of the Boule council, where a dark-haired young soldier had attempted to define virtue. Pericles knew him. He'd intended to stop only for a moment, but the words and ideas held him transfixed. Socrates had a mind like Zeno or Anaxagoras, as if the city brought forth genius from her very stones.

Pericles paused on those same steps, thinking of Aeschylus. The playwright had crossed the river at last, old and white-haired, all his strength drained away. It brought a pang to remember the first plays they had put on together, with Pericles risking his family fortune to bring *The Persians* to the great theatre of Dionysus.

From that height, he looked out on the city he loved. Death was there, of course, in the midst of life. He remembered a couple of lines from the *Iliad*, ones Aeschylus had loved: 'If men were gods, they would not make war. They fight because they are mortal.'

Pericles had not understood that in his youth. After the loss of Cimon, he had a better sense of what it meant. The future was in his sons. He was merely the steward for those who would come after him, a gardener tending vines, cutting some away and bringing forth the best and strongest. That was a good thought.

His scribes were waiting in a little group, like geese with parchment rolls. Pericles nodded to them. His tribe was back on the rotation, which meant he might know the epistates for once. Perhaps he would get through the mountain of discussions and proposals waiting for him, from a new dock on Salamis to a trial for murder he had agreed to prosecute. Then there was the administration of the new colonies to the west. Zeno would surely speak on that subject, as he had been born there, in reach of Rome.

Pericles turned to enter and heard a low sound echo across the Agora. It had an extraordinary effect, as if thunder had cracked overhead and frozen the scene. He paused and turned back, seeing thousands of people standing still, all looking north and west. As half the city asked the other half what was happening, the horn sound came again, from another quarter. In the eerie silence, Pericles thought he heard yet a third, almost in echo from the eastern wall.

He felt his stomach drop away as he understood. Alarm horns blew on the city walls, joining one another in a great lowing cascade across the city. He had overseen their installation himself, along with the archer towers.

The noise was taken up, from the walls of the city right down to the port. There was a new sound running alongside the emergency note. He could hear it like the sea, louder with every moment. Voices and tramping feet. People were coming in, exactly as they had been told, as they had planned and practised. Pericles felt a chill at the thought. The gates were open. They were shut each night, but never during the day.

His scribes were looking to him in horror, waiting for his word. He made himself smile.

'I think I should go and see what's going on, don't you?'

Perhaps it was the way they clustered, but they reminded him of battlefield messengers and he looked at them with new interest.

'You – run down to the port. Make sure we are not under attack by sea. Use my name to speak to the port master and then find me.'

The young man pressed a bundle of scrolls into the arm of the one next to him and raced off.

'You,' Pericles said to another. 'Go to the walls and locate the senior officer. Find out what started the alarm.'

A third stepped up then, bright-faced and ready. Pericles nodded to him.

'Go inside, Petros. Tell the council to call all the strategoi and pass war command to them. I am heading to the walls. When they are ready, they might see fit to join me.'

He knew he spoke sternly from the way they reacted, but he could not shake the feeling of dread rising in him. Across the city, men would be scrambling to fetch their shields, spears and armour. Every shopfront would be coming down, with workshops, taverns, homes and gymnasia all emptying onto the streets. They had practised and drilled for this a hundred times, he told himself. He had overseen runs from the demes all around Athens, with thousands of families grabbing up bags and racing for the city.

It had seemed a game then, with mothers and their children walking in together, staying to purchase pots in the Agora or see a play. Yet he could not escape the sensation of fear and fury mingling. There was only one enemy who would dare approach the walls of Athens, who could drive villagers and farmers like sheep before them, racing for the safety of the walls and gates. He dropped his hand to the blade on his belt. In that moment, he wished Cimon could have been there, or Themistocles, Aristides, Ephialtes – his father Xanthippus above all. Yet they had crossed the river, one by one, their labours at an end.

Pericles stood first in Athens. He saw it in the nervous eyes of council members as they came out onto the steps to see. He understood then what those heroes of his youth had surely known. He was alone, and all men looked to him. With a darker expression than he knew, he strode out across the Agora, heading for the walls.

When he reached the high walkway, Pericles could see the curve of the city stretching into the distance. The gate was open beneath him, a great banded thing of bronze, iron and oak. He could see an archer tower further along, busy as a bird's nest. Six men were stationed there in shifts, ready to defend their city. More stood on the walls with spear and shield, their helmets high on their heads while they waited for orders.

At that height, the breeze was pleasant, far from the odours of cooking and sweat below. Pericles could see trails of people approaching his city, like ants across the land, burdened with their possessions. He could hardly believe the sheer numbers coming in. On the road below, crowds were already pouring through the gateway, on horseback, mule, or on foot, with all they owned wrapped in huge bundles of rope and cloth. Some carried statues in from the cemetery, to be buried. He wondered how many still lay in the earth, lost to memory after the invasion of the Persians.

It seemed his people had thrived in the years since Athens had built her walls. Half the crowd seemed to be carrying infants. They had brought new children into the world, secure in the knowledge that if they were ever threatened, they could all rush to the sacred city and be safe. This day was the test, he realised.

The refugees raised dust as if they were marching on a battlefield. Despite the breeze, Pericles could see a pale haze rising, drawn into the city with them. His people: rich and poor, young and old. They passed the tombs of the cemetery. They came from villages and towns around Athens, abandoning farms and mines, even estate houses like his own. Slave and free too, they mingled in their rush to gain safety. His mother would be somewhere among them, just as she had practised.

They were all desperate and exhausted by the time they passed the gates, with dark circles of sweat showing on their clothes. Already, husbands and wives huddled all over the city in every doorway and temple, guarding even a simple place to sit with blades or clubs.

Still they came, driven before the threat of war, a great flood of humanity that poured in, with no sign of any end to it. Pericles wondered how he would ever shut those gates – and what would happen when he gave the order. Every man, woman or child was one more to feed and shelter. He reminded himself of the long walls down to the port. Athens could not be put under siege. He could bring in whatever they needed.

Pericles heard his name called. He leaned over and looked down on the inner gate, blinking at the sight of a strange group clustering there. He nodded to the hoplites at the bottom of the steps, giving permission.

Zeno and Anaxagoras trotted up the stone stairs, with the architect Phidias a step behind. Pericles saw Aspasia was with them and felt a clammy feeling under his robe as he recognised his first and second wife were talking together. His sons Xanthippus and Paralus brought up the rear, glowering at all the noisy strangers in their city. It was hard to reconcile his sense of being nobly alone with the actual reality of his life. Ephialtes had said something similar once. Like it or not, they were all part of who he was.

As the group reached the walkway, they fanned out, unable to tear their gaze from a view only rarely seen. Pericles raised an eyebrow in silent question and Zeno was aware enough to look embarrassed. The little philosopher blushed as he halted. Pericles saw he had donned his old breastplate and greaves, ready to defend his chosen home. Xanthippus and Paralus had no shields or spears. Pericles whistled up another of his scribes to run and fetch spares from the council store. He suspected they would be worth a fortune before the day was over, despite all his preparations.

'Put my name to the order!' he called, before the scribe had reached the bottom of the steps. No one would begrudge the use of kit at such a time, but nor would he leave himself open to accusations of favouring his own sons. Debts had to be paid.

Pericles looked over the group that had gathered in his name.

'Zeno? Why have you brought my wife . . . and my ex-wife?'

Before Zeno could reply, Pericles noticed an absence and spoke over him.

'Aspasia? Is Peri safe?'

'He is being spoiled at the hetaira house. Don't worry about him. We wanted . . .'

She trailed off for once, unable to explain how they had all thought of him when the world was flung upside down. It was echoed in their faces, sons and friends alike.

'We wanted to know you were ready . . .' Thetis added.

Pericles looked at her. A simple gaze could be a strange thing with an ex-wife. It opened him to all the years they had been together, good and bad, to joys and arguments and children born. He had to wrench his gaze away.

'As ready as I can be,' Pericles said. 'We had scouts watching the isthmus, waiting for any sign of their army. That should give us a day in warning, perhaps two. The result is in what you can see – every deme and district around the walled city, all emptying through these walls. If the Spartans have come, they will find our countryside deserted.'

'Can we even feed so many?' Thetis asked over the noise of the moving tide below.

Pericles heard an old note of criticism in her voice. Yet he realised the soldiers on the wall were listening as well, desperate for news. He raised his voice for them.

'I have not been idle, Thetis. We can feed them – and we have the fleet still, under Myronides. We can close the gates and life will go on. Everything will be a little harder and there will be sacrifices, but we can wait them out. If they don't come, this will be just another drill. The people are rushing in because the walls work. Athens may be the only city in the world that can't be taken in war. The Spartans can shake their spears outside our walls for a month. I hope they do! I hope they look up at us and understand at last that they are yesterday's men, every last one of them. We are the future – in youth and trade and ships.'

Pleistonax loped alongside his men, his uncle Nicomedes at his shoulder. He thought the older man would have preferred to mount one of the warhorses he had taken to breeding, but Pleistonax had only raised an eyebrow when Nicomedes had mentioned it. That slight disapproval had been enough.

The ephors and his civil king were at home with the new generation of helots. Pleistonax imagined they could handle any lack of discipline from children and young women. It meant he could stay in the field longer than any Spartan leader had ever dared, a strange blessing after all the bloodshed, after the death of a Spartan king and his own rise. Perhaps it was some plan of Ares, he could not say. Pleistonax was in the prime of his strength, grown to manhood in war and trials of the earth. He had rebuilt the army, and if it had taken longer than he had hoped, they were more his men than the generation before it. Half the eight thousand who marched to Athens with him were sixteen to twenty-four – men who had been just boys when the eruption threw down their city and set the helots to savagery and spite.

'There she is, the whore,' Pleistonax murmured, as the walls of Athens rose into view before them.

Still distant, he had asked a hard pace from his warriors. His true Spartiates were determined to prove their worth to a new king. The perioikoi who walked with them were older men for the most part, trained in Spartan skills, but not of the first quality. It led to prodigies of valour, as Nicomedes had explained it to him. Spartiates would not be shamed in front of those who had been driven out. In turn, the perioikoi strove to prove themselves worthy. Each year, Nicomedes had said, a Spartan battle king could promote from the perioikoi if he chose to.

'And send Spartiates down to them, for dishonour?' Pleistonax had asked in his innocence.

His uncle had shaken his head. Of course not. No Spartan would accept such a stain on his honour. He would take his own life first.

Pleistonax watched the walls grow wider and taller. He saw lines of people entering the city through gates that were still open. An urge built in him to increase the pace, to drive them like sheep or goats before a raging fire. He took a sharp breath at the thought.

'Orders, Majesty?' Nicomedes asked.

Pleistonax looked at him. The man was experienced, which was why he was there.

'At this moment, the truce is unbroken,' Pleistonax said. 'We merely approach an ally, in good faith.'

'They will close the gates,' his uncle said.

Pleistonax nodded.

'They are afraid of us. With good reason. Well, I came to see the pride of this city that sits on our flank like a running sore. I came to let them see our strength restored!'

He spoke as confidently as he could, but every step seemed to raise the walls. They grew as he marched towards them, looming at impossible size. He could make out small figures in hoplite gold on its top, even mules walking the crest, carrying bundled supplies. There had to be a road up there, with buildings on it.

He revised his understanding once more and felt his heart sink. The walls were both taller and thicker than he had imagined. When he looked to the east and saw the line running down to the coast, he could only swallow. There was no city wall in Sparta! Until that moment, Pleistonax had not quite appreciated how intimidating they could be.

'They might come out to face us . . .' his uncle murmured.

'I don't think so,' Pleistonax replied. 'Would you? No, they will pull those gates shut and sit behind them.'

'What will you do?' Nicomedes asked.

His nephew was quiet for a long time. The city lay not six hundred paces away. The refugees in that part had vanished, hurrying around the city to some other point.

Where Pleistonax stood was not open countryside. On one side, the road led past houses and farms, with fenced pastures and horses cropping grass. On the other, a host of tombs spread by the thousand, right to the city walls. Even as Pleistonax gazed around him, he saw the gates move at last.

They were pulled in by oxen, slowly at first and then faster. The edges were of thick bronze and overlapped to make a seal, striking one another with a bell note that must have sounded across the city. Hoplites raised spears in challenge then on the wall road, high above. Pleistonax heard the people shouting, the sound like a distant sea as it rose and fell away. He could not tell if it was in triumph or fear that they cried out, only that he was the cause.

'What will I do, uncle?' he said, showing his teeth. 'I will make them *want* to come out and face me. I will burn their land to ash.'

26

Pericles breathed deeply. He had told the others he wanted to walk up the Acropolis to get a view of the land and the fires, but the truth was the breeze was clean up there. Down in the city, air lay like bitter broth, especially in the mornings. Along with the smell of open sewers and far too many people crammed in, fires still burned right around the city. The Spartans had destroyed entire towns and villages, ancient gymnasia, anything to hurt those who hid behind the walls. The only part they had spared was the cemetery, perhaps for fear of offending the gods. They were not Persians, after all.

From that height, Pericles could see huge plumes still rising, driven south on the wind like fox tails. He'd heard the Spartan king had made his men catch stray dogs, tying smouldering branches to them and letting them run through fields, driven to shrieking fear and madness. Farms and shrines and woodlands had all been consumed. For a day's march in any direction, there were only crackling beams left, and the stubble of crops. The air itself was thick with it, so that Pericles could smell char in his robe. When he coughed, he spat dark brown flecks onto his palm.

Pericles grimaced at the thought. Some of the people had taken to wearing strips of cloth around their mouths. It made them strangers, somehow, just when he needed to know them. Arguments had begun as the Spartans arrived and not stopped, as far as he could tell. Some wanted to ignore their presence, to remain safe and sound until the enemy soldiers were forced to head home again. They were the majority for the moment, but there was another faction growing, led by Myronides of all people. It seemed the cautious strategos had decided the insult was too great to bear for the heart of the League.

Pericles heard raised voices and looked over to the steps, groaning softly to himself. Myronides too had decided to make the climb to that point. With talk of Spartan spies, he had been stopped from approaching, of course. Even then, as he gestured and pointed, the hoplites looked back for Pericles to give permission. He was sorely tempted to ignore the man. Was it too much to ask, for one hour of peace before the tumult of the day? The entire city seemed to expect Pericles to solve their problems for them – with triple the number of people and not enough food. Every day revealed something he might have foreseen, if he'd had the wisdom of the gods and a dozen more years. At times, he wished for Ephialtes to have lived, so he could have handed all the problems over to him.

Crushing a yawn into his fist, Pericles gestured with his free hand. Myronides walked stiffly towards him, his dignity ruffled. He even glared back at the hoplites as he went. Pericles could only stare at the bristling cockerel, ready for a fight. Of all those he had known, he would never have picked Myronides as one to yearn for war. Perhaps it had been the death of Cimon that changed him, he didn't know.

'Who told you I was here?' Pericles said before he could speak.

Myronides blinked at him.

'Is it a secret? Half the city knows you make an offering at Athena Parthenos each morning.'

Pericles nodded. It did not seem wise to be so predictable, hoplites or not. If Myronides could find him so easily, he would change his routine.

'I came to say there will be an emergency meeting of the council at noon.'

'Another one,' Pericles murmured.

Myronides coloured, though whether it was from the steps or his frustration was hard to say.

'Is it so surprising? We have an enemy army destroying our homes, raiding around our city like a fox sniffing at a henhouse – and you will not let us answer.'

'I am not a king, nor a tyrant, Myronides,' Pericles reminded him. As he felt his own anger growing, he made an effort to gentle his tone. It may have been the smoke in his lungs or the sheer closeness of people wherever he went, staring, staring. He felt rubbed raw, somehow, always close to anger. It was an effort, but he smiled.

'If the council votes for what you want . . . if the Assembly agrees, I cannot stop it. Please don't give me powers I have never had.'

Myronides mastered himself in turn.

'Let me speak the truth, strategos, so we both understand. The council look to you for guidance, whether they call you tyrant or not. You are the son of Xanthippus, after all, as well as the great-nephew of Cleisthenes. Yours is a line as old as any of the Eupatridae. More, your own estate was burned, so they see you as one of theirs. They stand with you. Yet true power lies with the Assembly. Whether it is because of the plays you put on, or because they heard you speak with Ephialtes, or because they see the Long

Walls as your great work, it does not really matter. They also look to you, Pericles. So speak not to me of what you can and cannot do. If you gave the word, I could take every hoplite in Athens out against the enemy. I could do it tomorrow morning and put an end to this fear.'

'That would be an ending, without a doubt,' Pericles said. 'But not the one you want. You were at Tanagra! You saw the damage just a few of them did to us. Now they have eight thousand?'

'I can bring twice as many out,' Myronides said. 'That is what Cimon would have done, if he had lived.'

'Well, you are not Cimon,' Pericles snapped.

The words seemed to wound the older man, so that Myronides closed his eyes and swayed as if he had been struck. After a moment he nodded.

'That is true. But if we just wait, if we do nothing . . . the Spartans will come back, again and again, year after year. Do you think our people will run for the walls every time, that they won't raise a great howl of protest? Being made to live like cowards shames us now, but if we have to do it every spring? We'll lose the League and all our authority.'

Pericles listened, though he didn't want to. He had seen Spartans fight and he knew the army waiting outside their walls would destroy them. He was absolutely certain of that, with their young battle king just itching for a chance to prove himself.

'Do you know who leads them, Myronides?' he asked softly. 'The Spartans? Do you know their battle king?'

'Only his name. He has no battle honours yet.'

'Pleistonax is the son of Pausanias, who came out to lead the League fleet years ago, over Cimon and all the senior captains.'

'I remember . . .' Myronides said.

He turned to look into the distance, to where Spartans strolled along the borders of their camp. Dawn sun flashed off their shields and spearheads, like jewels.

'There were accusations made,' Pericles said, 'that he conspired with the enemy to free prisoners, that he had taken bribes. Just enough to send Pausanias racing home to defend his good name. And what did they do? They walled him into a temple to die of thirst. It is his *son* we face, kurios! A man who blames Athens for his father's destruction. If we go out to face the battle king of Sparta, we will be destroyed.'

'If we are forced to hide like children, the result will be much the same,' Myronides said stubbornly.

'Perhaps,' Pericles replied. 'Yet I choose this path for now.'

He didn't bother to defend the accusation he saw rising in Myronides. The man's assessment had been broadly accurate. Pericles controlled the council and the Assembly, at least for that year. He believed in the Long Walls – and so they did as well.

'Your father would have gone out,' Myronides muttered.

Pericles winced.

'Perhaps. Perhaps I am a lesser man. We are the only city in the world that cannot be put to siege, Myronides! Our merchant ships deliver food and water at the port every morning. Should I not at least prove the worth of that? Or should I ignore those walls the Spartans hate and just go out as if we had never raised them up? You know, if the Spartans win against us, my walls will be pulled down, every last stone. They stand today as a symbol – our skills and craft, against spears. That is worth something. Every day the Spartans are forced to burn farms and wave their swords in helpless fury is a *victory*. Tell the people that, if they ask. The walls are our strength.'

Pericles waited until the older man bowed his head, frustrated, but accepting there would be no more. Myronides made his way back to the soldiers and Pericles saw two of them went with him, keeping him safe. There had been more murders of council members. The men responsible had been caught and torn apart by a crowd before they could even be questioned. Pericles had no doubt there were Spartan spies in Athens. Men like Myronides were no longer allowed to be alone. He clenched his jaw at the thought, staring into the distance at a Spartan king who burned with grief and resentment, who dared to threaten all Pericles loved, all he had made. The seeds of it went back a long way. That particular fire had crackled underfoot for years – sprung from rivalry and arrogance. Well, he had planned for it. Pericles clenched his fist, holding it up to the enemy in the distance. The air tasted of smoke and rot, even at that height. When fires rose so high, when they burned so very hot, even those who set them could be consumed.

Thetis looked up in irritation as her sons came clattering in. Xanthippus looked pale and Paralus was talking in a serious tone to him, his head low. She shook her head.

'The city under siege and you two are larking around like boys!' she said.

It was not a fair description, but she didn't like to see them so serious, made old before their time. Both of them wore armour, with the helmets shoved back on their heads. The spears and shields they bore were new and they placed those down carefully. In their presence, the town-house suddenly felt cramped and busy, though she could not escape the sheer relief just to see them whole and untouched by the war.

'We went up to the wall,' Paralus told her.

Thetis tutted. She took his helmet when he offered it with his cloak, folding it in her arms and placing it ready for him to snatch up if there was an alarm.

'To stare, I suppose,' she said. 'Or was it your father you wanted to see?'

Paralus flushed at that and she rolled her eyes. Pericles had his new wife and son, of course. They were his family. Yet her two boys, her brave sons, needed him still. There were times when she could have killed Pericles for the way he treated them.

'Was he there?' she asked.

Paralus shook his head, stiff as he sat to remove his sandals. A house slave came to bathe his feet clean of the road dust and he concentrated on that for a while.

'He said he would be,' Xanthippus said suddenly. 'But the wall officer told us he was called away.'

He sounded bitter and Thetis understood that all too well.

'He forgets his priorities, your father. That was always a flaw in him. Not the only one, either.'

She saw both boys exchange a glance and reminded herself not to be too harsh. They hated it when she criticised Pericles, as if she overstepped somehow in her anger. They didn't know the half of it, nor how she had controlled her temper a thousand times. They had seen her weep and shout over him, and now they were wary when she even said his name, as if it might lead to worse.

'At least you are both safe,' she said. 'I heard those three councillors were killed yesterday, murdered in the street! I don't trust all these new people. They knock on the door here, begging for food and water. I dare not answer – not when you are on patrol, chasing your father's approval. Which you will not get, because he is a selfish man who thinks of no one but himself . . .'

'Mother, please,' Xanthippus began, holding up his hands. 'Is there anything to eat?'

'A little broth, nothing fresh. No bread, with the baker and his wife both ill. The market is empty, at least of food. Oh, there are people enough, all with their hands out, all calling. Not too thin though, some of them! No, I think they're eating better than I am.'

As she folded her arms, she had some sense of her own well-fed frame, so grew pink.

'And the smell! I have to hold dried lavender to my face when I go out, or a cloth wrapped around me. They just shit where they stand, some of them, or in any doorway. I swear I've had our own step cleaned twice today. It is disgusting – and your father let them all in, without thought for where they would sleep or empty their bowels. The whole city stinks and still we have those Spartans sniffing around, looking for a way in. I tell you . . .'

Xanthippus reached out and kissed his mother on the forehead, silencing the stream of words.

'We're only home for an hour or so. We're on shift again after that – and there won't be anything to eat until morning. So yes, please. If there's stew and a little watered wine left, I'll try some. In truth, my stomach is aching from hunger.'

'You are good boys,' Thetis said. 'You take after my side, I am certain.'

They exchanged another glance as she bustled away, but there was as much affection as anything. Xanthippus saw his brother rubbing his gut.

'You too?' he asked.

Paralus shrugged.

'Just a little pain. Bowels are a bit loose. I think . . . yes, I'll need to go again.'

'You've been half a dozen times already!' Xanthippus said, shaking his head. He saw his brother was sweating and his smile faltered. 'Seriously, are you all right?'

'I'll be fine. I just need to find a pot before it all starts running down my leg. And I might visit the baths afterwards.'

'Closed, I'm afraid,' Xanthippus said.

He watched his brother walk away, holding himself clenched. His own stomach was oddly tight and swollen, he realised. Perhaps it was the lack of food, or that piece of fish they'd bought earlier. That would be it, he thought with a groan. Fish could cause upsets in the gut.

'I think it was that fish!' he called after his brother.

Paralus had found the little room where they kept a pot for visitors. He was making horrible sounds in there and Xanthippus winced. That would have to be emptied into the street trench before he was able to use it, he thought. He recalled the slow-moving mass of filth he had seen, baked in the sun and making the air so thick his eyes watered. His mother was right, perhaps. There were just too many people crammed into Athens that month, under a fierce sun, with neither space nor clean water.

'Are you finished in there?' Xanthippus called. His own stomach was making unpleasant sounds and he could feel sweat breaking out on his skin. He was suddenly so thirsty he could hardly bear it and hopped from one foot to the other. 'Come *on*, would you!' Only a deep groan came in reply.

The coast was dark and still as the fleet rowed along its reaches. Experienced sailors guided them around the headland and wherever they saw an inlet or the boats of a fishing village, they went in, ready to burn and destroy. The Spartan army was in the field, after all. Those who lived on the southern Peloponnese were defenceless against the League. The order was to send up a cry that would bring the Spartan king running back – and so there was no mercy in them.

Ships beached where they found shoaling sand, though that was rare. More often, boats full of men in hoplite armour went up creeks and streams wherever they could be seen in the moonlight. That was a risky business, but they were grim and determined. The Athenians in particular had left their families with the threat of slaughter hanging over them. They were unforgiving as they stepped into shallow waters and walked inland.

Patches of light sprang up in the places where they brought fire. Shadowed men walked along streets of ancient houses, setting each one alight. For those still landing, screams could be heard in the distance. The actual killing was a silent thing in comparison. Those who stumbled out, coughing and flailing, were put down and left where they fell.

There was fighting too, but sleeping fishermen were no match for soldiers. Village after village was set afire and those who had done the work returned to their boats with bloody swords, wiping them clean with oil and cloth, checking them for nicks or weakness, and then climbing aboard to be rowed back.

Where a main vessel had landed, that ship had to be dragged off by two more, with ropes scattering drops of sea like pale rain. The work of the sea was of knots and ropes and weights and sticky blood on the hands that took bucket after bucket of seawater to clean off.

Many of those crews had known war in some form. Against a Persian host, they would have laughed and joked and talked of their luck, just to hear their own voices and know they had survived. That night, they were silent. They knew the orders of the Assembly and the fleet navarch. They did not question the rightness of them. No one who had seen the Spartan fires around their city thought the work was unnecessary or unduly harsh. War was brutality and it fell on women and children as much as men with iron in their hands. If some of them winced or sat with eyes closed, it was from the sting of sea salt. When one man made a sobbing sound, his friends looked away in the dark, ashamed for him.

Any fishing boats they found had clay oil lamps tossed into them. Flame spread beautifully there, like flowers opening. What survivors there were would starve on that coast in the months to come, but that was part of it. The Spartan king had to hear a great wail of pain and grief if they were to bring him back. He had to feel a rare and righteous fury to leave the side of Athens and race home. The crews of the fleet were there to bring it about, to raise it up until the heavens themselves trembled with it.

As the sun rose, villagers woke to smoke and fear. The slaughter continued in daylight and there was more resistance. One Spartan appeared from a doorway in full kit, with a kopis in his hand. They never learned why he was there, though he was older than the men who faced him in

343

a ring. They cut him down, but not before he had killed two and ruined one more, spattering Athenian blood. They gave the Spartan's kit and cloak to the injured man and burned the house behind them.

Day after day brought savagery and killing, continuing into the nights. No one sobbed or wept by then on the dark decks. They had been hardened like arrow points in fire, stained in soot and blood and all they had done. Nor did they laugh. They went about their task with eyes like lead, chopping, burning, destroying. They left ruins and corpses all along that coast, until it seemed like nothing lived and even the lizards had been spitted through and left to dry in the sun.

27

In the council building, Pericles raised stiff fingers, bending each one to count off his points.

'My priorities? One, the Spartans who are not going home. Two, more murders and thefts in a single month than the whole of last year. It's not just the ones trying to bring the city down for Sparta, either. With all the newcomers, tension is running high. People are fighting like wild dogs and we need to do something about that.' He looked around the council, seeing how many empty seats there were. 'And three, this blasted sickness is spreading. Do we have reports from the doctors? Numbers? Confirmation it came from the port? I had to call out the Scythians yesterday to put down a riot, with a crowd trying to kill new families for bringing it in. If it gets much worse, we won't be able to man the walls or the gates. The spies in the city will just be able to open them up and the Spartans can walk right in.'

The man who rose to speak in reply was Apollodormus, an archon and nobleman of great experience. He looked ill, Pericles saw, with a grey pallor and sweat bright on his skin. The man was old enough to be of his father's generation, and yet he would not be denied his chance to speak. His voice and will were still strong.

'It was my understanding that the Spartans could not spend a full season in the field, yet they remain. Has the strategos any explanation for this? I brought my family behind these walls on the understanding that it would not be for long. Here we are, even so, without proper lodging or a place to wash. The fountains are fouled, the wells are poisoned with filth. Without the barrels delivered from the port, the city would be gasping for water, or dying for lack of it.'

He might have gone on, chewing words in his rising wrath. Pericles rose from his seat and the older man subsided, perhaps more willing than usual to rest on the cool stone. He panted as he sat down and Pericles winced for him.

'Archon Apollodormus asks why the Spartans remain. I can only conjecture. In the past, they feared a rebellion of their slaves. We suspect they have culled them back to manageable numbers now, reducing that threat. That has allowed them to remain outside our walls this long.'

'And what is the strategos doing about it?' Apollodormus called without rising. A few voices echoed his question and Pericles bowed.

'Our fleet ravages the coastal towns of the Peloponnese, gentlemen. That news came faster to us than it will reach the ears of their battle king. It is my hope that when he learns of it, he will be called home by his ephors. We tear at his flank every day he remains here. It may be enough.'

He doubted his own words and he thought they could see that in him. Pericles still remembered how Cimon had described King Pleistonax of Sparta. The young ruler had been scornful, rude, arrogant: as typically Spartan as if formed from a cast. There had been no weakness in him, however, no bluster or threats. Pleistonax had taken silver for a truce, but then thought nothing of breaking it. If the

Spartan blamed Athens for his father's death, Pericles could not imagine him going meekly home, no matter how they stung him.

'As for keeping order . . .' Pericles went on.

He stopped as the archon slumped sideways, his robe falling open to reveal a bony chest and an expanse of skin with a bluish tinge. Those around the old man tried to rouse him, but he was senseless. Pericles watched in grim horror as the chest rose and fell . . . rose . . . and fell, emptying. The man's head lolled and he was gone. His bowels released in a thin brown trail that spread down the rows and resulted in exclamations of disgust. The benches cleared around him and someone began vomiting nearby.

Pericles felt his throat dry, so that his voice became a creaking thing.

'This meeting is suspended, in recognition of the emergency and in honour of Archon Apollodormus. May he cross the river in peace.'

He signalled to the Scythian guards. The officer only backed away a pace, his eyes wide. Pericles cleared his throat in irritation. There was a new fear in the city and it was spreading even faster than the damned pestilence. People hid their faces and leaned away from one another, convinced bad air was the cause.

'Lochagos!' Pericles managed to snap to the Scythian guard officer. 'Do your duty. Fetch cleaners and make the archon presentable. We cannot leave Apollodormus where he is. Understand? The rest of you, clear the room, please. Allow the archon his dignity.'

Pericles looked with distaste at the brown line that ran down half a dozen rows. They could not leave the city for cremations. Instead, greasy pyres burned in courtyards, with men watching in case the sparks spread. That smoke just added to the choking air. He sighed, exhausted. There was not much dignity in death, no matter how it came. Yet the archon had looked fit enough just a few days before.

His own sons had come down with some disturbance of their bowels, Pericles thought. Xanthippus had been certain it was just some bad fish he and Paralus had eaten. That it might be this same, foul thing was like a cold hand in his chest. No. Xan and Paralus were strong and fit. It would not touch them, would not hurt them. Perhaps they had already recovered! He decided he would find time to go over to their house and make sure they had the best of care.

Pericles felt the weight of years on his shoulders, with an accompanying fear. Plagues came most summers in cities, that was known. They arrived on the air or in the holds of ships and they spread like fire for a time, killing off the old and very young. Not grown men, not strategoi! Pericles was needed. The gods knew, he was the only one who could keep the city safe. It would not be his time either. It could not be. He told himself that over and over as he tied a cloth over his mouth and hurried away from the council building, looking for cleaner air.

Pericles glanced around him as he knocked at the door of the town-house he had known as a boy. His father had stayed there when he was away from his family. Of course, it had been rebuilt after the Persian fires, but it had been his home as well for a time, before the divorce. He patted the door frame in affectionate memory. As he waited for it to be opened, he kept an eye out for any threat. There had been many reports of attacks on men and women. It didn't matter if those who stole or murdered were trying to feed their own family, not to the victims. He kept one hand on the knife belted around his waist, glaring at the families huddling nearby. The day was hot and they were beaten down by it, gasping as they stared. The smell, too, was a living thing in that place, as thick as sour broth. The cloth around his face didn't seem to help. He thumped on the door again, harder.

It seemed an age before he heard steps. The latch rattled and the door opened slowly onto a gloom and a rush of colder air, like a temple of stone. He breathed in relief at that, stepping inside and making sure to replace the bar.

He almost didn't recognise his first wife as she stood before him, her hands trembling. Thetis had lost an extraordinary amount of weight since he had last seen her, so that flesh hung in folds under her chin and her arms were wrinkled like linen. Her eyes were bright enough, but it looked more like madness than health. Pericles swallowed, pulling down the cloth on his face to speak.

'Thetis? You look . . . when did you eat last? Where are the boys?'

The air was cooler in the house than on the sun-baked street, but the smell was still there. It had become familiar, he realised. The pestilence ripping through the population had a particular odour as well as the bluish tinge to the skin he'd seen on the archon. He tried to look for that in his wife's face and throat, but the light was too dim.

'Thetis?' he said again, more gently.

He took her arm and she slumped, as if his touch was all she had waited for. Pericles found himself bearing her weight, though it was not what it had been. He walked with her across the hall to a bench, lowering her onto it with as much care as he could. The smell of bowels and corruption was sharper around her, as if it had seeped into her hair and skin. Vomit rose in his throat and he saw a pot by the window. Yet as he bent over it, a glimpse of the slurry within made his convulsion more violent. He could not stop adding to the mix until his stomach was completely empty, and even then the spasms went on, until he was in great pain.

'Where are the servants?' he managed at last.

'Gone,' she whispered.

'Run away?'

When she shook her head, he felt a twinge of panic.

'Where are the boys, Thetis? Where is Xanthippus? Paralus?'

Her eyes raised to the stairs and he almost gave up his thought of emptying the pot into the street trench outside, adding to the foulness. He'd already seen a dead dog blocking a drain on the way there. The resulting flood had been so appalling he'd almost wished for a fire to begin. The sun still shone. Until it rained again, those open gutters would be jammed and reeking all over the city.

With a stifled curse, Pericles went out with the brimming pot, trying to hold his breath and making himself dizzy so that he staggered. He emptied it into the trench in the street, disturbing a cloud of flies lost to feasting, driven mad by it. What he poured out just glistened and steamed with all the rest. He had no cloth to rub the clay clean and so he carried it back and placed it by his first wife. She stared at him and he saw the fear in her.

Pericles took a breath as he climbed the stairs, his heart fluttering in his chest with odd thumps and drops. It was both strain and disgust, as if he was trapped in horror and could not leave.

There were four bedrooms at the top of the house, under eaves. He opened one door after another, finding beds stained by fluids and fat flies buzzing in looping circles. It had been just a few days since he'd seen Thetis last, when she'd seemed fine. This plague was fast in its effect. Perhaps that meant it would pass quickly through the people and be forgotten. Some of them were like that, these summer fevers. It was odd, but when he'd held Thetis, she had felt cold, not feverish at all . . .

He opened the third door and saw his son Xanthippus lying on the bed. The young man looked thin and the room reeked of vomit and excrement. Pericles had thought he would be getting used to the worst of it, but each new breath brought some sharpness back to his senses.

'Oh, son, I'm so sorry,' Pericles said.

He went over and sat on the bed beside him. Xanthippus blinked slowly and raised a hand. Pericles took it in his and felt a terrible heat. He had seen fevers from wounds before. They rose and rose until either death came or Fate intervened.

'Where are the doctors?' Pericles asked.

Xanthippus only shook his head. His eyes were oddly wide, his mouth slack. Pericles felt a touch of fear seep in, a blade of ice that made it hard to breathe.

'They . . .' He bent to hear the whispering voice as Xanthippus struggled to speak. 'They won't come out. Offered . . . gold. I'm so thirsty . . .'

Pericles looked for water, a cloth, anything to moisten his son's lips. He cursed his thoughtlessness. In normal times, one of the house servants would have gone out early to collect water at a fountain, or in times of drought from the river that ran to the south of the city. Those fountains were choked dry, though whether it was the Spartans cutting the supply or just that they were blocked, it didn't matter. Pericles understood he had to send someone to the port, to fetch new barrels from the boats coming in day and night. He could do it. There was little point in leading this city if he couldn't.

'I'll fetch water, Xan. I promise. Can you wait a little longer?' His son nodded and Pericles backed out of the room. 'I'll be as quick as I can.'

He put his head in the room next door and found Paralus in slightly better form. The young man was in bed, but he pushed himself up when he saw his father was there. Pericles saw he'd been reading and felt a touch of pride.

'Xan and mum are very ill,' Paralus said. 'I think I'm all right, though I've given up trying to stop it coming out.'

He looked embarrassed suddenly. Pericles saw the bed was wet, sodden with liquid that had the same sour stench as the rest of the house.

'I'm here now,' Pericles told him. 'I should have come before, I'm sorry. I didn't know you were all so sick.'

'It hits fast – and hard,' Paralus said.

His eyes were shadowed with painful memory and Pericles felt fresh guilt surge. He had been busy with the city. It did not seem like an excuse.

'I'm going for water,' Pericles said firmly. 'There's none in the house and the fountains are all fouled. I can get some at the port, but it will be a few hours.'

'Thank you,' Paralus said.

He slumped back as he spoke and the relief was clear in

him. Pericles nodded. This was something he could do. The city would just have to wait while he looked after his sons.

He clattered down the stairs into the gloomy entrance hall. Thetis still sat where he had left her. He knew in the moment that something had changed. The stillness of the dead is unmistakable to those who have known it. Pericles stopped by her, reaching out to touch her face. He did not expect the sadness that washed through him then. There was always something more he wished he had said, he understood that. He reached out and closed her eyes, half-open and staring. Gently, he picked her up. She was no weight, really. He carried her up the stairs, but found her bed was unclean, dark and dried. Laying her down on the wooden floor, he stripped the bed and flung open drawers and chests in his search.

Every last piece of cloth had been torn up for strips. He was on the point of giving up when he opened the last drawer in her room. The dress she had worn at their wedding was still there, untouched and musty. She had not ripped it up with all the rest and he found himself weeping as he laid it out on the bare boards of the bed and her on top.

As he went down the stairs again, he thought he heard Paralus calling, asking what was happening. Pericles made no reply. The door latch could be lifted and then shaken down from the outside, but if no one was strong enough to answer his knock, he realised he would have to break it in when he returned.

There were eyes on him as he came out, desperate, thirsty eyes. He ignored them all as he hurried away. At the bottom of the street, he passed a fountain that had run dry. Muck had been baked to cracked earth in its bowl. People stared at the strategos there as well, gasping like crows in the sun.

Pericles had thought his priorities were clear enough when he'd explained them to the council. Yet the plague had come to Athens. While it roared and tore at them, they needed water.

The road between the Long Walls down to the port was shadowed while the sun still rose. Only noon rays could light that ground and it was oddly cool there compared to the rest of the city. Pericles passed archer towers above and saw hoplites on guard up there. They watched him and he wanted to shout at them to face outwards, but he did not.

On any normal day, he might have met a thousand of his people coming into the city, or leaving it, with as many carts and draught animals pulling in goods. It was a vein of life, and the Spartans who camped outside could not choke it off.

Pericles met only a few people on the road. They drew back from him, pressing sleeves to their mouths and shrinking away. Whether they knew him or not, he could not be sure. The sea glittered ahead and he could see ships out there, with oars sweeping. It was a sight to raise the heart as he came out into the great port.

The Piraeus had been transformed over a dozen years, rebuilt in better stone with more docks and quays than ever before. His father would hardly have known the place, but Pericles had overseen every step of the designs with Phidias. It was a wonder, and he turned right as soon as he reached the main concourse, heading straight for the port master. The Piraeus was busier than the road that led to it, almost a town on its own. Perhaps they were less afraid of the pestilence in the city there, or perhaps it had not taken such a grip on them. He thought of Thetis, her image flashing into his mind. He shook his head hard, putting it aside. He had a task.

A queue of people stood and chatted in the sun by the port master's station. Pericles was walking past them when he stopped and turned slowly. A cart was there, laden down with what looked like amphorae for water or wine.

'What's in those?' he asked.

The owner looked him up and down before deciding whether to reply.

'River water,' he said, holding up a token with a mark carved into the wood, a crude thing. 'All bought and paid for. You with the council? I'll sell you the lot for thirty drachms, if you want.'

'Thirty?' Pericles said in astonishment. It was many times what they might have cost in a normal year. He firmed his mouth, suddenly furious.

'Don't look like that, son. These are war prices. You'll get sixty for them if you go into the city. Probably more by now.'

As Pericles looked along the quayside, he saw a ship unloading the precious supply of water they needed so desperately in the city. More carts stood untended, piled high with sacks of grain. He frowned.

'Very well,' he said to the waiting man. 'I'll buy them. I'll need your cart as well.'

'The cart is not for sale,' the man said with a laugh. 'I can't keep making a living without a way to carry the jugs, can I?'

'Then wait here. I'll fetch another.'

Pericles walked past the line, ignoring their protests and angry words. He went inside to find the port master drinking from a cup of wine. A burly hoplite stood on either side of his desk, their presence explained by piles of coin. Pericles saw silver and gold and he felt the hoplites watching him for any sharp movement.

Standing before the desk, he lifted out a token of his own, a bronze disc that confirmed him as strategos.

'I am Pericles, strategos of Athens. Stand up in my presence.'

The port master gaped as he rose, his eyes darting to the piles of coins he suddenly knew he might have to explain. The hoplites exchanged a worried look.

'I see water on the docks and on carts outside. Yet the city is dying of thirst – and you seem to be doing very well.'

Pericles swept the coins from the table with one gesture. The man gave a cry, but he did not reach for them.

'Strategos, I've tried! No one wants to go into the city. The water supplies pile up here and I can't get men willing to take them in. They are all too afraid of the plague.'

'It hasn't stopped you selling council property, I see,' Pericles said. 'In time of war? Your life is forfeit.'

The port master pushed past his table to sink to his knees.

'Please, strategos! How can I make men move when they are afraid?'

Pericles thought of Thetis, gasping for water at the end.

'You make an example,' he said. 'Bring him outside.'

He snapped the last to the two hoplites and turned on his heel. The man began to weep, but they dragged him out even so, bumping his knees on the stones.

The crowd were utterly silent, as if a wolf had come amongst them. Pericles glared at them all. He saw the owner of the precious cart was edging away and raised his voice once more.

'Stand where you are. On my authority as strategos of Athens. We are at war. Disobey my orders on pain of death. Is that understood?'

They nodded, held in place by fear. Pericles saw some of the ones at the edges were glancing around, wondering if they could run.

'Kill anyone who leaves,' Pericles ordered the closest hoplite. The man glowered at the crowd in turn, cowing them further.

Pericles sent the other hoplite to the closest ship, summoning their officers. They came out into the hard sun with visible reluctance. Yet order held. They may not have been Spartan in their obedience, but he was a name in Athens and he called them.

The port master squirmed where he knelt as more of them came to line up before Pericles. The man was used to holding the reins of power in that place and he stared at the ground in humiliation.

'Whatever you came here to do, whatever your rank, put it aside,' Pericles said. 'My orders are to take water into the city. To fill every cart on these docks and get them up the road as fast as you can, then to return and do it again.'

'What about sacks of grain? We have a hold full of it.'

It was the captain of the ship who spoke. Pericles glanced at a man used to authority. He held the gaze for a moment, until the fellow quailed and looked down.

'Put it aside or leave it for rats, I care not. That is a problem for tomorrow. For today, the wells are dry in the city and people are dying. My orders are as the representative of the council. The authority of the Assembly is in me.'

One of the new hoplites was edging away. Pericles increased the volume of his voice as he rounded on the man.

'Stand still!' he roared. 'Don't take another step, or I'll spill your life on this dock right now.'

'Please!' the hoplite said. He was very young, Pericles saw. More, he was trembling. 'Please, I can't go in. I've seen the plague and I can't.'

He had not stopped moving and Pericles gestured to the men closest to him. Two hoplites from the ship grabbed his arms. One of them hissed in his ear to be quiet, but he kept wailing and pleading.

Pericles waited, thinking of Thetis, wondering if Aspasia too might die. He felt a coldness settle upon him, a tightening of the skin and heart.

'Very well. By the authority granted to me by the people of Athens in time of war, I sentence you to death. Carry it out.'

He spoke to the ship's captain. The man was pale, but his mouth became a thin line. The hoplite held by the arms began to make a wild sound as the captain drew a knife from his belt. The others held him tightly and it was quick enough, though they were all spattered with his blood by the time he'd finished flailing.

Pericles looked down at the port master, watching with huge eyes.

'Do I need another example?' Pericles asked.

The man shook his head.

'No, kurios. I'll get water into the city, I swear.'

'Then move! All of you! Fetch it from the holds. Go in groups of four – and if I find any of you slinking away, I will hunt you down myself and there will be no mercy. Move!'

They broke into groups like a hive coming apart. Pericles saw the captain of the ship sending two hoplites with each group, to direct their strength as well as making sure they would not run. The man himself remained until Pericles turned to look at him.

'If you are going to complain about my actions, I suggest you take it up with the council . . .' Pericles said.

The captain grimaced.

'No, it's not that. He disobeyed. You were quite right. I just wanted to ask, strategos. I came in this morning and all we hear is that there's plague in the city. I've kept the men out of the whorehouses here, but you've seen it. Is it bad?'

Pericles considered. He needed the man's help.

'We've known worse. It is a plague summer, that's all. We need water – and we'll need the grain from your hold and more like it, every day until this is over.'

He glanced at the only other figure still with them, the port master, who had not dared to rise. The hoplites had taken the corpse away, leaving only a slick of blood on the stones.

'Get up,' Pericles ordered. 'You must know this place better than anyone. Be my right hand, today. Help get it moving.'

The man rose in desperate relief.

'They're just afraid,' he said. 'It's hard to make them work when they are afraid.' He glanced at the blood. 'You can't kill everyone who refuses.'

'You are mistaken,' Pericles said coldly. 'Though it won't come to that. Our soldiers have given oath to follow orders, even until death. There is no difference between facing Persian Immortals and this pestilence. Tell them that, if they ask. Now, come with me. I want a line of carts trundling up that road – free for the asking.'

It was night by the time Pericles came back to the townhouse. He was sunburned and aching from standing on his feet and bending men to his will the entire day. Even the walk back to the city hadn't loosened him up. Yet a full cart stood outside on the street. A crowd was forming there, with his hoplites handing out clay amphorae and even skins of wine he had found in a warehouse. More like that one would be coming at sunrise. It was a start.

Pericles knocked on the door before he remembered the latch had fallen on the inside. He scowled at having to do it, but he would just have to find a carpenter before he went to sleep. It was one more task to add to the hundreds he still had to do.

With two kicks, he broke the door in and stepped into the gloom. He held an amphora of cool water under each arm as he climbed the steps.

Xanthippus' room was black without the lamp lit. Pericles sat on the edge of the bed and found the lamp by touch and memory. He struck flint and iron into a little wool, blowing on it and setting the flame to the wick. It spluttered and crackled, spreading gold across the night's dark.

His son was dead, his mouth open and the tongue showing dry. Pericles felt grief wrench at him with appalling violence. He reached out to touch and shake the young

360

man, but he was cold and the flesh stiff. With a cry, Pericles picked up the lamp and crossed into the other room.

'Paralus! Your brother!' he cried.

There was no reply and when the light fell across the second bed, he saw Paralus sprawled there, all life gone. Slowly, Pericles sank to the floor. He put one hand on the lamp and snuffed it out with his palm, feeling the sting of the burn but not caring. Some things deserved the dark.

28

Spartan soldiers halted the party of Corinthian horsemen outside the camp boundary. Nicomedes sent one of his personal guard with word for them to enter, though it was not without suspicion. Neither the uncle nor the young king had summoned them to Attica. Nicomedes could see no good reason why a dozen riders would come racing out from their city across the isthmus when Pleistonax was in the field and facing the old adversary. There were more than a few dark expressions in the Spartan camp as the Corinthians dismounted. Whatever the reason for their arrival, it was unlikely to be good news.

The camp outside Athens was a bare place, without embankments. Lines of tents and toilet pits were the only mark on a land that reeked of smoke, where ash drifted on the breeze and collected wherever there was something like shelter. The walls of Athena's city were close enough to loom and press, so that it was hard not to sense them. They filled the eye, from the city to the distant sea.

Pleistonax saw his uncle approaching from an angle as the men of Corinth were directed across to him. His own tent and kit were the same as any other, with nothing more personal than a razor and a second set of sandals. In the summer heat, Pleistonax stood wearing only a simple tunic that left his legs and arms bare. A kopis blade lay flat against his thigh in a sheath of tanned goatskin, but his helmet, cloak, shield and sword rested in a neat pile by the tent, ready to be snatched up.

He gave no orders for the men of Corinth to be searched for weapons. They were all armed, that went without saying. In time of war, nowhere was safe. Pleistonax showed no sign of nervousness. He folded his arms as the Corinthians drew close, ready to hear, but a long way from offering trust or welcome.

His uncle managed to reach him first, in time to murmur a few words before they were in earshot.

'Remember these men are allies,' Nicomedes said.

Pleistonax nodded for his benefit, though he could not help making a reply.

'So were the Athenians once.'

The young king was unhappy at the mere idea that men of Corinth had seen Sparta at the lowest point. He knew by then that half the reputation of his people had been earned the hard way, in skill and battle. The rest was more complex, a combination of threat and mystery. It could not be given up. That half of their strength had to be maintained, even in war, even with men of the Peloponnese who had proved their loyalty. Sparta was more than strength of arms: it was an idea, a legend. On that day, Pleistonax was its avatar.

He said nothing as the foreign soldiers dropped to one knee in front of him, their heads bowed. That much was due his title and rank. He was the commander in the field and a king. It fell to Nicomedes to speak first.

'His Majesty Pleistonax, son of Pausanias, bids you welcome.' His uncle paused then, peering closer and smiling. 'I know you of course, Nestos. I remember your unstinting service after the earthquake. Truly, Corinth are allies of note. Your companions are strangers to me, but if you vouch for them, they will be made welcome. Will you gentlemen share food with us? There is a nourishing stew almost ready for the evening meal.'

Pleistonax watched the strangers exchange wary glances and repressed a smile. Spartan food was famously bland, always without salt or honey. Yet it built muscle and bone well enough. Pleistonax was pleased to discover he was both taller and broader than the men of Corinth, even the veterans.

Nestos was the first to straighten up as Nicomedes spoke, showing he had authority in that group. The man bowed deeply to Pleistonax to be sure he gave no offence, then replied.

'Majesty, Regent Nicomedes, it is my honour. It is true I came when Corinth sent me to support our most ancient ally and friend. I fought alongside the royal Spartan whose shade has crossed the river. It was a dark time, but I find I treasure those memories when I wake in thc small hours. To fight alongside a king is something I hope to tell my grandchildren.'

Pleistonax frowned until he could see the ridge of his own brow half-obscuring his sight.

'Is that why you have come here? To relive old memories?'

He saw his uncle wince out of the corner of his eye and sighed. Pleistonax knew he was brash and quick to anger. He counted it as a strength, whereas old men like Nicomedes seemed to think it was a dangerous thing. The young king shrugged as Nestos looked at him.

'Well? You rode here, which suggests you have something

urgent to say. Would you prefer to wait until we have all eaten, or perhaps until you have accompanied my uncle on a tour of the walls tomorrow? I am less patient. This is a war camp, in territory hostile to us all. Say what you have come to say or leave.'

Nestos dipped his head quickly, accepting the young man's assessment and moving on without hesitating. In that moment, he would have given his right arm to deal with the king's predecessor. Pleistarchus had been a battle king worth the name, a son of Leonidas. To have to address one younger than his own sons was a poor exchange. Still, he had to spend the coins he had been given.

'I speak not for myself, but His Majesty King Aleuses. I have been told to say first that an act of honour does not require payment. When Corinth sent men to stand along-side Sparta at Plataea, to accept the command of your father Pausanias, that was not in expectation of a favour returned, but in reply to a greater threat. Corinthian ships rowed too at Salamis – and I myself fought to contain your helot revolt and restore order. These were no more than the actions of a trusted friend and came with no cost or price expected.'

'And yet, somehow, you repeat each one,' Pleistonax said.

Nestos paused, the older man flushing in what might have been a surge of quickly controlled anger. Pleistonax felt himself respond, leaning forward on the balls of his feet, ready to attack. That had been beaten into him a thousand times over by the trainers of the agoge camp. A battle king of Sparta could not flinch from threat, or when he was struck. His reaction had to be to surge forward at any provocation. In that, Pleistonax carried with him the honour of his people.

'Majesty, I mention the past only to show we have been allies for many generations. Corinth considers Athens an enemy, as you know. We will support Sparta in alliance, in any form you allow. In men, or ships or silver. Let it be . . .'

Once more, Pleistonax spoke over him.

'That was something I knew yesterday, Nestos. Nothing you have said would bring you from your city to this desolate place. If it is to offer strength, I might have expected more than a dozen horsemen, but then I did not ask for reinforcements. I wanted the Athenians to see my army, my red-cloaks, standing outside their walls.'

'And they have,' Nestos said gently. 'War is made in the spring, is it not? The summer's height is already past. The days are shortening once again, Majesty, and yet the walls still stand.'

It was Pleistonax's turn to be uncomfortable. He made himself unfold his arms, though it was probably just a coincidence that it left one hand in range of his kopis hilt.

'Do not question me, Nestos, if that is your intention. I have challenged the hoplites of Athens – and they have kept their gates closed, yes. Their cowardice is revealed to those they call the League.'

He spoke with anger, revealing much to the Corinthian. The months of frustration and impotence had not sat well with a young king armed for battle and determined to prove himself at last. Nestos chose his words with care, as if he sought to persuade a lion not to snap at him.

'Majesty . . . your point has surely been made. They cannot take the field against your army. You are free to burn and destroy the region around the city, while they tremble and are afraid.' He paused, taking a deep breath. 'But they have not lost, and neither have you won.'

'Nestos, you overstep your bounds,' Nicomedes said roughly. 'You have no right to say . . .'

'Let him speak, uncle,' Pleistonax said, waving a hand.

Nestos saw the older man shut his mouth with a snap and nodded.

'Thank you, Majesty, for your patience. I came here only to say your purpose has been achieved. They hide behind their walls and there is no one in Attica to tell you where you can stand. That is a victory, I believe – in what it tells their allies, in the revelation of strength. No one will say Sparta cannot field an army to make the whole League tremble. Not any longer. You can return home in honour, while they pick over their burned fields for food. Athenians are an arrogant race, Majesty. Perhaps it is time to let them starve.'

Pleistonax said nothing for a time. To Nestos' surprise, the young king began to pace back and forth before the group. Eleven of them still bowed their heads over one knee and he had not invited them to stand.

'Tell me, Nestos, how bad is it?'

'How bad . . . ? Majesty, I do not understand.'

'Did you think I was blind and deaf here? I have spies in that city, as well as messengers on the road back to Sparta, men in Argos to report all they hear. Friends in Corinth even! Tell me why you want me to leave this place, Nestos. Speak the words you have been told to say.'

Nestos understood. He firmed his jaw and spoke.

'Majesty, their fleet raids the coast at home. You have heard of that, I see, though perhaps not the full extent. They burned my home port, so that ships of Corinth can no longer seek a safe berth in a storm. Nor can my captains remain at anchor with League ships ready to ram and board. The League – led by Athens – has attacked every village and town on the Peloponnese coast, except for Argos. Those bastards reap the benefits, of course, raising cups of Lemnos red to friends and allies as they row past!'

The Corinthian realised his voice had risen and that both Spartans were watching him with a more predatory interest. He controlled himself before he spoke again.

'Majesty, yes, I was sent to ask you to come home. The presence of Spartans on the Peloponnese would change the balance overnight. Your men would make these raids too costly for them. It is we who pay the price of each month you spend here – and the season for war is at an end.'

'At last, the truth, uncle,' Pleistonax said. 'Can you hear it?'

Nicomedes nodded, though he looked shaken. His nephew smiled in a rictus. His hands trembled, Nicomedes saw, as strong emotion washed through him.

'Why do you think the Athenians raid our home coast, Nestos?' Pleistonax said.

The man was held by the king's gaze as if trapped under glass. When he spoke, the words seemed dragged from him.

'They want you to come home, to be called back. But Majesty . . .'

'No, you have it right. They burn and kill so that men of Corinth will ride out here and beg me to turn away from their walls. You, Nestos, are doing exactly what they want you to do by coming to me. Do you understand that?'

'Majesty, the season of war . . .'

'Do you understand, Nestos? You coming here, to me. It is what they want, what they desperately need. Do you see it?'

'Of course, Majesty, but it does not change . . .'

'So you will be able to predict my answer, will you not? I am the battle king of Sparta. My father was Pausanias, who was brought down by the whores hiding behind those walls over there. So tell me, Nestos of Corinth, will I be coming home with you? Or will I ask you – and Corinth and all the rest of our allies – to *endure*? Which do you think it will be?'

Nestos raised his head, recovering a cold dignity.

'I believe you will remain, Majesty.'

'You are correct,' Pleistonax said softly. 'Now, we are low on food, Nestos. If you wish to do me a service, to renew the bonds of loyalty, you might arrange for supplies to be brought out. That would be welcome.'

He saw the man was taking the rejection without further drama and warmed to him. Not that Nestos had any choice, of course.

'I will come home for the first frosts,' Pleistonax added, 'though their fleet will do the same. Do not imagine I am content, Nestos. We cannot match the League at sea, and they will not face us on land. It is a stalemate of a sort.'

He growled five more words then, an afterthought, his head lowered like a bull facing the knife: 'We should build a fleet.' The idea pleased him. 'Take that home with you, Nestos. Could Corinth build ships to match the League? It might change the balance of power.'

'If Persia couldn't beat them . . .' Nicomedes murmured.

'*We* led the fleet against Persia!' Pleistonax snapped. 'Before the damned League even existed. My father commanded hundreds of ships before his disgrace. *We* are the inheritors of those victories, not Athens!'

Pleistonax was shouting. His uncle had taken a step back from his wrath and half the camp seemed to be watching and listening. The young king made a disgusted sound. The day had grown cold, he realised, as if in response to the Corinthian.

'Corinth can build warships,' Pleistonax said. 'So let them find a quiet place, far away from Athenian waters. They can create a fleet there, ready to destroy the Athenians when they come again. A ship is just a ship, Nestos! It is the crew that matters. I can give you warriors born.'

He was clenching one fist, raising it at the city that sat closed before him, at the great gates he could not force open. Nestos was nodding, his eyes wide. Spartans had never understood ships, he knew that. They saw them as transports for their warriors, not as weapons in their own right. Yet if Pleistonax was serious, Corinth would turn her labours to building a fleet.

'What would my father have done, Nicomedes?' Pleistonax said.

His uncle smiled in memory.

'My brother? Pausanias would have agreed with you. War is to be waged to the utmost, until our enemies are broken, until they are unable to raise spears again. There should be no respite given, no mercy offered or accepted. He would say that – and that he is proud of his son.'

'Well, you have your answer, Nestos of Corinth,' Pleistonax said. His voice was hoarse, almost a growl. 'Go home now. I will stay.'

The sun was rising, but Pericles did not look up as he left the town-house. He had spent the night with the dead, in prayer and apology. He could not remember all the hours of darkness. Some he did not want to remember. He had wailed and cursed and shouted terrible things when no one could see, when night covered him.

As he stood before the door, he tried to settle the latch back in place. It was broken and he stared at it for an age, trying to understand why it would not sit straight. His mind was slow, from lack of sleep or the grief that lashed at him like a great fish passing by. It brought back a memory of childhood, when he had been very small. A fish had brushed his chest as he swam, reducing him in an instant to helpless terror. He remembered how it slid past, a dark length he could not avoid or turn away. He knew it had grown in memory, as fears will. There were no fish in the river of that size, that gleamed and rasped his skin.

He shook his head, unsure why he was even thinking of a day so far in the past the rest of it was lost. He blinked at the broken lock. Ah, he had kicked it in. It didn't matter. There was nothing left worth saving. His hands were filthy, he thought. He needed to bathe in the river once again.

He was three steps away from the door when he remembered the Spartans had closed the city. He could not get out. He looked back. The thought of someone entering while he was away overwhelmed him. His boys were inside. Thetis was there. They could not protect themselves any more. They depended on him. Pericles blinked, his grief moving past like a shadow, like the fish against his childhood skin. There had been no flurry, no flapping tail and scales. It had moved without even knowing he was there. Or it had not cared one iota for his terror, as if he had no more worth than dust or rain. No. He could not let thieves see the door open.

He looked around blearily. Where were his friends?

Were they all gone? The city seemed quiet for an hour with the sun showing. Was everyone dead? He turned to a flicker of movement and saw one woman had come out to clean her step.

Pericles walked towards her and she cringed away. There had been too many robberies, too much violence, he remembered. People were desperate and afraid, beset on all sides while a Spartan king prowled around their walls.

'Please!' he called. 'I won't harm you. I just want someone to watch my door. My sons . . .' He could not say it as his voice suddenly choked off. 'I just need to find someone to repair the door.'

The woman remained, though she looked warily at him, judging. She looked as if she wanted to help, he thought. His hands reeked, but he fished in his mouth for a coin. The action made him gag and yet he held it out to her, a little drachm of silver, the size of his smallest fingernail.

'Please,' he said, holding it up. 'Would you do that? My sons are inside.'

He wasn't sure if she understood. She came closer and took the coin from him, darting back like a wild bird being fed from the hand. He did not know her. Yet in that moment, it was as if they were the only two people in the world.

'My sons are dead,' he whispered. His mouth hung open as he breathed. Her eyes filled at what she saw in him.

'I'm sorry,' she said. 'Go. I'll watch the door.'

He nodded. It was a small thing, but he felt oddly proud to have achieved it. He was not helpless. He had lost . . . more than he could bear to think about. In that moment, he needed Aspasia, to know she was safe, with his young son. The hetaira house was not far away, closer than the

Agora and the council building. She would be there. He had to see his wife and son, to embrace them, to know they were alive.

He ran through streets that were still a desolate shadow of what they had been before the Spartans came. Pericles felt himself sweating, his heart racing, his lower back sending shooting pains into his legs. Of course, he hadn't slept. He remembered how that went from his twenties, when it had seemed like stealing time from the gods to go without sleep. They always came with a price, those extra hours! What still seemed easy as the sun rose became hard. Sweat and aches were followed by the lure of a bed or couch and complete unconsciousness for an age. That too had been a lesson. All things had to be repaid.

The hetaira house looked as it always did, as if the pestilence had passed them by. Pericles paused before the door, his fist raised. It was early still and he felt a twinge of guilt. No, he had to know they were all right. His eyes swam as he hammered on the door, calling her name.

He stood in the sun for an age, weak with exhaustion. He would have to cremate the boys, he thought. He could get what he needed from the port, easily enough. Perhaps it would be better to do it there on the quayside. It was not easy to burn a body to ash. It took a huge amount of wood and perfumed oil and it had to burn for a day, hot enough to scorch stone. He would . . .

The door opened and Aspasia was there. She carried their son on her hip and she looked horrified at the state of the man on her step. The little boy held out his arms for his father, recognising him.

'Pericles?' Aspasia said. 'What . . . what has happened? What is it?'

'Xan and Paralus are dead,' he told her, forcing the words out. 'Thetis with them.' He cleared his throat, wincing as his stomach suddenly ached. He rubbed the spot, without being aware of it. 'I'll need to build a pyre for them. I'll need . . .'

She came out and embraced him, the child between them. Pericles clung onto them both, lost in grief, breathing them in, needing them.

29

Where the sea met the docks at Piraeus, the waters had a coating of oil. It was bitterly cold in the shadow of warships, but steps descended below the surface. The structure allowed Pericles to scrub himself clean for the first time in days. That was a relief, from the sour smell always in his nostrils, from the ingrained filth on his skin that needed more than just a jug and cloth. Though the wind had a hint of autumn, Pericles rubbed himself all over with blocks of clay, ash and sand. The abrasives left his skin scraped and raw, but it was still satisfying. When he climbed out, Aspasia handed him a flask of oil and he rubbed himself down with Athena's gift to the world, working it between his fingers and down his flanks. When he was finished, his wife passed over a fresh robe and sandals, then helped him fix it all in place.

She looked worried at how thin he had become. Aspasia was no cook, but she had the recipes of the hetaira house. She had tried everything, from root broth to bitter greens that were said to nourish the blood. Pericles had tasted it all, but could not keep anything down.

When he was ready, the man who was first in Athens stood with his feet shoulder width apart, skin oiled and clean. He raised his head, unflinching. Pericles looked at the two massive pyres constructed around the bodies of his sons. No sign of Xanthippus or Paralus could be made out beneath the layers of cedar, pine and oak. It was all seasoned wood, broken up from fleet boats, against the objections of their captains. Cimon would have been furious, Pericles thought, but there was little wood left in the city. Roofs had fallen as families tried to take one beam in two to burn their dead. He could hardly send carts out of Athens for fresh wood, nor wait for ships to return with holds full of lumber while his sons rotted on the docks. The city he loved, that he had rebuilt and fashioned for years, was still under siege.

Pericles looked again at the pyres, taller and wider than a man and drenched in the same oil that protected his skin. It would all burn well enough when the priests were finished with their prayers. Pericles breathed slowly. His sons were already free, he reminded himself. They would not feel the flames.

Zeno and Anaxagoras were there, as well as Phidias the architect and Damon, who could play any instrument. Zeno's wife had come down with the sickness. Pericles had tried to send the man home when he heard that. His friend had argued long and hard that it was all right, she was recovering. They had all heard by then how Pericles had left his sons to fetch water. As he told it, he had spent too long solving the problems of the city, finding the boys gone by the time he returned. It was a burden he had made for himself, as no one really knew whether they would have lived or died. His friends saw the guilt that burned so terribly in him, robbing him of strength and will.

Yet some did recover, without a doubt. Perhaps Zeno's wife would be one of those. Pericles had found his own mother was on the mend as well, after two bad weeks of illness. Agariste had outlived one husband, a son and two grandsons – as well as a daughter. Pericles had heard his sister Eleni had succumbed two nights before, held in the arms of her husband and children at the end. The plague that year was a thing of teeth and claws, without pity. It left some families untouched and swallowed others whole. It ripped away some in just hours, while others lingered, growing slowly weaker, taking the hope of those they loved with every ache and cramp. The coldness and blue tinge was the final sign, that seemed to mean no hope was left. Pericles had not heard of anyone surviving that. If they were to have a chance, the recovery had to begin before then. He rubbed his own stomach under the robe, hoping he would not disgrace himself.

The group that gathered by the pyres was small compared to what it would have been before. Pericles saw Aspasia had brought his little son, neat and clean for once, though the boy had the most extraordinary ability to find dirt and roll in it. Young Pericles held his mother's hand that day and stared at the pyres, asking over and over if Xan and Paralus were inside.

Two other children had joined their household. It was an arrangement that had become increasingly common over the crisis, mingling children of relatives and friends as one. The older boy, Alcibiades, was a son from his mother's side, a cousin to Pericles though he was very much a child. His little brother was named Ariphron, a family name. They were strangers and very wary of the man who had lost his own sons and had such red eyes. Pericles sighed as Aspasia gathered them in, brushing marks from their tunics and hissing at them to be still.

The council had sent the epistates for the day. He was another one Pericles did not really know, who bowed his head and looked awkward whenever their eyes met. Strategos

Myronides had come as well, though his gaze always seemed to need something. Pericles had no answers for anyone. He could hardly look away from where his sons lay, wet with oil.

Two priestesses of Athena and a follower of Hades completed the rites. Pericles had a sense of the boys around Aspasia losing that fidgety energy in sudden stillness. The representatives of the gods lit torches from an iron brazier, approaching the pyres.

Pericles could not see clearly for a time then. His vision blurred as two patches of brightness sprang into being, reaching up and up. He had carried Xanthippus and Paralus on his shoulders. He had instructed them in their letters, thrashed them for lying or theft and told them a thousand stories. He had let them down when they needed him. Oh, he understood the plague might have taken them if he'd returned hours before. He could not completely explain the strange state that had settled upon him in his father's house. He had seen Thetis was dead and then . . . He shook his head. He knew he had walked down to those very docks and yet he remembered almost nothing of what had followed.

The pyres had grown tails, the fires reaching up into the wind like souls. They breathed, he realised. Fire was a liquid thing, not yet black or ash, but so clearly alive. It gave him hope.

Aspasia touched his arm and murmured something. She brought his new wards over to say how sorry they were. Pericles nodded to them and she took the boys back to the city, his own son with them. Little Pericles was sniffling by then, rubbing his stomach. The sight of that little boy watching lads like Alcibiades for how to behave was a knife in his father's chest, a sudden sharpness.

One by one, they all came to him and said their good-byes, heading back to a city where houses were boarded shut and life had been cheapened. Pericles glanced to the ships at anchor. He could leave, he knew. He could just walk on board and show the seal of a strategos and any one of the captains would take him wherever he wanted to go. He shook his head as the flames roared at him. This was his city. His sons had needed him; Athens still did. He would not let her down.

'I thought the temples were all closed,' Myronides said, standing at his shoulder. 'I have a dozen petitioners complaining they cannot get a single priest to say prayers over the dead, never mind three.'

Pericles felt himself hauled back into the world, like an anchor rising from a green deep. He blinked slowly at the older man.

'Phidias asked them, I think,' he said.

Myronides peered at him, judging his strength.

'I suppose you are the closest they have to a patron, for the Parthenon. I went up on the scaffold to see the frieze, Pericles. Truly, it is a great work. It will stand for ever.'

'Perhaps,' Pericles said.

He did not want to be talking of such things while his sons were burned. He knew Myronides wanted someone to tell him what to do, but on that day, Pericles felt empty. He looked back at the pyres and saw the outlines of ribs. The priest of Hades had stayed to tend the dead, he noticed. The man's acolytes carried long rods of iron and Pericles swallowed as they poked the fire, shifting remains until they were all consumed. Some of them carried hammers on their belts. He did not want to know what they were for. His sons were beyond pain. He did not want to see their bones broken even so.

Pericles turned to Myronides. As he did so, pain cramped his gut and he groaned, rubbing it with a thumb.

'I'm sorry. I have had it and survived,' Myronides said softly. 'A month ago. It was a bad time, but here I stand. I know . . .' Myronides looked at the pyres, suddenly aware of them once more. 'I know it will be hard, but you can take hope. If it can't kill old Myronides . . .'

He broke off. Pericles almost laughed at his awkwardness.

'You have known plagues before, Myronides. I know I have. They tear through the people in the summers, but then they vanish. I admit, I have never known one like this before. It seems so . . . fickle, almost. Some years, old men and women all go in a month, or some spotted fever steals children in the night. We endure. Those who survive grow strong again. It is the way of things, though at times, it is . . . hard to bear.'

'This is worse than any fever I ever saw,' Myronides said. 'It should have burned itself out by now, but I have reports of bodies by the thousand. We have lost as many as one in three, Pericles. Those who survive are . . . more angry than anything. They want to strike back.'

Pericles pinched the bridge between his eyes with finger and thumb, rubbing the skin there. He had known why Myronides remained behind, of course.

'If you take the army out, the Spartans will destroy them.'

'I don't think you understand how much anger there is in the city.'

Pericles opened bloodshot eyes.

'You think that is some substitute for fitness or skill? How many trained men have we lost in the last few months? A couple of thousand? More? If you march out of this city, half the men will be emptying their bowels down their legs as they march. They wouldn't last an hour. This damned plague hasn't touched the Spartans, has it? They sit on open ground, with the breeze taking all the bad air away, while we have corpses rotting on every corner. And you would take the army out to fight them? *No*, Myronides! There is my answer.'

'We cannot endure this again. You must see that.'

Myronides waved a hand in the direction of the pyres and in a flash of anger, Pericles almost struck him for using his sons to make a point. He held himself very still and the older man kept talking.

'There are reports of supplies being brought across the isthmus. Our scouts say it could be enough to keep the Spartans in the field all winter. Yet we will have to bring back the fleet as the season turns and storms come. Do you think we can endure till spring, trapped as we are? Or last another year if they leave and return?'

'The walls keep us safe!' Pericles snapped. 'They and the fleet keep us safe. This is the *only* thing that works against Sparta, Myronides. We can trade and live free with these walls and this port. This pestilence will die away over the cold months, as they always do. In the spring . . .'

'In the spring, we will still be trapped in here, with too many people, too much shit and blood on the streets – and some new plague to kill us!'

The older man was wild-eyed, Pericles saw. He suddenly recalled Myronides had lost his wife to it. It was like dipping into the sea once more to wonder if the temples had sent priests to dedicate her funeral pyre.

'Your wife . . . I was sorry to hear . . .' he tried.

Myronides shook his head.

'This is not about me. It is about the survival of this city. If we stay behind your precious walls, we will be ruined. The world will call us cowards. No, if I have to die, I would rather it was holding a spear and shield against a noble enemy, not alone and forgotten, without even prayers said over me.'

Perhaps he meant his wife, Pericles did not know. It could also have applied to Xanthippus and Paralus. Pericles closed his eyes until he could breathe again. When he opened them, Myronides looked aghast at what he had said.

'I – I didn't mean . . .'

'Forget it. It is a hard path, what I ask. I know that. When men call to take up arms, when they shout on the hill for vengeance, it is the hardest thing in the world to *think*, to wait and plan and consider the best course. The blood grows hot, the call to honour tugs at our hearts, but that is the most dangerous time. Listen to me, Myronides. Sparta cannot commit their army to stand before our walls for much longer.'

He saw Myronides might object and held up a hand, though the pain in his gut was worsening.

'Every month they spend here is one where their power is reduced at home. Can you see that much? If they come each spring and summer, we will burn towns and villages of the Peloponnese in reply. We will demonstrate their weakness to those who look to them for leadership. It *will* hurt them! It will weaken them! I know wars are won in days or weeks. Yet this is Sparta, Myronides! The greatest fighting force ever assembled, the victors of Plataea – against a Persian army so vast they were like grains of sand. Give me time and I *will* break them, but it cannot be on the field, not in a single year.'

He hoped for acceptance. Instead, Myronides looked away and Pericles knew he had lost the man.

'We were there as well, at Plataea,' Myronides said at last. 'Athenians too stood against Persia. Now our city is dying – and the Spartans are the cause. Some say it is a curse we can lift only by courage. If you are too sick, let *me* lead the army out. Let me arm all the able men! We have the spears and shields of those who died. The council can take them for the greater good. I tell you, if we go out, if we engage them, we could change the balance of power for ever. We could put an end to the threat of a Spartan army.' He saw Pericles was unmoved and spoke with a world of bitterness. 'If Cimon were here, he would hear me. He would agree with me.'

Pericles might have replied, but the pain in his stomach surged, making him gasp. He reached for the older man as he bent over, trying to steady himself. Myronides took a step away.

'The council won't vote without you,' Myronides said, staring coldly. 'I could end it this year, but you have them all following your bidding, too afraid to make a decision on their own.'

Pericles found the strength to speak, though his voice was a growl.

'Numbers don't matter against the Spartans, Myronides. The Persians had a huge army, but they were like waves on a rock. I'm sorry, but I cannot do what you want. You *will not* open the gates. Keep order in the city. That is . . . your role. Acknowledge my orders, strategos.'

Myronides shook his head in disgust.

'The dead watch what we do,' he said.

'Acknowledge my orders, Myronides,' Pericles whispered, gasping.

The other man walked away, leaving the priests tending the fires and Pericles doubled over, knotted with pain.

Pericles stayed there for a long time, watching as funeral fires died and ashes were sifted. He found the sight of bones being hammered into chips and fragments brought no new pain. Whatever they were, they were not his sons, not any more.

It was deep in the afternoon by the time he looked up and saw Aspasia had returned. She had brought servants from the hetaira house, including the deaf one. Pericles glanced at the spot where the fires had burned. The stones there had been made darker, stained somehow with heat. He wondered how many would walk across that spot unknowing in the years to come.

The acolytes were readying urns to hold the ashes and bone chips, collecting every speck that escaped the wind. Pericles was sweating again by the time Aspasia took his hand. She nodded to the others to collect the urns and handed coins to the priests, an offering for their work.

'Your robe is wet,' she said. 'Did you go back in the sea?'

He did not want to tell her how he had been forced to empty his bowels again. The cold water left him numb, though something moved within, slowly easing through his gut.

'Is it so bad?' she murmured.

He nodded.

384

'Well, the town-house has been cleaned. I could tend you there.'

'No,' he said with a shudder. The place where his sons had died would be sold or burned, he did not care. He would not enter there again. 'Our home is better. The sun is warm on the bedroom side.'

Aspasia took his arm and held it tightly. He saw how she let one hand drift over her belly, pausing for a moment there as if to rub away pain. He prayed then, to Athena and Asclepius, the healer.

'I saw Myronides on the way down,' she said as they walked between the walls. 'He looked in a great fury. He hardly glanced over when I greeted him.'

'He has . . . lost much,' Pericles said. 'We have to make allowances for that. He'll apologise in time, I don't doubt. This is just a plague year. When it has passed, we'll rebuild.' He thought of Cimon then and the words his friend had once said to him. 'There will never be a time when we sit in the sun, with wine and cheese and olives. We are born to struggle, Aspasia. It goes on, until we are too weak. Then our sons . . .'

He stopped, holding back a tide.

'Come with me,' she said soothingly. 'You must rest and recover. I will tend you and spoon broth into you and oil your skin. I will rub your back and read to you. Let me help, Pericles.'

He looked at her with affection. He had carried the city on his back for a long time and he was weary. He nodded.

'You are a good wife,' he said. 'Though I saw you touch your stomach. If you have this thing as well, perhaps I will be the one looking after you.'

She sighed and rubbed a hand over her womb.

'It's no worse than a monthly cramp, so far at least. But yes, if you want. I will look after you – and you can look after me.'

At their home, she brought him a clean pot and boiled water on the fire to clean himself when the runs came. The boys had to be told to shut up as they clattered around, though little Pericles was glaze-eyed and hot to the touch. Aspasia grimaced at that as she told him to rest in his room. The other two were strangers to her and yet she fed them and told them they needed to be quiet in a house of the sick. She told them too that if she grew too ill, they were to make their way to the town-house, where Pericles' mother had taken up residence. They nodded at that, all big eyes and serious expressions, until Alcibiades jabbed his brother with an elbow and they were off again, wrestling and knocking things over. Aspasia left them to it. The crisis had come to her household and she felt lost and terrified, as alone as she had ever been. She kept all that to herself as she went to check on her husband and son.

Aspasia woke in the night. She had heard a cry and sat up, feeling drunk or still asleep. Her limbs ached, her mind was fogged. Yet she threw back the covers and got out of bed, heading to her son's room. His fever had built and built in the night, until the sweat dried on him and he'd grown delirious, calling out and thrashing in his blankets. She'd meant to close her eyes for just a moment, but she had drifted off.

She dipped a cloth into a bowl of water and pressed it to his skin. The night was chill at least, with a touch of winter in the air. The moonlight was enough to show his face, the tousled head that lolled against her arm. Her son was so very small and she felt helpless against whatever had him in its grip.

She saw his eyes were open. Aspasia touched a hand to his forehead and felt the heat was less.

'It's all right. I'm here,' she said.

He nodded, sinking into sleep.

30

Myronides went to the walls, looking out on the glitter that was a host of Sparta. Every evening, he climbed those steps with a combination of hope and fear. Hope for an end to the threat, but also fear that nothing would be resolved, that the battle king of Sparta could hold Athens hostage for half a year and then just walk home, unchallenged, unpunished. With the sunset turning the day's gold to grey, Myronides stared into the breeze until his eyes stung. Below, hoplites in full war armour waited for him. There were traitors in the city, he did not doubt that. There had been too many murders and blocked water supplies to refuse to believe any longer. It showed at first in the choice of targets. Only Spartans could have thought a mere epistates worth a knife in the ribs, when he would be replaced the following day. Whether the damage was by sympathisers or actual Spartan spies, Myronides did not know, but the streets had never been more dangerous.

The enemy were still there, in their neat encampment. Eight thousand of them! It brought a chill to see so many in one place. Nor were they ever still, as far as Myronides could tell. They trained and ran around the perimeter, in battle armour or naked, at all hours of the day and night. They seemed to stop only to eat and he honestly wondered when they slept.

He knew an army in the field was not a culture, not even a Spartan one. He would not have expected to see religious ritual or stories, or hear voices raised in song. In more normal times, they would have brought twenty thousand helots with them to tend the kit and prepare meals. There was no sign of those. This was the city of Sparta stripped to its bones, a cold, bare thing compared to Athens. The Spartan king made war, and nothing else.

Myronides knew how they thought. They believed the privileges of peace came from strength of arms. Everything worth having – trade and women and temples and voting and slaves – to the Spartan, those things sprang first from the ability to take and hold them.

Myronides sighed as he squinted into the distance. He could no longer see figures on a clay pot, but his eyes were sharp enough for this. Old men learned from experiences, he reminded himself, as he had learned from seeing Spartan soldiers battered at Tanagra. That had been glory then! If Pericles was wrong, he was squandering the prize of a dozen lifetimes. If they took the army out and actually *won*, it would mean . . .

'Myronides,' another man said in greeting.

The strategos felt his thoughts break apart and dropped a hand to his sword hilt. Fear stalked them all in the city. He relaxed as he recognised another of those the Assembly had appointed, knowing him in the fading light. The strategoi were all experienced men, though they felt the loss of Cimon still.

'Andreas,' Myronides said, bowing his head. The man had fought at Tanagra without a mark on his character. Myronides trusted him, though he looked along the wall to see who else stood close enough to overhear.

'I take it Pericles won't move?' Andreas said softly.

Myronides shook his head.

'He can't see past these walls. Of course, the people bless his name every day for building them. As far as they're concerned, Pericles is Theseus reborn.' He made a sound of irritation. 'And down in the Agora, the council follow his lead: for his father, for the friendship he had with Cimon, I don't know. Yet . . . I look out on that small force of Spartans over there – eight thousand of them, no more. I see how many men we have in Athens who would give their last breath for a chance to send those bastards running. And I despair, because an opportunity is being thrown away. If we do *nothing*, they will have shown the world Athens cannot protect herself. If they leave and we did not go out, they will take our honour with them! I tell you, Andreas, when they return in spring, we will not be men.'

'Then call the Assembly!' Andreas said, responding to his exasperation. 'Say what you just said to me and call for a vote.'

'I have done so twice,' Myronides reminded him. 'A third time will change nothing, except make me look weaker still. Pericles has convinced them to endure. Even with him sick, they will wait for him to recover . . .'

'Pericles has the plague?' Andreas said quickly. 'I hadn't heard.'

Myronides waved a hand.

'We should post lists in the Agora, if we could keep up. There are too many. Yes, the pestilence has him.'

'Well, if he is ill, Myronides, he cannot lead the city. If Pericles is . . . delirious with fever, say, *you* are senior strategos, appointed to act in time of war. You say a third vote will change nothing, but what if that much has changed already! Call the Assembly. Call your vote, Myronides, for the emergency. The city is with us, I'm sure of it.'

Myronides looked at his colleague in wild surmise. The sun was setting and he would have to call out the guards to summon the Assembly. More, a general call would cause chaos in a city already afraid of an invasion or a summons to arms. Yet if Andreas was right, if Pericles could be ruled out of the process, a single vote might bring the army into play. The army that had beaten Persia at Marathon and Plataea, that had sent the Spartans running at Tanagra! He swallowed. It would be a victory to mark a thousand years.

'Do it,' Myronides said. 'It has to be worth the attempt. I'll rouse the guards. You announce our intention to the council. Don't ask their permission, Andreas! We are strategoi and this is the crisis. Pericles is too ill to respond. *Tell* them what we are going to do.'

The Pnyx hill was ringed in torches, spluttering and crackling. It would be visible to the Spartans as a golden ring above the city, Myronides realised. They would be out there on the desolate plain they had created, staring into the night, wondering what the Athenians were up to. The thought made him bare his teeth. He'd had enough of that threat.

Myronides stood at the speaker's stone, looking out on his people. They had come by the thousand, tousle-haired and ill some of them, tumbling out of beds as Scythian guards hammered on their doors. They had answered the call. Myronides thought he could see his own certainty growing in them as they whispered to one another. The whole city was awake and children could be heard crying in the streets below, asking why their fathers had gone away.

'I am Athenian,' Myronides said. 'And I have endured

this humiliation long enough. Does anyone doubt this plague is a sign from the gods? Our wives and children die while we hide. We looked to the walls for safety, but perhaps that was arrogance. We make our own safety by being willing to stand when the call comes. By taking up spear and shield and a place in line with our friends.' He looked around at them, feeling his chest swell. 'No matter which enemy comes against us.'

He saw hands and voices rise as others tried to join in, to support or object, he did not know. Myronides continued, carried on a great wave.

'I thought those walls were a wonder! When they first rose, I thought we might be free of war, that we could close our gates and let the world howl. Well, I was wrong! Now we know the reality. We shake in our beds while dogs sniff at the door – and we do nothing. I understand now why Sparta has no walls. They make us weak. If I could tear them down and bring back all our dead, I would do it.'

More voices were raised. Myronides saw red-faced objection in some of them. He wished he could order the Scythian guards to sweep those men away. The time for debate had passed. Most of the crowd were with him still. He could sense it.

'Some of you speak in hushed tones of Spartans, of battles like Thermopylae or Plataea. It is your fear that speaks. I was at Plataea. I saw an Athenian square hold back the Persians. We formed our shield wall and our square and we were a golden stone in the flood. Let the Spartans talk of us! We were there!'

Thousands of them cheered the sentiment or the aggression in it. Myronides felt his senses swim. In all his life, he had never felt this! He had commanded men on the field of battle, but not seen them so determined, as if they just waited for the order to pour down the hill and onto the plain. It was red wine in the blood and it fired him up in turn, inspiring him to find the right words.

'They are eight thousand?' Myronides said. 'Well, we are a city, a people apart. We have suffered plague and despair while we tried to wait them out, but they are still here. And so are we. We are the Assembly of Athens, with all power and authority.'

He patted the air to calm them and the noise level dropped back just a touch.

'I ask then to be appointed polemarch, in the absence of Strategos Pericles. Grant me command and I will take out twenty thousand men to destroy the wolf outside our walls. Close the gates behind us. I will take our honour and our courage and I will show them what it means to attack Athens. What it must mean!'

They roared assent – and a few streets away, Pericles woke from a fever dream in the darkness. The room was stifling hot and his thirst was terrible. He had to work his mouth and lips before he could call Aspasia. He was slumping back when she appeared, her hand gentle on his forehead. She held a cup to his lips and watched him sip it.

'I thought I heard the crowds . . .' he croaked.

Aspasia smoothed his hair with her hand as he slumped back.

'It was nothing,' she said softly. 'Sleep, rest. Your fever has passed, I think. You'll be better in the morning.'

He spoke with his eyes closed, not quite fully conscious, as if he muttered in a dream.

'You'll raise the boy if I'm gone. My mother will help . . . Don't let her be too hard on him.'

'Don't say that,' she whispered. Her eyes filled. 'I *can't* go on without you. I won't.' She lowered her head to his chest.

'Tell him I tried to be like my father, the man they needed.'

'You are,' she whispered. 'Try to sleep, my love.'

His chest was cool against her cheek. The fever had certainly broken, but she did not know if he was resting or dying.

Myronides bowed his head. The Assembly had voted him as polemarch in time of war. In that moment, that very instant, he assumed the powers of a tyrant, of life and death in the city. He knew it came with terrible risks, that they would examine every decision he made when it was over. What he did that day would make him a figure of legend or see him banished, even executed. He felt strong as he gathered the strategoi around him. There was no dissent in them. This was the crisis.

It was like dipping into a pool he knew and loved, to ready an army for war. He had done it before Tanagra and on a dozen other occasions over the years. A great deal of the organisation could be left to the strategoi, but for Myronides, it felt like the sun would rise twice. While the Assembly went home to tell their families what was happening, the streets filled with running men, gathering kit and weapons, heading to the assembly point. For months they had discussed what they might do if the call came. In a night, in an hour, it was upon them.

Myronides saw a sort of brittle joy in his people as he came down from the Pnyx. Some of them recognised him and called blessings on his name. They wanted to go out.

He had known it, argued for it. They hated the cowardice of sitting safe inside Pericles' walls as much as he had himself. Perhaps they too saw the plague as a curse from the gods, a judgement on the unnatural order of their defence. Or maybe some of them had lost their wives and sons and sisters and wanted revenge so brightly they could taste it, so strongly they could hardly bear to remain inside the walls a moment longer.

In the darkness, the guards came down from the walkways around the city, forming up with their officers and strategoi. They seemed pleased to be going out at last. Myronides knew the frustration they had endured, month after month, watching an enemy burn farms and homes from the walls. There had been no honour in safety then. They had yearned to go down with the rest, to attack the ones who stung and wounded them, who scorned their strength. He had given them the chance and they loved him for it.

Before the sun rose, Myronides stood before the great Dipylon gate, looking back on streets filled with hoplites in war armour. Each strategos would command two thousand, with a hundred lochagoi captains in each group. Myronides heard them respond, voices clear. He wondered if the Spartans would hear, on the plain. It didn't matter. He wasn't making the mistake of the Persians. They had thought numbers were the most important part of an army's power. Sparta and Athens had shown them what an elite phalanx could do, what a shield line could do.

Myronides was bringing out the best soldiers in Athens, men trained from childhood. They had endured months of fury. He saw a host of spears forming in the roads stretching back and back, all the way to the Agora. These men would never run from a Spartan line. No, they would break it.

The sun was rising. Myronides had not slept and neither was he young, but he felt alive that morning, lifted by the men with him.

'Open the gates,' he shouted. 'We are going out.'

Aspasia woke with the sun's light reaching into the room. She had fallen asleep on her husband's chest, listening to his breathing. She must have moved again, she realised. The night had been very warm and she had no memory of slipping apart.

She heard a strange roar in the distance, like waves crashing on a shore almost, or a thousand hammers beating metal. It was not a sound she knew and it made her afraid. She sat up and turned to Pericles. She grew still then, until her face crumpled. He was gone.

Slowly, she reached out and kissed his lips, shuddering at the cold there. It was him and not him, her greatest love and just flesh. Her eyes flared open and she flung herself out of bed, crossing the hall to her son's room.

The boy sat up when she clattered through his door.

'What is it? What's wrong?' he said.

Aspasia collapsed, her legs betraying her. She pulled herself up and hugged her knees, while her son came over and tried to give her comfort. She put her arms around him almost from instinct, feeling that his fever had truly broken. His eyes were clear and she looked into them in wonder. She wept then, in joy and sadness.

Myronides formed his people before the walls of Athens. Ahead of him, the forces of a Spartan battle king looked small in comparison. Eight thousand was not so very many. In ranks eight deep, it was only a thousand men across. Yet there was no one there who saw those red-cloaked men and thought victory would be easy. Many of them had fought alongside Sparta and seen their extraordinary fitness, their skill at arms. Expressions were dark as Athenian strategoi dressed their lines.

The Spartans were ready for them, Myronides saw. It was almost eerie to see them in battle array before the new dawn, as if they had heard the shouts and alarms within and quietly taken their places. They made no move to surprise those coming out, as he might have done. Instead, they waited in silence, watching the gates open of the city they had besieged for months, watching the Athenian army pour out, then at last watching the gates close once more.

Behind his back, Myronides saw the walls fill with lines of his people. There were no guards left to stop them climbing the steps, of course. He could hardly blame them, but it would make the men awkward. They needed to be killers, that day. The gaze of wives and children would tug at them, calling them to be husbands and fathers. Myronides scowled. Husbands and fathers could not beat an army of Sparta. He needed soldiers, as ruthless and sharp as those who faced them.

Myronides grimaced at the silent lines of the Spartan king. Just waiting, the bastard. They wanted him to come out, of course. He had a sudden pang of doubt, but it was too late. The gates were closed and they had taken the field. There would be no return to the city, unless it was in victory.

Twenty thousand, he reminded himself. He had twenty *thousand* Athenian hoplites. He had refused thousands more who had come to pledge support without kit. No, the Persians had made that mistake. The battlefield was no place for a mob.

The spears around him were a forest and the morning sun was bright on their shields. They wore greaves to protect their lower legs and helmets to save them from head wounds. With the shield between and the spear jabbing out, they were armoured men, untouchable.

Myronides swallowed hard, raising his hand. His strategoi were all looking to him, ready to march as one. Before he could give them the signal, the Spartans lurched into motion, coming forward, eager for the fray. Myronides showed his teeth and dropped his hand.

He had wanted this, begged for it. It was the path of honour, he was certain. His hand shook as he wrapped his fingers around the shield grip and walked forward with the rest.

At a hundred paces, both sides adjusted their lines. The Spartan king knew by then that he faced a number he could not match in width. Those who would be overlapped kept their shields high on the wings. They marched on without the fluttering of fear that experienced soldiers could read in an enemy. The Spartans had come to that place for war and it had reached out to them. They were loose-limbed and ready, for whatever the day would bring.

Epilogue

As the sun set, all the noise and killing died away. One army had been broken and in the end, darkness hid them from those who watched from the walls. Inside the city, shadowed figures came out from a dozen different streets, working in unison, joining together as they approached the Dipylon gate. There was no one left to stop them and though they wore no sign of Sparta, they were of that city. Slowly, they heaved the gates apart. A fearful moan went up from the people who saw it happening. Outside Athens, red cloaks formed into ranks once more, ready to enter.

There were fewer of them than there had been that morning. They had been battered and wounded, reduced in pride as well as number. Yet it was King Pleistonax who passed through, his personal guard carrying torches around him. That light spilled gold on empty streets, as those who had watched melted away into the night. They had sent an army and seen it broken. There was no fight left in them.

Pleistonax stood in what felt like a deeper dark, with the walls at his back. He could see the Acropolis in the distance and he took a moment to breathe the sight in, though he ached in every joint. The Athenians had fought hard that day. He wondered if they had not been weakened by plague and months of poor food whether he would have been the victor. He smiled. Of course he would.

'I claim this city by right of conquest,' he called out.

His voice echoed back, but there would be ears to hear him, he was certain. It was a shame their officers had all been killed in the fighting. There was no one to formally deliver the city's surrender.

He turned to his uncle Nicomedes and saw something like awe in the man's eyes. That too had been a long time coming.

'My first command is to pull down the walls, uncle – all of them. Tomorrow will be soon enough to begin the work. Drive the people here like slaves until every stone and gate and tower is broken. I will not let them stand.'

His uncle bowed his head and Pleistonax hoped his father could see what they had achieved. He knew he was weary. His thoughts were slow and leaden as he began to consider the aftermath of a battle for the first time. He was no Persian, to burn Athens to the ground. He too was a Hellene. His purpose was to extend his will, his rule, over them.

Pleistonax yawned into a fist.

'Secure the port in the morning. If the League captains have any sense, they will accept a new authority over them.'

'I'll send men now,' Nicomedes said. 'What about their council, the Assembly?'

'Disbanded,' Pleistonax said curtly. 'I will appoint my own . . .' He thought for a moment. 'Some of my officers distinguished themselves today, uncle. Take . . . thirty of the most senior and set them to rule over this city. We'll make it a second Sparta, in time.'

'You know, the people here are not used to our ways,' his uncle said, a note of caution in his voice.

Pleistonax glanced sharply at him.

'Then set up blocks for executions, ropes for hanging.

Set a curfew and have them understand they are all helots now. There will be no more talk of votes and free men. Instead, I will give them peace – and order.'

He looked around at the empty streets and chuckled.

'I have already brought them silence. At last, their voices have been stilled.'

Historical Note

The 'Thirty Tyrants' imposed by Sparta managed to rule Athens for just a year before they were overthrown in bloody insurrection. The Long Walls had already been destroyed – and were never rebuilt. Sparta can certainly be said to have won the Peloponnesian war, though perhaps not the war of ideas. (Living under tyranny may be a natural state, yet democracy still offers something more for those who have known it. In the end, the Spartan elite were always too few to hold against rising tides of freedom and individual responsibility.)

Athens would experience both triumphs and disasters as the centuries passed, from being eclipsed by ancient Rome, to nineteenth-century Ottoman soldiers firing their cannon at temples on the Acropolis. Yet the city endures. I recommend a visit – also to Sparta, which is, after all, still surrounded by the same bowl of hills Leonidas or Pausanias would have known. The smaller acropolis there is in ruins. It is an eerie place.

The earthquake that struck around 464 BC destroyed most of the city of Sparta. The civil king Archidamus is said to have saved part of the army by leading them away from the epicentre, though it is hard to pin down details of such a chaotic event. What is certain is that the helots then began a revolt so serious that Sparta was forced to ask for help from allies. The helots slaughtered many, reducing Sparta's military strength for vital years. Many of them fortified a position on the slopes of Mount Ithome, a foreshadowing of the Spartacus rebellion centuries later, when a slave army hid on the flanks of Vesuvius.

Sparta asked for help from traditional allies like Corinth, but also Athens, which shows how seriously they took the revolt. Sparta and Athens are approximately 112 miles apart, a distance a modern ultra-runner could cover in fifteen to twenty-four hours. I have used the lower figure here, assuming that a Spartan messenger would consider it a matter of life and death. However, it would have taken longer to march a large force back – twenty-five miles a day was the ordinary long-distance pace, or thirty under pressure. Athens did respond relatively quickly, but when Cimon arrived with around 4,000 Athenian hoplites, he was sent back, humiliated and scorned. Perhaps the Spartans had their rebellion under control by then, or perhaps they just didn't want their competitors to see the extent of the damage. Spartan numbers were always small – the birth rate was low and they lost many soldiers in training.

Note: The term 'lady of the good death' or some variation of it was not uncommon in Mediterranean societies of this period – and right up to the early twentieth century in Sardinia, where the title was 'femina accabadora'. Usually but not exclusively women – dark midwives – they would despatch the elderly or terminally ill with a hammer or strangulation, saving families from having to tend to them. The past can be a hard place.

*

Cimon had staked his reputation on very public support of Sparta. Being rebuffed led to a banishment vote – one he lost, like Aristides, Xanthippus and Themistocles before him. The greatest general of Athens found himself exiled from the entire region of Attica – with war coming.

Whether Pericles was on that march to Sparta is unknown, but it was that year that he became certain war with Sparta was inevitable. He began to build the famous Long Walls, as described here, to keep Athens safe. It is simply extraordinary to consider that the Spartans were so perfect a military land force that even allies with the same weapons and equipment were certain they could never be beaten on the field.

Sparta had no catapults or siege engines of any kind, so massive walls were the best defence. (It is, of course, the origin of the Olympic pole vault that warriors used spears to leap over lower walls.) The walls Pericles built had archer towers and must have stood at least the height of three or four men. That would have taken huge sums and thousands of men to build at speed. The Spartans ordered them taken down as soon as they heard. They knew very well what such walls would mean to a sea-trading state like Athens. From the moment they started to rise, war became inevitable.

The battle of Tanagra is not well known today, perhaps because it was a stalemate. Yet Athens and Sparta faced one another on a clear plain – and both sides were so damaged they could not continue. The plan was to destroy a small force of Spartans, but if anything, it just reinforced Pericles' belief that they were too strong. It is true that

Cimon returned from exile to take part in the battle – and that he was rebuffed by Myronides, the Athenian or League commander. Cimon had broken the terms of his exile to stand with them and so could have been killed. Instead, he was ordered to withdraw. His offer was, however, seen as both noble and romantic and certainly played a part in his being recalled.

I've compressed some of the years after 464 BC, especially ones where little happened. It is true that Pleistarchus, the battle king of Sparta and son of Leonidas, had a short reign of around twenty years and may have been as young as thirty when he died c.460/458 BC. A heart attack seems most likely, but the true cause is unknown. It is satisfying that his successor was Pleistoanax, son of the regent Pausanias who commanded at Plataea and was bricked in to starve in a temple. I have used a simpler form of his name throughout with 'Pleistonax'.

In the interests of maintaining a coherent plot line, I have omitted some actions, skirmishes, insults and general breakdown of good relations between the two states and their allies. Athens fell out with both Corinth and Megara over these years, to name but two. Pericles moved the League treasury from Delos to Athens a few years after I have it, around 454 BC. He was accused of spending that huge sum on rebuilding Athens and in particular the Parthenon on the Acropolis. He denied it, but also argued that Athens kept League members safe, so League tithes belonged to Athens – a strange point to make if he hadn't done exactly that.

Aspasia is an intriguing character. There are always gaps in the record of ancient Greece, especially when it comes to women. We know she was much younger than Pericles and of foreign birth – probably from the Ionian coast cities. She was a *hetaira*, though the word did not imply simple prostitution. As the role involved dance, conversation and the ability to read and write, *hetairai* were closer to the Japanese geisha than *pornai* – bought women. Certainly, Aspasia was educated, which was rare at the time. Her salons and symposia became famous in Athens and were attended by Socrates among others.

Whether she ever married Pericles is unknown, but she certainly did bear his third son, known as Pericles the Younger. My feeling is that he would have wanted that son legitimised. I haven't made too much of it, but Pericles originally made a law that citizens had to have two Athenian-born parents. At the very end of his life, he pushed for the law to be changed back – allowing children with one Athenian parent to become citizens and so giving his third son full rights.

The details of the famous funeral oration by Pericles are from Thucydides, the historian and later, general, who was present at this time. Some war dead were buried, but cremation and a buried urn of ashes was also common. As with so many things ancient sources took for granted, details of funeral rites are thin.

Herodotus was also in Athens then. In fact, the city was enjoying the beginning of a cluster of great talent that would take it from a single city to the heart of a nation – and, of course, the greatest single influence on Rome. Not just democracy and plays, but western civilisation began in Athens.

Rather than try to match the style of Pericles as recorded

and translated, I have merely summarised the points he made. His speech was an extraordinary statement of confidence – in his culture and city, in his people.

Note: The Athenian Assembly faction of 'The Fine and the Good' was indeed led by a firebrand named Tolmides. For fear of muddying the plot with too many events, I've omitted his early raids against Spartan positions. Against the advice of Pericles, Tolmides called for young volunteers to intervene in a Boeotian dispute. About a thousand went out with him. Tolmides was then killed in an ambush by various forces. Giving a formal name to his faction makes it one of the first – if not the first – political party. As an aside, another man to die was a relative of Pericles. His young children were accepted as wards into the household of Aspasia and Pericles. One of those boys was Alcibiades, who would become a famous warrior and general. That is a story for another day.

Cimon's ending was, in many ways, a perfect story of the man. He took the League fleet to relieve Cyprus and in the fighting either took a wound or fell ill. Carried back on board ship, his final order was not to tell the men he was dying, in case they lost heart. They triumphed over Persian forces and then learned they had lost a great son of Athens. His life – unknown to me before I began this – has been a great joy to discover.

Ephialtes too was an interesting man. Unfortunately, the identity of whoever killed him on the street will always be unknown. It may have been an assassination or a simple street robbery, but it took a key player from Athens at a crucial time.

By the time Sparta rebuilt its city and martial strength, Pericles was first in Athens. He knew the enemy could not be beaten on the field of war and so when they came, all the demes and villages around Athens pulled back behind his walls. As a point of interest, it's true that Athenians used to bury their best statues when war threatened – a little like the diarist Samuel Pepys, who buried his valuable Parmesan cheese when London was on fire in 1666. That practice is one reason why, even today, Greek statues are dug up miraculously whole.

The numbers of citizens in Athens had grown enormously with the trade and wealth that flowed in. Sewage was usually either washed away in street trenches or physically carried out of the city for disposal elsewhere. With overcrowding and the closing of the gates came a terrible disease. We can't know for certain what it was – and opinion seems to be split between typhoid and cholera. Cholera seems the best bet in those circumstances. That occurs when water supplies are contaminated with sewage, and it remained a terror in cities like London right into the nineteenth century. For Pericles, the plague was the end. He lost his sister, his two oldest sons and his first wife, as well as his own life. His youngest son survived with Aspasia, as did his mother.

The Spartan threat to Athens actually went on for years, with all the farms and villages around the city destroyed each spring. I have simplified that period to keep a thread of plot that didn't also involve a dozen side tales or a host of new characters.

There was a truce negotiated for five years. In Athens, Pericles was asked about a cost of ten talents in the city accounts and it is testament to his authority that he was able to say it was for 'what was necessary' and have that be the end of it. In Sparta, the young king Pleistoanax was banished for a few years, as punishment for taking the bribe. Unlike his father, the accusation could not result in his execution as they had no alternative. Pleistoanax actually did have fair reason to consider Athens his enemy.

In reply to Spartan forces burning crops across Attica, Athens did send out the fleet to attack Spartan allies and interests, raiding the Peloponnese coast. They managed to force a truce for a few more years by holding Spartan prisoners as hostages.

The ephors and kings of Sparta realised they were never going to win against a city they could not breach. The answer lay in sea power. In secret, they built their own fleet and launched it, winning a sea battle at Aegospotami. Athens also lost a huge part of her military strength in a failed invasion of Sicily – and was forced to surrender.

The moment when the gates of Athens were opened to Spartan soldiers does not seem to have been recorded. Pericles certainly did not live to see his walls torn down, nor the rule of the Thirty Tyrants. He died around 430 BC and the war went on without him. I wrote of Myronides going out to face the Spartans in the same year, but the history is more complex. Those Athenian city gates were opened when they could no longer be defended. Sparta won the Peloponnesian war – and they won because the Athenians tried to take the war to them. They ignored the advice of Pericles and paid the price.

That chaotic series of conflicts between the two super-powers of the ancient world came to an end around 404 BC – an easy date to remember. The Spartans were well suited to military struggle, but not ruling a huge city. Though they destroyed the walls, trade and wealth and genius would not be tamed for long.

When the Thirty Tyrants were overthrown, both Socrates and a young man named Xenophon were in the city. It might just be possible to read the two Athenian books about Themistocles and Persia, then *Lion* and *Empire*, before going on to *The Falcon of Sparta*.

There are two surviving stories of Pericles as a senior officer, but no mention of where and when they took place. Yet they point to a particular type of personality – and a man trained by philosophers and problem-solvers like Anaxagoras and Zeno. In the first, his soldiers are panicking in a thunderstorm. Pericles made a spark and suggested it was nothing more than that, but on a greater scale. The second is similar, where his superstitious men are driven almost to madness during an eclipse. Pericles held his cloak over one cowering man and said it was merely a shadow. There is no reason to doubt either tale, but they reveal an extraordinary mind – the sort that might lend his name to a golden age. I suspect Julius Caesar was a similar type. Every age has its Newtons and Hawkings. It is one advantage of an increasing world population that we might see a few more of them. On that optimistic note, I will finish. It has been my privilege to tell the stories of both Themistocles and Pericles, in two parts, all the way from Marathon to the Long Walls. There is never a single ending. Nations and empires are never complete, nor safe enough to rest.

If you have come this far with me, thank you.

Conn Iggulden, London, 2022

Travel to the heart of a **Roman dynasty drenched in danger,** in Iggulden's thrilling new novel, *NERO*

Read on for an exclusive extract

NURTURING WRITERS SINCE 1935

I

The light was all wrong. With the sun low on the horizon, it was that strange, tainted gold that comes only in the dying hour. Black clouds swelled as if a hand reached over the hills, clawing and flashing with sudden violence. In the last moments before it struck, in the stables, the couple faced one another.

Gnaeus squinted against that sickly sun. He made himself busy with the third horse he had brought out to draw his racing chariot. The first two were snorting, held by the straps and central bar. The whole contraption weighed no more than a child. It was painted black and gold and every part had been made lighter, shaved down by masters. When he whipped those reins and drove the four horses to a gallop, no one in the world could catch him.

The mount was skittish and tried to rear. Gnaeus slapped it hard across the nose. He had no time for its foolishness. They were prey animals, stupid creatures. The horse was afraid of him – right to be if he lost his temper. Gnaeus had to lead it in a tight circle as it skittered and stepped, refusing to stand alongside the others. Those two were a matched pair, named Castor and Pollux. He had been offered a fortune just to breed from them – and turned it down. The senator he refused had made some comment about his family under his breath. Gnaeus had bedded the fellow's wife a week later. He smiled at the flash of memory, though it was laced with bitterness.

The air was humid and dense with heat. It seemed to press him down, so that his anger grew like the storm clouds. Gnaeus looked at his wife and knew she hated him. Yet somehow he was still expected to die for her.

'Are you not going to speak?' she demanded. 'Let the boy see to your horses. Are you going to Rome or not? If you run, Barbo, you'll kill us both.'

She pressed a hand to the womb they had thought would never fill, that had been empty for nine long years of marriage. He looked where she touched. She twisted him like a rope sometimes.

'Don't call me Barbo,' he muttered. 'That is for my friends.'

As he spoke, he accepted a set of reins from a slave. The third horse had quieted, allowing him to back it into the traces. Gnaeus heaved the straps tight and three mounts nodded and snapped at one another as the fourth was brought out, whinnying, calling. They wanted to run, just as he did.

Gnaeus waved the slave away as he took the last one. He needed no help! He rode every day, as befitted one of his class. Perhaps too, he was aware of ears listening to every word. Half the city seemed to know his business, he thought sourly. Nothing was private. That was another thing Agrippina would not understand.

'Should I call you "dominus"?' she asked with deceptive sweetness. 'Or should I greet you with "Salve, magister", as my teacher? I was but a child when we met, after all.'

He rounded on her, fast enough to make her flinch. Gnaeus was a man of great physical strength, but he moved with unusual grace. He saw the way she flushed and thought how beautiful she was, how afraid. He grabbed her wrist with his free hand and felt bones move under his grip. He was a soldier, an equite, a wealthy man. Though she was twenty-two years old, there were times when she was still the girl of thirteen her family had given to his.

'I never asked for you, Agrippina. It was your mother who flattered my family until the milk curdled, as I recall. So play no games with me. Not when you are asking me to go to my death for you. Or you might just find it is a little too much.'

'Then if you won't do it for me, do it for the child *in* me.'

She took his hand and moved it onto the swell of her, pressing too hard. There was madness in this woman, he thought. He wondered if the child would even survive its mother. When he felt a kick in the womb, he pulled back with a jerk.

'You know what will happen, *wife*, if I ride up the Appian Way into Rome? You know what Sejanus will do?'

'I know what he will do if you run,' she said.

She was very pale. He ached for her arms around him, just once, some sign that she had any affection for him at all. It would surely make it easier. His mother had told him she would grow to love him in time, but that had been false. For all Agrippina was afraid of him, she still treated him with contempt. Gnaeus had lived with neither love nor kindness from his wife. All his anger was not much comfort in comparison to that.

'Gnaeus?' she went on. 'Sejanus is the emperor's voice in Rome. If you run, he will declare you outside the law. He will take everything you own: the land, the mines, this house – me. The child and I will have no protection. How long will we last then, with the prefect of Rome as our enemy?'

With quick gestures, Gnaeus put the reins on the last horse. He drew the long strap back to its peg on the chariot. All four horses raised their heads, sensing the chance to run before the storm. There was such power in them, it made his heart race. Gnaeus was ready to leave, and yet he stood there as lightning flashed and thunder sounded to fill the world. He looked up, breathing air that seemed more alive. A breeze was blowing and it felt cooler than it had in weeks. They were certainly due a storm, a cataclysm. The land cried out for it.

'You know, Agri, I am just a youngest son. I was never in line for anything important. All I am is a grandson of Mark Antony. I race chariots and I oversee my estates, but I don't threaten men like Sejanus or the emperor. *My* family had wealth and, yes, they wanted to join our line to the divine blood of Augustus, but that was meant to be the end of it! Then Tiberius left for Capreae and this *Sejanus* . . .' He clenched his fist on the reins. 'Sejanus looked at the few left in his way and began to cut them down.'

'You don't know that,' his wife said.

Gnaeus looked at her in disbelief. He had spoken. That should have been the end of it. Other husbands did not have to put up with insolence. Yet she had to have the last word, always. He rested his forehead on the horse's shoulder. Gnaeus was thirty-nine years old. He had married Agrippina when he was thirty, and she had always been a child to him. Perhaps she always would be.

'Are you honestly so blind?' he demanded suddenly. 'Emperor Tiberius only knows what Sejanus lets him know. Do you understand that much? Since the death of his son, that vicious old spider has been lost on his island, withdrawn in grief. There is a great silence in Rome now. And his trusted friend – the beloved "companion in toils" he left in charge – saw his chance and took it. Of *course* Sejanus is responsible for your brothers, Agrippina! He destroyed Nero with an accusation. Is it not strange that such a healthy young man took his own life? Was it the terrible shame Nero felt? You tell me, Agrippina. He was your family, after all. None of you seem to feel shame. I tell you . . .'

He stopped for a moment, unsure if he should go on. The scorn on her face drove him further. He leaned in, his voice dropping. Even in his own house, he had to be careful. Sejanus paid an army of clients, so it was said, all to convey whispers and secrets back to him.

'Nero was accused of being a woman to other men. Do you think Tiberius cares for that? He is so deep in cruelty . . . Agrippina, I could tell you things that would sicken you. No, if Tiberius signed that order of exile, if he even saw it, it was at the request of Sejanus, driving a competitor out. I heard they let your brother cut his throat, but there was no choice in it, do you understand?'

'Don't you dare speak of him,' she said. She trembled then, but with frustration. Gnaeus was a powerful man, used to frightening those around him with the possibility of violence. She always had to struggle not to show fear in his presence.

He shrugged.

'I did nothing to your brothers, Agrippina. All I did was take a wife who was cold to me. It is Sejanus who saw a path to power, who made me another stone he could kick out of the way.'

He saw her glance around, looking to see if he was overheard. Gnaeus laughed, suddenly sick of it all.

'Oh, did I speak too loudly?' He raised his voice further. 'Did I say Sejanus has killed your two brothers, one by his own hand, the other starved to death? The third one might have been next if he hadn't vanished – for his own safety, I am certain. What was his name? Yes! Gaius Julius Caesar. Like Nero Caesar and Drusus Caesar. I wonder if it ever occurred to your mother that she named them all to be killed. And then *I* am accused! Of adultery with a senator's wife, as if half of Rome are not scratching at each other's doors every night. Sejanus attacks you through me with his accusation. I will be put to trial and sent, where, to the island of Pontia to starve, or to Capreae, perhaps, to be made a whore for Tiberius? Or just given a knife and told to do the job in my cell? That's what he wants. Or perhaps he *wants* me to run. Sejanus is killing his way to power, Agrippina. If you can't see it, I can! That is what you are asking of me! *If I ride into Rome, I am riding to my death.*'

He was shouting the last, battering words at her so that she leaned back and closed her eyes. The storm breeze too pressed at her, flicking her hair. Gnaeus felt he had almost raised the gale himself. He was breathing hard, as if he had run a race.

Agrippina stepped in closer, right into range of his fists, her voice a whip.

'You always talk of duty, Gnaeus, of the father of the

house being responsible for everyone within it. Well, that is your role. If you had not been so free with the wives of senators and consuls, perhaps Sejanus would have no nails from which to hang you. So do not come to me for forgiveness or sympathy. You have shown none to me.'

'You cold-hearted bitch,' he hissed. 'When did you ever welcome me to your bed? When have you opened your legs without being forced, without me demanding my right as a husband? Then you lie there like a dead fish until I am done? You head back to your room as if nothing has happened? For nine *years*, that is all I have had from you. By the gods, I should have known you would be twisted. Can you even love at all? Your father was murdered, your mother humiliated in the streets, beaten so hard she lost an eye. I've never seen you weep, Agrippina, not for them, not for your brothers. You're like a stone. So if I found a little warmth with normal women, with appetites as great as my own . . .'

She slapped him, suddenly and without warning, as if she had not known herself that she would. He might have ducked or stopped a punch from a man, but she had surprised him. It was a hard blow that knocked his head to the side. He moved in a blur then, raising one fist like a club.

Agrippina staggered, fearing he would kill her. Her foot caught and she fell onto the stones, landing hard, crying out in pain.

Gnaeus looked down on the young woman who carried his child, still aflame in his anger. He had *never* hit her, not once in a decade of marriage. She was half his size and weight and he was a soldier who had killed men, in battle and violent dispute. He had torn the eye from one equite who argued with him – and thought nothing of it. He had strangled another to death with his bare hands when that man refused to honour a bet. Yet he had never hit a woman.

Agrippina rose to her feet slowly, clumsily. She had paled even further and Gnaeus was suddenly sick of all her winces and spite. The storm cracked overhead and he saw fat drops falling into the dust, the rain beginning to drum in from the south. It would be a downpour. He could smell it on the air. He filled his lungs and stepped onto the chariot platform.

'If you run,' she said again, 'Sejanus will kill the child in me. Your child.'

He looked down at the way she stood, one hand supporting her womb. In nine years of marriage she had never held him as tightly as she held herself. Even then, she was manipulating him. She knew Gnaeus prided himself on his courage, that he held the name of coward as the worst a man could be called. He could not run, but by the gods, it hurt to give his life for one such as her. He wanted to live.

As he took a grip on the reins, the team whinnied, prancing on wet stones. They wore iron plates on their hooves, held by straps and grooves cut into each one. The sound was a clatter of knives. Gnaeus took his balance, ready. He felt strong.

'What are you going to do?' Agrippina called.

He shook his head like a twitch, sick of her voice. If he had married another, he would not be there, called on trumped-up charges into Rome. If she had not carried his child, he could have divorced her, but now they were bound. He found himself hoping the child would die, so he could be free.

Lost in fury, sick at himself, he turned the chariot almost

in its own length, dominating the quad with easy skill. He knew she would be watching to see which way he went, north to the city . . . or south, to live without honour, to abandon his wife and child.

Gnaeus didn't look back as he passed through the gate and went out to the road. The rain suddenly intensified, battering the ground and all those under it. He was drenched in an instant, his clothes sodden, rain plastering his blond hair to his head.

He did not see the red line that crept down the inside of her leg, or the way it mingled with rain and made it pink, so that Agrippina stood in blood. Something had torn as she fell and the pain was growing and already terrible. Yet she remained there, watching, knowing she could not leave. Gnaeus held her fate in his hands – and the fate of the child growing inside like a tumour. For all his anger and stupidity, she was almost sure which way he would go. That last, trembling lack of certainty held her, like a nail through the heart.

On the road, Gnaeus snapped the reins and roared. The line of animals sprang forward, the tiny chariot lurching off as if it had been released from a bow. Iron hooves sparked in the gloom and he was gone, heading to the city.

Agrippina collapsed then, crying out when Gnaeus could not hear, when he could not be there to lift her in his arms and lavish all the care that made her skin creep. Slaves from the house came rushing out in response. They sheltered her beneath blankets while others helped her inside and still more summoned the physician.

'Bring the midwife,' Agrippina hissed at them. 'The child is coming.'

She felt a great shudder take its grip and she was certain.

Lightning flashed again and again overhead, followed by thunder so loud they all jumped from the sheer power of it. She prayed Gnaeus had the strength to do what honour said he must. It was out of her hands. Agrippina was taken inside, to face her own trial.

Rain lashed the road as the quadriga chariot raced the storm. Lightning crashed over and over, whitening the entire sky with a skein of threads. Gnaeus could feel the thunder on his skin, he realised in awe.

The speed was dangerous on those stones. If he turned the chariot over, he knew he would be lucky to survive. At least the road was empty. Gnaeus felt he was the only man in the world, lost in a sort of madness where he saw every heave of the horses and felt his own heart beating.

He balanced on a tiny floor of painted wood, while his four horses tore through an artificial twilight. Each one infected the others with fear, so that they ran as if they were chased by lions, eyes wide, spittle flung like sea froth.

He passed huddled families on the side of the road. They stared at the madman, galloping in thunder and lightning. Gnaeus caught the flash of eyes as they turned, but he did not slow. He felt immortal. When had he ever run from a fight? From any man? For one who rode towards death, the air was sweet. He felt no pain in that moment, no ache of sorrow or ageing joints. All fears and worries were left in his wake and he was young again. He went like an arrow, and for a time he was lost in the joy of it.

Through the downpour, he knew the city by its light. The walls were manned by praetorians in all weathers. Oil lamps burned over gatehouses and all along the crest, like fireflies. Gnaeus smiled to see it. There was the city he loved, the order he needed.

It brought fear too. The strange peace that had filled him slid away like mists. The lights of the city meant strength and laws and praetorians standing watch. They also meant the end of his journey.

A man of Gnaeus' class could do whatever he wanted in Rome, right up to the moment of an accusation. That was all it took sometimes. Once they had him, Gnaeus knew he would never be free again. He began to curse and swear, trying to damn them all to Hades and eternal torment, every last one of them. Shouting tore through the last of his control. He howled for a time as the city grew before him.

His horses were running hot, steaming in the rain. Gnaeus detected a hitch in the gait of one and raged about that. Lame on the hard ground, of course. His fault, his fault, always his. He could imagine what Agrippina would say when she heard he had been so reckless. She was always telling him to *think*, as if he could somehow see what the day would bring before it came crashing down upon them.

He showed his teeth as the quad continued, slowing, the sound of their hooves like battle. He was not stupid, whatever she said. By the gods, how his life had twisted under him! He'd never even wanted to get married. Why would he, when women welcomed him so readily to their beds? They saw his blond hair and wide shoulders and, whether they were married or not, they whispered promises to make a satyr blush.

His mother had insisted, he recalled. The old woman had wanted a grandson and she'd arranged the union with the daughter of a good bloodline. The great-granddaughter of Augustus, his precious wife.

Gnaeus shook his head, wiping rain from his eyes. He had expected a docile little thing to bear him a brace of sons and perhaps a daughter to look after him in his old age. Instead, she'd come into his life like a polecat, all claws and fury.

He'd tried to train a vixen pup once, when he was just a boy. The estate slaves had dug out a burrow and killed the mother. Gnaeus had snatched up one wriggling little thing before they could put a spade through it. Foxes were so much like dogs, he'd thought he could tame her with food and discipline. He winced at the memory. It had cost him the tip of one finger and given him a scar that curled from elbow to wrist.

Agrippina reminded him of that little fox. Sleek and dangerous, beautiful . . . but when those dark eyes turned on you, you had to shiver just a little. He never knew what she was thinking.

The rain had settled to a drizzle. The gap between thunder and lightning seemed greater, which meant it was moving off. He was grateful for that, especially when he saw the queue of drenched travellers waiting to enter. Some fool even waved at him, shouting for him to slow down. Gnaeus made him jump clear before he was crushed, laughing as he went. A Roman summoned to his own death didn't have to follow petty rules, not one. It was a strange thought and he found himself smiling. He was Gnaeus Domitius Ahenobarbus! He was Barbo, of the races! They had chanted his name once, a long time ago.

He ran a hand through his hair, smoothing it back. Ahead, a child ran into the road. Gnaeus had time to judge the ragged clothes the boy wore. He caught a flash of a woman shrieking, her hands held out. She reminded him of Agrippina and he made a choice, edging the horses in.

Hooves struck the child and broke him, even before the chariot wheel flung him like a bundle of rags. Gnaeus heard the woman's wail beginning and he clenched his jaw, sick of pain and grief and stupid people who let their children wander into danger.

He dismounted by the gate to the city. An equite did not have to wait with shit-covered farmers and messengers. Gnaeus nodded to the praetorian guard. The man looked back at the woman weeping over her son, pointing in his direction. The two exchanged a glance and Gnaeus shrugged. It didn't matter.

'Prefect Sejanus sent for me. I am Gnaeus Domitius Ahenobarbus.'

A crowd had gathered around the dead child. More and more were pointing at Gnaeus, jabbing the air.

'You'd better come in, sir. They're working themselves up to a riot. Like children, all of them.'

Gnaeus chuckled. A sense of peace and purpose settled on him. He could face his fate with dignity. After all, he was home, amongst his own.

ALSO IN
THE GOLDEN AGE SERIES

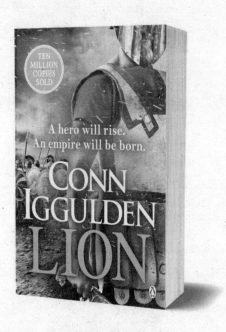

LION
AVAILABLE NOW

NURTURING WRITERS SINCE 1935

ALSO BY
CONN IGGULDEN
THE ATHENIAN SERIES

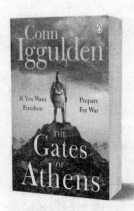

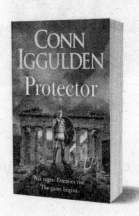

NURTURING WRITERS SINCE 1935

ALSO BY
CONN IGGULDEN
WAR OF THE ROSES

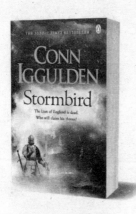

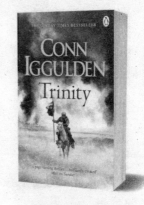

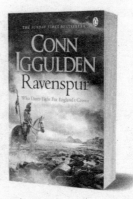

NURTURING WRITERS SINCE 1935

ALSO BY
CONN IGGULDEN

THE EMPIRE OF SALT TRILOGY

NURTURING WRITERS SINCE 1935

ALSO BY
CONN IGGULDEN

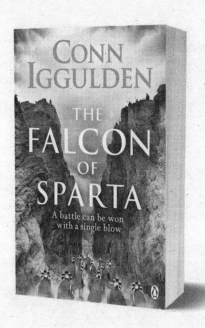

THE FALCON OF SPARTA
AVAILABLE NOW

NURTURING WRITERS SINCE 1935

ALSO BY
CONN IGGULDEN

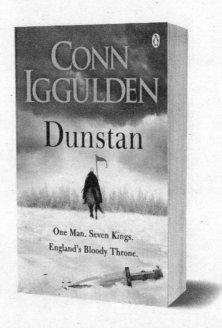

DUNSTAN
AVAILABLE NOW

NURTURING WRITERS SINCE 1935

He just wanted a decent book to read ...

Not too much to ask, is it? It was in 1935 when Allen Lane, Managing Director of Bodley Head Publishers, stood on a platform at Exeter railway station looking for something good to read on his journey back to London. His choice was limited to popular magazines and poor-quality paperbacks – the same choice faced every day by the vast majority of readers, few of whom could afford hardbacks. Lane's disappointment and subsequent anger at the range of books generally available led him to found a company – and change the world.

'We believed in the existence in this country of a vast reading public for intelligent books at a low price, and staked everything on it'
Sir Allen Lane, 1902–1970, founder of Penguin Books

The quality paperback had arrived – and not just in bookshops. Lane was adamant that his Penguins should appear in chain stores and tobacconists, and should cost no more than a packet of cigarettes.

Reading habits (and cigarette prices) have changed since 1935, but Penguin still believes in publishing the best books for everybody to enjoy. We still believe that good design costs no more than bad design, and we still believe that quality books published passionately and responsibly make the world a better place.

So wherever you see the little bird – whether it's on a piece of prize-winning literary fiction or a celebrity autobiography, political tour de force or historical masterpiece, a serial-killer thriller, reference book, world classic or a piece of pure escapism – you can bet that it represents the very best that the genre has to offer.

Whatever you like to read – trust Penguin.